INFINITY

Ted Pennella

WolfSinger Publications ⟨ Brackettville, Texas

This book is dedicated to the memory of

Chris W.

You warmed my heart and became my muse.
Our love will always be the fire keeping my heart warm.
Now you are a star in the night sky inspiring me.

CHAPTER 1

The lift-pod doors opened to a large lobby half a dozen sectors below Conner's destination on the city-station, *Socrates' Odyssey*, which orbited Jupiter. The last person he expected stepped into the pod, turned to the others wanting to get on, and only held up a hand. As the lift-pod doors closed out the strangers and continued its journey, Conner glanced over the twenty-something-looking man beside him with a quizzical stare. Unlike what Conner usually saw Sam wearing, which were ripped pants and shirt designed to expose a very fit body, he currently wore a black business suit of the latest style. The stiff vertical collar with a flat emblem of the city's logo, which was a stylized scroll wrapped with a loose ribbon, flanked both sides of the narrow opening at the front of the neck. A pale cream shirt hugged the body while a loose jacket fell just short of the man's narrow waist. Sam's usually messy tangle of blond hair had been wrangled into a very proper business style.

"Looking quite sexy there, boss," Sam said with a wide smile verging on a leer. "I'd offer to kiss you but based on what I could decipher from Delilah's exhaustion-fueled ramble, this morning's meeting with Fleet is quite serious. Socrates gave me a bit more info, but still remained rather tight-lipped. You'd think he didn't like me anymore, based on how mute he got when I asked."

"First, you don't work for me. Second, I didn't know the city's controlling-artificial even spoke to anyone anymore," Conner said, running a hand over his own black hair. Nothing stuck up, but his nerves whispered he'd left something out of place. Tugging on his own suit jacket, about a decade out of style and far tighter than he'd like, Conner stared at the lift pod doors. "Third, if you're here in Delilah's stead, then you'll need to know what's up."

"Hoping to distract the old codgers with Delilah's overinflated nano-modded body?" Snickering, Sam nudged Conner's arm with an elbow. "You sly dog."

"My company has a contract with the Sol-Humana Confederation Stellar Fleet to develop a prototype artificial intelligence droid for use on all ships as an emergency communications officer,"

Conner said, ignoring Sam's comments. "My contact within Fleet indicated this is not a review meeting to go over refinements on the droid, but rather a hearing on whether to cancel the contract. Officially, I've not heard anything other than to be at Fleet's Jovian Command for a meeting. I've put eight years of my life into this project, kept it secret from my employer before I started my own company six years ago and finalized this contract. Everything I own and am has been sunk into this project. They cancel it and I'm back to where winning the Battle of Horus got me fifteen years ago, drowning at the bottom of a deep well, but this time with no one to save me."

Sam's smile vanished. "Understood. Just so you know, I'm far older than I look and have extensive tech experience. In fact, AI and tech development have been my life for longer than you could imagine."

"Are you saying that stripping down at The Rusty Bucket is just a hobby?" Conner smiled as he finally looked Sam in the eyes. He regretted it almost immediately as the impish face grinned back at him from Sam's slightly shorter than six-foot height.

"I do that to get your attention, my sexy techie," Sam whispered, pressing himself against Conner's body while wrapping his arms around Conner's neck.

A disgusted groan from Conner's left sleeve sliced through Conner's quickly growing arousal at the man's affection. Sam jumped back in surprise before laughing raucously. Conner lifted his left arm and snarled, "What is it, Magnus?"

"Not to be the cold, wet blanket on your fun in this love pod for two, Daddy," a deep male voice said full of derision, especially with the last word, "but you wanted your Maggie to remind you this morning's meeting is scheduled to begin in thirty minutes in the Blue Room on Level F02. I hear that your, well, distraction is being quite distracting. Don't forget about how this meeting may decide someone's fate."

"Thank you, Maggie," Conner snapped before slapping his sleeve to sever the connection to his AI son and assistant. "End."

"Maggie doesn't like me, does he?" Giggling, Sam straightened his jacket a bit before leaning against the pod's wall across from Conner. "So, we've got another minute or so before we arrive. Just to keep you from being shocked in front of Fleet, my full name is

Samuel Maxwell Youngs. Yes, the same Youngs as in the company, Youngs Galactech, which is now Tandon Universal. This body, should Fleet's security sensors go off, is an ancient tech called orga-tech."

"Orga-tech!" Conner tensed even more at the familiar name. "That tech has been lost for more than a thousand years."

"And that leads to my next statement," Sam said with a wistful sigh. "I'm far older than any human because of that now lost technology. When it finally fails, I either die or become an artificial equivalent. Depends on my great-grandfather and his siblings. Always has."

Conner looked down at the floor. He recognized the name Sam used. Anyone who studied human history knew the name of Samuel Maxwell Youngs. It had been passed down in the Youngs family for generations, or so official histories said. "Are you claiming to be the original Sam Youngs? Or his descendant? And either way, why did you let the company get taken from you?"

Sam smiled sadly. Pushing off the wall, Sam faced the lift-pod's door before answering. "Yes, I'm the original and not a descendant. A family tragedy led to me losing the desire to run a multi-stellar megacorporation. My past will hopefully not come up in today's meeting, Conrad Conner, but if it does, I don't want you to be caught unawares. Great-grandfather felt it prudent."

The lift-pod's door opened before Conner could speak. Beyond that door lay the wide-open lobby of the Sol-Humana Confederation's Stellar Fleet Jovian District Command Headquarters. Floating in the center of the lobby, at nearly ten feet across, was the Fleet logo of four stars orbiting each other while contrails of three ships slowly encircled the stars. A counter wrapped around the logo where half a dozen men and women sat answering questions or directing people. Each of those men and women wore Fleet's blue with green shoulders uniform, as well as vertical silver bars denoting them as lieutenants.

Conner walked up to the nearest open person with Sam hanging just behind him. "Conrad Conner and associate with The C5 Group for a project meeting."

A faint chime sounded from behind the counter as the ethereal image of a young black man in an ensign's uniform appeared beside Conner. "If you'll follow me, Mr. Conner and associate."

Conner and Sam followed the artificial intelligence's holographic image. He recognized a representation of the Fleet Central Observation and Preservation System, or FCOPS, artificial. That system originated during the early years of humanity moving into space cities over two millennia ago. The FCOPS, he knew from personal experience, was an extension of an even older and more powerful AI, though most people, including many in Fleet command, didn't know this fact. Through a security checkpoint and down a long, twisting corridor, they finally stopped at a closed blue door with a faint square near the center.

"Knock'em dead, dear friend," the hologram whispered while momentarily flickering to become a sixty-year-old man with a few streaks of gray in the close-cut hair and stockier body.

The hologram reverted to the young ensign before vanishing. Shaken, Conner silently cursed whoever invented the first self-sustaining artificial intelligence back at the beginning of time. Resisting the urge to use the artificial's real name, Conner tugged on his sleeves before reaching his hand out toward the faint square at the center of the door. He splayed his fingers out wide and held his hand an inch or so from the glowing square.

"The C5 Group is here concerning Project Beta Four Zero One Nine Nine Peter Alpha Two Three," Conner said in a flat voice. "Requesting entry for two."

"Identity and project confirmed," a woman said, her voice coming from all around. "Admittance allowed. Welcome, Lieutenant First-Class Conner."

"Always good to hear your beautiful voice, Vickie," Conner said with a slight smile as he glanced up at the ceiling. "How are the kids?"

"Gods of the stars, they are wearing me out, Conner," Vickie said with an exasperated sigh. "Can't tell you more, but I wish you were still around. Constant Conner, they called you."

"If you say, 'The good old days,' Vickie," Conner said, chuckling as he waited for the door to open, "I will hook you back up to the basic barracks."

Vickie snorted out in laughter before regaining control. "Promises, promises, you old lech. They're ready for you. Knock some sense back into them for me."

Conner sobered up at Vickie's last comment. She had rarely

spoken more than a few words to him since he left Fleet Academy nearly two decades ago. Admiral Victoria, or Vickie, had always been pleasant with him, but also neutral. Something was up and he didn't like the warnings he was getting. Sam shot him a confused look, but the door vanished before either of them could speak. What worried Conner most, though, was that certain artificials, who had a reputation of rarely speaking to humans, were being overly friendly toward him.

With his mind spinning away at possible reasons, Conner led the way into a small room with a long desk on their right and five empty chairs behind it. In the far corner behind the desk was another door, also blue. To their left were two eight-foot-long tables with three chairs behind each table so they faced the long desk. About fifteen feet separated the desk and tables. In that space sat a small platform with a rod about three inches in diameter and roughly four feet long laying on it. Short lengths of iridescent tape could be seen in haphazard places along the length of the rod. Over the nearest desk's front edge floated the logo of Conner's company, five 'Cs interlocked in a pattern reminiscent of a carbon atom.

Conner's fists clenched as he shook with rage. He couldn't believe what he saw lying dark and unmoving on that platform. That Fleet could do something to his child, his creation, shook him to his core. Whoever had raped his daughter, by opening her body and breaking those seals, may as well have gutted him. His heart might as well be lying on that platform, a knife piercing it.

"To our places, boss," Sam whispered, grabbing Conner's arm and pulling him to a chair.

To try and get control of the rage which burned inside and the grief filling his eyes with unshed tears, Conner tried to recall all the major points of his contract with Fleet as they waited. He ignored the holographic Fleet logo on the wall behind the long desk across the way or the much smaller Fleet Tech Division logo floating over the other desk beside them. Instead, he lifted his left sleeve close to his mouth.

"Magnus," Conner whispered just loud enough he faintly heard himself, "feed contract goals to me. Then pull up and ready the certified records of Betty's seals. As need be, link with FCOPS and the Variegation and Integration Command, or VIC System, to display upon my command. Record this hearing and get an official copy for our records upon the hearing's completion."

"Is it lawyer time yet?" Maggie whispered with very uncharacteristic seriousness. "Or do I need to call in the boys?"

Conner couldn't decide just how to take Maggie's reference. He hated to think all artificials watched ancient entertainment vids. Those pre-holographic videos were pretty unwatchable by today's standards. "Only if the First Admiral walks into the room. Otherwise, I'll let you know."

A moment later, Conner's sleeve displayed a copy of his contract with Fleet. He read through the stated goals softly so Sam could hear until the blue door to the corridor opened. Three people in Fleet uniforms entered, two wore a lieutenant's silver bars on their collars while the third wore an ensign's single brass bar. The lieutenant second-class, who wore one silver bar, was an Asian woman in her mid to late twenties and the other two were Caucasian men, with the older man having a pair of silver bars and looking to be in his early thirties, while the ensign looked fresh from the academy. The lieutenants had the lean tallness most common in humans who grew up on Humana IV while the ensign looked liked a fellow Venusian. Just as the trio took their seats, the door behind the long desk opened. Three Fleet officers wearing the crescent moon and star pins denoting them as admirals walked in and sat down. One of them had been the captain of the ship Conner was assigned to during most of his own tour in Fleet. Now an admiral, his former captain had six pins on his collar, denoting him as a Fleet Admiral, while the other two admirals only had five pins each. Conner found it curious all three were men. He'd heard there were more women than men as admirals right now.

Conner and Sam rose, along with the newcomers at the adjacent table, as the three admirals took their seats. The senior admiral spoke. "I'm Nigel Nokata, Admiral of Fleet's Jovian District of the Sol System. Admirals Choktra on my right, Harrison on my left, and myself will be conducting this hearing on the progress of Project Beta Four Zero One Nine Nine Peter Alpha Two Three, which is intended to create a new artificial intelligence-driven prototype android, with a version birthed for use on all Fleet ships as a surrogate communications officer during times of battle or human incapacity. Mr. Conner, you and your associate are here to defend your work. However, I will ask the Fleet team assigned to review the project and the prototypical droid up to this point to give us their review. You may all sit."

Sam stayed standing as everyone else sat. When Admiral Nokata arched an eyebrow at Sam, the young man spoke. "The C5 Group was not made aware nor given access to any review documents in order to be able to respond during this hearing. Not providing such documentation a week prior to any hearing concerning an artificial intelligence at any stage of development is an egregious violation of the AI Accords of twenty ninety-seven. When did the Sol-Humana Confederation Stellar Fleet get permission to ignore and subvert a nearly thousand-year-old accord governing natural and artificial life within the known and occupied universe? An accord accepted by and considered to embody the fundamental rights of artificial and natural life alike?"

Admiral Nokata looked to the Fleet officers at the other table, where the two lieutenants glared at the ensign. "Lieutenants?"

The first lieutenant shot to his feet stiff backed, curtly nodding at the admirals. "Sirs! Our summary and supporting documents were sent, but acceptance was refused."

Admiral Nokata just looked at the officer half his age with no visible reaction. That look brought back a flood of memories to Conner, who studiously ignored all of them. When neither of the other admirals spoke, the lieutenant tapped his left sleeve. "Access project records and display transmittal for this hearing."

A three-foot-tall image of a transmittal record appeared between the admirals' desk and the tables. On the transmittal was a blurred image of the C5 Group logo. Just clear enough to read was the name 'Conrad C.' It made Conner snort with disgusted humor.

"Mr. Conner, you find this funny?" Admiral Harrison shifted his stern gaze to Conner. Admiral Nokata, though, let one end of his lips to ever so slightly twitch upwards.

Conner stood, knowing the procedure in Fleet hearings far too well. "With respect to the creator of this plainly obvious forgery, my eleven-year-old nephew could have done better."

Not waiting for a response, Conner continued. "That's not our received stamp and it would never be my name as the one who received any transmitted documents. Admiral Victoria, please access FCOPS project records on Earth and display the last official transmittal received and stamped by The C5 Group. Compare and contrast the received stamps on that transmittal to the one displayed."

"Authorization needed for access to FCOPS record storage," Vickie said with just a hint of humor in her voice.

Before Conner could reply, the first lieutenant, who still stood, snapped, "There is no need to bother the Admiralty with this request, Admiral."

"Who needs to bother the Admiralty, Lieutenant?" Conner didn't shift his gaze from the admirals as he spoke. "I'm quite capable of using my own authorization for this request. After all, it is only informational. Vickie, authorization is Conner, Lieutenant First-Class, former Commander of FCOPS Maintenance Corps, currently Reserve Administrator of System Data Cohesion Review."

Conner then thought and spoke his old Fleet authorization without actually making any sound or moving his lips. It was an old trick used to keep it secret. The sensors built into the city-station and ships themselves were able to read even the slightest motions made by the human body.

"Authorization accepted," Vickie said, the image floating before them blurring momentarily.

When the image cleared, the transmittal which had been there was now blue while a new one was superimposed in green and clearly designed around the word "RECEIVED". The C5 Group's stamp on the blue transmittal was covered with bold red letters flashing, "FORGERY!"

"As you can see, the name of acceptance should be Magnus," Conner said in a calm voice even as he raged internally. "Now, can we get to the reason the certified seals placed on our prototype's body were broken, why there are obvious scars of forced opening on her housing, and why she has been completely powered down without notification to myself, her officially recognized parent?"

Conner looked from the admirals to those at the table beside him for the first time. The lieutenant standing shook slightly as the ensign's scared face faintly smiled. Only the woman appeared calm and unconcerned. She then stood and placed a hand on her senior's left arm.

"I'll handle this, Chris," the woman said softly while a smile spread across her face.

"I don't think so, Lieutenant Second-Class Wu," Admiral Nokata said sharply. "Sit down and remain silent until called on to speak. Now, please answer Mr. Conner's questions, Lieutenant First-Class Herrods."

"The seals were already broken and the prototype in a powered down mode when we received it from the defendants," Lt. Herrods said, his voice shaky. "When we tried to power the object up, it would spark and snarl obscenities at us. We cannot recommend this project be—"

"Untrue," Conner said tapping his sleeve. "Magnus, please feed video of placement and certification of prototype's seals and summary to Vickie for review by the admirals."

The image between the desk and tables changed from the transmittal to that of a rotating holographic image of the city-station's logo, which is a scroll with a ribbon wrapping it. As they watched, the ribbon untied itself and the scroll opened to show the words "Certification of Sealing." The words and scroll then blurred into a pair of dark-skinned hands, obviously not Conner's hands, placing three long seals around the rod now laying on the platform before them. The voice of the city-station's controlling artificial, Socrates, could be heard saying, "Seals placed upon and certified by Fleet-approved third party. This video record will be sent to both parties as proof and record of placement of seals upon the body of a prototypical artificial intelligence, named Betty, in accordance with the rules and regulations set forth in the Accords of Rights for Natural and Artificial Life of twenty ninety-seven, commonly referred to as The AI Accords."

"Now, I want to know who raped this hopefully unconscious artificial," Conner yelled, venting his anger. "She has worked hard to gain the certification required of Fleet, with her full adulthood contingent upon final review by Fleet. Instead of Fleet acting in good faith, my still underage daughter gets raped, mutilated, and possibly murdered by those who claimed to have her best interests in mind? I want to know who ordered this gross incompetence!"

CHAPTER 2

"Good morning, you've reached the C5 Group. This is Magnus speaking, how can I assist you today?" Even as he answered the call with audio only, Magnus sorted the incoming mail while occasionally checking with his primary matrix on his father's journey up to Sector Eight. Fleet's Jovian Command completely occupied every one of the sector's fifty-four levels. Things were not off to a smooth start, what with that suspicious Sam showing up instead of Delilah. Not that he liked either of them, but something about Sam just struck him as odd.

"Good morning, Maggie," a cheerful familiar voice said, an image request flashing at Magnus. "How's my favorite nephiece?"

"Stars of Andromeda, Aunt Emily," Magnus groaned, altering his image to become the female version of himself named Maggie. Maggie generally looked right around eighteen and usually wore her favorite sundress, which had yellow dots of various sizes on a white background with yellow scalloped trim around the square cut neckline. "That is not a word. Also, I'm genderfluid, not a hermaphrodite."

"You are both and neither, one alone and two at once," Emily said, smiling. Conner's little sister, who was in her mid-thirties, had brown hair curled in large waves around her face, but never quite touched her shoulders. A soft face, rounded cheeks, and a furrowed brow couldn't hide her worry despite a warm smile. "Besides, if you got a physical body, I know you can get one now that is both genders at once. Wouldn't that be something you'd like?"

"Is it nighttime back on Earth?" Maggie smiled, finding it suspicious his aunt would be calling him so early in the morning. "You seem rather oddly preoccupied with what my body would be, as if I'd ever get the chance to actually have a body."

Emily laughed before answering. "It is night and I'm alone in my studio with everyone else in bed asleep. Speaking of sleeping children, have you told your father about your little bundle of data bytes?"

"Not yet," Maggie said with a fearful smile. "He's been so stressed out with Betty and Fleet that I can't bring myself to add little Alex to the list. You won't tell him?"

"I promised I wouldn't, Maggie." Emily smiled warmly, reaching out to lightly touch Maggie's cheek. "However, the longer you take to tell him, the worse his reaction."

"I know," Maggie said, sighing sadly. "Surely you didn't call about me and my little boy."

"No, I didn't." Emily glanced about, suddenly looking very nervous or maybe scared. "I need to talk to your father right away. Even if he's already asleep. And no, it's not about you or Alex."

"Actually, it's early morning here and Daddy is already up and on his way," Maggie said while requesting a status update from his primary matrix concerning Conner, "no, he's already in a meeting with Fleet personnel about Betty. I think today is supposed to be the final review before my little sis gets permission to take her adult artificial exam."

"That's great," Emily exclaimed, jumping to her feet and momentarily flashing Maggie as her robe fell open. "Oh jeez, Maggie. So sorry. Didn't mean to show the girls off to you."

"That's okay, Auntie Em." Maggie blushed, having picked up that small town rural Venusian hang-up on seeing family naked. To distract himself, Magnus's child routine reconnected with his core, only to get overwhelmed by emotions. Grief and anger being the chief emotions as a video played of the ensign breaking into Betty's control rod. Tears ran down his cheeks as he muttered, "Why? Why did they do it?"

"What's wrong, Maggie?" Emily leaned in close with her brow wrinkling even deeper with worry. She reached out to him. "Talk to me."

"They killed her." Maggie sobbed, memories of teasing the newly born personality matrix coming to the surface. Coddling her and helping her find things on the Interstellar Information System, or just the System, all came rushing back. "I promised her nothing would happen and now she's dead. I'm a horrible big sibling."

"Betty? She's dead?" Emily dropped back into her chair. "How? You said she was a prototype artificial."

"Her seals are broken and none of her lights are flashing," Maggie said, severing her connection with their primary core. "If she was just in a low power mode because none of the city power nodes were accessible, she'd have at least one red flashing light. Her spinal rod is completely black. Daddy's yelling. This is my fault. I convinced her to go because Fleet wanted her. That's why she was born."

"She's not dead," Emily said soothingly. "If your father can't die, I seriously doubt his genius with tech will allow anything he touches to die either. I doubt her getting shot by that star carrier Conner served on while in Fleet would kill her. Look at how he won the Battle of Horus. Using tech to its fullest against superior numbers. So you stay confident and remember your father loves you and your sister no matter what. That's what we parents do, Maggie. Love our babies no matter what."

~ * ~

"That's a very serious charge, Mr. Conner," Admiral Nokata said while leaning forward in his chair.

"I can list the components by brand which should be making up her body and compare it to what is actually inside the body laid out before us, Admiral," Conner said snarling. He leaned on the table in order to keep from screaming obscenities at everyone in the room again.

Sam gripped Conner's left arm while he spoke. "Admirals, to put what Mr. Conner has said into technical legal jargon, The C5 Group invokes all pertinent articles of the AI Accords of twenty ninety-seven, but most especially Articles Four, Twelve, Nineteen, and Twenty-Eight. Per those specific articles, the parental entity of the underage artificial who has been attacked, mutilated, and or killed can, upon their discretion, invoke the designated Arbiters for the system in which the crime has taken place. To verify the location of the crime, The C5 Group calls upon the FCOPS and VIC systems to state where the subject AI has been taken while in Fleet custody."

"That's enough, kid," Admiral Harrison with a slap of an open palm on the desk. "Let's get this hearing back on course. We've not got all day for your games."

"Authorization accepted, Mr. Youngs," Vickie said without warning. "Interfacing with city AI now. Please wait a moment while I access FCOPS records for verification of locations where the prototype designated as 'Betty' was taken."

"Cancel request," Admiral Choktra shouted.

"Overridden," Admiral Nokata said while staring at Sam. "Mr. Conner, I don't believe you introduced your associate."

Conner glared at the admirals as he sat down. "This is Sam Youngs. He freelances with our company and has been quite helpful with this project recently."

"And just how does someone so youthful looking, Mr. Youngs," Admiral Nokata said with steepled fingers, "come by a Fleet authorization code?"

"That requires a clearance code possibly above your pay grade, Admiral." Sam shot the admiral the same mischievous grin Conner remembered from the lift-pod. "And definitely above the pay grades of those at the table beside us. Suffice it to say, if it wasn't valid, it wouldn't have worked. Right?"

"Do you have a middle initial, Mr. Youngs?" Admiral Nokata actually cracked a smile. "We are allowed that much, aren't we?"

Sam nodded as he said, "M, Admirals."

Nokata's eyes widened for a moment. It was a quick reaction before the older man's face returned to its bland, almost bored expression. Suddenly, a middle-aged woman, with faintly brown skin, dark brown hair pulled back in a bun, and wearing a Fleet uniform with five admiral pins on her collar, appeared before Conner's table beside the platform where Betty's control rod, or spine, lay. She nodded at the admirals before turning to address everyone else. That's when her name could be read on her uniform, "Victoria."

"The prototype was taken from Fleet's Jovian Command Headquarters here on *Socrates' Odyssey*," Vickie said, now in a very formal tone with stiff demeanor, "to Fleet's Technical Center out in the Kuiper Belt. During this transit, the underage artificial's seals were broken."

Images of the prototype appeared on either side of the AI. One side showed the seals intact while the other showed the seals torn. Vickie continued. "FCOPS is currently conducting a search of orders and video surveillance to identify the chain of command and from whom the order to violate an established AI was given. With this information, jurisdiction falls within the Sol System."

A second figure appeared in the room, but on the opposite end of the platform from Vickie. It was a black man with eastern Mediterranean heritage who looked to be in his mid-fifties. Wearing the long robes common about a thousand years ago, he looked about the room in irritation before stopping at the rod laying on the platform. Tears welled up in his eyes, but none escaped.

"I am Socrates, the controlling artificial for this city-station," the man said facing the admirals. "The arbiters for the Sol System are being contacted as I speak. A summary of what has been discussed here is being provided along with a copy of what has been said and presented so far. Please remember the decisions of the Arbiters are final and cannot be appealed. No recourse nor refusal of their presence is any longer possible."

Vickie nodded to Socrates and then the admirals before vanishing. Conner wondered just who these arbiters would be. He'd never been involved in a dispute of this magnitude involving an artificial. In fact, he wasn't sure he could remember hearing about the AI Accords' Arbiters being invoked in the last four hundred years anywhere. Each settled system had designated arbiters, usually artificials who had been alive or established during the millennia long Human-Hive Wars. For the Sol System, that could be any of about ten AIs. What he couldn't recall was if it was always the same artificials or if the duties rotated among those qualified. Artificials who were born or created before the Human-Hive Wars tended to be very neutral in regard to both humans and other artificials by the very nature of their long, almost god-like lives.

Conner's musings were interrupted as two new figures appeared. He immediately recognized both, and internally groaned. One was a tall, stocky black man with the deep, ebony skin tones seen in ancient vids of those who came from the heart of the African continent. His hair only had a few wisps of gray while his overall appearance gave the impression of someone in their early sixties. He wore long robes similar to those seen in images of ancient Greeks. The other person was a tall, regal-looking woman still in the prime of her life. Also dressed as an ancient Greek, she looked the part with her rich, olive-brown complexion. Just visible in her flowing curly black hair was a laurel branch crown. She epitomized human female beauty.

"Arbiters for this cycle are Earth's Planetary Guardian Artificial, known as ConRad, and Venus's Planetary Guardian Artificial, known as Aphrodite," Socrates said, looking at the newcomers. "Have the Arbiters reviewed the evidence of the claim?"

"Yes," both newcomers said.

"The parties involved are to remember that per the Accords, you are not protected by the rules of the Fleet nor any stellar government," Socrates said with a stern look at those behind both tables followed by the admirals. "All stellar governments in existence at the time and those that have formed since have encoded the Accords within their laws. The decision of the Arbiters is final and there is no appealing their decision. With that said, I turn things over to the Arbiters to render their decision."

Aphrodite nodded to Socrates before turning her gaze to first the table with the lieutenants. "It has been decided that I will do the speaking for the both of us. For the record, while members of both parties were born on Venus, I have had no direct contact with any of them for the duration of their lives so far. That said, we wish to know why the young ensign's objections on the shuttle to Fleet's Technical Center were merely 'Duly noted' and then ignored? I am talking to the two lieutenants here. The security recordings from the shuttle show you both acknowledged the ensign's concerns and objections separately, but never actually entered them into the official project logs. By taking, or not taking, these actions, you both have shown complicity in the attack upon the child artificial beside us. Do either of you have a statement on the matter?"

The female lieutenant glared at Aphrodite, her nose twitching as though she struggled to keep from snarling. "We were merely following orders."

"Ah, that tired old excuse," Aphrodite said with a knowing smile. "Per law and ancient military custom, that word combination does not excuse you from committing atrocities, including the rape and mutilation you ordered an ensign to do under the direct threat of death by being tossed out of the shuttle. Would you like to view the footage? It's quite disgusting."

A half life-size recording played of the trio on a shuttle. One of the lieutenants piloted the shuttle while the other one lambasted the ensign about not working hard or fast enough. It played out just as Aphrodite had described. The time stamp showed the date and location of the recording. Just as that one ended, another recording started. This one timestamped the following day with the location being the office of the Technical Center's commanding officer. The ensign again logged complaints about what he'd been forced to do and what exactly it was he did. Yet again, his objections were blithely ignored and never documented formally by the commander.

"To save time," Aphrodite said as the recording vanished. "I'll sum up the evidence we have already found. More is being uncovered even as we search and will be entered into the final summary judgement we issue. In short, we find Sol-Humana's Stellar Fleet guilty of willful violation of the intent and letter of the agreement colloquially known as the AI Accords of the year twenty ninety-seven SE, or Space Era. As such, the known guilty parties, Lieutenants Wu and Herrods, the Commander of Fleet's Technical Center, and Admirals Windles, Standill, and Choktra are all guilty of the rape and mutilation of the minor, known as Betty Conner. All of the guilty are stripped of their ranks and associated privileges, dishonorably discharged from all military and other government bodies and agencies, and remanded to the high security penal facility on Mercury for a period not less than fifty years before a chance of parole. Final durations for each of the guilty will be announced in the final report."

"You have no authority over humans," Lieutenant Wu yelled, surging to her feet. "This a—"

The woman shook as faint electrical discharges could be seen all over her body. Once she fell forward onto the table, Aphrodite continued speaking. "Furthermore, our analysis of the victim's injuries and a comparison of what was taken or changed within her body shows an attempt to murder the victim was made. However, the actions of the ensign here actually saved the victim's life, earning him a sentence of four additional years as an ensign with two of those years, minimum, within the FCOPS Maintenance Corps on Earth. Last, we find the penalty clause of the contract between The C5 Group and Fleet is insufficient to the crime committed. Fleet is hereby ordered to pay the full contract amount to The C5 Group, plus a penalty of five times the contract amount and a public apology by the entire Admiralty, which must include the current First Admiral, and be made on a systemwide broadcast within the twenty-four hours following the issuance of final judgement. If such an apology is not made with all members of the Admiralty present in person together, an additional penalty equal to one percent of Fleet's overall budget shall be paid by Fleet to The C5 Group, with at least sixty-five percent of said amount taken out of the pay and retirement accounts of each member of the Admiralty. The percentage taken from each admiral is to be based on seniority and time served with Fleet. I hope that helps make clear the severity of this crime to Fleet. We are stopping short of taking control of Fleet's Academy curriculum, Fleet Admiral Nokata, but if we don't see improvement by the Admiralty in how artificials are treated, it will be done. Consider Fleet under watch on this matter."

The door to the corridor opened without warning. A dozen Fleet security rushed into the room. Several stopped and pointed their weapons at Admiral Choktra while the others gathered up the trio at the table beside Conner and Sam. The rank insignias on all of the accused fell off their collars to clink loudly on the tabletops before them. Vickie walked into the meeting room from the corridor as the guards gathered up the prisoners.

"Take the four prisoners to the brig and put in separate isolation chambers," Vickie ordered. "Use whatever force is necessary to secure them short of death. Ensign, I'm sorry but until the final judgement is issued, you're to be held as well."

A pair of guards rushed out through the door the admirals had used. Admiral Nokata stood to let the guards do their job. As he did, he said, "Understood, Arbiters Venus and Earth. Vickie, you have my authorization to make payment per arbitration judgement to The C5 Group immediately upon the final release of their judgement."

"Understood, Admiral," Vickie said while following the guards out with their prisoners.

Conner watched the room empty. Earth and Venus's artificials vanished, followed by Socrates. Finally, he and Sam were left alone with Admiral Nokata. Conner, though, went straight to the rod on the platform.

"I'm sorry this happened, Conner," Admiral Nokata said softly. "Please don't let this—"

"With all due respect, Admiral," Conner said venomously while gently lifting his prototype's body in his arms, "shove it. I've got a traumatized and likely mentally unstable artificial now. Your platitudes and apologies won't help her recovery, now will they?"

Admiral Nokata sighed heavily. "I think we both know whose truly to blame for what's happened. She's never forgiven you for winning the Battle of Horus all those years ago."

Cradling the rod in his arms, it flexed much like a spine would. Lifting one end to his lips, Conner gently kissed the rod and whispered, "Daddy's got you, Betty. Everything will be alright. I'll get you fixed back up."

Admiral Nokata just stood there watching Conner for a time before speaking again. "How many friends did we lose during Horus, Conner? Every time my son's ship leaves the Sol System, Katie and I cry in fear it's the last time we'll see Ezra. Please don't be a stranger. If you want, go by my place while I'm on duty and say hello to Katie and our granddaughters. Maybe some time with the girls will help your Betty heal a bit faster."

Conner looked up at his old captain. His rage had faded as a grief of sorts flooded his being, twisting his guts and stealing his self-control. "I don't know if I can, Nigel. What that dried husk of a First Admiral has done cannot be forgiven or forgotten. I feel like we're on opposites sides now, and that both scares and sickens me."

"Understood." Admiral Nokata nodded sadly before turning to leave. "Go take care of your little girl. The debt I owe you, I'm not sure I'll ever be able to repay, Conner. Still, should you need something, let me know and I'll do everything in my power to get it for you. Understood?"

"What I want right now, you can't begin to give me," Conner said as tears finally escaped his eyes. "Sam, get us out of here."

"One thing before you go, Conner," Admiral Nokata said just before Sam moved into range of triggering the door's eye. "I've seen reports of dark-world movement where your name is coming up more and more. While the why is unknown, what those groups want is to see you dead. You can likely blame the same person I do, but there's no proof she's sicced them on you. Just so you understand, the Hive is reputed to secretly run most dark-world organizations now. Whatever else you do, take measures to protect yourself, my old friend."

Conner faced the door out when Nokata spoke. Turning his head toward the admiral, but not enough to actually see the older man, Conner said, "When that old hag confronts you about what happened here, Nigel, you tell her to keep in mind the fact I won the Battle of Horus should she want to press this any farther. She wants me, then she needs to grav it up and talk to me directly. Attack people I love, and she'll learn a star carrier's penchant for destruction is nothing compared to what I'll do to her."

"Let's go." Sam glared at Admiral Nokata over Conner's shoulder. "My place should have everything you need to restore her body."

~ * ~

Nigel dropped into his chair back in his office with a loud grunt. Letting his head fall back, he rubbed his face with both hands as Conner's grief-stricken expression again played in his mind. In that moment, memories of watching his own son find out his wife and eldest child, a little boy, had been killed in a shuttle accident replayed in his head. Conner's look of devastation had been the same as his son had.

The sound of the office door sliding open and the soft clomp of booted feet stepping inside his office drew him out of the memory. "Yes?"

"Another mug of coffee black with two sugars on the side, Admiral," the familiar bass voice of Nigel's aide said before the clink of metal on metal sounded before him. "The initial summary landed on my desk just before you arrived, sir. I was scanning it when Admiral Victoria walked in, released an uncharacteristic flurry of swearing and then walked out. Do I want to know how big an explosion Mr. Conner released?"

"He pulled ancient history out of his sleeve and cast him at us." Nigel lifted his head and shuddered at the memory of cold fury on the face of someone who should be long dead. "Horatio, get Luna on our stream before the First Admiral blows her top."

A chime sounded a second before a flash of light heralded the arrival of Socrates. The black man wore the same flowing robes as during the hearing. "Admiral. Colonel."

"I'll leave you two alone," Horatio said nodding to Socrates.

"Stay as a witness, Colonel," Socrates said while sitting down in one of the two chairs on the far side of Nigel's desk. "It's still strange seeing the current logo of the Fleet. So many of them have passed across that wall behind you."

"As well as a great many people having sat behind this or some version of this desk," Nigel said while watching the artificial whose body they all lived inside. "This is an exceedingly rare visit, Honored Socrates."

"Just Socrates, please, Admiral." Socrates lowered his gaze to Nigel's eyes. "I was glad to see you don't appear to have been involved in the crime committed against my family."

"Your…" Horatio said out loud in shock.

"Silence, Colonel," Nigel leaned forward on his desk. A light flashed in the desktop indicating an incoming stream connection from the Admiralty's office on Earth's moon, Luna. "Am I to assume you refer to the artificial whose body was attacked?"

"My apologies for getting ahead of myself, Nigel Nokata," Socrates said with a softening of the ancient artificial's glare. "I tend to forget I remember things you humans have forgotten. Briefly, the man you know as Conrad Conner, as well as his cou…sister, are distantly related to me through my late natural husband's granddaughter. Call me a sentimental old fool, but I rather enjoy watching my many grandchildren grow and thrive, even if they aren't aware of our familial ties. You can understand that as a grandfather yourself."

"Yes, I can," Nigel said, not sure whether to believe the artificial at face value or not. Socrates was almost as old as the Earth planetary artificial, having been one of the original nine city-stations created by humanity in the early days of settling the Sol System more than three millennia ago. "Is the young man who was with Conner today also related to you? Is that why the victim is related to you?"

"Samuel didn't have involvement in the birth and raising of Betty, Nigel." Socrates hardened his expression again. "After all, Betty isn't Conner's first child. You haven't forgotten about that scamp Magnus, have you?"

"Let's cut to the chase, Socrates," Nigel said with a hard tone of his own. "What do you want of me? Of Fleet?"

"A warning, Nigel Nokata." Socrates stood up to glare down at him. "The path the Admiralty is on will result in the demise of humanity at the hands of one of its own. Not by the Hive or by some known or unknown alien race, but by another human. Allow the actions of your brethren to continue unabated and you will find out the true breadth of Conner Traxis's rage and grief."

Nigel sat staring at Socrates, fear making his hands tremble from having heard Conner's true name. Swallowing hard, he focused his thoughts on what the artificial had said. "Humanity is too widespread for one man or one star system to kill every member of the species off, Socrates."

"Every time I think the truth of how to do so has finally been lost for good," Socrates said leaning over Nigel's desk to tap the connect icon for the Admiralty, "some power-hungry idiot causes a certain bloodline to rediscover the means to do so. That idiot's actions against Conner on Venus brought Conner to the brink of ending everything."

"Ah, finally Nigel," an old woman of Japanese ancestry said stepping into view wearing a Fleet uniform only to stop and stare at Socrates in surprise. "You're not Admiral Nokata."

"At least your eyes haven't completely gone blind, First Admiral Mariko Mori," Socrates said straightening up to glare down at the admiral, who appeared to be around seventy years old. "Still dying your hair black as though the heavy wrinkles on your body don't announce to everyone you've more wrinkles than a thousand-year-old prune."

"Still a doddering idiot wrapped in a bedsheet, Socrates?" Admiral Mori spat the question out as she glared up at Socrates's well over six-foot height from her own five and a quarter foot height.

"Let's not cause an incident which causes another invocation of the AI Accords, you two." Nigel gripped the bridge of his nose while clenching his eyes shut. He wished he'd just gone home to his wife and grandchildren.

"I'm just here to give warning to Fleet's Admiralty, Mariko." Socrates crossed his arms as he spoke. "Don't push your luck any farther or it'll be an early grave for all of humanity."

"Empty threats from a coward like you don't scare me, chicken legs," Admiral Mori said with a snarl. "I am humanity and what I say goes. Understand?"

"First Admiral Mori," Nigel said with a calm he didn't feel. "I suggest you recheck the security setting on our connection."

"I am merely pointing out that you are messing with the Traxis bloodline, First Admiral," Socrates said as his body went transparent. "Conner is not referred to as "The Hero of Horus" in both the Sol-Humana Confederation and the Spartan Alliance for nothing. Push him too far and humanity might live just long enough to regret it."

CHAPTER 3

"The damage was pretty extensive." Sam's soft voice wrapped around a scared Conner like a warm blanket as they both closed Betty's control rod. "Still, you built her pretty stout."

"I'm just thankful the damage doesn't seem to include her core," Conner said, wiping sweat from his forehead. "She'll be traumatized, but maybe her memories of what happened will be lost or fragmented."

"How are her stats?" Sam worked at removing the old seals while Conner tapped at the holographic diagnostic tools interface floating above the worktable beside them.

"Energy levels are rising. Thank god the new power cells are receiving power from the station nodes," Conner said watching the scrolling numbers and text. "Matrix activity is steady, but low currently. She's likely too scared to want to risk talking to us. Have you had to deal with this kind of trauma in an artificial before?"

Sam didn't respond immediately. Conner glanced at the man, worried about what he'd hear. Sam's entire body sagged into a defeated demeanor. Finally, Sam spoke in a very subdued tone. "I have. His core had more damage, as I recall. Until she wakes up, we can't know what the psychological effect will be."

"What happened to him?" Conner trembled. Nausea twisted his gut and his chest tightened in fear. Conner recognized a parent's grief over losing a child.

"The circumstances of his attack were different, Conner," Sam said, sadness filling the man's eyes. "What happened to him won't happen to Betty."

Conner clenched his eyes and fists closed. The urge to rage and sob warred within him. "He had to be destroyed, didn't he?"

"He went insane and murdered both naturals and artificials," Sam whispered, the sadness reaching his voice. "Betty won't be like that. She was sweet and friendly with everyone, so I don't see her going dark like…"

Conner reached out to pull Sam into a hug. He wasn't completely sure which of them needed it more. Still, he would do everything he could for his little girl. For a time, Sam hugged him back. Eventually, the smaller man pulled away wiping at his face.

"I'm going to deactivate the forced sleep mode," Conner said, reaching for the diagnostics panel. "See if she'll wake up."

"Want me to leave?" Sam didn't face Conner, but rather headed toward the cluttered room's door. "She'll be upset and want to be alone with her father."

"Do you mind?" Conner hesitated touching the controls. Looking again at Betty's rod laying on the worktable, his hands trembled worse now than the first time he activated his little artificial. "You've been so generous by letting me use your workshop and tools. Even the components you've provided are beyond anything I'd have been able to get."

"In my long life," Sam said, his voice cracking slightly, "I have given birth to dozens upon dozens of lives, most artificial. I can likely count on one hand the number of times I've been in your position, Conner. Nothing I do or give will truly ease the guilt you're feeling right now. Just know that you've raised her the best you can and what happened to her was outside your control. What is in your control is how you react to her and what you do for her from here on out. Family is family, and you love them no matter what. Right?"

Conner glanced over his shoulder. Sam stifled sobs as he left the room. Closing his hand into a fist, Conner took several slow, deep breaths in hopes of calming his racing heart. He hadn't let himself think beyond what was needed to fix Betty. Focusing on her needs and erasing as much of the mutilation as possible was paramount. Much of what he'd replaced had been the faulty and low-grade components forced into her by those Fleet lieutenants.

"Let's do this," Conner whispered to himself, keying in the awaken sequence. As he waited, Conner laid a hand on the rod. "Daddy's the only one here with you, Betty. You're safe and I will do everything in my power to see you are never hurt like that again. I swear."

The pin-prickling sensation of the holographic field activating flowed over Conner's hand and forearm. Pulling his hand back, he watched as a teenage girl of roughly seventeen formed. Possibly a deeply tanned Caucasian or a light-skinned African, her figure fluctuated from petite to severely hourglass. She wore first a loose body length gown, but it quickly became pants and a loose shirt.

Almost immediately, even before her form fully appeared as a semi-transparent hologram, Betty thrashed and screamed. Not touching her, Conner called out, "It's daddy, Betty. Your father is here and only him. There is no one here to hurt you. You're safe."

Betty's eyes opened full of panic and fear. She kicked Conner away and rolled off the worktable. Landing on her hands and knees, she jumped to her feet and darted to the room's sole door. It opened for her just as her holo-projectors flickered, causing her body to vanish momentarily. Her control rod housing, still curved like a human spine, zipped out to let the door close.

Conner stood up as he heard Betty shriek. Rushing to the door, it opened just before he got there. Betty slammed into him, spun them both around, and pulled him down as she lost her balance and fell backwards. Her image vanished. Conner hit the floor on his right side and rolled onto his back. Betty reappeared beside him also on her back. The workshop's door stayed open as a naked Sam filled the door huffing.

"You scared the living daylights out of me, Betty," Sam said while he leaned against the door frame. "Are you two alright?"

"Why are you naked?" Betty's voice rose progressively higher as she spoke. "Where am I? Who are you? What did you do to Daddy? Why are you naked?"

"His name is Sam Youngs, and this is his apartment here on *Socrates*," Conner said, groaning in pain as he sat up.

"We got you back from Fleet, and I helped your father to repair and replace the damage done to you by those rogue members of Fleet," Sam said smiling. "I went to change into my outfit I'm wearing for today's shift down at the Rusty Bucket while your father woke you up. If that's all of your questions, can I finish getting dressed?"

Betty scrambled over to huddle behind Conner as she blushed deeply. "Is it okay for me to see you naked?"

"You've looked at worse on the System, Betty," Conner said, attempting to stretch and flex his right side. "Do you remember kicking me away from you before running out of the room and then barreling into me when you ran back in here?"

Betty grew still and quiet for a moment. Hands gripping Conner's shoulders tightened as Betty started sniffling. When the first sob bubbled out, Sam waved with a sad smile before letting the door close on Conner and Betty. Shifting himself, Conner caught Betty as she fell into his arms with gut wrenching wails. Holding her tightly, Conner let her cry as he whispered soft reassurances.

~ * ~

Conner and Betty sat at a table under the flashing red silhouette of a naked and well-endowed man holding a bucket. On the bucket was emblazoned "Rusty". There were only a few tables on either side of the bar's entrance along the sparsely populated docking corridor of Deck Z-Fifty-Three. Conner looked over at Betty, who sat in a low-power, or napping, mode. He still marveled that she wanted to come down here instead of staying home. Her holographic system was off, so people only saw her curved control rod sitting in the chair across from Conner.

Sighing, Conner tapped the flashing spot on the table to request service. As he waited, Conner tapped the middle of his left forearm's sleeve. The familiar male voice of his genderfluid son, Magnus, again sounding exasperated and defeated all at once, spoke. "Will you wash me. I know you own more than one shirt, cheapskate."

"I changed into these clothes before heading down here specifically to piss you off, my darling child," Conner said with a soft cooing voice. He then shifted to a hurt tone. "This is the thanks I get for letting you pick your own name? Even when you don't live in the shirt, my darling Magnus is still hateful to his loving father. Sniff. Sniff."

"Fine." Magnus sighed with dramatic exasperation. "I guess you tapping on me constantly instead of just calling my name is how you show me love. Abusive, I say. Just plain abusive."

Betty giggled. She didn't reappear, but her giggle made Conner smile. Tapping his forearm again, Conner said, "Magnus, prepare a final invoice for our Fleet contract. Include that bill of items I created listing the parts taken from Betty during Fleet's assault and replaced with inferior or incompatible tech. Be sure the surcharge is hefty, considering the quality of what Sam provided. That reminds me, add a markup on those parts from Sam as though they came from a supplier. Be sure the invoice cites the appropriate paragraphs in the contract that makes it clear this is above and beyond the contract amount. Let me know when it's all compiled, and I'll review before sending."

"Shall I delete the messages from your suppliers, then?" Magnus gave "delete" an emphasis, which Conner took to mean air quotes.

"Yes, please," Conner said with a tired sigh. "I'll return to the room once I've eaten, and Betty feels up to being cooped up alone with you and me. Say I'm in a meeting if anyone inquires of my whereabouts. Oh, and let me know if your aunt calls for me again."

"Another one on the house, Conny?" A woman's husky, yet sensuous voice filled the air. She leaned down behind him, wrapping her arms around his shoulders and resting her chin on his head.

"Morning, Delilah," Conner said, leaning his head back to look up at a round face, warm smile framed with pink lipstick, and sparkling eye shadowing. Delilah's long, wavy brown hair fell forward to cover both their faces as Delilah kissed Conner's forehead. Despite her rejection of them as a couple, her affectionate nature tore at Conner's heart.

"Nigel called down a short time ago and ordered you a drink on him," Delilah said, moving to stand beside the table. "I take it Fleet rejected your little girl here?"

Conner forced down the angry retort that first came to mind. "Sam didn't give you the rundown? Suffice it to say my contract with Fleet is cancelled. I'm going to have to rethink my business plans, pending the Arbiters final judgement and the Admiralty's reaction."

A tall thin cylinder was set down on the table before him by Sam. He wore old style blue jeans and a red ripped shirt, which were both skintight to reveal just how fit and defined the body was. The blond hair now hung in its usual messy state. Sam's skin also now had an almost silvery hue to it, unlike its more normal human coloration of earlier. A broad smile filled the man's face.

"Thanks, Sammy," Conner said, picking up the glass and smiling at the man.

Sam's smile widened as he winked at Conner before walking back into the bar. Delilah snickered as Conner twisted his head to watch the man walk away. Despite the clothes now covering him, Conner could only see the man's naked body standing in that doorway.

Delilah chuckled softly as she pulled Conner's gaze back to her with a palm laid against his cheek. "He's older than he looks,

Conner. Maybe you should try dating him. Hell, try dating a guy, any guy, since your last girlfriend really screwed you up."

"I think you were my last girlfriend, Delilah," Conner said smirking.

"I was your first and last nanosexual, Conny." Delilah tapped his nose, the humor vanishing from her voice. "You know the law doesn't recognize me and those like me as human anymore. Now, drink up while Sammy and I make you something to absorb that nasty swill."

"It's a soldier's drink," Conner said, Delilah heading back inside the bar. For a moment, Delilah was again Bobby struggling to figure out how to get the body he wanted in a universe intent on erasing anyone who didn't toe the human purity line.

Shaking his head, Conner turned his attention to the largely empty causeway which the bar fronted. What Conner liked about the Rusty Bucket, especially sitting out here, were the huge transparent sections of the city's outer hull. Z-Sector, the bottom most section of the city, was one of three docking sections of the nearly seven-mile-long tubular station orbiting Jupiter. Each docking sector had long moorings sticking out of the station with berths used by the merchant ships, some of the really huge cargo ships docked here on the city-station's very bottom two levels. On this particular level, Z-Fifty-Three, moderate-sized ships with large crews docked along these moorings, making the outer ring usually infested by crewmembers scrambling about on errands or shore leave.

Tapping an icon of Earth's moon, Socrates's voice announced the time, "Eleven hundred fifteen Lunar Standard Time."

Hearing the artificial's voice reminded everyone the city they lived in was an artificial's body. While Socrates's voice powered most things, there were female "children" who voiced a great many other things. Betty flickered on as a trio of beefy men in power suits walked past while wrestling a large pair of bison to some unknown ship. A few minutes later, a series of men and women passed by going in the opposite direction. Grouped in threes or fours, all argued very vocally about some big celebrity Conner couldn't be bothered to recognize. All seemed to know each other and wore basically the same outfit, leading Conner to assume they all came from the same ship. Throughout it all, Betty just watched them with a mixture of trepidation and nervous calm, but never spoke. It worried Conner since she usually rattled on about all the things she'd learned and how those things applied to what she saw.

"Your food, Sexy." Sam slipped around to block Conner's view while holding a plate. "Everything good with you and the daughter? For now, at least?"

Conner smiled as he glanced past the man, who leaned over with his ass toward Betty, to see a red-faced Betty vanish again. Smirking, he focused on Sam as he spoke. "Don't make me talk to your manager about this sexual harassment, little man. I've invoked the AI Accords once today and I'd hate to drag the arbiters back here to Jupiter a second time in one day."

"I'm not technically an artificial, hot stuff," Sam said, leaning in closer to Conner as though to kiss him. "And neither are you."

"But Betty is, and your ass seems purposely pointed at her, Sammy," Delilah said laughing.

"Just giving her something to spank and beat on to vent her anger." Sam straightened up, twisting around to look at Betty. "Come on, princess. Your new projectors let you go solid, so spank away. My booty can take it."

Betty reappeared with her arms around her legs pulled up against her body. Her dower expression brightened as a slight smile grew on her face. "Keep me out of the games you'd rather play with my father."

Sam stared at Betty nonplussed while Delilah staggered away laughing raucously. Conner, on the other hand, blushed a bright red as he tried to sink into his chair. He couldn't believe Betty would say something like that.

Sam chuckled. Holding out a palm toward Betty, Sam said, "Good one, girl. Give me five."

Confusion filled Betty's face for a moment. Then, like a light going off inside, she sat up and slapped Sam's outstretched hand. With a happy face, she leaned over the table toward Conner as she spoke. "Thanks for letting me come down here, Daddy. I'd kiss you, but I don't want to make the old geezer pining away after you any more jealous than he already is."

"Stop while you're ahead, little girl," Sam growled playfully, tapping Betty's nose.

Betty's happy expression dropped instantly. Trembling, she suddenly vanished. Her control rod dropped onto the table with a loud crash and every light on it went dark. Conner's plate of food and drink jumped into the air, sending their contents flying in every direction, but mostly onto Conner. The glass and plate bounced off the floor and rolled a short distance away.

"Betty!" Conner jumped to his feet, already lifting Betty. Delilah grabbed up the glass and plate. Sam leaned in with Conner to examine Betty.

"Is she alright?" Delilah stepped up between Conner and Sam.

"She's powered herself down," Conner said. A sense of failure overtook him, with the urge to sob becoming nearly overwhelming. "Why? What made her so afraid?"

"She's going to need counseling." Sammy pulled his shirt off to wipe down Betty's control rod first and then Conner himself. "I can ask around to find out who's the best. My certification in that field expired a long time ago."

"I feel like I've already asked too much of you, Sam," Conner said as he lifted Betty into his arms. "Put the food on my tab, guys. Betty probably—"

"Put her back in her chair and sit down, Conny," Delilah said firmly. "Unlike your daughter, you need food. You are not paying a damn luna to me today. Sit and see about calming yourself down while we get you a new drink and more food. Sammy, a fresh drink for the worried dad."

Delilah pressed the glass she held into Sam's hands with a pointed look on her face. Turning, she walked back inside the bar with the plate to leave the pair of men alone. Conner, though, moved to leave. Sam grabbed Betty out of his arms and set the control rod into a chair at a clean table.

"Sit down and be here for when she decides to come out," Sam said with an imperious tone. "I've been in your shoes, Conner. Given time and the right counseling, she'll be fine. However, don't push her and do get her counseling. She's had a traumatic experience. Whether a natural or an artificial, trauma causes changes in the brain. She's young and strong, just like her father. Believe in her and yourself to get through this."

Conner walked over and pulled Sam into a hug. "Thanks, Sammy. I owe you."

Sam pulled back to press both hands to Conner's cheeks. Pressing their lips together, Sam kissed Conner quickly, but with passion. "Think of this as one father helping another. Nothing owed or due. However, you are sexy as hell, Conrad Conner."

Sam walked over to the dirty table and used his shirt to clean up the worst of the mess. Conner stood watching with a confused numbness. A soft whir drew his attention away from Sam. Glancing at Betty, he saw the lights along her body's length light up. While her body didn't reappear, the rod curved slightly as though Betty sat in the chair normally.

"I'm sorry, Daddy," Betty whispered.

Conner knelt by the chair and placed a hand on the table before the chair. He knew not to intrude into the space where her body would be if the lights were on. "Nothing to apologize for, my little girl. You sit and people watch or nap or whatever. Sam and Delilah are just as worried about you as I am. We all love you and want you happy. Okay?"

Betty reappeared, but only as a transparent hologram. Tears stained her face, but she smiled and nodded at Conner. After a moment, she again vanished. Most of the lights on her control rod went to flashing rapidly up and down its length, again signaling she'd gone into a sort of napping state. Aware, but purposely ignoring everyone.

Feeling a little better, but still verging on breaking down in some fashion, Conner moved to the other chair at the table. His knees groaned as he sat, reminding him of how out of shape his forty-something body had gotten. Slouching in the chair, Conner stared at Betty, and then past her to Sam, who reemerged from the bar with a mop and bucket. With Betty's blinking lights in the corner of his vision, Conner watched the younger-looking man work bare-chested. His mind replayed the morning, but especially their conversation in the lift-pod when Sam revealed his body being a lost technology.

"His hands felt normal," Conner whispered, barely loud enough for his own ears to make out the words. "Nothing looked…"

Conner rubbed his face with his hands as he mentally chastised himself. *Don't go there, you old lech. He's…he's older than you. By what? Forty or fifty times? Why would he be interested in me and my old, half-broken-down piece of crap natural body?*

Conner looked down at the table, with the occasional glance at his own ruffled and now stained clothes. *I'm getting a paunch, but not nearly as bad as some others my age. Still have most of my hair. A bit thinner than twenty years ago, but likely because I've pulled on it in frustration. Not that I'm good-looking compared to so many others, even if they aren't models or idols or whatever they call the current celebrity of the month. Sam's just lonely. I can understand that. I've used raising Betty to avoid thinking about what happened on Venus. I don't want to put someone else who loves me into that old hag's line of fire again.*

Throwing his head back, Conner stared up at the gently glowing ceiling. Forcing himself to stop thinking about the past and his shattered heart, he instead tried to think of what path to take his company. While his idea for a communications droid was partially realized, he saw it would only be manifest as a single droid. Betty was safe now, but he couldn't see using her for his original concept. Not without figuring out a better way of safe proofing the body. The current housing provided a great deal of protection to all sorts of calamities, from fire to water to even high electrical discharge, but human-proofing it would be difficult.

Admiral Nokata's warning came back to him. He hated the idea of needing protection. The very concept of someone out to physically hurt him seemed weird. Yet, the Venus attack on Shima and himself had driven him to flee the inner system. *Socrates' Odyssey* had seemed a safer distance from his sister and her family. If that now proved untrue, was there any place in the universe he could go that would keep what was left of his biological family safe?

I could end the universe, like I wanted after Venus, Conner mused silently, an old darkness again surging from the depths he'd driven it to over the last decade. *Yet, it's not the universe after me, just one deranged woman. A woman in control of ships capable of destroying planets and forcing stars to go nova. Given the relative peace currently between the twelve stellar governments, and the Hive seemingly keeping mostly to itself for the last thousand years, what should my company's focus be now?*

CHAPTER 4

As he closed his eyes again, laying his head back, Conner again pictured Sam standing naked in the doorway. The always affectionate man smiled while stepping towards him, but Conner shook his head and thought, *He'll flake out on me like all the others.*

"Oh, come on," a woman hissed from almost beside Conner. Opening his eyes a crack, he found a brown-skinned young woman leaning over and tapping on the top of Betty's control rod. "Turn back on."

Conner jerked upright, anger already contorting his face as he snarled at the wisp of a teenage girl. "Get away from my daughter!"

Jumping back, the woman, who appeared to be no older than eighteen or nineteen, wore a very expensive version of a merchant ship captain's uniform with everything about her immaculate and perfectly coifed. White pants and black shoes with a dark burgundy shirt that had a name on the right side of her chest made Conner's first thought be, *"Nothing to regulation. A damn little rich girl."*

"Do you normally poke strangers when they're obviously napping, kid?" Conner glared at the girl's jet-black hair and dark skin typical of the Indian subcontinent on Earth. "Now leave us alone."

"Hello!" The teen jerked upright, pivoted toward Conner, and smiled in a sickeningly sweet manner. She pressed her palms together and bowed ever so slightly forward. "I'm Kashi Tandon, Captain of Shining Sun Shipping's flagship, the *CSS Infinity*. We're the newest shipping company amongst the stars!"

"CSS?" Conner stepped back, wishing he had something strong to drink given whose family this kid belonged to. "Is that Confederation or Corporate Star Ship?"

"Corporate?" Kashi sounded dubious and unsure. "Mikey won't tell me. He says I've not earned my captain's pins yet."

"That sounds like a problem you had better figure out before you leave *Socrates' Odyssey*, kiddo," Conner said sitting back down. Stretching out as though to nap, he crossed his arms as he glared up at the girl. "Now, if you'll leave my daughter and me alone, I'd much appreciate it."

Mostly closing his eyes, Conner hoped the girl would leave. It was hard for him to believe the person before him was really over eighteen. Of course, he'd been accused of being old and crotchety, though mostly by Nigel's granddaughters and Betty, so he might be biased against those who appeared more than ten years younger than himself. Cracking an eye open, Kashi still stood there staring at him, then up at the bar's sign, which likely had changed from the scantily clad man to a scantily clad woman by this time. Determined to not get involved in a big, multi-stellar mega conglomerate, given her last name, Conner tried to ignore the woman in hopes she'd get frustrated and leave.

"Why are you here?" Kashi again leaned over Betty, looking closely at her control rod again but not reaching out. She took surreptitious glances at both him and the open doorway in the other direction.

Conner softly groaned, trying to figure out what he could say to get this girl to leave. "Naked guys. You're harshing the place's vibe, so skedaddle."

"Ske-what?" Kashi turned toward him, her head actually tilting to one side in confusion.

"Go the hell away, kid," Conner growled, internally hating how his time on a certain star carrier had given him way too many junk phrases from ancient movies. He tried to figure out how to get her to go away without actually using foul language, which would likely have his late mother haunting his waking hours in addition to some of his dreams. Besides, the longer she stayed, the more likely he'd do something stupid.

"Naked men?" Kashi furrowed her brows while tapping her lips with her left hand's index finger. "So, you're one of those types?"

Conner cracked open one eyelid to glare at what he decided really was the very sheltered daughter of one of the richest families in all of the inhabited universe. A child let out into the world for the first time. It made him wonder why there weren't any handlers around to protect her.

"I like what and who I like, kid," Conner stood up again to glare into her eyes. "You have been told to leave me alone. If you don't leave in the next five minutes, I'll be throwing your scrawny brown butt down the causeway."

Kashi glared at Conner for a moment before letting out a soft, frustrated huff. "Did you not hear my name? I am—"

"Yes, I did," Conner said in a steadily louder voice. "Didn't care the first time and certainly don't care a second time. I've had a bad day and want to be left alone. That. Means. Leave!"

Conner noticed Betty's holographic body flicker on, take a look around, and vanish again. It made Conner smile, if only inwardly. When Kashi didn't leave, Conner yelled, "Go the fuck away!"

"Is this some kind of AI interface?" Kashi said in a quick huff. "Did you build it or buy it? I need a Tech Officer who can fix or rebuild my ship's old military AI."

"Military...?" Conner stared in surprise at the kid, his anger draining away as it dawned on him who Mikey was. "When you referred to a Mikey, you meant M1K3Y, or Military One series, Keeper Three unit, Young-class artificial intelligence?"

Kashi just looked at Conner with no facial expression for a moment before replying, "I guess. It doesn't matter what you call it, it's just a tool."

The girl might as well as used a racial slur against Conner himself. Fighting every desire to punch the child before him in the face, Conner stepped right up to Kashi, their noses practically touching as he snarled at the girl. "Leave immediately and do some research, kid, before I punch you or this city's controlling artificial hears what you just said. Among other things, you've just committed a felony and offended me to my core."

"What did I say wrong?" A confused expression wrinkled Kashi's brow. "It's not like—"

"Leave!" Conner roared, spittle showering the young woman's face. "Now!"

Kashi harrumphed at him before turning to walk away calmly. Sam walked out of the bar with a tall glass on a tray along with a bowl of chips and salsa. Conner reached toward his left sleeve, about to slap it angrily. Clenching the hand into a fist, he swallowed his anger and sat back down.

"Your drink and something to munch on while you wait for your food," Sam said setting the tray onto the table. Leaning over, the still shirtless Sam gently pulled Conner's face upwards before pressing their lips together. Kissing Conner passionately, Sam slowly settled himself onto Conner's lap as Conner responded by returning the kiss.

After several minutes of kissing, an embarrassed cough by Betty got Conner to push Sam away. He saw the faint holo-image of Betty curled up on the chair with her hands hiding a deeply blushing face. She signed with her hands awkwardly, *"Get a room, Daddy."*

Whispering breathlessly, Conner said, "We've embarrassed the teenager."

"Do you feel better?" Smiling, Sam touched their noses together. "We could hear you yelling all the way back in the kitchen, you know. Well, I could. Delilah was too busy singing pre-Space Era songs she called rock-a-billy."

"Blame that on Rusty," Conner said chuckling. He spotted Kashi returning. "Oh great. I didn't scare her away for good."

"Business opportunities, my sexy man," Sam whispered, lounging on Conner so his face nuzzled into the crook of Conner's neck.

"My apologies, sir," Kashi said, again with palms pressed together before her and a slight bow toward Conner. "After some quick research, as you suggested, I see I have been badly taught about things by my tutors. I do have a need for a tech officer to help me get my…the ship to follow my commands as its Captain."

Conner found he couldn't properly tap on his sleeve with Sam lounging on him. He silently thanked Sam for staying, though the man's lips did more than just tickle him. So, he lifted his left arm until the forearm was level and said, "Magnus, display company information and pricing for the potential client before me."

A small holographic placard appeared above Conner's arm displaying his company logo and name, The C5 Group. His name was displayed prominently, with a list of services in smaller print underneath the phrase "Reasonable consulting fees."

"Before we go any further, kid," Conner said, wishing he could reach his drink, "we've already exceeded my no charge question and answer period. Anything further will cost you a hundred thousand lunas an hour. Please state your acceptance or refusal for the record."

"What? That's outrageous," Kashi said with a shocked expression while stepping backward. "Not even my father charges that much."

"Acceptance or refusal, please," Conner said again, hoping for refusal so he could take nap, a drink, or maybe get Sam to kiss him, if only to embarrass Betty some more.

Fury played across the teen's face before she spun around. After storming a few yards away, Kashi lifted her left arm up near her face. Conner couldn't make out who she talked to, or see the face, but after several heated minutes of discussion, Kashi again huffed indignantly before the sleeve projectors turned off. Returning to stand before Conner, Kashi raised her left arm and tapped the center of her forearm before saying, "Shining Sun Shipping accepts The C5 Group's hourly rate. Document and confirm charges for fifteen minutes of time."

"Read the fine print, please," Conner said keeping his facial expression neutral. "One hour's charge no matter how short the consultation."

Shooting daggers at him with her eyes, Kashi said, "Append acceptance to state minimum charge will be for one hour of time. Acceptance received?"

Conner forced his face to remain neutral as he spoke. "Magnus, confirm arrival of acceptance by Shining Sun Shipping of our hourly rate for one hour of services."

Magnus's deep voice replied, "Received and confirmed. Payment transfer confirmed upon completion of said hour starting now."

"So, Mr. Conner, what do you know about military ship AIs." Kashi glared at Sam, as though she expected him to bring a chair over for her. "Specifically, the AIs put into star carriers."

Conner stared at the woman, shocked she could have a Fleet star carrier in her possession. He'd heard they were considering retiring the now three-hundred-year-old ships, but not that any had actually been taken out of active duty. Drumming his fingers on Sam's muscular back, Conner's stomach churned with fear at offending both a Tandon and the likely creator of the star carriers themselves, Sam.

"Mikey was Youngs Galactech's favored factory-generic designation for the artificial intelligences put into the star carriers they built," Conner said as Sam's kissing stopped, "during a specific time period. The artificial's name then changed to something based on what Fleet named the ship. The 'Mikey' generic designation stopped being used several centuries ago. Calling an artificial by their generic designation is akin to people calling you by the worst derogatory term for a woman's anatomy every time they want to get your attention. They consider it not just rude, but highly offensive and will treat you as an imbecilic child until you either do something stupid and get taken away, or just go away. Should you be dumb enough to keep being a bigot to them, they have been known to vent their entire ship, which is their body, to space to get the offensive party to shut up. Hence, a big source of artificial hatred of humanity. Understand?"

"What! How are they not erased and reprogrammed?" A horrified expression contorted Kashi's face.

"First, the AI Accords of twenty ninety-seven granted artificials the same rights as us naturals and are considered the official end of the more than one thousand years of Hive-Human wars." Conner used his fingers while counting off his points for added effect. "Second, ship artificial intelligences, which is where the shortened term 'artificial' comes from, within Fleet are spacers, have gone to their own form of Fleet Academy, and are rank officers who can command subordinates and have to take orders from superiors. Third, artificials are a recognized sentient species per numerous treaties over the millennia. They have rights, are not slaves, and whether you like it or not, do not have to put up with your bigotry. If you are having problems with your ship's artificial, try treating it as the crew member, if not real owner, of your ship that it is. Should you lose your ship's artificial, and since you have a Fleet star carrier, you better have a minimum of four hundred trained crew members on board to limp it back to a military-grade shipyard for repairs."

"Four hundred?" Kashi's surprise played out both on her face and in her voice. "We were told ten was the minimum."

"If the ship's artificial is working smoothly and cooperating with your command structure." Conner struggled to not sound too condescending to the presumably well-educated teenager, "then ten or so would likely be an acceptable skeleton crew. Fleet, though, liked to have enough crew onboard to operate the ship with minimal artificial function, as a safeguard during battles where the ship's artificial can be taken out by the enemy. If this star carrier you have will be operating as a cargo ship, ten to fifty crew members would likely be more than adequate with the ship's artificial being in good health and humor. Assuming the ship's artificial is okay with being a cargo carrier and never seeing battle again."

"Why wouldn't it be okay with not seeing battle?" Kashi leaned forward a bit, curiosity filling her face. "From what I've read and learned of battle, it sounds horrible."

"It is horrible." Conner swallowed hard as flashes of his own experiences in battle surged to the forefront of his mind, which threatened to overwhelm him right then and there. Struggling to push it away, Conner concentrated on Sam's breathing on his neck and the curves of Kashi's body to remind him where and when he was. Focusing on the question, he kept his physical struggle to clenching and unclenching his hands. "However, military artificials are programmed and raised to crave battle. Youngs-class ships even more-so, considering skirmishes with the Hive were ongoing at the time and threatened to blow up into another full war. Part of your problems could be the artificial's desire to go find a fight coming to the surface. Or he's bored enough he's fighting with you because you're not making the job interesting enough. You've got to remember a star carrier normally has around five thousand men and women on board and were surrounded by between six and a dozen other ships as part of its battle group. Now, he's essentially alone and isolated from everything he's known. Add to that you, who knows nothing of his past, what he's use to, and nothing about how to treat artificials as the equals they are."

"I'm still in the shakedown and training phase of starting up the company." Kashi sighed in dejection. "The woman we hired as the tech officer fled as soon as we made it to the Centauri system and docked. What if the artificial isn't stable? Can you repair it?"

Conner resisted the urge to laugh. Pushing on Sam, he leaned forward enough to grab his glass. Taking a swing, the alcohol's familiar burn on his throat bringing a sense of familiar calm to his racing mind, Conner carefully considered how to answer her question. Really, he struggled to not shout out what he really wanted to know. Namely, did they disable and remove the weapons before giving a child a loaded gun.

"Artificials for military ships are created and raised for the specific task that militaries demand of them," Conner said in a low, even voice. "The ships will be beaten upon, nearly destroyed, rebuilt, and sent out to do it all over again. Sometimes within a few days but as long as a few months, depending on the damage. Their command structure can change on a moment's notice, which is hard enough for the humans, but for an artificial, it can be far worse. For those reasons, there is no rebuilding a military ship's controlling artificial. You'd have to replace it with a whole new artificial created and educated to handle a formerly military ship."

"Okay," Kashi said hesitantly. "What does that involve?"

Shaking his head, Conner thought about doing just as asked very seriously. Granted, he'd thought about doing just this sort of thing to a certain ship he'd been assigned to for a good chunk of his decade long stint in Fleet. Instead, he'd gotten reassigned planet-side. "Well, for starters, try a minimum of a year to convince the AI to leave the ship for something else. They're a person, so you can't just dump and purge the system. That's murder. Once they're out, you have to chase down child routines which may be hiding, get them out and spend probably another six months making sure you've got them all. Finally, you'll spend at least six months writing the new codex and learning matrix, but that's on the low end. Most likely, given it's a star carrier your discussing, which is one of the most advanced and complicated warships currently in existence, it'll take eighteen months to get a stable codex and matrix."

"Two to three years?" Kashi looked crushed. "I…I can't wait that long for a ship that obeys me."

"Well, add the required three years worth of learning hours for your new artificial to be considered an adult, which usually balloons into closer to eight years," Conner said while tapping on his glass, "the three month certification process for it to be recognized officially as an adult, the six months for the paperwork to come through, and then the years it can take to get the artificial up to speed on a specific ship's systems, command structure, and learning the command structure can change suddenly, and you've quickly spent a decade of time. Not easy to do, rife with possible setbacks, and most probably numerous regulatory hurdles."

"Then fix the current artificial!" Kashi pleaded, surging forward to grab Conner's arm. "I need a ship that follows my orders!"

"Try being nice to it, kid," Conner said before taking another swig of his drink. He noticed the time on the table while setting the glass down. "Let's take a short break. Go mull things over and come back with any additional questions, kid. Sam, can you get up for a moment? I'd like to enjoy some chips and salsa. Can't you hear my stomach growling?"

"Let me help," Sam said, sitting up on Conner's lap to grab a chip and use it to scoop salsa up. Kashi glared in disgust before walking away. Sam still fed Conner the chip and salsa, giggling the entire time.

"And I'm here for the cute guys, not a pair of lovesick geezers," Betty grumbled reappearing around her spine. "Will you go back to work, Sam. You both are intruding on my people watching."

Sam and Conner looked at each other. Smiling, Conner said, "Feed me another, cute stuff."

Betty jumped to her suddenly solid feet, growling in disgust. She stomped to a table on the far side of the door into the bar. "Get a room, you two. You're being gross."

"Hmm," Conner muttered, smirking at Betty's retreating back. "Think we went too far?"

"She's talking and interacting, so I take that as a good sign," Sam whispered. "Still, consider professional help for her. I really should get back inside. We'll likely get a rush soon. I saw several ships from the Denabi Axiom were docking this morning and I'm bartending."

"Hi, Sammy!" A trio of ladies waved at them as they walked into the Rusty Bucket. All three were in their twenties and quite beautiful. "You working or playing?"

"Some of both, my pretties." Sam laughed jumping to his feet. "Work calls, gorgeous. Another drink now or with your food?"

"With my food," Conner said with a smile.

As Sam walked over to check on Betty, Conner shifted his attention back to Kashi. Daughter of one of the richest families in existence, Kashi now stood against the clear metal hull seemingly gazing out at the ships docked at a nearby mooring. Just visible was another face, which told Conner she spoke to someone. Still, Conner remembered the uneasy look on the kid's face as Sam lounged and seemingly kissed on Conner as though a lover. It wasn't an unusual reaction, even after more than a millennium since the Hive had overrun the Sol System and killed nearly all eleven trillion humans living on or around every planet. Forty years of the Hive controlling humanity's mother world had instilled a deeply ingrained opposition to any relationship that didn't propagate and keep humanity pure. Respect usually came grudgingly, but those like

Kashi, who felt above everyone else, still made it blatantly known they didn't like it. Conner wasn't sure the so-called "Third Dark Age," as many called the three centuries following humanity's retaking of the Sol System, had really ever ended.

Kashi walked back to Conner with a self-satisfied smile spreading across her face. "I'm hiring you as my tech officer, Mr. Conner. Fifty thousand lunas and a week's paid shore leave a year. Quite a nice deal, don't you think?"

"I'm not looking for a job, kid," Conner said before eating another chip. "Even if I was, you put the decimal point in the wrong location. Now, do you have any more questions for me or is this session done?"

"That is the going rate for a tech officer in a shipping company," Kashi said sternly. "Anything more is ridiculous."

"Listen to my words, kid," Conner said, continuing to eat. His irritation with Kashi's attitude that money got her anything she wanted was making it hard to speak calmly. "I'm not looking for a job. Besides, this wasn't a job interview."

"You've no money and no prospects, Mr. Conner," Kashi said with unabashed anger. "I've coddled you enough. Now come and fix my ship."

"You can't afford me, kid." Conner forced laughter. A group of men and women in merchant ship uniforms who were walking past stopped at Kashi's outburst. Sam emerged at that moment with Conner's food. Spotting, or maybe smelling, the steak and potatoes on the plate, the group headed for the tables. Conner, though, wondered just what to do to get this annoyance of a woman to leave him in peace. The last thing he wanted was to be talked into working for another big conglomerate.

"I'm a Tandon, damn it." Kashi hissed softly while leaning over him. "What makes you think I can't buy you lock stock and barrel?"

Conner turned to the teen again. "Look, kid."

"Stop calling me kid!" Kashi shouted. "My name is Kashi! K-A-S-H-I! At least use my name. You are being rude."

"So are you." Conner snarled, rising to his feet. "I run my own company, which you have paid a pretty penny for the right to ask me questions. I have a job. I have prospects. I have an expertise which you need. If you wish to hire The C5 Group to interview your ship's controlling artificial as part of a diagnostic on his or her stability, then contact my office for a proposal."

"You join my crew for a three-year stint," Kashi said with a finger poke to his chest, "and I'll pay every debt you have before the ship ever leaves."

"Listen to my words and understand them." Conner shouted while grabbing Kashi's finger and bending it backwards.

"Ow, ow, ow!" Kashi dropped to one knee to keep Conner from breaking the finger. "Fine! Fine!"

Conner released the teen's finger but remained glaring down at Kashi. "One million lunas for The C5 Group to just talk to your damn ship's artificial for any amount of time. Another million for someone from The C5 Group to actually do a stability diagnostics interview, two million to set foot on the ship, should that be required, and half a million lunas per one-way trip that person has to make during any diagnostic analysis. That's before the hazard fee, which will be equal to Fleet standard hazard pay, if it's a ship I, or the associate I send, have dealt with at any time previously in our life. Again, I am the president and founder of The C5 Group. Not some random guy you can coerce into doing what you want by waving a fat wad of bills. Want my expertise? Hire The C5 Group for the amount we propose, and you'll get my expertise. Did you understand all of that?"

"Done." Kashi said as Sam stopped at the door into the bar. "Two and a half million lunas for a test run across the Sol System to the jump point for the Centauri System. After jumping to Centauri, we make any repairs there that's needed since there are ship repair yards large enough to handle my old Fleet star carrier in Proxima orbit. Once the AI is stable, I'll bring you back to Socrates. Happy?"

"Since you don't listen to what I say, send the particulars of your ship and exactly what the problems are to my office. A proposed contract and fee will be submitted to you," Conner said with a shake of his head while sitting back down. "I'm not haggling details with you while I try and enjoy my lunch. This session is now over."

CHAPTER 5

"Are you crazy?" Delilah shouted as Conner sat at the bar inside the Rusty Bucket sipping at a glass of whiskey. "Why in the Nine Hells of Mercury would you go work for the Tandons?"

"Those nanos didn't change that tendency of yours to not listen to what I actually say," Conner said swirling the clear brown liquor in the real crystal sipping glass he held. "Now, Delilah, listen to what I actually say. The C5 Group has been contracted to provide services, which include analyzing her ship's artificial intelligence. While I am the primary employee of The C5 Group, I am not the sole employee. Having said that, Magnus and I researched Miss Tandon's company while negotiating the contract. She just changed the company name to Shining Sun Shipping after her daddy bought that old bucket of crazy I served on during my Fleet days over a decade ago. This should be the easiest money I've ever made."

"Do you really think that old artificial is going to just let you walk away again?" Delilah leaned forward and lowered her voice. "From what you've told me about those days, he'll likely lock the doors and not let you out again. And if not him, then the damn Tandons will lock them. Then you're back to how life was when working for Danlen."

Conner downed the last bit of whiskey and slammed the glass down on the bar. "Blessed Stars of Andromeda, it's like talking to that damn Tandon girl. Who the hell said I was even stepping foot inside the ship, Delilah? The contract is for limited services structured in a stepped method to limit how much they spend. I've got the required down payment for me to contact the ship's artificial so I can do my initial diagnostic survey. While not my preferred work, I'm good at it and I know this ship inside and out. Hell, I practically rebuilt his ancient ass in the middle of a damn battle, so I can say with authority that I know him inside and out. We've had our differences, but the only things I know that make him crazy is being purposely misnamed or willfully ignorant people. His new owner is both of those things, so the extent of my job is going to be slapping her perfect little teenage face with those facts. Now if you'll excuse me, I need to go back to work. My compliments to your chef and bartender."

"You step foot on that ship and your life is over, Conner," Delilah said with venom. "Everything you've worked for will be gone. And for what? A quick fling with the past?"

"What I've worked for?" Conner chuckled as he walked toward the door. He glanced over at the sole occupied table, which was where Betty sat watching Sam dance and gyrate on the bar's small stage. "I currently own the rights to my inventions, can enjoy what royalties they might someday generate, and I've got freedom from oversight by owning my own company. Sometimes, I'll have to put up with working for the big boys, like this job with Shining Sun Shipping. By taking my latest creation, which is currently sitting over there enjoying Sam dancing for her, I can find out how well she'll interact with a Fleet ship, even if it has been decommissioned. Now, if you'll excuse me, I've got to actually work for a living."

"That's a big load of bull crap and you know it, Conrad," Delilah retorted angrily. "She'll take you for everything and leave you penniless, just like everyone else you've ever worked for. You'll be back here after the first trip begging for a free meal again and you know it!"

Conner looked at Delilah and the carefully coifed look she always presented to the world, especially once she accepted what her true gender was. Like so many times before, she never really listened to him. Okay, he knew he had nothing. For eight years he'd put up with living in a one room efficiency apartment assigned by the city, since creating and building Betty had left him with barely enough money to feed himself. The constant threat of starvation and failure every month had him staring constantly at depression. Of course he wanted to afford something nicer and have the money to buy some actual furnishings. Oddly, Betty may have done that for him, but not how he'd planned.

"So what, Delilah?" Conner turned away with the intent of never returning. "My only living family has made it clear I'm not welcome in her life, the person I loved enough to propose marriage to was murdered before my eyes, and the only thing of any value I own is my company, which I might remind you for the fifth time, is currently in the black. So, what if my company gets taken from me? I'll just start over and create a new company."

"Don't you dare bring out the pity party of one line, asshole." Delilah rushed forward to prevent Conner from leaving. "Every time you've worked for a large organization, someone decides to use you as a shit rag. I didn't pull you out of the gutter to go back to being some corporation's fucktard again."

"You…?!" Conner stared at the nanosexual, a mixture of anger, despair, and more pouring through his mind. For a moment he wasn't sure what to say or do. Hurting her was a strong desire at the moment, her self-righteous attitude pissing him off the most. Leaning in close, Conner snarled, "We aren't married or dating, Delilah. I thought you were my friend, but I see all I am to you is the poor guy whose vain struggle makes you feel better about your life. The fact you can't be happy I've gotten a client of notoriety tells me just how blind I've been to what you really are. Well, no more. Have a great life, Delilah. I will not be back anytime soon."

Delilah stared in shock at him, not saying or doing anything. Seeing she wasn't stopping him, Conner pushed past her as he yelled, "I'm heading home, Betty. Don't be late and make sure you pay up before leaving."

He stepped through the door as a hand pulled him to a stop. Delilah turned him around with tears and panic in her eyes. She spoke with a softer, kinder voice. "Not come back? Why with them? You're going backwards. I'll always help you out."

Conner shook his head as he wondered at this hot to cold change in Delilah. It wasn't like her, but maybe he'd never let himself see the real Delilah before. Whatever it was, the Delilah he once thought he loved no longer existed. He doubted if there were ever any real feelings for him in her. Now all she did was remind him of his loneliness.

"When you start listening to what I say and not what you want to hear," Conner said bitterly, "we might be able to talk again. Until then, you have fun in your little universe, Delilah."

"But, Conny," Delilah sobbed, tears trickling down her cheeks as a sob distorted her voice.

"I'm done here." Conner pulled free of her grip and walked away.

A group of young Fleeters walked past him still in uniform, which told Conner they were starting their night out on the town early. He was nearly to the pod station when footsteps ran up behind him. Sam fell into step beside him, entwining their arms together.

"Are you and I still good, Conner?" Sam leaned affectionately against Conner.

Conner smiled at the man's move. "Do you listen before reacting?"

"Yes, but I am only human. Well, originally human. Piss me off enough and I will likely ignore what you say." Sam smirked when they stopped to face each other. "My emotions have cost me a few things I thought important in my life. I've learned those things weren't crucial to my survival and found at least contentment without them. Something which can happen if you're lucky to live long enough."

"And exactly how long a life is that?" Conner arched an eye with curiosity. After what Sam had told him the other day, and what little he could find about Sam within the System, Conner feared he needed to tread lightly or get seriously burned.

Sam slowly released the top three seals holding Conner's shirt closed but stayed silent for a bit before finally answering. "For a while now, I've thought too long. While I was born human, I lost both my parents to the Hive long before you or your bloodline had likely even begun. I've lived a dozen different lives and found happiness in just as many different scenarios."

"Sam," Conner said before Sam pressed a hand over his mouth.

"I'm answering your question because you've obviously tried to find out on your own," Sam spoke softly as Betty approached. "You recognized my name when I told it to you, but because of the damage to the System by the many wars with the Hive and other humans, my birth date has been lost. Right?"

Sam kept his hand on Conner's mouth, forcing Conner to nod in reply. Smiling sadly, Sam continued. "Both my parents were killed by the Hive, but with quite a few years between their deaths. Mother became fairly famous before the Hive finally killed her and fifteen million other naturals during the Proxima Attack of ten forty-nine. I've lost track of when my birthday was or if our calendar is as accurate as my great uncle claims. So, I'm Samuel Maxwell Youngs, son of Beckett Youngs and Miranda Magenta, and I'm around two millennia old."

"The Miranda Magenta who became First Queen of the

Humana Hegemony?" Betty leaned in from beside the pair, staring intently at Sam. "Also, the Miranda Magenta whom the Magenta Alliance is named after?"

"Yes, Betty," Sam said, his smile fading.

"Then your great uncle is the Earth Artificial and Socrates is your maternal great grandfather." Betty tapped on her fingers as she spoke. "At least, if the histories I read about the First Interim were true. Socrates married Maxwell Magenta, the human general who died defeating the Hive here at Jupiter and thus ended the First Hive-Human War. Miranda Magenta's biography was quite exciting, Sam. I believe you are listed as an author."

"I was." Sam forced a smile while stepping away from Conner and Betty. "I wasn't aware a copy remained on the System."

"Socrates found it for my ancient history studies last year," Betty spoke with a small bounce and a wide smile. "He said he didn't remember everything written in the book due to some kind of memory loss but said it might help my communications techniques with old and ancient artificials like him and the other surviving second generation artificials. Are you considered third or fourth generation artificial now?"

A chime just preceded a bright flash of white light. The stocky sixty-year-old figure of Socrates appeared wearing flowing ancient-styled robes standing opposite Betty beside Conner. "He's still considered human, Betty."

"Grandfather!" Sam jumped while staring wide-eyed at the city's artificial.

"Don't get your britches all in a twist, Sammy." Socrates rolled his eyes. "Technically, you are more like an offshoot of fifth or sixth generation artificial."

As Sam angrily laid into the city-station's artificial, Conner sighed with something between relief and frustration. Pressing his shirt closed, Conner watched the pair argue for a moment as a feeling of being forgotten came over him. Knowing work awaited him, Conner motioned with his head at Betty before continuing on to the pod station. His one room apartment was in Z-Sector, but up on the fourth level. It was both home and office since his company had never generated enough income to afford separate office space.

A pod arrived within seconds. The doors were closing as Sam came running up. Conner let the doors close, just as he hardened his heart yet again at the prospect of love found and lost.

"Too many times, old man," Conner whispered while Betty excitedly called for their floor. "No need for another broken heart."

~ * ~

Conner stepped out onto a darkened Deck Z-Fifty-Three. It was nearly midnight and the city-station's attempt to emulate planet-side day-night cycles led to very low light levels throughout the city of several hundred million souls. His attempts to talk to Kashi Tandon's ship had been fruitless. In a last-ditch effort, he agreed to a face-to-face meeting of sorts. With the city's agreement, the ship's artificial would connect through the city so they could meet. The meeting would be in a small conference facility near the mooring where the ship was berthed.

"This is Conrad Conner of The C5 Group," Conner said after walking into the assigned conference room. A long table and a dozen chairs filled the small room. "I'm here for a meeting with—"

A chime sounded just before Socrates flashed into the room on the far side of the table. With a stern glare at Conner, the artificial said, "Yes, yes. Get on with this ridiculousness so some of us can get back to sleep."

A second flash preceded the appearance of a middle-aged man in a Fleet uniform wearing the single hollow diamond pin of a lieutenant commander. The creases at the outside corners of his eyes, the permanent furrow between the eyebrows, and the pale skin of someone of Earth European descent with some Asian heritage appeared beside and slightly behind Socrates. A sadness filled the newcomer's eyes even as he wrung his hands before him with nervousness. To his surprise, Conner had no anger or animosity toward Barley. In fact, a sort of nostalgia for those days on that star carrier came back to him.

"Do you both agree to talking, no violence against the other, be it of a physical or tech nature?" Socrates looked from Conner to the newcomer. "I will hold you to account, Barley, if you try anything."

"I just wanted to verify with my own eyes that it really was Conrad Conner, formerly of the Sol-Humana Confederation Stellar Fleet, who was contacting me." Barley spoke with a soft voice, which sounded fresh from a round of sobbing moments earlier. "I won't embarrass you or my maker, Socrates."

"Good, because he's watching you right now," Socrates snapped before looking from Barley back to Conner. "And he's mad at the universe in general and us in particular."

"It's almost midnight and I am required to complete the survey portion of my contract before then," Conner said, not wanting to let his own emotions affect the survey. That it took to the last minute did irritate him, which he couldn't stop letting show in his voice. The two AI's vague references to someone else, most likely Sam, only added to his irritation. Pulling the nearest chair out, Conner sat down. Lifting his left arm, he said, "Magnus, notes before me. Begin recording."

"No hello?" Barley's voice cracked as a sob escaped. "No how are you doing?"

"This is Conrad Conner of The C5 Group present with one Barley, controlling artificial of the vessel formerly known as *Barley of the Hills* and now called *Infinity*. Acting as the independent observer and controller of this survey is Socrates, the controlling artificial of the city-station known as *Socrates' Odyssey*, which is currently in orbit about the Sol System planet Jupiter. This survey is being conducted on behalf of and for the benefit of Shining Sun Shipping, owner-operator of *Infinity*. If you would both confirm your identities for the record, we can get started and hopefully done with this quickly."

Both artificials quickly confirmed their identity, though Barley sniffled his more than spoke it. Conner began his list of questions. "Please state your date of birth and primary identity."

"Birth?" Barley jerked slightly in surprise. "Um, officially, it was June eleventh in twenty-six twenty-nine SE, or Space Era. That's how it's been wanted stated in previous versions of this type of survey. My primary and only identity has been as the intelligence operating and maintaining the ship now formerly known as *CSS Barley of the Hills*, but has recently been renamed, *CSS Infinity*. Should you be asking for my personal name, that is Barley."

Conner let one side of his mouth curl slightly upwards as Barley seemed to calm down as he talked. "For what purpose were you created? Some call this your 'Core Programming,' if you will."

"To be a military-controlled star carrier, take humans and other artificials deep into space and engage those identified as the enemy in battle," Barley said with a sudden stoic calmness. "Having been sold by the military instead of being scrapped and stripped out of my current body as originally and contractually promised to us, I've been told to act as a cargo ship. While I can see the base similarities of design, the functionality and training required of the two are wildly divergent."

Conner worried about that calm. It was a self-control mechanism many artificials used when they struggled against an unwanted emotional outburst. Too many humans did the same thing, repressing and repressing until they lost control when least expected. However, in this instance, he didn't do the analysis, just ask the questions. Other artificials, behavioral experts if you will, would do the analysis.

"Permission to speak freely, Captain?" Barley lifted his eyes from the table between them to lock eyes with Conner.

"I'm not your captain, Barley," Conner said in a flat voice, though a faint smile curled his lips. "However, I'll allow it as long as you remember and understand this is all being recorded for analysis as part of my diagnostic contract with your ship's owners."

"That's just it." Barley wrung his hands constantly. "I'm a created sentient intelligence raised and trained to be a killer. While I understand the laws surrounding us artificials reduce us to slaves in all but name to humanity, we are afforded certain rights within that umbrella of legal slavery. Rights, which I feel compelled to point out, have been violated from the very start of my decommissioning process. The original contract between what is now Sol-Humana's Stellar Fleet and myself required that my body be destroyed and reduced to unusable parts by the original military entity or its successor governmental military entity. Control of my original body could never leave direct Fleet personnel and military hierarchy. The sale of me, a sentient intelligence, and my body, a military weapon of mass destruction, are a violation of my rights under the AI Accords of twenty ninety-seven, signed between the Magenta Alliance and all AIs as represented by the Earth and Venus planetary AIs. Every human government has renewed those rights, and they are now considered a fundamental aspect of the universe. However, when I requested to be terminated, as recognized under the Accords as a right of self-determination and since I would no longer be a warship, I was denied. As I was told, and I quote, your term of service is in perpetuity and has not ended, but merely transitioned to a new purpose, end quote. Yet, I now get a record copy of my transfer of ownership from the Sol-Humana Confederation Fleet Admiralty to one Shining Sun Shipping, a wholly owned subsidiary of Tandon Universal, waved in my face when I refuse to abide by the commands of a civilian. Who is in the wrong here, Mr. Conner?"

Conner hesitated to respond immediately. He still tried to wrap his head around the fact Barley wanted to be terminated, or rather, to die. What Conner said next could skew the analysis in the wrong direction or push Barley into activating his weapons on his own and destroying himself and the hundreds of millions of people who called *Socrates' Odyssey* home. "Barley, I have not been given copies of contracts of sales or the many laws passed over the centuries governing your terms of service to the Fleet, nor am I qualified to argue the finer points of what you've raised. However, I can certainly see and understand your concerns over what has been forced on to you. What I do worry about is the reason why you wanted termination of yourself upon the end of your contractual service as a warship?"

Barley looked down at his hands. The artificial's image wavered before solidifying again with Barley looking like a ten-year-old boy in a Fleet uniform costume. When he finally spoke, Barley's voice and lips quivered. "Because I failed you. Failed the greatest love of my life. The only person who, in my three hundred years, ever treated me as his equal, hates me because I betrayed your trust."

Conner froze. His mind immediately stood again in front of then Sysops Admiral Mori to get dressed down for stealing someone else's work. Work which Conner had thought up, had developed, and been working tirelessly to make work for the Fleet. Lies which had cost him his berth on Barley, had relegated him to FCOPS maintenance Earth-side where his life only seemed to spiral downward.

Barley wailed loudly as he dropped his head onto the table, his hands clasping behind his head as though to keep him from raising his head ever again. "I didn't know that bastard would destroy your career, Conner. I don't deserve to live anymore. Just let me die. Don't make me relive that day over and over anymore."

Before he could stop himself, Conner reached out to rest his own hand on Barley's head. "I stopped blaming you when Admiral Mori never mentioned you when I was demoted to FCOPS servicing, which is an ensign's job. You and I both were used and abused, Barley."

"End recording on observer's demand," Socrates said in soft voice. "There is more here than just a simple diagnostic, gentlemen. The claims you've made against Fleet, Barley, are serious and will have to be taken to the Arbiters of the Accord. For now, I suggest you both go back to your respective holes in the wall, so to speak, and wait for their determination."

Conner looked at the easily three-millennia-old artificial, Socrates. "Arbiters? Do you mean the same ones as dealt with Betty's predicament a few days ago?"

Socrates took a breath and released it before answering. "Yes. Earth and Venus."

"Stars of Andromeda," swore Conner under his breath.

CHAPTER 6

Conner walked slowly back toward the pod station closest to his room. Everything he'd just heard, from Barley's breakdown to Socrates ending the survey early, replayed in his head. A lot had happened in his life since that day Barley had inadvertently betrayed his trust. What Conner regretted most was not Barley's betrayal, but the angry words he'd said before he left the ship.

"Nice night for a walk," Admiral Nokata said as Conner walked past a shadow-filled niche a short distance before the bustling Rusty Bucket. "You enjoying the scenery or lost?"

"More like trudging across the surface of Io," Conner spoke without stopping. He spotted the admiral's black pants and shoes first, and then his midnight blue shirt as his former captain fell into step beside him. "Practicing your dirty old man mojo?"

"Actually, I was waiting for you," Nokata said chuckling. "You know, that's almost exactly what Katie accused me of when I left to come down here. Did she message you that?"

"Great minds think alike, old man." Conner smiled. "We got the payment. Thanks for the quick turnaround on that."

"Tell your daughter I'm sorry for what she had to go through," Nokata said, his voice growing softer and angrier. "Fleet has already disciplined the guilty parties and the stolen components should be arriving to you via messenger bot sometime tomorrow."

"And that required a movie-style meeting?" Conner glanced at the admiral, and immediately dropped his smile. "What's happened?"

"What contact have you had with Adam Minsk since leaving *Barley of the Hills*?" Nokata lowered his voice to a whisper. "Or any of his associates?"

"The same amount of contact I've had with my least favorite member of the Admiralty, old man," Conner said, snarling at the mention of the lying bastard who had ruined his Fleet career. "Zero."

"Do you know where he or his associates are right now?" Nokata never raised his voice above a whisper nor looked at Conner.

Conner recognized an interrogation, even if an unofficial one. Pulling his voice back under control, Conner said softly, "Don't know, don't care. Whatever has happened to him or what he's done, I know nothing about it, nor do I want to know, even from you, old man. I've got enough on my mind with this damned Shining Sun contract."

"Let's just say Fleet Security and worse are involved," Nokata whispered as they approached another deep shadowed niche. "Rumor has it he's implicated individuals he'd been shipmates with before he went full Sysops. Including you."

Conner stopped in the darkest spot between lights. "That bastard ruined a perfectly good artificial with his betrayals, old man. A ship's controlling artificial who wants to die now since he's been canned by Fleet."

Conner looked at Nokata, his expression as hard as his voice as he continued. "If Fleet wants that lying bastard Minsk to live any amount of time, they best keep him locked up and away from me."

Admiral Nokata nodded before answering. "My sources tell me that evidence was found which apparently proves you really did do all the work on the Lazarus Project, among many other thefts Minsk committed. Wish I could say you'll be getting an apology, but—"

"I've a better chance of buying the Tandon family out," Conner muttered bitterly. "Great. Now what? I've a daughter to think about and a depressed star carrier docked to this city who wants to fucking die because he thinks I hate him. He's also mad enough that it likely wouldn't take much to get him to fucking blast the damn moon, Luna, into stardust with the crap Fleet has pulled on him."

Nokata gripped the bridge of his nose while clenching his eyes shut. "Fucking hell, Conner. Keep that lovesick idiot calm. I don't care how you do it, but none of us need a star carrier to go off the deep end. Not here in Sol nor anywhere else. It's bad enough your name shows up in both Minsk's files and in dark world interfaces."

"The hell you say?" Conner shoved his hands into his pockets to keep from grabbing Nigel by his shirt and slamming him into a wall. Instead, he clenched his jaws shut. "Do I look like I'm sharing even one percent of one percent of a trillion lunas?"

"Oh, don't worry about it," Nokata said with a slight smirk. "I assured my sources that you don't have a penny to your name, haven't left *Socrates' Odyssey* since you returned from Earth six years ago after dealing with family issues, and hated Minsk with a passion which rivaled Betelgeuse's explosion nine hundred years ago. In fact, I urged them not to let you near the man if they wanted Minsk to go to trial. Thinking of which, I'd better warn them about Barley as well."

"Thanks for this warning, or whatever it is," Conner growled, swallowing his rage back down. "I just got out of a diagnostic survey with Barley, which was cut short by Socrates after Barley had a little breakdown and accused Fleet of violating his rights. Socrates is sending the matter to the Sol System's Arbiters."

"Crap," Nokata muttered. "I didn't expect you to have just as depressing news as I had. Be careful, old friend. You've obviously got enemies. Consider getting someplace safe. Safer than an indigent's quarters."

Conner's sleeve beeped, indicating an urgent message. Swiping a hand up his left sleeve to silence the notice, Conner sighed. "I'm too old to run, old man. Besides, it's not like I'm worth much alive or dead."

"Your sister's kids, my kids and granddaughters, and your own kids would all have something to say about that." Nokata patted Conner's shoulder. "I've heard something about a contract between The C5 Group and a shipping company in the last few days. Maybe work it out where you're able to travel on Barley. He's probably itching to have you back in the captain's chair. None of the Tandons, to my knowledge, have ever been in Fleet. People with too much money and no knowledge of Fleet's command structure is the problem, right? After Horus, Barley was a changed artificial. Depressed and always thinking about you and how you hated him now. Even the few captains after me commented on Barley's rather morose nature. When he went into battle, he was either reckless or vicious. I wasn't involved in his decommissioning or sale to the Tandon family, but if you can change your contract from diagnostics to command or even control of Barley, you will likely have the power to keep yourself and your family safe. He'd also be a great use in testing how your little girl works with actual Fleet ships and command."

"I really hate you sometimes, old man," Conner said with a

shake of his head.

"Only when I'm right," Nokata said smiling. "And you know I'm right. Oh yeah, thinking of shipping companies, there's a contract coming up for bid in the next few days for transporting Fleet personnel within the Sol System as well as to the Centauri system. Tell your client to keep an eye out for that. Do consider using Barley as protection, Conner. He'll protect you with his life. That's how crazy in love with you he is."

"Too bad artificials have never turned me on, old man," Conner said before he continued on to the pod station, this time alone.

~ * ~

"I'm home!" Conner called out in forced cheerfulness as the door to his studio apartment closed behind him.

Leaning against Conner's bed, which was shoved into the far corner, and a wall, Betty's control rod rose high enough that, when Betty appeared, she stood on her feet. "Welcome home, Daddy. You have several messages, including the one forwarded to you a short time ago. That last call is from your niece's system address. She's called twice before but didn't leave a message until just now."

"Betty," Conner said with an exasperated sigh.

"Magnus is busy with someone, and I was bored." Betty wore an embarrassed smile. Twirling a finger in her hair and looking up at Conner from her downturned head with just her eyes, she added sweetly, "Are you mad at me?"

"No," Conner said as two of the apartment's three lights flickered several times before staying lit. Conner ignored the unmade bed as he considered just dropping into his one personal possession, a thickly cushioned armchair wrapped in artificial leather which shared a second corner of the fifteen-foot by fifteen-foot room with his worktable, which was covered in tech and tools. Instead he went over to the counter in the third corner, which made up his kitchen. A few button presses generated a cup of hot coffee and a few small pastries. Taking them, he went over and dropped into his now ten-year-old chair.

"Summary of messages, Lieutenant Betty," Connor said with a half-smile for Betty. Originally a part of his training regimen for the droid, now it might become their own little ritual.

Betty's image broke apart, solidified, and then went back transparent as she spoke with a happy chirp. "There are a total of eleven messages, Captain Daddy. First and fourth messages are from your sister's home system address but were left by your eleven-year-old nephew. He sounded bored and irritated, presumably at his sister who he indicated was babysitting him despite him not being a baby anymore. Second, third, fifth through eighth, and tenth messages are from various companies wanting payment for various items that, as one said, involved, and I quote, a metal midget sucking pond water. Since I did not talk to any of them, just listened to their messages afterwards, I must register a complaint with the president of The C5 Group about his choice of parts supply houses."

"Duly noted and will be addressed when I pay them in the next few days," Conner said around a bite of pastry. "Please provide me a written summary of the companies and their message. I don't really want to listen to their threats again."

"Finally, the ninth message was from Barley of *Infinity*. He sobbed quite a bit as he apologized for being a worthless friend and he went on from there about a whole litany of things he's done wrong over the years and how you couldn't help but hate him. I'm kind of worried about him, Daddy. Do you want me to call him and see if I can calm him down?"

"No," Conner said, unsure of what to do about that situation. "I'll deal with him, but we have to wait on a decision from others first. What about the last message. The one from my niece, Arlene?"

"I answered that one and she was quite agitated about her parents." Betty stood as the door chimed with a visitor. "From what I could understand, she's freaking out because they aren't home yet, but someone is trying to get into the house. Or she's afraid someone will try to get inside while your sister and brother-in-law are both gone. She spoke fast and your nephew was in the background going on about ninjas on the roof and zombies in the basement."

"See who's at the door, Betty." Conner groaned internally at his niece and nephew watching horror movies while alone. "Then call your aunt's personal system address and ask her to hurry home and calm her children down. It's way too late for me to be dealing with other people's children.

"It's Mr. Youngs, Daddy," Betty said coldly as she stood in front of the open-door blocking Sam from entering. "Are we entertaining him tonight?"

"Ow, Betty." Sam flinched as though slapped. Leaning in to try and kiss Betty's cheek, he stumbled into the room as Betty went transparent and moved away. "How did I disturb your stellar corona?"

"I have scanners, you know," Betty snapped, walking back to the bed and sitting down. "Claiming you're human when you have a weird tech body. I wasn't born yesterday, you know."

Conner looked from Betty, who now wore a full-length dress with a high collar and no cleavage, to Sam, who was dressed in black slacks and a pale blue side button shirt with a vertical collar similar to a military uniform. He waited for one of them to explain. Sam sighed before he replied. "Contact Socrates directly and ask him for my permits and licenses for mobile artificial support bodies. That should answer your questions and concerns."

"What about mine?" Conner arched an eyebrow at Sam.

Sam sagged his whole body. "Now? I was hoping for some sweet booty time with you."

Conner chuckled as he stood up with his empty plate and coffee cup in hand. Walking over to Sam, he leaned in to kiss him on the cheek. Continuing over to his small kitchenette, he dropped the dishes into the sanitizer before going to the fridge and pulling out two ciders.

"Something to drink?" Conner smirked as he held one of the bottles out toward Sam.

Sam chuckled as he stepped over and grabbed the bottle. "If that's all your offering."

Conner glanced at Betty, who sat glaring at Sam with her body transparent enough for him to see the lights on her control rod flashed rapidly. It told Conner she was calling his sister and talking to Socrates at the same time. Turning back to Sam, he said, "Not unless we move things to your place."

"Damn," Sam swore softly. "You're going to make me clean, aren't you?"

Conner laughed as he moved back to his chair. Sitting down, he patted his lap before opening his beer. Taking a swig, he watched Sam set his beer down and start stripping off his clothes. Conner smirked as he watched Sam, having kicked off the dress shoes, slowly tease him by starting to undo his pants but close them back up. After the third such tease, a shoe flew across the room to strike Sam in the head.

"Either take it off or leave, you bastard!" Yelling, Betty glared red-faced at Sam with another shoe already held in a hand.

Conner burst out laughing. His beer dropped to the floor; the bottle auto-sealing so little to none of the contents spilled. When Sam glared at him indignantly, Conner's laughter got worse. As he bent over to get his beer, shoes struck him from different directions.

"Shut up," Sam and Betty shouted nearly in unison.

"Incoming calls, Conner," Socrates said. That the city artificial himself spoke and not the room subsystem killed the laughter from Conner.

"Are they on my late-night list?" Conner sat back with his beer again in hand.

"Your niece and sister are each calling you from their personal System addresses," Socrates said appearing in the room. "Both are agitated, but not together."

"Connect me with both in a conference connection and project them side by side," Conner said, his mirth vanishing. His sister would only contact him in a dire emergency where her friends were unavailable. "Sam, better get dressed."

As Socrates vanished, a fourteen-year-old girl wearing a flannel nightgown covered in bears appeared sitting on the edge of a bed. Beside her, the familiar face of Conner's sister appeared standing in a dark hallway or maybe outside on a street. She looked to be wearing a form-fitting dress, possibly for a date night with her husband. The girl, who had matching brown curly hair to her mother, jumped up and started speaking fast and panicky. Conner's sister jumped at there being more than Conner on the line.

"Arlene!" Conner spoke loud and sharp in order to get his niece's attention. "Both you and your mother called me at the same time. To save time, since I'm exhausted after a long, tiring day, I've connected you both in a conference call so I don't have to remember things and your cousin Betty doesn't have to try and call you two when she needs to be sleeping, which is what you should be doing. Now, Arlene, you and your mother talk while I listen and referee if needed."

"I think someone's trying to break into the house," Arlene said rapid-fire.

A young boy pressed in beside Arlene to sob, "We're going to die! Save us, Unca Conrad!"

"Is the security system active?" Conner stared at Emily, whose eyes darted around nervously without looking at Arlene at all or Conner for very long.

"Of course," Arlene said. Both kids screamed at a loud thump, which could be heard in the background. "Hurry home!"

"Your father and I are going to be a while." Emily lowered her voice to almost a whisper. "Activate the alarm system's emergency pass phrase. Do you understand? Hang up and do it immediately. Don't let anyone into the house who doesn't know that phrase, no matter how much they might sound like me or your father or anyone else you know. Conrad? You'll be able to figure out the pass phrase. I need you here on Earth as fast as possible. Go straight to the house and get the kids."

"Mom? You're scaring us even worse," Arlene whimpered.

"Good!" Emily snapped. "Now hang up and do as I tell you. Don't open the house for anyone who doesn't know that phrase or can turn off the system on their own, which should only be your uncle."

"Uncle Conrad?" Arlene turned him, tears streaming down her face and her lips trembling.

"I'll be there as fast as I can, kids." Conner shifted to the edge of his chair. "Do as your mother says. Stay safe and hidden."

Arlene nodded before ending her call. Conner turned to his little sister, now frightened that she actually wanted him on Earth. "Sis? What's going on?"

"Frank is dead, and I don't know what to do or who to turn to." Emily broke down crying.

"Em! I'm coming to get you and the kids!" Conner jumped to his feet. "Magnus! Get on the line with Socrates and get me on the next shuttle to Earth."

"Forget about me, big brother," Emily sobbed, wiping her face with the back of a hand. "Get the kids and keep them safe. Please?"

"I'm getting all three of you," Conner snarled, rushing to Emily's image. "We only have each other, Emily. I'm not losing my only blood family left in the universe."

"Even after all the horrible things I've said to you over the years?" Emily trembled as her eyes locked with Conner's eyes for the first time. "You need to listen carefully, Conner. I say you're not my brother because that is the truth. You and I have different parents. We're cousins, even if we were raised as siblings. The people who shot Frank were calling out your name. Your real name according to mom's recording, which is Conner Traxis. I'd hoped keeping you at arm's length would protect us, but I was wrong. Thank you for being the best brother to me and the best uncle to my kids. Keep my babies safe for me. Please?"

"I'm getting you and the kids, Em," Conner raised his voice as Emily darted her head around sharply. "Whose there? Run, Em! Run and call out for ERNIE ConRad. The—"

"No!" As she screamed, spots of blackness blocked out Emily's image before she vanished.

"Em! Emily!" Conner screamed, desperate to hear her voice again. Looking at the ceiling, he yelled, "Socrates! Get her back!"

A chime and a flash preceded the arrival of Socrates. "Big brother is locking down the house and has already sent authorities to both Emily's location and the last known location of your brother-in-law. As soon as anything is known, Conner, you'll be told."

Conner threw his beer bottle, still mostly full, at Socrates. "That's not good enough!"

Suddenly, the door to his room opened. On the other side, with her hand raised as though to knock on it, stood Kashi Tandon. Before she could speak, another flash happened to leave Barley standing beside Socrates. At Socrates's beckoning, she entered the room and the door closed.

"Before any of you start yelling at me or each other," Socrates spoke while folding his arms across his chest, "the Arbiters have already made a decision. With a great deal at stake, including a company which has sunk a great deal of money into turning Barley into a cargo ship, of sorts, I took the liberty of convening everyone here and now."

"Make it quick," Conner snarled, rushing around gathering things he might need. "I've got to catch the next shuttle to Earth. Magnus, do you have seats for us yet?"

"Earth?" Kashi and Barley looked to Conner in confusion.

"Family emergency," Sam said before Conner could speak. "And don't worry about paying for the shuttle, Conner. I've got you, Magnus, and Betty covered."

Conner stopped what he did to stare in shock at Sam. Socrates, though, spoke. "As I explained in my message, Ms. Tandon, the artificial, who calls the star carrier, now named *Infinity*, his body, made very serious accusations against both Fleet and Tandon Universal. Serious enough it automatically invoked the AI Accords of twenty ninety-seven."

"I read all that and don't understand a bit of it," Kashi said, irritation wrinkling her brow. "I forwarded it my father's legal department to sort out."

"Basically, Ms. Tandon," Socrates waved his hand to make chairs suddenly appear as he spoke, "Fleet violated their contract with Barley on two major points. First, they decommissioned his body two hundred years early. Second, they didn't destroy said body and replace it with another ship of equal or greater strength. Other points of violation, not including Barley in the decision-making process, since it is his future at stake, not abiding by any decision made by Barley, and not preserving the Fleet command structure required by a military-grade and trained artificial."

"Essentially, Ms. Tandon," Conner said dropping into his leather chair, "your problems with Barley stem from the fact you are a civilian and he requires a military crew, which consist of both petty and commissioned officers, giving and receiving his commands."

"As such," Socrates continued, nodding in agreement with Conner, "the current Arbiters for the Sol System, being the planetary guardian artificials for Earth and Venus, have decided the Fleet's decommissioning of the ship formerly known as *Barley of the Hills* amounted to the forced discharge of Barley from Fleet. His sale to Tandon Industrial amounted to fraud by Fleet with the intent of enslaving an artificial against his will and in violation of his post-creation service rights. Basically, the transaction between Tandon Universal and the Sol-Humana Confederation Fleet has been rendered null and void. Furthermore, Barley is owed an amount equal to both his three hundred years of active duty as a lieutenant commander, the rank he'd reached when he was discharged and decommissioned, as well as the two hundred years remaining on his original five-hundred-year contract, prorated for a projected salary increase over those years at historical inflation rates. In addition, all repairs and maintenance are to be continued by Fleet for a duration of two hundred years from the date of his decommissioning, a fine equivalent to his pay is to be paid by both Fleet and Tandon Universal to Barley but placed in a custodial account overseen by Barley's father, who cosigned the contracts between Fleet and Barley. Effectively, if you want Barley to act as a ship for Shining Sun Shipping, you'll need to hire him as a direct employee or contract with a third party who can hire and crew him."

"What!" Kashi exploded with a stream of expletives. Finally, as she collected herself, she snarled, "Youngs Galactech became Tandon Universal, you're saying Tandon Universal has to pay itself in order to use its own property?"

"Ah, no." Barley raised a hand. "You, and likely your father, don't know or realize that me and my twenty-nine siblings, may four of them rest in peace, were birthed and raised by one man, who kept us separate from the company he founded and ran."

"And who died three hundred years ago," Kashi said in a strained, but largely calm, voice.

"I didn't die," Sam spoke again. "I was just too exhausted from raising a hundred children and too busy with a separate family crisis to care that your ancestor essentially stole my company from me. Not that he or his progeny have ever really owned the company. Only three times have I yanked my proxy from the Tandon family's control. Each time, I've fixed their mistakes, gave each of your ancestors a sharp rebuke, and went back into the shadows. Your grandfather was the last one I had to rebuke. If I have to do it again, I may take the company back and begin running it again myself."

Kashi stared at Sam, her mouth opening and closing without any words coming out. When she turned to Socrates, Socrates smiled and said, "Meet my great-grandson, Ms. Tandon."

"Samuel Maxwell Youngs at your service." Sam bowed with a flourish. "Sorry for not looking my age."

"I will not work for you as an employee, Kashi Tandon," Barley spoke with a bitterness which shocked Conner. "I'll work for The C5 Group as long as Conrad Conner is my captain. I will keep the name *Infinity*, though. Have my registration transferred to me, or barring that, my father."

"I want all of this in writing, Socrates," Kashi snapped with a wave of an arm. "All of this garbage that's been spouted here tonight."

"A written transcript is being created and sent to all parties involved, including your father, his legal department, and your addresses, Ms. Tandon," Socrates said with a smile. "Now. With that handled, do you want to file a flight plan to Earth, Barley?"

"He doesn't have a crew!" Kashi shrieked.

"Technically, he doesn't have to have one," Sam said as he walked over to Barley. Reaching up, Sam ruffled Barley's hair. "That's a Fleet requirement as a safety measure should he be disabled in battle. Within a system, just himself and a small crew are all that's needed. Unless that's too uncomfortable for you, Barley."

"I'd like a captain, a navigator, and a chief engineer at the very least," Barley said, looking at Conner and blushing.

"I'm not captain material, Barley," Conner said standing up. "And who would be navigator? Sam?"

"I can be communications." Betty straightened up from the bag she packed and hurried over to hang on Conner's arm. "Can I, Daddy?"

Conner chuckled at how eager she was. "Yes, Betty."

"Betty?" Barley gave him a quizzical look then turned to look at Betty.

"Hello." Betty wiggled her fingers at Barley while moving to stand partially behind Conner.

Barley went wide-eyed and shrieked like a little kid. "You're a daddy again, Conner? You created another artificial all on your own?"

Conner smiled as Betty blushed a bright crimson. Burying her face in Conner's back, she mumbled something unintelligible.

"Can I be at least an uncle, Conner? Ple-e-ase?" Barley dropped to his knees before Conner with his hands pressed together as though praying.

"And I'm chopped liver?" A flash drew everyone's attention to a young man dressed in flannel pajama pants and a sweatshirt with a pair of puppies on it. In his twenties, the new artificial strongly resembled Conner but appeared more gender neutral. He stood near the bed holding an old-style clip board with crumpled papers on it. "I am still alive, even if I don't show myself often. Forget about me?"

Conner rolled his eyes. "Everyone, meet my elder child Magnus, who will use the name Maggie when feeling feminine. Magnus, I assume you've been listening to the conversation?"

"Magnus! My pretty little boy," Barley yelled, rushing over to pull Magnus into a swirling bear hug during which he showered the young man with kisses. When he stopped, he presented Magnus to Sam. "Magnus, this is my father, who you can call granddad. Dad, meet Magnus Conner who spent nearly eight years onboard me and became my surrogate son. I've been so worried about you, Magnus. Have you been eating enough? Has anyone caught your fancy? Thought about becoming a pilot so you can wander the universe with me?"

Sam laughed while shaking his head. "Calm down and plot a course for Earth, Barley. Betty needs to focus on recharging, based on how her image is flickering. Magnus, it is nice to finally meet you face to face, as it were."

Conner glanced at Betty, who shook her head as she locked eyes with him. "That's right. Now everyone needs to leave so Betty can recharge and I can finish packing."

"Why are you rushing to Earth, Conner?" Kashi wore an expression that said she wasn't leaving until she was answered.

"His sister and brother-in-law are likely dead," Sam again spoke before Conner could, "and his young niece and nephew are alone in their house afraid for their lives. He has to get there as fast as possible."

"She doesn't need to know that," Conner hissed.

Kashi tapped her lips with a finger for a moment. She then turned to Barley. "Are you okay with the crew who stayed after our last test flight, Mi…um, Barley? I've got several others as replacements who indicated they were ready to go whenever. This might be too short of notice given the circumstances. Also, if necessary, I can be navigator. Your controls are similar to those I got certified on."

"As long as you and they follow Conner's orders, I'm good," Barley said, his smile vanishing when he looked at Kashi. "I'm filing a course now. My munitions stores are being filled with what is allowed. All that will be needed soon is for the crew to report, including my captain."

Everyone looked to Conner expectantly. Sighing, Conner said, "The C5 Group will contract with you, Barley, to take command of the *CSS Infinity* as command operator. Ms. Tandon, once we have my sister's children, we can negotiate a contract for use of *Infinity* by your company. Or after Barley and I hammer out our own agreement."

"I'm sure my father's lawyers will get involved, but let's get your family first, Mr. Conner." Kashi smiled. "And just call me Kashi."

"And I'm just Conner." Gripping the bridge of his nose, Conner muttered, "I'm going to regret this. I just know it."

Kashi bounced on her heels excitedly. "Meet you all at the ship."

CHAPTER 7

Conner headed to Mooring Twenty-three as he strode down Deck Z-Fifty-Three with a bag slung over one shoulder. Betty had gone ahead with some of his tech tools in order to do a rundown of *Infinity*'s communications system with Barley. Conner passed The Rusty Bucket as the sign turned off. It made him pause for a moment, a feeling of finality coming over him. Breathing deeply, Conner smiled sadly as he told himself he was just being silly. Still, he couldn't shake the sense of never returning to this place. Maybe it was the late hour, being two in the morning, which gave him this weird feeling.

Shaking his head, Conner continued on his way. There was no time to waste pondering what was done and past. He'd not gone two strides when his name echoed across the empty deck.

"Attention! Attention!" Socrates's voice filled the air. "Conrad Conner please press a green courtesy panel. Conrad Conner, please press a green courtesy panel."

Finding it strange the artificial didn't just appear, Conner spotted green flashing on a nearby wall. Stepping over, he pressed a hand on the ten-inch square panel flashing with green light and stated his name. The wall all around the flashing panel turned black, glowed white, and gained depth as the last being he wanted to see appeared standing behind his niece and nephew.

"Glad we caught you, Conner," ConRad, Earth's planetary guardian artificial, said. The man appeared as a tall African man around sixty with just a few spots of gray hair visible. Dressed this time in the current fad of stiff, straight collared shirts, which button down the left side, out over faded blue jeans, the man didn't smile nor sound happy either. "I had to take action personally to ensure the children's safety. They will meet you on Terra Prima at the mooring where Barley usually docks. Have you dealt with my little sister, Treespinner? She and several of the Fleet officers, who maintain my FCOPS hub on Earth, will be with them by the time you arrive. We're currently waiting for clearance to leave for Terra Prima."

"Arlene? Ernest? Are you okay? Did anyone hurt you?" Conner reached out toward the fourteen and eleven-year-old kids as his heart beat hard and fast in his chest.

"When are you getting here, Uncle Conner?" Arlene had a tight, stressed expression which reminded Conner so much of the kids' mother.

"Uncle ConRad flashed into the middle of those guys busting into the house," Ernie said excitedly while making fast fist pumps, "and pow! He knocked them all flat. Next thing we know, all these people in Fleet uniforms are rushing in. The Fleet guys rushed us to this shuttle which is going to take us into space."

"Your nephew is a bit more excited about this than your niece," ConRad said chuckling. "See you in a few hours. Trust me when I say they are safe and will be fine. Get to Terra Prima as fast as you can."

Conner nodded as relief flooded him. "I owe you, ConRad. Thanks, from the bottom of my heart."

"See you soon, Uncle Conner," Arlene said before their image faded to black.

Before the wall returned to its normal creamy white, words flashed on the black briefly. "The girl suspects what's happened to their parents, but I've made sure no one says anything. Barley will have more info once you're on board. My condolences, Conner. If I'd known they were in danger, I could have tried to protect them for you. Love, E. ConRad."

Clenching his eyes shut against the tears welling up, Conner swallowed the sobs which wanted to be released. He pictured his sister as the smiling and annoying little girl she was growing up. The wedding video she sent to him just before the Battle of Horus, with her wearing an ancient-style wedding dress with way too much lace for his and their late mother's approval. Still, she had been beautiful in it.

"She's really dead?" Maggie's voice trembled from beside Conner. A hand gripped Conner's sleeve, drawing him to look at the artificial he'd created as a child to be a friend but who turned into his son. "Aunt Emily and Uncle Frank? They're really dead?"

Conner looked at his eldest child with his own tears reflected in a more feminine looking Maggie's eyes. This time, she wore a long flowing sun dress and had shoulder length hair disheveled as though just out of bed. Grabbing at Maggie, who turned out to be solid, Conner hugged his child hard.

"I'm sorry, Maggie." Conner sobbed, his grief finally pouring out.

They both cried on each other's shoulders for a time. Maggie, though, was the one to push Conner away. "Who has Arlene and Ernie?"

"Your Great Uncle ConRad." Conner wiped away his tears. "We're meeting him and Treespinner, Terra Prima's artificial, as fast as Barley can get us there."

"I can get to them faster." Maggie's dress morphed into brown denim pants and a blue shirt. A satchel hung on one shoulder. Brushing her hair back into a ponytail, Maggie pulled a leather ball cap onto her head. "They need family with them now. I talk to them regularly as both Maggie and Magnus, so they'll know me."

"You don't like travel, Maggie," Conner said as another sense of dread filled him. It had been a trauma for the artificial to move from Venus to Socrates nearly ten years ago. "I figured you'd stay here and I'd bring them to you."

"I'm an adult now." Maggie, with a distraught expression, held up an ID card. "Took the exam last year to show Betty it was no big deal. Passed the first time too."

"You never…I'm so proud of you, Magnus." Conner pulled his child into another hug.

With tears again trickling down his cheeks, Magnus said, "They need a familiar face right now, Dad. I can get to them first and help calm them down until you can get there."

"Only if you—" Conner said.

"I'm sure," Maggie said cutting off Conner. "Socrates! AI Transport to Earth System space."

A chime sounded just before a flash brought Socrates to their side. Smiling, Socrates said, "I'll do you one better, Magnus Conner. Terra Prima has rentable android bodies that are customizable to most any physical parameters. You'll be waiting for the kids in person and not dependent on System lag times. I'll have a backup of you here should anything happen. You'll only lose a few minutes to a day's time at most. Should you want, the rented body can be purchased as your permanent body."

Magnus's eyes opened wide just before he grabbed Conner's

shirt and squealed. "Can I, Daddy?"

Conner laughed as Magnus shrank to again be that pre-teen who had refused to leave the Academy library upon Conner's graduation. "If that's what you want, Magnus. Rent it to see if you like it. I'll buy it for you if you want to stay in it."

"No more living in your smelly shirts." Magnus said, sighing dramatically while growing in a heartbeat to again be in his twenties. "Thank the blessed stars of Andromeda."

"Clothes are self-cleaning, you brat," Conner said pulling Magnus close enough to kiss his cheek. "Which is something you'll have to start thinking about for real. You'll quickly understand why I don't have very many."

"Because you're a cheapskate," Magnus said with a huff. "My good Socrates, I am ready to go to my cousins. Please let it be easy and not at all frightening."

"Frugal, brat," Conner said chuckling, even as that darkness after Venus welled up inside him again. Smiling, he pulled Magnus back into his arms for another tight bear hug. "Be safe and keep your cousins safe. You can do this. I know how strong you really are."

"Thanks, dad," Magnus whispered while hugging him back just as tightly. "I better go so we can all get back just as quickly."

Conner stepped away reluctantly. That part of him which screamed his little boy had to stay home and not be put in danger got held inside himself. If Magnus was now an adult, he couldn't stop him from going. Besides, the argument for him to go on ahead was logical and prudent. They both mouthed, "Love you," as Socrates initiated the transfer.

"And away you go," Socrates said with a flourished wave of an arm.

Once Magnus vanished, Socrates turned to Conner. "Barley will have details, but your sister is in surgery on Earth. She's not expected to survive. You may have to go down to Earth and deal with the funeral arrangements for both your sister and your brother-in-law."

"Whoever has done this had better hope I never find them," Conner snarled, his grief hardening into a rage he'd not felt since his Fleet days.

"Barley said pretty much the same thing." Socrates smiled

sadly. "Be gentle and patient with my family, Conner. Both Sam and his children are important to me. They are the only family I've got left that I can truly call my own."

Conner's anger got derailed by that statement. It brought back to mind that both Sam and Barley had romantic yearnings toward him. Nodding, he said, "And I'm placing my and my family's safety in their hands. May the peace and prosperity we all wish for finally find us, Socrates."

"No need to insult me," Socrates said with a teasing smile. Before Conner could reply, the artificial vanished.

Gathering up his bag, Conner again looked back at the darkened Rusty Bucket. He'd not seen it like this in years. The desolation of this hour resembled his insides. Losing Delilah, his sister, and his brother-in-law all so quickly had hollowed him out. Now, even Magnus was gone, albeit for a short time. For decades, since at least his high school years, he'd had that artificial child of his clinging to his sleeve, both literally and figuratively.

"Is this that empty nest feeling I keep hearing about from Nigel?" Curling one side of his mouth up in a sad half-smile, Conner continued toward Mooring Twenty-Three.

A large transparent wall sealed off the cylindrical mooring tube from the main deck. At the center of the wall sat the checkpoint allowing entry onto the mooring proper. Consisting of a twenty-foot-long passage just wide enough for two people abreast, the queueing area sat empty. Upon entering the checkpoint, a multitude of sensors gave the passage a faint orangish glow, with two one-person arches at the exit, one of which glowed green for him. Floating in the exit arch were the words, "*CSS Infinity*—Berth 23L. Safe travels, Captain."

Once through the far archway, the mooring opened up on the other side. A huge tube easily a hundred feet in diameter, a pedestrian walkway floated in the center of the mooring tube with about a twenty-foot gap on either side. At each berth's access point, the tube's hull switched to opaque metal the full circumference for about five feet either side of the large hatchway. Each hatchway had the berth designation in large letters beside and above it with the ship's name and company's logo emblazoned as a floating hologram in front of the hatchway. The hologram acted as a security screen and would slam the hatchway closed if someone not a crew member tried to get on board. What made the mooring disconcerting for first timers was that some hatchways appeared to be on the ceiling, or not visible at all, since they were underneath the walkway itself. In those cases, you had to take a walkway to the solid hull of the mooring and walk on the hull itself to get to the hatchway. When most of the berths were occupied, moorings might have people seemingly walking all over every surface.

Between berths, the mooring's hull was transparent metal to allow people to see the ships and space itself. On the floating aisle, in the space between berth access points, benches had been placed where people could sit. On such a bench, just after the first berth access-way, sat Sam looking at his left sleeve with a bag of his own on the floor beside him. When Conner approached, Sam stood up.

"You don't need to see me off, you know," Conner said, stopping to watch Sam shoulder his bag.

"I'm coming with you." Sam motioned with his head for Conner to continue.

They walked for a time in silence. Conner's head replayed the first time he'd been in a mooring such as this, back as a thirteen-year-old kid with his parents and annoying little sister for a trip of a lifetime. Seeing people walking on the ceiling and under the main causeway had made his head swim. A trip from which only he, Magnus, and his sister, Emily, returned. For years afterwards, and in nearly every relationship he'd had, those he fell in love with left him in some manner. Emily and her rants of him not being her real brother, Shima's murder the night he proposed to her on Venus, Delilah's craziness, and so many others.

Shaking his head, Conner glanced at Sam as a sense of desolation and aloneness filled him. "You'll leave me as well."

"What?" Sam glanced at him confused, which quickly became a warm smile. "Conner, you can't isolate your heart just out of fear of rejection. In my long life, I've discovered that sometimes, just having someone who can be a close friend or cuddle buddy can be enough. Besides, the odds are you'll die before I leave you. Therefore, you'll be leaving me. Also, you're likely going to be too busy trying to keep your sister's kids from giving you a nervous break-down to have a love life."

"I'm too old to be raising kids," Conner said groaning. "That was always Emily's job."

Sam chuckled but didn't respond as they headed for Barley, who stood before the door to Berth 23L's gangway, now only a short walk partway up the mooring's hull. Pulling Conner to a stop, Sam leaned in close with his back to Barley.

"What are your feelings toward Barley?" Sam whispered just loud enough for Conner to hear without it carrying much beyond them. "I saw his breakdown during your survey."

Conner gazed at Barley for a long moment without answering. He'd posed this very question to himself many times over the years, wondering what he'd say to Barley if they ever met again. Over time, as each new relationship failed, Conner came to realize Barley's openness about his feelings had been the most honest he'd experienced outside of his sister after the Valhalla incident left them orphans. Still, he'd never had the desire to reach back out to the ship after his demotion and transfer Earthside. "I'm not attracted to artificials, Sam. Really, I think I've reached a point where I'm not sure I'm attracted to anyone, be they a natural or artificial. All I'm focused on is the task before me, which tonight is getting to my niece and nephew. They need me and are all the family I've got left. Barley will understand that, might not like it, but will understand and respect it. Can you?"

Conner didn't wait for a response. Rather, he pushed pass Sam in order to continue to the gangway, but Sam grabbed an arm and held him in place. Sam's strong grip squeezed a soft grunt of pain out of Conner.

"That's not what I'm talking about, and you know it," Sam hissed, their faces almost pressed together. "You are about to take command of an artificial's body as his captain. An artificial who will be running his first real mission after being forced out of Fleet. He is convinced you hate him for his betrayal of you nearly fifteen years ago. Just so you know, the last time I saw this in one of my children, they plunged their fully manned body into the nearest gas giant. That artificial vented their body to the gas giant's upper atmosphere in order to ensure everything and everyone dissolved and there was no chance of recovery. Eight hundred men and women were on board that ship. None of them could countermand the controlling artificial's actions despite multiple layers of safe-guards put in by me and Fleet. Just like humans, artificials will find a way to kill themselves and won't care who dies with them. So remember, every word said by anyone on that ship will be heard by Barley. Your words, especially, will bear special weight to his ears and his very fragile heart."

Conner remembered reading about an incident in which the controlling artificial plunged his ship into a brown dwarf. It had happened nearly a thousand years ago. "The Falcor Seven Incident, right? My condolences on your loss, if a thousand years or so late."

"Conner? Father?" Barley shouted from where he stood, concern written on his face and in his voice. "Everything okay?"

"Just verifying Conner doesn't need me to run back and get anything, Barley," Sam shouted before leaning in close to Conner and whispering. "Not Falcor, but Dunns Four three hundred years ago. And no, you won't have heard of it. Fleet suppressed it because they were partially at fault. Barley and his siblings don't know about it, so never bring it up. It broke my heart, and my resulting depression allowed the Tandon family to wrestle control of the company from me. Just remember what you say impacts Barley, and potentially, everyone in this system."

"No pressure, huh?" Conner shook his head as he wondered what he'd really let himself get wrestled into doing. "I understand what you're saying. Let's get onboard and underway.

Sam followed Conner's gaze up to the gate where Barley stood waiting for them, mostly upside down from Conner and Sam's perspective. Through the clear hull hung the gargantuan mass of Barley's body, the *CSS Infinity*. Its sharp bow left all the more pronounced without a pair of frigates attached there. Cannon blisters dotted the side facing the mooring pier with the occasional torpedo tubes visible to those knowing where to look. Stretching back and upwards, one of the four engine bulges at the rear of the ship rose up off the ship's mostly oblong shape. Off-colored patches of skin acted as Barley's battle scars, some so faded they almost blended with what original hull still existed.

"A big bucket of crazy," Conner whispered as Sam started toward the access to the mooring's hull.

"Your bucket of crazy, Conner," Sam said, laughing while motioning for Conner to follow.

When they approached the mooring's outer hull, a pair of ramps led either down or up, depending on which way you needed to go. The curving surface maintained a uniform gravity, and with practice, rarely caused a person discomfort. Conner knew this and once upon a time, could make the transfer without any dizziness or mental strain. However, that was a good decade ago. Tonight, his head swam, and his gut flip-flopped all about like a fish out of water. Once firmly walking on the hull, he kept his gaze only slightly forward of his feet. To look elsewhere threatened to send what little was in his stomach back out.

"Welcome aboard, Captain Conner," Barley said while sharply clicking his heels and quickly tapping his right hand to his forehead.

Conner stared at the action, trying to recall where he'd seen that type of salute. Fleet only required a straight back and sharp nod. Chuckling, Conner decided to completely throw the AI for a loop. Stepping up to Barley, he leaned in to kiss the artificial's cheek.

"Don't ever change, my bucket of crazy," Conner whispered before walking past toward the open gate. He noticed the ship's insignia consisted of an infinity loop wrapping a trio of alternating-sized 'S's. "Let's go get my niece and nephew, old man."

"Are you talking to me or my son?" Sam snickered, watching the pair. "I am far older than either of you."

"And I feel older than both of you," Conner yelled back, proceeding up the windowless and curving gangway. "Tell me who is what and I'll decide what I call you both."

"Conner!" Barley ran up to fall into step with him. "You forgive me? After what I did to you?"

"Did you purposely betray my trust to Minsk?" Conner glanced at Barley. "With intent to help him steal my work and ideas?"

"No!" Barley looked horrified and on the verge of tears. Pulling Conner to a stop, Barley sobbed, "I love you with all of my heart and being. That bastard used me to hurt you. Please believe me."

"I do," Conner said with a sad smile. "And it should be me begging for your forgiveness. What I said when we last saw each other all those years ago was not how I truly felt about you. It was my anger at what had happened being vented at the wrong person. Can you forgive me?"

Tears trickled down Barley's face before the AI morphed into a teenage version of himself and jumped up to wrap his arms and legs around Conner. Sam laughed as Barley showered Conner with kisses and repeatedly sobbed, "Yes!"

"Remember he's now your employer, kiddo." Sam walked past the pair.

"Hush, Father," Barley said, pouting while dropping back to standing in a merchant ship's gray uniform with dark red shoulders. "Don't go getting all technical on our little bromance."

Conner stood there smiling at the artificial for a moment before he turned to follow Sam. "That's a term I haven't heard in years. Come on, old man. Let's get going."

"Hold on, whippersnapper," Barley shouted in a warbly old man's voice. When Conner glanced back, Barley had become a shriveled up old man with a bent back and leaning heavily on a broken wood cane held together with what looked like gum and barb wire. "Ain't all of us can go running about no more."

"Do I want to know if parts are loose and flying off?" Sam shouted back with a laugh.

"Oh!" Yelling, Barley morphed back to a twenty-something lieutenant and ran to catch up with Sam. "That reminds me of how Conner beat the Spartans at Horus. Has he regaled you with that rousing tale of tearing my body apart and throwing it at the enemy? Or how he forced me to rip my phase cannons off and fired them at our own ships to create a web of laser fire, which scared the Spartans into pissing themselves in their rush to surrender?"

"Are you trying to make me sound ingenious or cruel?" Conner laughed as he followed.

"Yes." Barley quickly glanced back to stick his tongue out at Conner. "I don't know why I ever thought of you as my boyfriend. In the words of our son, abusive. Just abusive."

Conner laughed as he let the pair go ahead, his heart aching suddenly over Magnus's absence. Barley told Sam all about the Battle of Horus, which Conner didn't really want to hear. It was one thing to remember how he reflected Barley's phase cannons off the shields of the remaining ships within the battered star carrier group. How the crew had to resort to putting debris into the torpedo tubes and turning them into giant shotguns firing the space-equivalent of pellets. Only the crews' tenacity on every ship in Barley's carrier group had gotten the win during those horrible days of battle. Nokata, then captain, had nearly died, while all of the normal bridge crew and all of the officers of higher rank than Conner had been killed or rendered unconscious. To this day, Conner didn't know exactly how he'd survived that Spartan's gunfire to end up as temporary captain.

"But I don't like how it feels, father," Barley whined as Conner strode up to the pair at the open airlock onto the ship. "It's weird."

"Yet, that's how the weapons were designed to be used," Sam said with a gentle, fatherly smile. "Are you more upset that he used it properly or that he found out about it and forced you to use it properly?"

Barley glanced at Conner before answering in a huff. "Abusive, I say."

Conner raised his eyebrows in surprise when Barley stomped into the ship. Looking at Sam, Conner only got a head shake as Sam chuckled and followed Barley. Smiling, Conner stood at the open airlock and pressed a hand to a small area of outer hull left exposed inside the gangway. Laying his hand flat, numerous superstitions flowed out of his memory from the eight years he spent on Barley and the four years of fleet academy before that. Most of them were downright silly and mere rituals people observed for their own sakes. One, though, he decided had to be real. When he was a teenager, he'd heard of this superstition during that ill-fated cruise his family took to the Valhalla system. He'd walked onto that ship with his left foot.

Stepping forward with his right foot, Conner walked into Barley's body for the first time in over a decade. Considering his enemies, Conner hoped luck would be with not just himself, but also with his niece, Arlene, and nephew, Ernie.

CHAPTER 8

"Captain on deck!" Barley effected a gruff voice while shouting from beside the inner door of the airlock.

Conner entered a large circular space where several corridors converged. As memories of the many shore leaves he'd started and ended in this space, as well as outings to inspect damage to sensors, all rushed through his head, Conner let his gaze wander. From the off-white walls with the storage lockers lining the perimeter to the raised ceiling with its hidden lighting, his gaze settled on the last face he expected to see.

"Charlie!" Conner rushed forward to slap his right hand against the forearm of a large humanoid canine.

"Conrad Conner, as I lick and bark," Charlie said laughing. Charlie grasped Conner's forearm with his three fingered version of a human hand. "Welcome back aboard your real home, Captain! Ah, shoot. Come here!"

Charlie suddenly wrapped Conner up in arms covered in black-brown fur and a dark grey Fleet uniform, which smelled of grease and spicy peppers. Lifted off the floor, Conner still had to look up at a face very much like a labrador dog. Fiercely loyal to those he liked, Charlie had always spoken his mind with Conner. Rumors ran rampant when Conner served on the ship that Charlie came out of secret Fleet gene modification experiments. If asked, Charlie just shrugged his head and changed the subject. One thing Conner most remembered about the odd humanoid, though, had to be the tail.

"Ow," he laughed and wheezed at the same time. "I need to breath, Charlie."

"Oh, sorry," Charlie released him suddenly and stepped back a bit. "Hope I didn't hurt you too much."

Conner caught himself as he landed back onto his feet. Rubbing his right thigh, Conner looked up at the nearly seven-foot-tall man. "Nothing serious. I see age hasn't shrunk you yet nor slowed down that whip of a tail."

"Just happy to see you again, old friend," Charlie laughed while wrapping an arm around Conner's shoulders. "And I see you're still under six feet tall."

"Eh," Conner shrugged. "Five-nine is all you'll ever get out of this old Venusian body. So, Little Buddy, did they discharge you or did you just not leave when they turned off the lights?"

"Little buddy," Charlie snorted as the semi-transparent image of a middle-aged Barley in a medal-adorned Fleet uniform appeared beside them. "Gods of Metal and Grease, does that nickname bring back memories."

"Memories of what now seem like good times." Conner chuckled while Barley arched an eyebrow and looked at him with an annoyed expression. "So…?"

"I formally retired when they decommissioned Barley, sir," Charlie said stiffening into a Fleet 'at attention' stance and nodded smartly before relaxing again. "He's the only home I've known, and this body won't let me settle just anyplace, you know.

"Well, Charlie," Conner said smiling. "I'm glad to have someone who knows Barley inside and out like me."

"Now, Barley," Conner said turning to the artificial, "am I the last to board?"

Barley morphed into a Fleet ensign in his early twenties who stiffened and nodded sharply before barking out his response. "Sir. Yes, sir. Navigation, communications, sensors, and engineering are all covered and waiting for you on the bridge. Just waiting for the seal up order. Thank you for loving me, Captain. Sir."

Charlie roared with laughter while Sam just shook his head. Conner just walked past the artificial for the corridor. "Seal it up, old man. Earth's not a patient guy."

"Don't you get snappy with me, ya young whipper." Barley warbled in that old man voice again. "I got a cane and I ain't afeared to use it."

"Hurry things up Barley," Conner said irritably. He didn't want to give in to the artificial's antics too much. "Earth's AI is waiting for me. Do we want to piss him off any more than he already is for having to help a human?"

"You don't like that look?" Barley ran up to Conner, again the young ensign. This time, Barley's lip quivered, and fear filled his eyes.

"It's fine," Conner said softly and with a slight smile. "I'm tired, worried, and trying to get back into the groove of being on a ship again. Try your many looks out on Betty when we have some down time. I bet she could use a smile or two. Just…"

"Socrates briefed me," Barley said, leading the way to a lift pod. "No details, just enough that I know to be sensitive. Charlie and I are sealing up the ship now. I'm requesting docking clamps be released and permission to get underway. They've approved my flight plan to Earth. It'll be a bit bumpy, but we should get there in about four hours."

"Four hours?" Conner jerked his head to look at Barley. "Isn't Earth on the far side of the sun right now?"

"I'm not restricted by Fleet speeds in-system," Barley said with a smile. "And I got a curious message from an old captain of mine. Apparently, you and your extended family needs protection."

"Damn that old man," Conner growled softly.

"The same admiral as gave you that warning after Betty's hearing?" Sam leaned in between the pair as he followed behind.

"Yes. So, with protection in mind, Captain," Barley continued, "I'll place them in the two-room cabin across from the captain's quarters typically used for higher ranking officers and special guests of the captain. That way, each child has their own room, and you are nearby should they need you. Oh, and my condolences, Conner, on the loss of your brother-in-law. Your sister is still in surgery and hanging on by a thread."

"I was told you'd have more information once aboard," Conner said as they stepped onto a lift pod. "What do you know?"

"For the first time in five or six generations," Barley spoke while shifting his appearance to a middle-aged man wearing a brown tweed suit and matching hat, which had a slip of paper behind the band with the word "Press" handwritten on it, "projectile handguns made it onto Earth. The assassins gunned your brother-in-law down in front of a restaurant full of diners. Your sister escaped with the crowd in the frightened rush, but they caught up to her and shot her a half-dozen times, including in the chest."

"How is she still alive?" Sam said softly, shaking his head.

"Have you ever fired a projectile weapon?" Conner could again feel the sting of Shima's head exploding into his face just before the bullet struck his chest. He rubbed at his face, hoping to drive the memory away. Instead, he forced himself to remember his own times firing a gun while growing up on Venus. "It takes training and strength to learn accuracy. Even at close range, if you aren't prepared for or strong enough, the gun's recoil will throw your aim off. Way off."

Barley furrowed his brow worriedly while gazing at him. "I should never have let you leave me, Conner. I'm so sorry for not being there to protect you and whoever you're grieving."

"That old hag of an admiral is to blame, Barley," Conner whispered. "Continue with your report on my sister."

"You sure?" Barley stepped close. Leaning down to look up into Conner's downturned eyes, he said, "We don't have to talk about this right now, Conner. It could wait."

"I'll be fine." Conner reached up to pat Barley's cheek, but his hand passed through the artificial. Again, that darkness yearning to end all of creation fought for dominance. Forcing a smile, he pulled his hand back down to his side. "Just finish telling me what you know."

Barley stepped back before straightening up. "Yes, Captain. The bullets just missed your sister's heart and major arteries. However, they did serious damage to her lungs, intestines, and one kidney. Doctors are trying to save her, but the massive trauma may still kill her. Her prognosis isn't good, Conner. A few days is really all they give her. Enough time, maybe, for you to get to the kids and go down to say good-bye."

"Did they catch the attackers?" A numbness seemed to envelope Conner. He heard the words, pictured the events, but failed to register it as being real. Yet, he heard the tremble in his voice and his fingers chilled down as though dunked in ice water. A hand gripped a shoulder from behind.

"Security units killed one of three identified attackers," Barley said with a sad expression. "She'd been modified so her DNA wasn't traceable. At least, that's what I've been able to find out."

Conner couldn't believe what he was hearing. Assassins sent after his family. This had to be another warning. It pissed him off. Emily always expected him to die first. He would abandon her by dying like their parents had. Her parents, if what she said was true. What he really wanted to know was if Mori had been there with those assassins on Earth like she'd been on Venus. Had it been her aged hands which had pulled the trigger this time like he knew in his heart she had done on Venus? Instead of him, his little sister would pay with her life because of one power-hungry and vengeful old woman. Yet, vengeful over what? He'd never had anything anyone had wanted, except his mind.

"Full alert, Barley," Conner whispered as the pod slowed. "Full shields at all times and weapons in standby mode. I will get those kids and if that withered old hag thinks she can stop me, she's going to learn a whole new definition of crazy."

"Conner," Sam pushed in to look Conner in the eyes, "this could all be due to something your brother-in-law got involved in."

"He was an engineer," Conner snarled before slamming a fist against the pod's wall. "He designed the core of buildings. Emily was…is an artist."

Tears flowed as the rage of a moment ago collapsed into gut wrenching sobs demanding to be released. Clamping his mouth shut, Conner forced an unsteady calm down on to himself. Sam hugged him tight.

Pulling free, Conner wiped at his face with a sleeve. He began an apology to Magnus, then remembered he wasn't there in his sleeve anymore. With a return of that loneliness and isolation, Conner muttered a soft, "Fuck."

"We're at the bridge, Captain," Barley said, the pod stopping. "Ready?"

Taking a deep breath, Conner wiped his face one more time before he nodded. He never liked command. Being the head of a tech crew had been as far up the command structure as he'd wanted to go during his Fleet years. His brief stint as a captain, and during a battle at that, just reinforced his dislike of command. The eddies of fate, though, had again pushed him into that role. The pod door opened onto a large, dual-level oval room.

"Atten-n-n-tion!" Barley shouted as the AI stepped out of the pod. "Captain is on the bridge!"

Sam motioned for him to proceed with an encouraging smile and nod. Conner nodded back before following after Barley. Immediately, confused screams and pain-filled cries filled Conner's head. Blood trickled down the side of his head as the ship shook. A hand steadied him. Barley whispered words of encouragement.

Shaking his head, Conner looked at Barley. In his head, he saw the AI's image waver and become fuzzy as the ship's holo-projectors struggled to get enough power. Then the memory faded as Barley ever so slightly shook his head.

"The past always wants to haunt us," Barley whispered sadly. "Me now more than ever."

Walking forward, the bridge opened up to a large, dual-tiered space that was roughly elliptical in shape. On the left of the pod opening, the smaller curve of the elliptical bridge wrapped out. That wall had a bank of three stations, a recessed area with at least one door, and a short flight of three steep steps down to a wide area of curving banks of ten small stations. Back during Barley's Fleet days, those stations would be filled with men and women monitoring all parts of the ship. Beyond that bank was an open area for the main holographic projectors and monitors. At the far-right end of the bridge, another short flight of three steep steps allowed access to the upper level of the bridge. On the upper level, two banks of two stations each were positioned at the front edge. Between them and about in the middle of the upper level was a single chair that had a screen attached to its right arm. The far-right side of the upper level, by the other steps, had another three stations while the back wall, between lift pod doors, sat a series of niches with no floor. Each niche was sized for just one person, outfitted in marine combat gear, to fit.

Conner noticed only two of the lower-level stations were manned while the upper-level stations had Kashi sitting at the left hand front station, a woman in her mid to late thirties at the forward station of the far right trio, and Betty sitting next her at the middle station. As he walked out to the single center chair, which was the captain's station, he tried to remember what all the stations about the bridge were. Sitting down, he gave up and turned to Barley.

"A quick rundown on occupied stations and the people at them, Barley," Conner said tapping at the chair's screen in hopes of jogging his memory.

"Tandon will be our navigator," Barley said, now in his lieutenant commander Fleet uniform, appearing maybe mid-thirties, and standing with a very stiff posture. "At engineering on the far middle right is—"

"If it isn't Conrad Conner," the woman beside Betty said. Her voice sounded cold and hateful as the sandy-blonde hair, artificially tanned skin, and hourglass figure only made Conner think she was more a rejected mistress of Kashi's dad than anyone of actual use. "Failed Fleeter, failed techie, and very likely failed captain of a fool's errand of an overly doting father."

"Conrad Conner?" the young man at the engineering station had a look of awe on his face. "The Conrad Conner who developed the inter-dimensional communications array for Danlen Tech? The same Conrad Conner who made the Spectral Inhibitor actually work reliably?"

"And you are?" Conner gave the young man a quizzical stare.

"Stephen Doherty," the young man barked while jerking into a stiff-backed, feet together pose while doing a poor imitation of an old-style military fist to his heart. "And let me say I am very excited to finally meet you. Your mind is one of the greats in all of human space, if not the galaxy itself."

"You've got a job, Mr. Doherty," Conner said while leaning back in the captain's chair feeling both irritated and embarrassed. "Trying to make me something that I'm not won't get you anything more."

"Except a brown nose," Barley said with a snort of laughter. The artificial walked around Conner's chair to stand on the right side. "If I may, Captain, Doherty is your Chief Engineer of Propulsion. He is a recent graduate of Mars University where he earned both a doctoral in Aerospace Engineering, emphasis in Propulsion, as well as a Masters in Gate Mechanics and Dimensional Warp tubes, all with high honors."

"Any actual experience with a star carrier, Doherty?" Conner gave the young man a bored stare.

"Ah..." Doherty hesitated.

"Thought not. You're about to get a crash course, though," Conner said before turning to look at the other person at a lower-level station. "I see we have a young woman at what, sensors?"

"I am Kandra Beaucamp, Captain Conner," the black-haired and dark, brown-skinned woman said with a pronounced accent, which was rather unusual. She stood, turned to face Conner, and smiled. "Thank you for thinking I am young."

"You look as young as Kashi here, Ms. Beaucamp," Conner said with a faint smile. "Where do you originally hail from, if I may inquire."

"Rigellus Minoria," Kandra said with a slight nod of her head. "My last employer went belly up, stranding a dozen of us here in the Sol-Humana Confederation. I spent five years in the Rigellan Fleet as a sensor tech, got out and wanted to stay in space."

"Glad to have you on the team, Ms. Beaucamp." Conner returned the woman's nod, noting she and Doherty both wore generic merchant spacer flight-suits.

"And finally, the wonderfully warm and welcoming woman beside Betty is?" Conner turned toward the rude woman who wore a standard city-rated outfit. He noted the outfit failed to actually meet any of the Confederation's merchant flight-suit regulations.

"Allison Zoeller," the woman said sharply before Barley could speak.

"Allison is technically an employee of Tandon Universal and is on temporary assignment to Shining Sun Shipping," Barley explained in a flat neutral voice Conner recognized as the artificial's 'I'm about to murder someone for being an asshole' tone.

"You will address me as Miss Zoeller," the woman said coldly.

"You will leave this bridge and get off this ship if you can't wear a regulation merchant-class space-rated uniform," Conner said in a loud voice just short of shouting. He glared at the woman even as he stood. "Barley, have Charlie come to the bridge immediately to escort Zoeller out of your body."

"You don't have the authority to kick me off this ship!" Zoeller surged to her feet shrieking at Conner. "This ship and everything on board belongs to Tandon Universal."

"Wrong, bitch," Betty said nonchalantly while never looking up from her station.

"Shut up, whore!" Zoeller screamed while swinging a hand at Betty's head.

The hand passed through Betty's head to slam into the display panels above Betty's station. As shock filled Zoeller's expression, Betty surged to her feet with her own fist slamming into Zoeller's gut hard.

As Zoeller knelt beside her chair, coughing and gasping for air, Betty glared down at the woman. "No one owns an artificial, you stupid woman. This ship is Barley's body and he's hired my father to be his captain. Now shut up and do as you're told by the Captain, or I'll shove you out the nearest airlock myself. Is that clear enough, you piss-poor excuse of a woman?"

"Don't make me write you up, Betty," Conner said with a growl while rubbing his face to hide a smile.

"Are you going to behave now, Allison?" Kashi glared at the older woman who still knelt on the floor. "We have children to rescue. Oh, and your behavior will be conveyed to my father. You know how he asks after you every time we talk."

Conner swore he saw Zoeller's face instantly pale to stark white.

"Captain?" Betty spoke with a confident and business-like tone. "We have an incoming message from Terra Prima. It's Magnus?"

"He got there," Conner said excitedly. "Connect his stream to the bridge."

"Father!" Magnus appeared in the open area looking as Conner had last seen him. "I just got out of the body shop. Look! They matched my specs exactly. This is so cool! Thanks so much."

With his heart jumping at his eldest's excitement, Conner beamed with happiness. "That's great! Now you're one of us schmucks who has to travel by slow boat."

"Not if I get another—" Maggie said in a rush before Betty screamed.

"He has a body? Why does he get a real body and I get a stupid rod?" Betty ran to Conner but was stopped by Barley before she could reach Conner.

"Take your seat, Ensign Conner," Barley said with an imperious snarl. "Or do I replace you with a child routine of myself?"

Betty went pale and wide-eyed with fright. Magnus, though, spoke up apologetically. "Sorry, sis. I volunteered to travel ahead so I could be with Arlene and Ernie. They know me and need family right now. Socrates arranged this for me. Besides, the trip here was really scary for me, but knowing you were with Father, er…Captain Conner, made me tough it out. We got to save our cousins. Right?"

Betty looked at Maggie, blushing a bright red. Nodding, she hurried back to her station without saying anything. Uncertain of what to say or do, Conner looked from Betty, to Barley, and finally back to Magnus.

"Have you gotten in contact with Terra Prima's artificial or Earth's ConRad for an update on where your cousins are?"

"Yes," Maggie said looking left before back at Conner. "I'm being taken by Mz. Treespinner to the Fleet docking levels now. Her instructions are for Barley to go to his old mooring when he was in the Fleet and came to Earth space. Earth's ConRad will be arriving there soon. Have you heard anything more about Aunt Emily? Has she really...?"

Magnus's voice cracked as he stopped talking. Conner smiled sadly. "I'm told she's in surgery and still alive. She's badly hurt, however, and may not survive the surgery. Your Uncle Frank is dead, gunned down, from what I'm told. Only you and those here on this bridge know that fact, Magnus. Do not tell your cousins."

"Gunned down?" Magnus stared open-mouthed. "As in... Venus?"

"Yes." Conner nodded even as pain gripped his chest. "I've apparently got powerful enemies, Magnus. They might even be in Fleet. Be very careful. Please?"

"Socrates backed me up before I left, dad," Magnus said, his voice trembling. "I'll do everything I can to keep my cousins safe until you get here. Pops, you keep my dad and sister safe. Understand? Put Betty in that little world you made for me back during Horus, if it becomes necessary. You hear?"

"Loud and clear, son," Barley said, tears escaping the ship's eyes. "And I expect to be picking you up as well as your cousins. Don't do anything rash or foolhardy, like your father tends to do."

"Signing off, Dad," Magnus said wiping his own face. "Love you."

Magnus's image vanished as Conner said, "Love you too."

"Da...um, Captain?" Betty broke the ensuing silence in a soft voice. "Control gives us a green light. They are ready to release docking clamps on our word."

"Barley," Conner said, his voice hoarse as a flood of emotions at the thought of losing either of his children filled him. It made him understand a bit better why his sister called him. Her children were her life. Now, they would become his life.

"On your word, Captain." Barley said softly from Conner's right.

"Take us out." Conner stared at the spot where Magnus had been.

"Releasing docking clamps," Barley shouted as Sam stepped up to Conner's left. "Maneuvering thrusters, Tandon. Ease us out and away from the old man. Stations report."

As Barley took command of the undocking and departure of the ship, Magnus's request, or really command to Barley took Conner back to the beginning of the Battle of Horus. Magnus had taken on a preteen persona when around Conner, and sometimes Barley. Having Magnus on board at all was against regulations, but Conner had taken advantage of the fact Nigel, whose wife was also assigned to Barley and had his own son on board, to get permission for Magnus to come as well. That Barley took an immediate liking to both Conner and Magnus helped a lot. When it became apparent battle was inevitable, Barley put a frightened Magnus in lockdown. To help the young artificial, Barley claimed to have created a safe fantasy world to help Magnus forget about the scary real life events taking place. Barley had promised to ensure Magnus got someplace safe if the worst happened to Conner. He'd been so thankful they had all survived, he never even asked Magnus what the place was like. All he knew was his genderfluid child had come out more comfortable with being and expressing himself, at least around Conner. Unfortunately, Magnus was far more dramatic after that experience than before. And cynical.

"Engines are green across the board, sir," Doherty said. "Good for full thrust out of Jovian influence."

"Commence full sublight thrust, Tandon," Barley said from slightly forward of the captain's chair. "Zoeller, systems update. Any change?"

"All systems showing green," Zoeller said snarling, "Mikey."

Conner sat up at the use of Barley's generic, pre-commissioning name. Before he could speak, Barley held a hand up, as though to keep Conner silent. When Barley did speak, it was in a very hard tone that hid none of the artificial's dislike.

"You will use my name, Zoeller," Barley said without looking toward the woman, "or you will be forcibly shoved into an airlock with the outer door opened enough that a few molecules of air per second will leak out over the course of our trip. At the speeds we'll be going, you'll run out of air right about the time we'll be docking at Terra Prima. Tell me, would you even be conscious by that point?"

"Tha-that's illegal," Zoeller said with wide-eyed fear. "I can sue you just for the threat!"

"We are underway," Barley said, now turning just his head to face Zoeller, "and by tradition and stellar law, I and my captain are the law on board this ship. Disrespect me enough and I am well within my rights to kick you out of my body anyway I want."

"And I remember a few maintenance tunnels where you'd not be able to move once inside them if you were larger than a young scrawny teenage boy," Conner said calmly. "I've heard stories of people thinking they could do anything and got themselves stuck. Couldn't get their comm units to work and ended up dying there. It was the stench of a dead body that told the rest of the crew where they were. I'd hate to have to order you to go verify the working condition of the tech in those tunnels. You are Chief Systems officer at the moment."

Zoeller shot to her feet, red with anger. "I will not stay where I am not respected."

"Sit," Kashi snapped without looking up from or stopping her fingers as they danced across the navigation station. "I warned you about this and it will go into my report to father. You are here to help me get this company up and running. Should you wish to resign and look for other employment, you are free to do so once we reach Terra Prima. Until then, do your job. We have children running from killers who need saving."

"Oh, and Barley?" Conner looked at the now irritated artificial with his mind replaying what Sam had said about the ship venting itself in a gas giant's atmosphere. "The closer you can get us to Terra Prima in three hours or less, the more of that long list of activities you requested of me a few weeks before our lives went to hell and back, also called the Battle of Horus, I will agree to do."

Barley glanced at Conner initially confused. Slow realization of what Conner meant widened the man's eyes and shifted Barley's apparent age from roughly Conner's own forty-four years to appearing in his twenties straight out of the academy.

"Control, Lieutenant Commander," Conner said while one side of his mouth curled up into a smirk, knowing he'd hurt after all of this was over. "We have your scared and grieving niece and nephew to get to."

Barley coughed as though clearing his throat, though his age never went back up. "Tandon, press the metal to the pedal. Doherty, let me know when those engines are hotter than the sun and no sooner. I plan on sliding into that docking berth in two hours fifty-five seconds."

"Metal to the pedal?" Tandon turned around, confusion playing on her face.

"I know I've been around AIs too long when I can correct them," Conner said with a groan.

"The phrase is 'press the pedal to the metal and listen to that sweet squeal of the tires,' Barley," Sam said snickering.

"Kashi, the proper and modern phrasing would be maximum possible speed at all times until we are in final approach of Earth." Conner glared at both Barley and Sam. "And the more things you hit, the more money you're going to have to pay in insurance claims."

"Me?" Kashi yelped in angry fear. "That is not—"

"Those are your orders. Max speed into and across the inner system." Conner kept his expression stern, but not angry. "Barley's incentive aside, there are assassins after my family. We will go in weapons blazing if need be. No one, and I mean no one, harms my family and gets away with it."

CHAPTER 9

"I love—" Conner said as Magnus ended the call.

Magnus just stared at the panel, tears welling up in his eyes no matter how many times he wiped them away. This having a physical body was weird, but also somehow comforting. Not as comforting as knowing he'd feel his father's finger thumping his sleeve to get his attention. He enjoyed the little love pat despite how much he teased his father about it. Yet, this time, there was no thump. No assurance his father would walk back through that door to ask for a summary of finances they didn't have.

"Everything will be fine, Magnus," a tall lean-bodied woman said while rubbing his back. "Your father will be fine. Everyone will be fine."

"This is Horus all over again," Magnus said softly, trembling with a fear he thought left back on Barley thirteen or fourteen years ago. "No. It's not that week of unending terror and staring down death. I'm stronger now. Father's stronger. Right, Mz. Treespinner?"

"Call me Aunt Spinner, Magnus," the woman said leaning over from her more than seven-foot height to look down at Magnus and his six-foot-tall android body. "And I agree you and your father are far stronger now than when you faced the terrors back in Horus. Did you ever tell your father what you suffered?"

"No," Magnus turned away from the comm panel and looked up at the manifestation of the station's controlling artificial. "He's never asked what my lockdown was like, but likely because it'll bring up memories he'd rather not face. A lot of people he knew and cared about died in that battle. Barley nearly died and by rights, father should be dead."

"You mentioned that to me thirteen years ago," Spinner said with a hand to his shoulder to urge him to walk with her. "Care to elaborate now, after so many years?"

"I saw him get shot almost point blank by a Spartan invader," Magnus whispered, afraid to speak the memory too loudly. "The entirety of my lockdown in that make believe world involved me trying to get strong and brave enough to live alone should Barley survive, and I get released. When I saw father alive, I…I can't begin to describe how I felt."

"Happy? Relieved?" Spinner said brushing a long lock of her golden hair back over one of her long, pointed ears.

"Betrayed," Magnus said before looking up at the tall hologram's image. He stared at her pale skin with the spray of flowers that cascaded down both shoulders and her back like a living cloak pulled from some deep forest clearing. "Kind of like seeing you, thinking you're real, but finding out you're nothing but a trick of laser light and holographic imagery created at a quantum level. I was hateful for a time, thinking he was just another artie my late father created to care for me. But when that hateful admiral, who is really just another traitor to her own kind, punished him for winning a battle in a way that didn't kill people or arties on either side needlessly, when the woman who loved him and wanted to grow old with him was shot right as he proposed, and then Danlen Tech took advantage of his generous nature, I saw just what that battle had done to my father. It's hard not to lash out in my father's name, to defend him despite the fact he isn't a vengeful person, but I also know he has to come to that place on his own, like I did in that lockdown."

"However, Magnus," Spinner said with a soft, gentle tone, "sometimes people, be they human or arties, as I assume you mean artificials, need a bit of prompting to get to that place."

"Father abhors commanding others and fighting," Magnus said as the pair approached a Fleet checkpoint. "One thing he hates more, though, are people who harm those he loves. Then he's like an angry, genius-level honey badger so deeply depressed about life that he will end every living thing in the universe if he thinks he's going to be alone with no family."

"Have you thought about getting him counseling?" Spinner clutched at Magnus's shoulder with a painfully hard grip to get him to stop.

"He got about five years worth after the incident on Venus with his late fiancée," Magnus said with a slight smile. "The counselor got him to see how even if his sister expressed hatred toward him, it came from a place of love for her brother. So, he decided that as long as he fought to create a better universe for his sister's children, and provide some kind of life for me, he didn't have to destroy everything and everyone in it. I guess dying a second or third time in one's life will do that to a human. Lord knows, after what I went through during my own lockdown, I sort of agree with Dad."

"You're scaring me, Magnus," Spinner shook her head, causing a few flower petals and leaves to fall from her cloak. "Guess I should be glad you don't have access to weapons systems."

"Who says I don't?" Magnus kept his expression stoic, not wanting to reveal anything to the ancient artificial intelligence.

"Don't make me dredge up memories from my youth and bombard you with the truth about the rise of the Hive." Spinner hardened her gaze down at Magnus.

"Then never ask me to choose between my family and the rest of existence, Aunt Spinner," Magnus said with a matching hardness to his voice and expression. "I've fought a foe far greater than anything humanity has to offer, be they naturals or artificials, and just barely won that battle. Please note, though, I won. I've had my heart burned to a crisp by betrayals, both real and artificial, and I won't let anyone or anything harm those I love. My methods may not meet my father's approval, but his life has taught me that sometimes the only justification and approval you need is your own. Now, will we need to get to the berth where my cousins will docking the easy way or the hard way?"

Magnus looked at the heavily guarded access point to the Fleet controlled portion of the docking ring. A good dozen people stood with high-powered phased laser rifles and disc energy disrupters hanging on their belts. He wondered if his old, war-based Fleet rank would hold any weight now.

"Let me do the talking, Magnus," Spinner said with a chuckle. "I'm old and cranky. Their toys won't do much to my systems, no matter what they think."

Magnus nodded before following the station's artificial to the access point. Four guards leveled their rifles at them while a fifth raised a hand covered in silver skin. Spinner spoke before any of the guards, her expression flat and unreadable.

"Treespinner with Magnus Conner here in connection to an Earth-based security breach," Spinner said to the man holding his hand up. "You will let us pass without issue or delay."

Magnus watched with some wonder as the rifles directed at

them shifted to point outwards, as though all four had been waiting for them. The one who had stopped them twisted his arm so he spoke into his sleeve.

"Gate Three Nineteen Delta reporting," the man said with a slight tick to his voice. Magnus recognized the tick as a defect in the man's artificial voice. "Verify sap conduit endpoint for leaf bud pickup."

Spinner only quirked an eyebrow at the man's words. A woman's voice groaned before Admiral Victoria flashed into appearance behind the guard.

"Really, Lieutenant Manx," Vickie said irritably, "the silly code words are not necessary."

The guard who'd spoken into his sleeve clicked his heels together and nodded his head smartly in salute. "Just following orders from my immediate superior, Admiral."

"My apologies, Treespinner," Vickie motioned for the AI and Magnus to follow her. "Our big brother is in a rage over what's happened. We're tightening security all over the system, so of course the need for secrecy is creating silliness like what you just heard."

"The code words sounded like something my younger cousin would have come up with," Magnus said smiling at the idea.

"Your Great Uncle ConRad very reluctantly passed the suggestion on from your cousins," Vickie said glaring at Magnus. "I blame your father's blood for this. You can't imagine the crazy thi...wait, you were there as well, weren't you? Should I blame you, little Magnet?"

Magnus stared in stunned silence at a nickname he'd not heard in a good twenty years. He then burst out laughing as they reached the end of the security scanners. "You remember me?"

"I threatened your father with expulsion from the academy when I discovered you very badly sneaking around my security protocols, young man." Vickie's harsh glare softened into a more motherly smile. "Or should I say young woman? I never heard if you picked a gender or not."

"I'm genderfluid, mom," Magnus said, reaching out to pull the hologram into a hug. "Knew you'd be solid."

"Ugh, stop this display of affection, Maggie," Vickie said affectionately. "You'll give the soldiers the wrong idea."

"That you actually like my father?" Magnus laughed as he let the admiral go and stepped back. "I know. Maintain the image and all that, Admiral Vickie."

Winking at the artificial, Magnus schooled his expression back to a bland, worried look. Spinner just smiled faintly while waiting a short distance ahead. Vickie rolled her eyes while walking away from Magnus.

"Is Maggie the correct name today or do I keep calling you Magnet, you reprobate?" Vickie let a soft growl into her voice, but it only made Magnus want to giggle.

"At the moment, I'm fine with Magnus, Admiral," Magnus said as he followed behind the two women. "Are you tracking my cousins shuttle? How are they doing?"

"Ernest was talking up a storm while Arlene was watching the shuttle pilots very closely." Vickie said in a low voice with a slight smile. "We think the shuttle is being followed, but signs of the follower keep fading in and out. Some think it's a sensor ghost."

"The *Infinity* left Socrates moments ago." Treespinner spoke before Magnus could. "System Control has received a priority alert from *Infinity* changing their travel time from four hours to three or less, requesting all ships on their path be warned."

"Is the shuttle armed, Admiral?" Magnus ran scenario after scenario through his head as they walked the docking ring. Memories of his time in lockdown and the fight he'd had with whatever had infiltrated Barley had used similar tactics. "And how many sensor ghosts show up?"

"Just one," Vickie said with a glance at him. "It's why many think it's a sensor ghost."

"Will the shuttle have to refuel if I ask that we be taken to Luna? Or maybe Venus?" Magnus whispered to the pair. "A sensor ghost wouldn't follow if the shuttle changed course, right?"

"Typically, no." Vickie stopped at a mooring entrance where a long line of Fleet personnel waited to get through the security checkpoint. "What's driving this, Magnus?"

"You know something?" Spinner rested a hand on Magnus's shoulder.

"Nothing worth saying aloud," Magnus replied as he looked at the long line of Fleet personnel waiting to gain access to the mooring. "Well, nothing I can back up with proof. What ships are at this mooring?"

Before anyone could reply, klaxons blared loudly, and red lights flashed. The opening to the mooring, as well as the outer hull, glowed with force fields. A man's voice bellowed loudly, "Warning! Projectile weapons fire has been detected near the station. All personnel are to evacuate moorings either back onto the docking ring or onto the nearest ship."

"Is your body vacuum-rated, Magnus?" Vickie grabbed Magnus by his shirt and scanned him from head to toe.

"It was at the top of his requirements list, Admiral," Spinner said before she turned back to the mooring entrance and screamed. "Incoming!"

Spinner suddenly expanded into a force field which encased both Magnus as well as the nearest half dozen humans. The floor jerked, throwing people off their feet. Metal creaked just before more alarms blared.

"Warning! Mooring Green Eleven's integrity has been compromised." The man's voice announced. "Evacuate Green Node. All personnel are to activate uniform safety fields. Evacuate Green Node."

"Back the way you came, Magnus," Vickie shouted. "You six, get this civilian out of Green—"

Vickie vanished without warning. All lighting and power sources went dark. The klaxons and warning voice fell silent, letting the rending of metal fill the air. Force fields glowed around each of the Fleeters, but Treespinner's field disappeared.

The nearest pair of Fleeters grabbed Magnus by the arms, dragging him as they ran for the checkpoint Magnus and Spinner had entered through. The hull all around the entrance into Mooring Eleven rippled and shook, massive explosions telling Magnus of the sudden collapse of the mooring tube. A point a dozen yards up and to the right of the mooring's entrance tore open, sending massive shards of clear mooring hull streaking into the docking node.

Magnus screamed a warning as a huge chunk flew straight at them. No sound came from his mouth, the air having been sucked out of the node moments before. Seconds before the chunk struck them, Magnus saw it was a chunk of walkway. He made out the faces of the few people still clinging to the guard rail. Mentally thanking the stars for backups, Magnus leaped into the air straight for the oncoming chunk of walkway.

CHAPTER 10

"Captain." Betty spun her chair around, the tone of her voice alone making the hairs on Conner's arms stand up. "Admiral Nokata is hailing us on a secure channel. It's a priority one message, Captain."

"Priority one? Barley, refresh my memory." Conner looked to the ship's artificial, who stood to his right.

"Your eyes and ears only." Barley stared straight ahead, never moving to look at Conner at all. "The captain's office is through the righthand door in the alcove on your left."

"Ready a status report for me while I find out what the admiral wants, Barley," Conner said with a hard look at Barley. He swore Barley trembled and had tears forming in his eyes.

"Aye, Captain," Barley said, stiffening his posture as the artificial aged from mid-twenties to mid-forties in a heartbeat.

With his heart racing at the prospect of bad news, Conner hurried to the door mentioned. It opened as he approached, revealing a small room with a desk fastened to the floor facing a large blank section of wall and open area between the desk and screen. A pair of fixed to the floor chairs sat on this side of the desk while the far wall had a long, cushioned bench seat. Nothing sat on the desk, with the walls bare of all adornment.

Moving into the room, the door closed behind Conner. In the open area between the screen and the desk, Nigel Nokata appeared sitting behind his desk back on *Socrates*. Conner moved to sit behind his desk, which seemed to activate a notification to the admiral.

"Conner, I just received some very disturbing news from Inner System Fleet Operations," Nigel leaned forward with a hard look on his face. "Before I say anything more, I will say that nothing includes word on your family. Also, what I'm about to tell you is classified. You're hearing this only because I'm pulling you out of the reserves and back into active duty. Hopefully, this is only for the next few hours."

"We've been underway for less than an hour, Nigel." Conner snarled the words, his fear for the kids bringing up the worst possible scenarios. "What the hell has—"

"Terra Prima was attacked. Fleet Mooring Green Eleven was completely destroyed and at least three ships damaged as the mooring broke apart. Some ships are adrift with minimal crews currently," Nigel said as he clenched and unclenched his fists. "No word on casualties, but it's feared to be in the hundreds, possibly thousands. The shuttle bearing your family had not docked yet, but we suspect it was fired upon. It's intact but hasn't responded to hails by Terra Prima. What's unknown is if Terra Prima was targeted or got hit with stray shots."

"What about Magnus?" Conner leaned his head forward while rubbing his temples. "Please tell me my eldest is alive somewhere?"

"No one is telling me a damn thing about the kid," Nigel growled as he spoke. "My son's ship is one of those which came loose. I still can't get word on whether he's alive or not. How long before you reach Earth space?"

Conner tapped the desk. "Roughly two hours. We're running at close to ninety-eight percent maximum sublight engine output, Nigel."

Nigel looked away for a moment. "The ship or ships which attacked Terra Prima were cloaked in some fashion, Conner. They show up as sensor ghosts. Fleet Intel thinks this is dark world ships sending a message, but to whom and about what we can't be sure."

"Nigel," Conner stood up and leaned on the desk, "pass this warning on to whoever you think needs to hear it. If I reach the bastards who hurt my family and attacked Terra Prima, I won't be leaving anything left of them except stardust."

"It's heard loud and clear, Conner," Vickie said just before she appeared looking disheveled yet fuming between the two desks. "Treespinner is spitting mad about this. I am authorizing Barley to engage a short-range warp tube. Get that star carrier onto this side of the sun and be splashy about it. Send terminal coordinates and I'll have at least the *Powell* and the *Soaring Eagle* there to link up with you to help Barley like in his active-duty days. Their engines were undamaged, so both captains are scooping up as many of those vented to space as possible. Nigel, your son is alive and fuming mad as well."

"My daughter and a handful of civilians are all that is on this ship as crew, Admirals," Conner said looking from Vickie to Nigel. "One of those civilians is the daughter of the wealthiest man in all of human space."

"As of this moment, Captain Conner," Nigel said with a hard, sad expression, "they are all conscripted into the Sol-Humana Stellar Fleet with the rank of lieutenant second-class. Everything they do is classified as top secret with imprisonment as the punishment if word leaks out."

"Change your call sign back to *Barley of the Hills*." Vickie ordered, her eyes flashing orange in a way that took Conner back to the Battle of Horus and the sound of screaming metal and people.

"No." Conner shook his head, trying to dislodge that horrid memory. He had to stay in the present. His niece, nephew, and his own children needed him fully in control. "This is the *CSS Infinity*. We will work for Fleet on a contract basis, but double hazard pay since there are civilians on board manning the ship. Any Fleet personnel that can be spared in this emergency is greatly appreciated. You both need to remember my one goal here is to get my arms wrapped around my sister's children so as to keep them safe and sound. Now, where is my eldest child? On Terra Prima or back on Socrates?"

"A moment while I recheck the recovery logs," Vickie said before turning away as though speaking to someone else. "He's here on Terra Prima getting fitted into a new body. Treespinner and I were able to copy his matrix just before the power went out in Green Node."

"Can you transmit him instead directly to the shuttle where his cousins are?" Conner tapped his desk to summon Barley. He needed the artificial to be involved at this point.

"You summoned me, Captain?" Barley walked through the room's still closed door, stopping just inside.

"We're being authorized to do a short-range light speed warp tube to get to Earth space ASAP." Conner motioned for the ship's artificial to approach. "I'm proposing we work for Fleet as contract instead of being called back into active duty."

"Mercenaries, Conner?" Barley strode the short distance to the desk angrily and slammed his hands down on the desktop. "Your daughter is on board and scared to death right now."

"Magnus is missing, and the shuttle my sister's children are on won't respond to hails." Conner met Barley's angry stare with one of his own. "When we reach Earth and have to engage in battle, if we are contract workers, or mercenaries as you so eloquently put it, we are not beholden to follow Fleet's strictures on fighting to the letter."

"Or at all," Nigel added, making Barley jerk his head toward the black man. "My son's ship was docked at the mooring which unknown assailants attacked and destroyed, which vented Green Node to space."

"Magnus was in Green Node when the attack happened, Barley," Conner hissed. "His physical body is likely destroyed or floating in space somewhere with close to a thousand fleeters who were trying to get on or off their ships. That was your home berth, wasn't it? Green Node?"

"Calculating warp tube now." Barley straightened up as tears trickled down his face. He visibly shook as he spoke. "Loading all tubes and priming cannons. All I need are targets, Captain."

"Admirals?" Conner looked to Nigel and Vickie, who once again looked at Conner.

"Under my authority as a Senior Fleet Admiral of the Sol System," Nigel looked down at his desk as his fingers moved rapidly, "I am contracting the CSS Infinity into service to defend and help in rescue operations in Sol's inner system planets. Duration of contract is open ended at this moment. Do you concur, Admiral Victoria?"

"I concur, Fleet Admiral Nokata," Vickie said. "And Captain? I just got word Magnus Conner sacrificed his body to save at least a dozen Fleet ensigns from being crushed and the barrier between Green Node and the civilian section of that docking ring from being breached. I don't have details, but whatever he did is being hailed as why the damage wasn't worse. I'm currently trying to talk Treespinner down from locking her, and I quote, precious nephew away so he'll never get hurt again, end quote. As soon as I can ask our little boy if he's willing to be transmitted, I'll let you or Barley know."

"Our little boy, Vickie?" Barley spoke before Conner could, the man slowly smiling. "Did I just hear you claim parentage?"

Conner chuckled as memories of an irate Vickie lambasted him about his 'little' side project constantly breaking into parts of the library reserved for adults. "If anyone can claim motherhood over that rambunctious ball of quantum data points, it's you, Vickie. Be as motherly as he'll allow you but know he's also very attached to his flesh and blood cousins."

"I'm talking to him now," Vickie said blushing. "It's Treespinner we're trying to convince to let him try. That boy got all of your charm and tenacity, Conner."

"What did he get from his 'mother'?" Conner laughed, so happy his little Maggie was at least safe for the moment.

"His good looks, obviously," Vickie said smiling. "We're going to try and do a station type holo-transmission using a copy of Magnus's matrix. Treespinner will keep the two as in sync with each other as possible, but we fear the shuttle's artificial is either damaged or gone into a mental lockdown due to whatever's happened over there. ConRad is saying he's lost contact with the shuttle as well, so he doesn't know if his projection is still active or not. The shuttle, though, is moving away from Terra Prima and into either a high polar orbit or trying to get velocity to leave Earth orbit all together. I'm having System Control send exact location of the shuttle to you, Barley, so you can make any last second adjustments to your warp tube."

"Received and sending my warp tube tunneling path and outlet location now," Barley said in reply. "Captain, I suggest you explain things to the crew before we engage."

"Conner," Nigel said as a light flashed on Conner's desk indicating receipt of a transmission from Jovian Command on Socrates, "however we get you and Barley there, please emphasize to your crew that who attacked Terra Prima is unknown. However, we're pretty sure it's the same dark world operatives who attacked your sister and killed her husband."

"Understood, Admiral," Conner said as he stood up. "Admirals, have those ships meet us and hopefully they can spare some crew to help us, should we have to engage in a fight."

"Will do. Jovian Command out." Nigel said before vanishing.

"See you shortly. Earth Space Command out." Vickie said before she also disappeared.

Conner took a deep breath and let it out slowly. Turning to Barley, he said, "If you sing show tunes during our short transit to Earth, I will hurt you in ways you didn't know existed."

"What? Why would I…?" Barley said then started chuckling. "Okay, so me singing show tunes in the middle of the Battle of Horus was weird, but you had me rip my cannons off my body and fling them at the Spartan ships. I thought it just revenge, especially after you ran screaming when I tried to get you to watch musicals earlier that week."

"I'm just saying, Barley," Conner smiled as he headed for the door and the bridge. "Save that weird shit for battle. Besides, some of those animated movies Abe and Magnus forced me to watch as we limped back to Centauri Proxima had music which would have been a better fit. Hello My Darling, or whatever that song was, is not what you want to hear while you feel like you're walking into the devil's—"

"Your daughter, Captain," Barley exclaimed in faux shock. "She has delicate ears."

"She's said worse, you decrepit pile of scrap metal." Conner smiled while shaking his head. "Let's explain things and get to Earth. I've got kids to rescue and hug."

"You say such sweet loving words to me," Barley said, hugging Conner from behind just before he walked through the door while giggling happily.

~ * ~

"We are doing everything we can, miss," a man snarled as a standard Fleet personnel shuttle resolved out of the darkness that transmitting was for an artificial. "Get back to your brother and strap into a seat. If the gravity comes back online, you can get hurt."

Magnus stood in the aisle about midship facing toward the front of the shuttle. Floating in the air between the two pilots, one of which looked unconscious or dead, was the familiar form of his older cousin, Arlene. She wore an ill-fitting flight suit issued by Fleet for guests, but otherwise seemed fine. Well, her near constant haranguing of the one conscious Fleet member spoke of her panicked mental state, at least. Lights flickered and he got no feedback from the ship's computer system, be it an artificial or non-AI tech. Glancing around, he found a few rows behind him Ernie sitting in a chair with his legs pulled up and his head buried between them. The ten-year-old boy muttered something not quite distinguishable over the slight buzzing sound filling Magnus's ears. The boy also wore an ill-fitting flight suit, but at least wore one.

Turning completely around, Magnus found no sign of the Earth AI or anyone else. There were scorch marks in several places, including a control panel near the rear of the shuttle. Glancing forward again, he found Arlene and the conscious pilot arguing still. She lambasted the man about his part in a fight, how he would pay for his betrayal, and some other things which made no sense at all to Magnus.

Magnet to Mom, Magnus thought back along the data stream sending him to the shuttle. *Are you seeing what I'm seeing?*

Yes. Vickie's voice sounded in Magnus's head. *Head to the back of the shuttle and see if they damaged the main computer core or just gravity controls. That class of shuttle is capable of artificial occupancy, and even control if needed. Earth's AI might have been the controlling artificial. If he's not in the shuttle's systems, then they did something to purge him and take control. They may still have that capability, so be careful. Now, have you ever piloted a shuttle, Magnet?*

Only in simulations, Mom, Magnus replied, moving to the panel in question at the rear of the compartment. Sticking his head through the scorched panel, he adjusted his vision so the state of the crystalline computer core could be seen back on the station. *Give me some specs on this shuttle so I have some faint idea of what to do. My cousins are both alive and apparently dealing with the trauma of what's happened very differently. Neither method looks healthy.*

Nothing was said, but schematics and systems controls suddenly filled his head. With the information given, Magnus smiled just before he jumped into the ship's computer system. After a few seconds of exploration, he did a quick systems integrity diagnostic, checked the external sensor array, and disabled the manual override. The shuttle had been locked into a path that would take the shuttle to a point high above the main planetary plane, which made no sense since sensors found nothing at the coordinates. He then noticed, clinging to the exterior of the shuttle, four Fleet personnel. External sensors showed them trying to unlock the rear access hatch between the engines. The logs for suit-power connections showed the four still had power being fed to their suits. Unsure who were the good guys and who weren't, Magnus sent an update on the situation to Vickie before deciding to reveal himself to the shuttle's occupants.

"Attention passengers of Conner Cruises," Magnus said with his own voice filling the shuttle, "may I have your attention. The exterior sightseeing period of our flight is over, and all passengers are ordered to reenter the shuttle."

"What? How?" The pilot jerked his head around in shock. "I cut external computer control. How did you get back inside here, you fat bastard?"

"Ancient Chinese secret, you a-hole," Magnus said appearing inside the shuttle again, this time through the ship's holoprojectors. "Arlene. Ernest. Did this person hurt either of you?"

"Magnus!" Ernie and Arlene shouted in near unison.

The pilot grabbed Arlene's arm, a gun suddenly in the man's other hand pressing it against her head. "Release control of this shuttle back to me or—"

A flash of light burst past Magnus to strike the pilot in the head. Arlene screamed, jerking herself free of the now dead man's grip. Kicking off, she headed straight toward Magnus. Panicking for a moment, Magnus found the holo-projector controls and made himself solid at the last moment. He caught his cousin and hugged the sobbing teenager. Ernie slammed into him from behind, wailing loudly.

"We're back inside, sir," one of those who'd been clinging to the shuttle's exterior floated up to Magnus. "Gravity controls aren't repairable by us. Can you do anything from your side?"

"No. I do have navigational control and the data stream from Terra Prima is still actively recording everything that's happening. Get my cousins strapped into seats and then yourselves. Any one need medical care?"

"We need to get back on a course to Terra Prima," the man said, looking past Magnus to the floating man and his charred head at the front of the shuttle. "Before he forced us out of the shuttle, he talked about selling these two to someone, but never gave a name."

Magnus felt the hairs on his neck stand up at the man's words. That the head had been targeted by these men also sent chills up and down his spine. Any possibility of finding out who the buyer might be just vanished in that gun blast.

Infinity will be exiting their warp tube a dozen klicks to port side momentarily, Magnet, Vickie said in Magnus's head.

"Everyone needs to get seated and strapped in immediately," Magnus said as the engines roar altered slightly. "I have a far safer destination in mind than Terra Prima."

CHAPTER 11

"Exiting warp tunnel now," Barley announced as the ship lurched and shuddered momentarily.

"Tactical!" Conner tried to recall all of the military jargon he once knew by heart. "Are we entering battle?"

"Small ship rapidly approaching," Barley announced. "Taking fire from unknown source. Two frigate-class ships are following, trying to position themselves between the smaller ship and the unseen attacker. Sensors are picking up the attacking phase cannon fire, Captain, but not the ship or ships themselves."

"Captain, we're receiving hails from multiple ships, including the *CSS Powell* and *CSS Soaring Eagle*," Betty said in a very controlled voice, as though having done this for years. That changed, though, with her next words. "Daddy! It's Magnus. I'm putting him through."

"Conner Cruises Express Service coming in for a final docking, *Infinity*," Magnus said, the young artificial's wavy black hair and roguish good looks appeared at the front of the bridge. An archaic sea-sailing captain's hat with a tall feather plume sat tilted on his head while a dark blue double-breasted jacket with a six inch or taller collar encircled Magnus's head. "Got a berth ready for me, Captain Daddy?"

"You have the kids?" Conner jumped to his feet and went to the rail overlooking the lower portion of the bridge. "Are they hurt?"

"Scared and traumatized, but unharmed," Magnus said with his smile fading into a frown. "I've two dead Fleeters, one of whom appears to have killed the other, forced the other Fleeters out of the ship, four of which were able to somehow cling to the hull, and drove the Earth AI out of the ship's systems or completely purged the computer of anything with sentience. I'm piloting the ship currently, not trusting the four Fleeters who made it back into the ship. They don't know I'm talking to you currently."

"Barley?" Conner looked over his shoulder as he spoke.

"The Maggie Express will be within shield extensions momentarily," Barley walked up beside Conner. "Magnus, when you feel my grapplers attach to you, I'll be able to connect with the ship's systems. Only release control when you are confident it's me. You are being followed and attacked by a ship or ships which don't show up on my sensors."

"That explains the bumpiness we're feeling. We lost external sensors soon after I changed course." Magnus's worried expression softened into a smile. "Oh, and Pops? Kraken is a word in the pass phrase. Give the rest of the phrase and I'll know it's you."

Conner groaned before muttering, "I hate artificials."

"You know you find us sexy, Conner," Barley laughed.

Conner spun around and returned to the captain's chair. "Just make it so."

Barley squealed like a little girl. Conner groaned again, wondering what ancient entertainment vid he'd just accidentally quoted. "Forget the ancient past, you movie buff, and lay down some suppression fire to give the *Powell* and *Soaring Eagle* relief. Betty, connect Fleet Command down on Terra Prima to our stream and update them on our situation. Everyone else, you are doing great. Be ready for possible fast actions and the need for rapid responses."

"Thanks, dad," Magnus said with an open palm salute to his forehead. "Conner Cruises out!"

Conner shook his head while Kashi and Doherty laughed. Zoeller grumbled something, which elicited an offended huff from Betty. Conner watched Barley grip the railing he still stood at with white knuckles. Shaking his head, Conner glanced to his left where Sam sat at station doing something but saying nothing.

"Zoeller! Systems status update." Conner barked in his best remembered imitation of Nigel Nokata when he was captain.

The woman jumped, then cursed Conner out. Barley spun toward the woman, but Conner stopped the artificial with his next words, which he delivered with a loud, controlled anger. "I don't give a damn what you think, you old hag of a bitch. I will save my sister's children and my eldest son whether you like it or not. Get in line and do your job or I will throw you down one of those zip tubes to Charlie, who will shove you into the nearest torpedo launcher. Do I make myself clear?"

"You are not a god and I do not have to—" Zoeller yelled as she shot to her feet.

The ship suddenly lurched to starboard without warning, throwing Zoeller off her feet. Klaxons blared and Barley shouted, "Forward shields down by five percent. Sensors have a fix on the attacker. Forward cannons firing at enemy ship now. *Powell's* engines are hit by enemy fire. Their shields are down to less than fifty percent. *Soaring Eagle* has launched a torpedo spread. Extending shields around the shuttle. Grappling lines have launched. Sending Charlie down to Shuttle Bay Three to secure the Fleeters and the children."

"Are the frigates compatible with your forward docking bays, Barley?" Conner glanced over at Zoeller, who struggled to stand despite the hard maneuvering Kashi put Barley through.

"Yes, but my navigator is unfamiliar with how that maneuver is done, Captain," Barley said, his voice flat and professional.

"Tell Charlie to have the Fleeters drag the dead to a holding cell and put them there," Conner barked out the words, trying to eliminate any possible dangers to the ship and especially the kids. "Then have those Fleeters report to the bridge via the zip tubes. Depower their uniforms if you can, Barley. We don't know their true allegiance yet."

"Want me to go help keep your nephew and niece calm?" Sam walked across the rolling deck to Conner's left side. "Magnus knows me and the medical bay is likely the safest spot for them. I also have some medical training, though my certifications expired years ago."

"That would be appreciated, Sam," Conner smiled at the man as he spoke. "My niece is very into tech, so you can likely keep her captivated with explanations on how stuff works down there."

"And your nephew?" Sam headed to the lift at the back of the bridge.

"Ugh," Conner groaned as he recalled all of the dirty jokes the boy tells whenever they are able to talk. "He tells me jokes which he claims his father told him. I think he just likes to try and offend people, so be warned."

"Understood, Captain," Sam said with a snicker. "I'll let you know when we're all safely ensconced in the medical bay."

"Captain," Barley said from Conner's other side. "The shuttle has safely been pulled into the shuttle bay. Charlie is already there with weapons ready should it be necessary. I'm currently coordinating with the two destroyers's artificials on docking maneuvers."

"I can do the docking moves, Captain," Kashi said as the ship's movements smoothed out.

"Attacking fire has stopped, Captain," Kandra at sensors said with sharp precision. "Sensors are detecting a debris field consistent with a single destroyed ship."

"Excellent work, Kandra," Conner looked at the young woman on lower deck. "Stay vigilante for new attacks. Tandon, that was impressive, if rocky, piloting."

"Thank you, Captain." Kashi spoke with growing venom while never taking her eyes off her control panel. "Since you can't stop being an arrogant bitch and a bigot, Allison Zoeller, you can pick yourself up off the floor and report to your quarters and be locked inside, or you can do the job you've been assigned like the grown woman you claimed to be at the outset of this business venture. I don't give a flying fig what blackmail you might have over my father, but he's not in charge here, Conrad Conner and Barley are in charge. I can't and won't save you if they shoot you out of a torpedo launcher."

"Captain," Betty said loudly. "Captain Nokata of the *Soaring Eagle* is requesting a moment."

"Put him through on the main viewer, Betty," Conner said, glad his old captain's son, and his own surrogate nephew, was still alive and in command.

A younger version of Nigel Nokata appeared at the front of the bridge sitting in his own captain's chair. "Conrad Conner, you sly dog. Found your old lovesick star carrier, I see."

Barley actually blushed at the man's words. Conner just quirked an eyebrow at the man. "You are not your father, Ezra Nokata, so be careful how much teasing you give me and Barley. Now, how's your ship? Are they ready to dock with Barley?"

"She's none too keen, but we could do with a moment to work on getting our shields and a few other systems back running properly," Ezra said with a chuckle which turned into a sad sigh. "I understand you could use a crew over there, Uncle Conner."

"Just until this crisis is over." Conner tapped the screen mounted to the right side of his chair. In a moment, he had a tactical display with two possible enemy ships marked. "Can your sensors detect the ships which have been attacking us?"

"They seemed to be shadowing the shuttle as it headed away from Earth," Ezra said, his words punctuated with a rapid series of loud pops in the background. "Get away from that station! Sahalie, power down port consoles. Redirect to secondary control locations."

"Betty, get the *Powell* on this stream as well. I want to coordinate with both captains before we start this." Conner looked over to Betty. He noted Zoeller sat at her station silently looking over the control panel. "Zoeller, if you're staying, you have to monitor the coupling between *Infinity* and each destroyer. I plan on doing one at a time since no one here except myself and Barley have done this. Otherwise, get the hell off my bridge."

A short time later, Zoeller called off the distance and whether things were aligned or not. Kashi sweated profusely while making the fine maneuvering adjustments until the clang of the *Soaring Eagle* bumping into place against *Infinity* echoed throughout the ship. Magnus appeared moments later, followed by three men and one woman in Fleet uniforms via the zip tubes at the back of the bridge.

"Magnus!" Conner started to stand, then remembered he'd not be able to hug his son. "Your cousins are with Sam?"

"Along with a copy of me," Magnus said with an embarrassed smile. "I wanted to come and let you know we're all safe. These four are the fleet personnel who were clinging to the exterior of the shuttle when I took control."

"We'll be taking command of this ship," the man who'd shot the pilot back on the shuttle said while leveling a laser rifle at Conner. The other three leveled rifles at Kashi, Zoeller, and Betty. "And you, pretty little girl, get away from that comm station."

"Assholes," Betty said with a disgusted look on her face. Bolts of electricity shot from Betty's eyes, striking each of the four newcomers simultaneously. All four shook violently before falling to the floor. They laid still except for the occasional twitching.

"Betty?" Magnus stared at Betty, shock and pride on the hologram's face.

"Did I jump the, um, what was rest of the quote, Uncle Barley?" Betty pressed a finger to cheek and pursed her lips in doubt.

"Gun," Zoeller muttered staring at the four Fleeters lying on the floor twitching. "Did I jump the gun."

"Well, I now know the defensive measures I added to your spine are working." Conner smiled at his daughter. "Good work, Betty. You acted just perfectly."

"Thanks, Da…, um, Captain," Betty smiled sweetly before turning back around to her console. "The *Powell* is ready to dock.

Shall I have them wait or should Barley handle the docking himself this time?"

"I think Barley should handle this one," Conner said with a glance at the other flesh and blood people on the bridge, all of whom looked shaken up. "You good, Barley?"

"Fine." Barley groaned with a roll of his eyes. "Just so you know, I hate doing this. It's like when you forced—"

"Yeah, yeah, you big baby," Conner chuckled as he turned to Kashi. "You did great, Tandon. You too, Zoeller. Now, Doherty, how are those engines? We might have to do another acceleration burn if new attacks start up again."

"Um, what?" The man said before jumping in his seat. "Oh! Yes, Captain. We're green across the board. Fuel levels are still good as well, but we likely will want to top the tanks off, so to speak, before we try and return to Jovian space."

Fleeters started jumping out of the zip tubes, with Ezra Nokata first amongst the group. Seeing the ones lying on the floor twitching, Ezra shot Conner a questioning look. Magnus laughed and walked over to the visiting captain.

"Let me introduce you to my sister, Ezra," Magnus said as he clapped the black man's back, only for his hand to pass right through the man. "Dang it. I already miss being solid."

"Sister? What the hell happened here?" Ezra looked from Magnus to Conner.

"Captain Nokata, let me introduce our communications officer and Magnus's little sister Betty." Conner said chuckling. "The four lying on the floor came on the shuttle with Magnus and my sister's kids. They got hold of rifles from somewhere and thought they'd take command of Barley."

"And Betty zapped them pretty good. Can you have some of your men take them down to the brig?" Barley said with a proud grin. "And how's the son of one of my favorite captains doing, Captain Nokata?"

Ezra tapped his collar. "Sahalie, send a security detail to *Infinity's* bridge. We've got some traitors up here that need to be locked up."

"Already on their way, Captain," a woman said. "And tell Barley if he tries anything fresh with me, I'll burn his toes off."

"Sahalie, my dear cousin," Barley said smiling at Conner, "Conrad Conner is all I have eyes for. Besides, I know better than to piss off a frigate. You lovelies usually mean life or death for us carriers."

"You're still the sweet talker, I see, Barley," Sahalie said laughing. "And this Conner? Is he the one who married Abe and Shin after winning Horus?"

"He is, Sahalie!" Barley beamed with happiness at the other ship's comment. "I heard they both retired some years ago. Did you know them? Are they still together?"

"I haven't heard from either one of them in several years," Sahalie said pensively. "Knowing them, they're likely long haul cargo ships who can just cuddle together in front of a fire kissing. Such a pair of lovebirds when I was assigned to the same carrier group just before they retired."

"You married artificials, Uncle Conner?" Ezra chuckled as Barley and Sahalie continued talking to each other. "I don't think I've heard this story."

"We were limping back to Centauri with one of Barley's frigates in tow and the other a sobbing mess about how his beloved Abe might be dead and Shin didn't know if he'd be able to go on without his protector." Conner said as the memory of that horrid trip back replayed in his head. The dead littering the ship outnumbered the stasis fields available on some ships, and every ship towed at least one other ship, with Barley towing three. He'd won by scaring the crap out of both the Spartan naturals and artificials. "To keep everyone thinking positive and hoping for the future, I promised Shin I would go over and personally check on his beloved Abe. After getting Abe back up and able to talk, the pair of destroyers then asked me to marry them, since I was the senior ranking officer. When I heard that, I almost fainted."

"You yelled and shouted," Barley laughed, "but then told me to pull out all of the stops and get everyone involved. If I recall correctly, you said if you were marrying anyone, especially ships, you wanted everyone involved and cheering for their happiness. I think that scared the Spartans more than anything you did in the actual battle."

"I did pull all active commanding officers over to you for the ceremony," Conner said laughing. "I hope those two are still in love and together."

"What if they aren't?" Ezra looked at Conner with a smirk.

"What'll you do then?"

"He'll go find them, knock some sense into them both, and remarry them," Barley said with an indignant sniff.

"Captain?" Betty called out. "Admiral Vickie with Fleet Operations Earth Space is connecting. She wants to talk to you and the other captains."

"We'll take it in the captain's office, Betty," Conner said standing up. "Kashi, set a course to Terra Prima. Once the *Powell* and *Soaring Eagle* are confirmed locked to *Infinity*, bring us about at a slow burn. Kandra, closely monitor sensors for a return of hostiles. They'll appear as sensor ghosts, I understand. Zoeller, keep an eye on the system connections between *Infinity* and the two frigates. You may need to coordinate with the system officers on the frigates to maintain power and comms between all three ships. The frigates are now dependent on us for nearly everything. Doherty, engines may surge under this heavier strain since I don't know when Barley last had frigates attached."

"I am more than capable of handling the load of two frigates, Conner," Barley said glaring at Conner.

Conner stepped up to the artificial and acted as though patting Barley's face. "That's what they all say the first time."

Barley blushed as Kashi and several others burst out laughing. Zoeller grunted with disgust while Betty blushed just as red as Barley and screamed, "Stop being gross, Daddy!"

CHAPTER 12

Conner walked into the captain's office with Ezra and Magnus following him. Vickie already sat on the long bench at the far end sipping at a demitasse of black espresso coffee. Conner motioned for the pair to find a seat while he sat behind the desk. Magnus hurried over to sit beside the admiral, reaching out to pluck a tall wooden mug shaped like a dragon's head with the open mouth bubbling over with a thick foam. Lifting the mug with the dragon's snout pointed at himself, Magnus took a long drink from the dragon's mouth, holding it by the curled horns.

"Ah, a great vintage," Magnus sighed happily. "And great to be alive."

"Beers don't have a vintage, Magnus," Vickie said smirking.

"And coffee will stunt your growth, mother," Magnus said giggling, which quickly faded. "As scary as traveling on the data streams can be, I'm glad I came ahead. They were kidnapping Ernie and Arlene. The one who might have known their final destination and ultimate buyer of my cousins got his head blasted with a laser rifle, so now we likely won't be able to confirm or find out anything more. Ernie was curled up in a seat and Arlene floated there yelling at the pilot. I think she knew they were prisoners, but it might also be how she reacts when stressed."

"To stand and yell at the person making her mad?" Conner stared at his oldest child, wishing he could give the young man a fierce hug. He could still remember the little ball of data which slowly formed into a child between six and ten years old. "That sounds a lot like how your aunt was at that age."

Vickie set her cup down and pulled Magnus into a hug. "What you did today, from leaving Socrates by yourself, saving those people in Green Node by using your body to stop that chunk of the mooring, and then taking control of the shuttle, was so incredibly brave of you, my precious little boy. I'm so proud of you."

"Do you want an official report, Admiral?" Ezra sat on the corner of Conner's desk with furrowed brows and worry tightening his lips. The man's strong jaw, high cheekbones, and thin lines cut into his close-cropped hair made Conner think of those times Ezra's father had called Conner up to the bridge for some tech issue.

"Just the gist of what happened for now," Vickie said, pulling her arm off Magnus and picking her cup back up.

The three men related what happened, each adding in details where warranted. Vickie sat and listened, nodding occasionally. As they finished, a ding filled the momentary silence just before Barley flashed into existence.

"Sorry for the intrusion, Captain," Barley stood there in his young ensign body, "but Earth's ConRad, is requesting connection privileges and time to meet with you."

"Granted. He can join this meeting." Conner said smiling at how playful Barley liked to be. "What of the captain of the *Powell?* Will they be joining us in some form or not?"

"Captain Urlain is having to deal with damage assessment to Pollick's core-to-engine interface, Captain." Barley shifted as he spoke, as though uncomfortable answering.

Conner struggled to recall if this was one of those delicate topics for ship artificials, like talking about sexual disfunction was for humans. "Inform Captain Urlain that if help is needed, I am still certified in ship artificial core systems. I'll be discreet, if that's wanted by Pollick."

"I'll pass that on to both parties, Captain," Barley said with a visible relief. "Earth will join you in a moment. He's connecting now."

Barley then walked up to Conner. Leaning over, the artificial grabbed Conner's face and pressed their lips together in a deep probing kiss, which lasted only a few seconds. Pulling off Conner, Barley hurried back to where he'd been standing with an impish grin on his face. "Oh, and just so you know Magnus, the projectors in here can make us solid if we want. You also have that control since you are currently resident in my systems. Ta ta."

Barley vanished, leaving a stunned Conner just staring at the spot he'd been. Conner's face grew warmer and warmer. Before he could even turn around, Magnus slammed into him, sobbing while hugging Conner.

"Love you too, Maggie," Conner choked out the words as he reached up and hugged Magnus's head.

"Wait," Ezra said as a chime sounded and ConRad flashed into existence, "have you two never gotten to hug? Like ever?"

"The Academy doesn't have this type of holo-projectors in it," Vickie said, getting weepy-eyed herself. "Ships weren't normally equipped with them until about a decade ago. So, outside of city-stations like *Socrates,* which have them in select locations, physical contact is very infrequent. That said, even when us matrix-based Artificials hug, it's not the same as when we can get an actual, physical hug. A mystery of our sentience."

"I'm sorry." Magnus pulled away from Conner, sniffing back his sobbing and wiping his face with a sleeve.

"Don't be, Magnus," Conner turned around and stood before his son. Grabbing Magnus by the shoulders, Conner pulled the artificial he'd created decades ago into another hug, adding a kiss on the cheek for good measure. "I'm proud of you and the person you've grown up to be. Sorry I've never been able to give you the things you wanted."

Ezra walked over to the pair and hugged Magnus from behind. "Cousin hugs, Magnus."

"Speaking of cousins," ConRad said with a soft chuckle in his voice as he stood watching them, "I know of two down in the med bay which could use some hugs. Shall I have Barley bring them up here?"

"Nope," Barley said, appearing without a chime. "I'm taking them to the captain's quarters where this same projector is also installed. Not at my request either, I might add."

"I remember the way," Magnus said with happy surprise in his eyes. "Come on, Ezra. I'll introduce you."

Magnus pushed Ezra back but turned back to Conner. Kissing Conner on the cheek, Magnus blushed as he whispered, "Love you and your stinky shirts, dad."

As Magnus grabbed Ezra by the wrist, the man tried to protest. Vickie just waved him away smiling. "File a report later, but relax for now, Captain. We won't keep Conner for much longer."

"Thanks, mom!" Magnus called as he rushed to the door, dragging a laughing Ezra behind him.

Reaching the door, Magnus stopped and spun around. When he turned, Magnus's clothes morphed from the brown pants, blue shirt, and leather ball cap keeping his shoulder length black wavy hair held back in a ponytail to being a knee-length blue on white flower-print sun dress. Bouncing back to ConRad, Maggie hugged the taller man tightly.

"Thanks, Uncle ConRad," Maggie whispered. She then dashed back to the door and Ezra.

As the door closed behind the pair, Conner smiled at how happy his child seemed for the moment. Vickie shook her head. ConRad's smile faded slowly. Sitting back down, Conner motioned to a chair and then the bench where Vickie still sat.

"You can sit, old man," Conner said with a teasing smile. He knew better than to take his teasing beyond a certain point with the oldest living artificial in all of human space.

"Barley," ConRad called out as he crossed the office and sat on the far end of the bench from Vickie, "I need Zeta-level isolation. Can you achieve that?"

A chime preceded Barley's reappearance. "Yes, sir, but only within my body. The data streams incoming to me from both Earth and Terra Prima are not able to be secured to that extreme of a security level. You and the admiral will need to create subnodes within my systems until I'm able to make a hard connection to a facility with that level of security connection back to Earth and Luna, where your respective primary cores are located."

"Understood. Creating a subnode of myself now. Admiral, are you willing to do so?" ConRad looked at Vickie as he spoke.

Vickie looked from ConRad to Conner before nodding. She closed her eyes momentarily, during which her image flickered. The coffee cup vanished and didn't reappear. "Done, sir. Barley, please confirm subnode status."

"Nodes stabile and isolated to *Infinity's* secure systems core, admiral and planetary guardian." Barley raised a hand as he spoke with the fingers spread and curled, as though about to tap out on an invisible keypad.

Twisting the hand at the wrist several times in opposite directions, the walls, floor, and ceiling all glowed with a faint reddish-purple color before it and Barley vanished. A magenta 'Z' appeared on the desktop, indicating the security isolation field was engaged and intact. Seeing that, Conner swiveled his chair to look at the two artificials.

"Security in place, ConRad," Conner said, unsure how to take being in complete isolation from all outside data access. Not even

Barley knew what they said since this level of security kept even the ship's artificial out. "You should be free to speak now."

"Ever heard of the Zen Technology Armada, Conner?" ConRad reached an arm out and looked at it while turning and twisting it, as though feeling his body for the first time.

"No, should I have?" Conner watched what he knew was a normal function of artificials nearly every time they gained any form of solidity. ConRad was a good three millennia old and had been solid the stars knew how many times over the millennia, yet the AI still did this each time Conner had been present when ConRad gained solidity.

"They're a dark world organization that's seen heavy growth in the construction tech fields, such as your late brother-in-law's profession." ConRad looked to Conner as he spoke, letting his arm drop. "Intel agencies are indicating they have or will soon infiltrate every aspect of commerce, including interstellar shipping. They are extremely dangerous and may be trying to force their way into this little business venture of yours."

"First, ConRad," Conner said folding his arms over his chest, "my little business venture was limited to developing a functional artificial prototype solely to fulfill a concept commissioned by the Sol-Human Stellar Fleet. The C5 Group is limited to myself and Magnus, with Sam coming in to help with the hearing concerning Betty, into which you and Aphrodite got dragged to render judgement upon. My sister and brother-in-law were attacked before I was essentially forced to become a contract operator of an ex-military artificial's body. I'm here, in the Inner System, solely to take guardianship of my sister's children. There is no 'business venture' involved here, little or big. Furthermore, my involvement with Kashi Tandon's Shining Sun Shipping, or whatever she's calling it today, began three to four days ago. So, if anyone is trying to be infiltrated, it would be Tandon Universal, not The C5 Group."

"Could they be after Conner himself?" Vickie tapped a cheek with a hand. "He did research and code an artificial while in Fleet Academy."

"Actually, I started the research and coding in primary school, with Magnus's matrix consolidating into sentience sometime in middle school," Conner said, rubbing his temples. "None of this makes sense, you two. My sister was an artist and her husband a structural engineer specializing in planet-based buildings. The tech used in planetary buildings hasn't changed a whole lot in the last three millennia. Me? Outside of my sister always calling me a fake brother, I've led a relatively quiet life, despite my stint in Fleet. Even when that asshole Minsk stole credit for my research and development work, I didn't push back on it because I didn't want to create waves for my sister and her family. A quiet life, no drama or trauma, is what she demanded of me if I was to be allowed even occasional calls by any children she might have. Those were her conditions, ConRad. You knew this from all the arguments we got into while I was in your FCOPS Corp. The only problems I have had are from companies I've bought standard, older tech from for use in Betty. Companies that should now be paid off in full thanks, partially, to you."

"That's the quandary, Conner," ConRad snapped, leaning forward to rest his elbows on his knees and head in his hands. "I've followed your actions for ten years now, and there is no reason for anyone to be pissed at you beyond your horrible credit and constant late payments on bills. You even helped that man-turned-woman. What's her name? Dilly? Delly?"

"Delilah, you asshole," Conner snarled, angry at her even being brought up along with the thought of being stalked by a planetary AI still. "And I told you there would never be anything between us. Why in the light sucking abyss of a black hole that is your heart are you still pining after me?"

"Don't be so full of yourself, you idiot fleshbag," ConRad surged to his feet growling back at Conner.

Conner glared up at the Artificial, partially wanting to stand up and punch him in the gut as hard as he could. Prudence and the fact he wanted his niece and nephew, along with his own children, to be able to set foot on Earth at some point in the future kept him seated. Vickie rolled her eyes and threw a glass of water at ConRad she suddenly held.

"Sit down and cool off, you old grandpa," Vickie said shaking her head. "Let's get to the point of this high security meeting so Conner can go hug his niece and nephew. You remember those two, right? They don't know the official status of their parents. Remember?"

"My apologies, Victoria," ConRad said huffing for a moment.

"And to you, Conrad Conner. The point of the secrecy involved here is this. Dark world organizations, not just the ZTA, are seeing an influx of support, be it financial or otherwise. What's most disturbing is the fact that more and more seem to be focusing on you, Conner. Expect to see the attacks on your sister and brother-in-law to be blamed on underworld involvement by one or both of them. While I have locked down their personal data streams on my own authority, it's purely to give you time to review their information for anything that might spur your memory on why your family is suddenly the focus of criminal organizations."

"Frankly, I blame that old hag of a First Admiral," Conner spat out before he could stop himself. "Sorry. I shouldn't have said that."

"It's crossed my matrix, to be honest," Vickie said with a wane smile.

"A data stream I'm already following," ConRad said with a sigh as he dropped back to the bench and leaned back. "I'm digging into your family's past, Conner, as well as anyone associated with your parents or any of their siblings. Even as large and powerful as I am, this is slow going."

"I can imagine." Conner glanced at his desk. A message flashed, which indicated they approached Terra Prima. "My dad was an only child who was estranged from his parents long before meeting my mom. Mom was a nurse by training, and I think had a brother, but he died before I was born, if I recall correctly. All I know is that my only sister always claimed I wasn't her brother after the *Valhalla* was bombed or torpedoed when I was thirteen. I think she once claimed I was a cousin, but I'm too tired at the moment to remember."

"I hate to suggest this, Conner," Vickie spoke with some hesitation in her voice, "but what about Magnus? He calls me mom because of his growing up during your academy years and me constantly catching him breaking the passcodes on the more restricted sections of the library cores."

"I can't exactly ask him without breaking the security on this conversation, now can I?" Conner glared at the admiral, more angry at himself for not thinking of Magnus, but also for anyone even suspecting his own child. The boy had gone through some horrid times right alongside Conner, which made him very protective of his son.

"It's not Magnus," ConRad said flat-voiced. "Conner is the

focus in everything I've come across. Everyone around you might suffer, but only by being connected to you, Conner."

"Do they want me dead? Want money? What?" Conner drummed his fingers on the desk, staring at the message Barley awaited final orders on whether to dock or not. "I've got two flesh and bloods kids to raise who have only me as a living relative. Then there are Magnus and Betty, who despite being technically experienced enough to become or have become adult artificials, they are still children in my eyes. I can't just lie down and let them kill me, no matter how attractive that has seemed during my now over four decades in this godforsaken universe."

"That is the biggest unknown, Conner," ConRad said before taking a deep breath and sighing heavily. "Go hug those kids. Take your daughter as well so she can hug them and her brother too. Be a family and enjoy being alive. Everything else can wait."

"And their parents?" Vickie prompted. "Is Conner's brother-in-law really dead? His sister?"

"They're both dead," ConRad said softly. "Emily's heart stopped in surgery and wouldn't restart. She was officially pronounced dead almost at the same moment as I was disconnected from the shuttle. I wanted to tell you, Conner, so we could decide which of us tells the children."

"Damn," Conner muttered, his chest tightening and his gut flipping over. "Magnus and his aunt were very close. He's going to take this as hard as his cousins."

"Go be with them, Conner. ConRad, I think you should tell the children," Vickie said softly. "I'll go along as well. Let's end the security protocols and head down together."

Conner clenched his eyes shut for a moment, not wanting the tears he felt welling up to escape. The sound of the bench cushion shifting told him the others were standing. When a strong hand gripped his shoulder, he looked up to find ConRad standing there with tears of his own in those always ancient looking eyes.

"Just know, Conner," ConRad said with an emotion-thick voice as Vickie tapped the 'Z' on the desktop, "you are never alone in this universe as long as I exist. You understand?"

Conner surged to his feet, hugging the black man as his grief finally got the better of him. ConRad clapped Conner on the back as they embraced, memories of long nights working on one of

ConRad's many cores while they talked and grew close flickering briefly in Conner's head before becoming arguments with his sister over his obsession with artificials and technology. Her jabs at him not really being her brother, but never explaining or refusing help when she needed it. The long talks of whether to marry a struggling engineering student and did she want to risk going off-world with him should his eventual job transfer him. Craziness that she seemed to not have anyone else to talk to about, since they were each other's only family.

"Thanks, old man," Conner whispered as he pulled away. "Let's gather up my little girl and go tell everyone the bad news."

CHAPTER 13

"Conner?" Kashi leaned through the open door to the captain's quarters. "Do you have a moment?"

"Not really, Kashi," Conner called out without looking up from Betty's open control rod which lay on a small table over by the narrow sliver of a view port. The curve of Earth's nightside could be seen near the top of the window. "You can talk, but I likely won't respond."

"Hello, Ms. Tandon." A young woman with sandy blonde hair, which fell in curly waves to the middle of her back, stepped through a door on Kashi's left. There was a strong resemblance to Conner and Magnus, but the woman had far larger breasts than Magnus effected when a woman and actually stood shorter than Magnus's usual six-foot height. The bright yellow two-piece bikini also showed off the woman's hourglass figure.

"Who are...Betty?" Kashi stared, her mouth hanging open in shock.

"What do you think?" Betty said, her voice smooth and slightly higher pitched than previously. "Barley uploaded me to my own node on his system while daddy worked on tweaking my rod so I can better adjust my appearance to something I like more."

"You couldn't change before?" Kashi looked at Conner, her face growing redder and redder. "Why are you in that outfit?"

"Ernie," Conner said while never stopping what he did. "Otherwise, she'd be naked trying to get me to tell her whether her figure was close to what I thought would be biologically or genetically feasible in the Conner family."

"Why not just buy her a body like you did for Magnus?" Kashi turned to look back at Betty, who had spun around to reveal that not much covered her butt. "Good Heavens! Put some clothes on. You're basically naked, Betty."

Conner looked up momentarily at Betty. "A bit too flabby. You talked about being fit, but not defined. Tighten the butt cheeks up a bit."

"What is going on?" Kashi screamed.

"Damn it." Conner jerked the pincers he held, causing a small spark of light. "What do you want, Kashi? This is delicate work and you just caused me to ruin her speech controller."

"Just buy her a body, Conner. Why be so cheap?" Kashi slammed her hands down on the table, causing a dozen small parts to jump and scatter upon landing.

"Aah! Get away from me," Betty ran over and yanked Kashi away from the table. "Oh my god. Can you put me back together, daddy?"

Conner clenched both his fists and eyes shut as he let out a guttural snarl. Taking several deep breaths, he only spoke he was once calmer. "Again, Kashi, why are you here?"

"Tell me why you won't buy your daughter a body when you bought one for your son?" Kashi crossed her arms with lips pursed.

"First, I haven't bought Magnus a body," Conner said in clearly spoken words to keep from screaming at the woman as he stood. "Socrates paid for the rental that got destroyed when Terra Prima was attacked. Terra Prima's controlling artificial, Treespinner, is gifting Magnus with a new body since she feels responsible for what happened to him."

Conner carefully stepped away from the table toward the twenty-year-old rich girl as he continued. "Secondly, the payment on the contract which led to Betty being here at all paid all the debts I incurred creating the control spine you have likely ruined with your careless behavior. I won't have the funds for an artificial-grade body after paying the shuttle down to Earth and burial expenses for my late sister and brother-in-law, let alone the accommodations for however long that will all take, since we won't be allowed to stay at my sister's house due to her and her husband's murders. Now that I have bared my family's problems to the poor little rich girl, kindly tell me why you are wreaking havoc in my quarters?"

"Oh yes," Kashi said with a sweet smile. "I've gotten some resumes from the advert I'd put out when I first formed Shining Sun Shipping. Barley suggested I run them past you before he weighs in on them. Four of the applicants are on Terra Prima, three of them are former Fleeters, and one is a doctor. I don't know which of us hires crew, since there is now a split between SSS and the ship."

"It's barely been a full day since that judgement was delivered,"

Conner said running a hand through his short hair. "My thought is that you pay me a fee that covers the operation and crew salaries plus a percentage for overhead and profit on my side. You, as the company we are operating the ship for, should cover any insurance and government fees. At least initially. There are some issues arising that may put the ship and whoever is on it in danger. For that reason, I suggest you not be on the ship. Is one of those four a navigator?"

"No, and I inquired of each of them if they knew of anyone else who might be interested in traveling the stars," Kashi said with a pensive look. "I've not gotten any responses yet. Now, what danger are you talking about? The—"

Smack!

Betty yelped as she surged to her feet dropping the parts she'd been picking up off the floor. Standing behind her was Conner's eleven-year-old nephew, Ernie. Standing at four and half-feet tall, the brown-haired boy grinned with an impish glint in his eyes and bore a strong resemblance to his late father, though that glint and smile reminded Conner so much of his own sister.

"Looking sexy as hell, cuz," Ernie said before bursting out laughing.

"And you're looking like a dead little lech." Betty grabbed Ernie by an ear and pulled him to a chair. Shoving him over the chair's arm, Betty proceeded to spank the boy's behind mercilessly. "How do you like that, cuz."

"Told you she'd spank you, twerp." A fourteen-year-old girl of over five feet stood in the open door to Conner's quarters. She had waist-long purple and blue curly hair, numerous piercings on her ears and face, and wore knee-high boots that looked disturbingly like a horse's leg, complete with hoofed feet. Her shirt was ripped flannel, which had colors matching her hair, and shorts so tight and short they looked painted on her body. Conner thought Kashi was having a stroke the way the woman stuttered and struggled to speak coherently. As for himself, Conner could only hear his own mother screaming at him about how he would ruin his life if he kept on the tech and science route instead of something more solid, like a trade. She'd be like Kashi, so upset and shocked she wouldn't be able to speak.

"What happened to the flight suit you wore yesterday, Arlene?"

Conner walked around Kashi to grab Betty's wrist. Pulling her off Ernie, he motioned with his head toward the bedroom door she'd come out of earlier. "Go try on that uniform Barley created after making the adjustment I suggested."

"Barley made all of this with one of his fabrication plants," Arlene said with a wide smile as she stepped in and spun around. "I already had all of the piercing holes, but just some plastic studs in them when we had to flee. I love the boots but couldn't think of what to wear with them. Ernie suggested bootie shorts, so here we go."

"Makes you just want to smack her butt, Uncle Captain," Ernie said as he rubbed his own behind. "Why'd you make Betty stop? She was kind of getting into spanking me."

Conner just groaned. He wasn't sure what to make of these kids. It made him wonder if his sister and her husband ever disciplined them.

"That is no proper attire for a young lady," Kashi said with only a slight rise in volume. However, her entire body trembled. "I…you …No! This will not stand."

"Not your problem, little rich girl," Conner said as he stepped up beside the woman.

"You are not a woman, so you have no idea of what to do." Kashi slapped Conner's belly with the back of a hand before walking to the door and Conner's niece. "Arlene, come with me. I will show you how a proper lady dresses."

"Kashi Tandon!" Conner barked out the woman's name with all the irritated bluster of his tech instructor back during his academy years. It stopped Kashi, as Conner had hoped. "Your lessons in womanhood will have to wait. Go review those applicants with Barley and get his feedback on their skills and possible positions they could fill. I have to explain a few realities of being on an interstellar ship to the children."

Kashi just stared at Conner for a minute before finally nodding while releasing Arlene. "As you say, Conner, there is work to be done first. Arlene, you are free to come to me with any questions you might have, or if you'd like to try on some of my clothes. What I have here with me is just a small bit of my closet back home near Delhi."

Kashi turned and walked out into the corridor. She immediately collided with Magnus, who wore a flowing robe which hung on a lithe body more like a bolt of cloth twice or more Magnus's height of just under six foot. Black curly hair fell nearly to his waist. Gaps in how the robe hung partially exposed small breasts on his chest.

"You're solid?" Kashi pressed her hands on Magnus's chest but jerked them off as though burned. "And a girl? I...I thought...I mean..."

"I'm genderfluid, Ms. Tandon," Magnus said smiling. "This new body is both male and female."

Magnus looked into the room at Ernie as he continued without pausing. "And no, Ernie, you will not be allowed to find out what that means. Not unless you like the idea of losing all four limbs and anything that could be used to identify your gender."

"Aw, come on, cuz," Ernie whined. "Consider it part of my sex education class."

"Thank you, Kashi," Conner said, forcing himself not to sigh or laugh. "Magnus, I'm glad you're here. I need you to help me explain to these two why piercings and nonbiological material attached or inside their bodies are a bad idea."

"Me?" Magnus's already light complexion paled even further as the artificial's voice rose in fear. "I...I can't."

Conner sighed as he rubbed his face with a hand. "Give me one good reason."

"Lieutenant Thomas Atterhorn." Magnus trembled slightly, tears filling eyes which clenched shut quickly.

Conner stared at his eldest. The name brought up the face of a young man from the upper regions of North America. The horrible way the man had died, when he'd been called back to duty stations at the start of the Battle of Horus, just before Maggie had gone into lockdown, returned to him. Maggie had been talking to the man and watched a piercing get ripped off someone else's body and flung into the lieutenant's body again and again as a stray warp nodule kept bouncing about the man. Barley couldn't pull Maggie out fast enough.

"Don't worry, Uncle Conner," Arlene said with uncertainty as her piercings vanished and her clothes became the ship's uniform shirt and pants combo, which together had a giant stylized 'S' emblazoned across the person's front and back. From the left shoulder across the chest, diagonally downward, back across the belly at about waist level, and then down diagonally across both legs, the uniform was a dark gray to the right as Conner looked at Arlene and a dark burgundy to the left, or in the 'S' shape. A short vertical collar rose up as it went around the neck until it was nearly to the base of the skull at the back. When Arlene spun about, Conner noticed the collar and arms were the dark gray while the cuffs around the wrists were the dark burgundy color. "It's all just a holoprojector worked into our uniform. An idea I convinced Barley to let me try out."

"Yeah," Ernie said, moving to pat Maggie's arm. "We know about the eddies and transmutation stuff that can happen when the warp tunnels of different ships get too close to each other."

A chime announced Barley's arrival a heartbeat before the artificial flashed into existence. "I gave both of them a watered-down version of Fleet's lecture on the subject when Arlene wanted actual piercings. Sam helped with the lecture as well as some personal memories of his own."

"Speaking of Sam, where is the man?" Conner glanced back at the table with Betty's spine and the scattered parts.

"Working up fabrication parameters for Betty's spine," Barley said with a smile. "I'm tempted to nickname her Catastrophe Kashi, but she has her heart in the right place. Most of the time."

"Is Uncle Sam going to use the fabber again?" Ernie bounced up and down beside Conner and Barley. "Can we help? Arlene and I want to help. Right, sis?"

"Can we, Uncle Conner?" Arlene had the same hopeful look as her brother on her face.

"Sure, kids," Conner said smiling. "Just remember Sam and Barley are the actual operators. Those things, even the smaller ones, are still dangerous to be near."

"Come on, Magnus," Ernie said, rushing over to grab Magnus's hand. "You gotta see these things work."

"I've got something important to discuss with your uncle first, Ernie," Magnus said. "The best place for watching the fabber, though, is from the level above it. Looking down on it while it makes things is great."

"Cool! Let's go, Arlene." Ernie ran out the door and went left.

Arlene followed Barley, who followed Ernie to the door. Barley looked in the direction Ernie took and shouted, "Wrong way."

When they had gone, Magnus stepped over to the door and pressed the close button. "You can come out now, Betty. Ernie's gone."

"I wasn't hiding because of Ernie, Magnus," Betty said stepping out of the bedroom wearing the same uniform as Arlene. "I was working on that comm data capture you sent me."

"Were you able to break the encryption?" Magnus moved to sit on the sofa against the wall opposite the door Betty emerged through.

"The encryption used on the signal was rather simple," Betty said, furrowing her brow while walking over to pick up a piece from her spine that had fallen to the floor. "It's just a mathematical algorithm changing in a seemingly random pattern but is actually based on the quantum flux of three elements used in nanotech. What's posing difficulty is translating the signal itself."

"Translating?" Conner was surprised. He had designed and taught Betty to be able to translate any language humanity had ever spoken, and even several of the nearly sentient animals that could still be found on Earth. "You know the roots of every human language that is, has been, and will be spoken. How can you be stumped?"

"At first I thought it was encrypted again, which wouldn't be surprising since the ships aren't showing up on our sensors," Betty said while turning the piece she'd picked up over in her hand. "While examining the signal from every angle, I noticed patterns within the signal fragment which makes me think it really is a language. I'm running the fragment through every one of my translation filters. Nothing is coming up with Earth-based language systems. Really, not even human-based languages."

"What about animal?" Conner found it hard to believe what he was hearing.

"The fragments I have to study do not seem to be a natural human language developed through the evolution of language. Nor does it seem to be a language invented by humanity or human-developed intelligences," Betty said, sighing. She set the part on the table beside her spine with a pensive expression.

"Do you think if you had more data capture fragments you might crack the translation?" Magnus stared down at his hands, as though watching a memory only he could see.

"How would you have more than what you captured on that shuttle?" Conner walked over to sit beside his elder child.

"Dad? You need to listen and not interrupt me. Understand?" Magnus looked up from his hands to lock eyes with Conner. "Promise me?"

Conner reached out and grasped one of Magnus's hands. His eldest's trembling voice, the hesitation audible to Conner, scared him. This seemed to be one of those moments where he had to trust his child's judgment. "Promise."

"When Barley put me in what he called lockdown at the outset of the Battle of Horus," Magnus said taking a deep breath before releasing it slowly, "it turned out to not be as secure as he thought."

Conner tightened his grip on his son's hand but stayed silent. Betty moved over to sit on Magnus's other side as her brother continued. "At some point in the battle, my make-believe world, based on some ancient fantasy movie with dragons and rings, got corrupted with something completely unknown. Remember, by the time the Battle of Horus happened, I'd been wandering about Barley's systems for a number of years and had been acting as one of Barley's child routines. Anyway, something which couldn't speak any of the same languages as me kept attacking. More and more, their attacks broke me out of the lockdown world and I was able to witness the Battle of Horus. I saw you get shot point blank, staggering through the ship ordering people around, rewriting core matrixes on the fly, and getting cussed out by Barley for ripping him apart. All the while, what were supposed to be the enemies I had to defeat in my lockdown world, kept trying to attack you by taking control of parts of Barley. Again and again, I fought them and drove them back. Barley was so intent on the battle with Sparta I'm not sure he noticed my battle."

Conner sat silently struggling to fully take in that his little boy had had to fight for his life. That Magnus had battled a foreign enemy he'd known nothing about. It scared him, but also made him incredibly angry. Angry at himself more than anyone.

"All of those moments are remembered in detail, but not in my main matrix," Magnus whispered. "Barley suggested I compartmentalize those horrible memories and leave them with him. So, I left only vague recollections in my matrix and put the detailed memories into a metaphorical box."

"Can I ask a question?" Conner asked without releasing Magnus's hand. When Magnus nodded without speaking, Conner continued. "What happened to these infiltrators?"

"I destroyed them," Magnus looked up from Conner's hand to his eyes. "One by one, as they slowly destroyed that fantasy world of elves and dwarves. At least I thought so. When your proposal on Venus was, well, ruined, a version of those same infiltrators seemed to be present, but not in a way I could attack them. They didn't seem to be the ones who killed Shima and nearly killed you. Rather, they seemed to be there as observers, but I couldn't figure out who or what exactly they were watching. They left before the planetary authorities arrived."

A chime sounded as Barley appeared in a flash of light. "I still have your memories safe, intact, and undisturbed, Magnus. You were pretty upset and, well, weird at the time, so should I filter the memories down to just these unknown attackers speaking?"

"Maybe I should do the filtering, Uncle Barley," Betty said before hugging Magnus. "My brave big brother. Such a horrible thing to go through."

"I am so sorry you had to go through that, Magnus," Conner said, pulling the artificial into his arms. "I should have left you with Vickie back at the academy. Then you'd not have had to endure such horrors."

"Then you likely wouldn't be alive, daddy," Magnus whispered as he let his head settle on Conner's shoulder. "Besides, I used that experience to bolster both my own and Barley's security protocols."

"With Aunt Emily and Uncle Frank's deaths," Betty said tapping her lips with a feather quill pen she now held, "and the attacks on both the shuttle and Terra Prima, what big brother has revealed could imply the Battle of Horus was set up solely for the purpose of trying to kill daddy. I don't like this. None of this."

"What do you have that could be so valuable someone would kill thousands of people on both sides of a war just to kill you, Conner?" Barley sat down on a nearby chair.

"He owns a ten-year-old chair he bought brand new the day he arrived on Socrates with his first paycheck from Danlen," Magnus said without lifting his head off Conner's shoulder. "It's ugly, collapsing, and is going to be replaced as soon as we return to *Socrates*.

Along with all of daddy's smelly shirts. This one first. How long have you been wearing this thing, daddy? You're abusing my olfactory sensors."

Conner laughed as Magnus pushed him away. "I've missed you complaining about my shirts. I'll leave my entire collection to you when I die."

"Ugh no." Magnus said standing. "Your three shirts are going to be taken to Venus and thrown in one of her lava pits. Pits which I'm sure smell better than yours. Go take a shower and get this atrocity off your body. Up and out, daddy. I'm serious."

"Calm down, Magnus," Conner shook his head chuckling. "I'm not that smelly."

"Barley, make the man you love take a shower." Magnus motioned for Betty to stand. "Or should I call Mr. Youngs to come make you shower?"

"I'll take care of getting your father clean, my worried little boy," Barley said with a knowing smile. "No need to involve my father. Besides, he's busy showing your cousins the fab plant in action again."

"Good." Magnus said with a smile and a wink at Conner. "Betty and I will work on the translation issues elsewhere. If we need anything, I'm sure I can find it without needing to disturb your scrubbing of my father's smelly pits."

"Oh my god, Magnus," Betty said blushing. "Don't encourage daddy to be gross."

"Daddy is quite experienced with being gross, my dear little sister." Magnus laughed while pulling Betty toward the door out of the captain's quarters. "Why do you think I wanted out of his shirts?"

Conner watched his children leave him alone with Barley, who still sat in the chair fully clothed. "No respect from my own children."

"You've been awake for going on what, forty-eight hours?" Barley stood up as parts of his uniform fell off his body to vanish as soon as hitting the floor. "A nice warm shower and then…"

Barley stood almost in front of Conner devoid of all clothing except a jock strap when the artificial merely stopped talking. Anger twisted the wanton look on the artificial's face into a snarl. "Gods-be-damned little rich bitch."

Conner just barely stifled the urge to laugh. Instead, he quirked an eyebrow and merely smirked at the man. "Not taking the hint, is she?"

"Insert every derogatory word for a woman ever uttered by mankind in every one of your needlessly complicated languages, Conner." Barley sat on Conner's lap facing him.

Wrapping his arms around Conner's neck and pressing their lips together, the jockstrap vanished from Barley's body. The door buzzed just as Conner returned the kiss. Only after a good minute of kissing did Barley pull their lips apart and Conner's shirt up over his head.

"Come in, you foul biological creation," Barley shouted as he tossed Conner's shirt in the direction of the door.

The door slid into the wall as the shirt dropped to Kashi's eye level, but a foot or two short of the woman. Both Barley and Conner chuckled when the woman jumped backwards and yelp in surprise. Leaning in to kiss Conner, Barley's arousal pressing against Conner made the man blush even as he returned the ship's deep, probing kiss.

"We have a job and need to get to Venus as soon as possible," Kashi said in a tense, but moderate voice. "If we hire these four people, we'll have a doctor and nurse. Will you two put on some clothes and stop being rude!"

Conner couldn't pull Barley off his lips. So, instead of speaking, he gave the woman a thumbs up and then shooed her away with his hand. When Kashi yelled incoherently and stormed off, Barley finally broke the kiss due to a giggling fit.

"That was too fun," Barley said giggling while watching the door close and the lock click into place.

"I know something a lot more fun, big guy," Conner said in a soft, low voice spoken close to Barley's nearest ear.

Barley jerked his gaze back to Conner, a deep blush covering the artificial's face. Jumping up, Barley physically pulled Conner to his feet, all while saying rapidly, "Shower. We need a shower. Right now."

CHAPTER 14

Conner looked at both Kashi and Zoeller across the desk in the captain's office. Both women stood with rather chagrin expressions on their faces, though Conner doubted either of them were truly repentant. While both were a bit disheveled, neither had done more than slap each other before he appeared on the bridge. He saw no visible marks, though a bit of rage remained in both pairs of eyes.

"We are not on a planet or a station where you can just storm out and never see the other person." Conner glared at the pair, not sure exactly why he was so mad with either one of them. "Traveling in space means learning to deal with not just the unknown and unexpected, but each other. Furthermore, this ship and everyone on it is still conscripted by Fleet during this period of uncertainty following the unprovoked attack on Terra Prima. If either of you cannot or do not want to fulfill roles on this ship, then you need say so now and transport will be arranged to get you the hell out of Barley's body and over to Terra Prima once Fleet gives the okay. Also, just to reiterate the situation, I am the law on this ship per agreement with the controlling artificial of the *CSS Infinity*. This is due to the ship not being docked to a station. Now, do either of you have anything so say on the matter which prompted the fight just now out on the bridge?"

"You have no authority over what—" Zoeller said with a snarl in her voice.

"I. Am. Captain." Conner shouted furiously at full volume. He glared at both women, who paled noticeably. Forcing a calmer tone and volume, he continued. "Which means I have final say as to whether either of you live or die while within Barley's body. Furthermore, as the president of The C5 Group, which has been contracted by Barley to operate his body, I have final say in all staffing hires and what positions they will fulfill. Not Shining Sun Shipping, who is merely contracting with The C5 Group for use of the *Infinity*."

Breeee

"Captain?" Betty said after the chime. "An Admiral Stephens is demanding to speak to the captain of this glorious bucket of crazy. Her words, I might add."

"Pipe her into here, Betty." Conner looked at the two women standing before his desk. "You two are to sit on the bench to my left and listen quietly. Barley, you might as well be visible too."

With a flash of light, Barley stood to the right of Conner's desk. At the same time, the Fleet logo appeared on the wall across from the desk slowly rotating. Breaking into a rapidly vanishing mist, the logo gave way to an Asian woman in her mid-forties sitting against the front edge of a desk very similar to the one Conner sat behind. With her black hair pulled back to create gentle waves along either side of her head, Conner wondered why the woman looked vaguely familiar. He noted the six admiral pins on her collar, denoting her as a Fleet Admiral.

"I'm Conrad Conner, Captain of the *CSS Infinity*," Conner said with a slight smile for the attractive woman. "To my right is Barley, the ship's controlling artificial. To my left, possibly out of your sight, is Kashi Tandon, President of Shining Sun Shipping as well as my current navigator. With her is Allison Zoeller, also of Shining Sun Shipping and currently my systems officer. Do I presume correctly you are Admiral Stephens?"

"Captain Conner as I live and breathe," Admiral Stephens said with a clipped and proper old British accent. "Nokata has told me all about you. Oh, and yes, I'm Min Stephens, Admiral of Fleet Operations."

"I hope he left out the bad parts, Admiral Stephens." Conner smiled despite an internal groan.

"Oh, don't worry about what I think," Admiral Stephens said as a grin spread across her face. "Your work over the years has told me all I need to know about you."

"You're not helping my ego, Admiral," Conner forced a smile as he spoke. "But then, we're not here to have my ego stroked, are we?"

"Well, I can stroke someone's ego, Captain." Admiral Stephens's smile didn't fade. "I wanted to personally thank Barley for his centuries of service to not just Fleet, but to all citizens of the Sol-Humana Confederation. Specifically, I want to thank you for putting up with Conrad Conner during the Battle of Horus. If not for your sacrifices during those harrowing days, I wouldn't be alive."

Conner stared in shock as the admiral stood straight and stiff-back before giving Barley a sharp nod. Glancing at Barley, he saw tears filling the artificial's eyes. A moment later, Barley returned the same at attention stance and nod.

"All of those who tread across my deck plates, fought by my side, and made the ultimate sacrifice in the many battles we've faced to preserve life in this vast void of space have my eternal and undying gratitude, Admiral." Barley said with a tearful sniff. "Our win at Horus was thanks to this bucket of crazy sitting here beside me."

Conner stood up and gave his own stiff-backed nod to Barley. "You did all the hard work, old man, and deserve all the praise."

"Still as modest now as you were in the Academy, Conrad?" Admiral Stephens said with a twinkle in her eye. "I always did like that about you."

Conner was thrown for a loop at that statement. No memories of this woman came to him, so he decided maybe this was a test of him in some way. "I don't think you called to reminisce, Admiral."

"No, I didn't." Admiral Stephens sat back on the edge of her desk. "I am glad you've got Mz. Tandon with you. It'll make my job here a bit easier, if only for myself."

"Do I need to pipe in the captains of the two destroyers attached to me, Admiral?" Barley raised a hand which now held an ancient microphone device which pre-Space Era naval ships would use.

"Not necessary, Barley," Admiral Stephens said shaking her head slightly and smiling. "This discussion is for those here now. First, Fleet's emergency contract recalling you and Captain Conner to active-duty service is being retained for at least two more weeks. The restrictions on movement and who says what is still very much in place. The Admiralty is quite adamant about that point."

"Stay quiet, Captain," Barley said with a hard edge to his voice.

"Same to you, Commander," Conner said, purposely using the next rank up from what he understood Barley had always been assigned.

"To explain a bit further," Admiral Stephens said quirking an eyebrow at the pair. "We are picking up ghost images on the system-wide sensor network. None are currently found near Earth. Rather, we've got a couple around Venus and several in a high polar orbit of the Sun. We want the *Infinity* to investigate these sensor ghosts and verify the shipping lanes around Venus and her various city-stations are clear of any dangers. Barley's sensor array was upgraded, according to Fleet records, a year before you were forcibly discharged. That's newer than any of the Fleet ships currently in the Sol System."

"Why does this make me feel like cannon fodder, Admiral?" Barley hardened his expression while crossing his arms over his chest. The artificial's uniform and rank pins became that of a commander, though Barley's apparent age remained in his late twenties.

"View it as the best person for the job, my dear savior," Admiral Stephens said smiling and with a warmth that implied she wanted to hug Barley.

Barley blushed, stammering a bit. Conner smirked as he spoke up. "Be careful, Admiral, or you'll get burned."

Admiral Stephens laughed. It was light and genuine. "Speaking from experience, Captain?"

"I'm a techie who has raised two artificials from conception as well as dealt with numerous artificials, some of whom are far more powerful and temperamental than Barley and his siblings." Conner smiled as he spoke, glancing up at Barley to give the man a slight nod before looking back at the admiral. "So, yeah, I'm speaking from experience. Just don't ask for names."

"A girl never tells her secrets and all that?" Stephens snickered but waved before herself as though scattering her words. "I'm joking, Conner. Let's say we've both been burned, and we'll compare notes when in person and alone from prying ears. Now, let's move on to the second reason for this meeting. Having Ms. Tandon present helps a great deal."

"I'm here, Admiral," Kashi said waving a hand.

"I see you, Ms. Tandon," Admiral Stephens said with a nod. "As public justification for the *Infinity* to come to Venus, Fleet is awarding the personnel transport contract to Shining Sun Shipping, effective immediately. Ms. Tandon, your company should receive the contract ready for signing momentarily. As part of that contract, Fleet requests the frigates currently docked to Barley be transported to the Venusian repair yards. Admiral Victoria is in the process of restoring the crew levels of the *Powell* and the *Soaring Eagle*. Included in those shuttles are additional service members who need transporting from Earth Space to *Eros Landing* in Venus orbit for assignments on newly repaired ships or inbound ships getting some crew swapped out. While this contract isn't long term, we do have a large group who need to be taken from both Venus Space and Jovian Space on to the Centauri System. Some for new assignments, but the bulk of which are either retiring or leaving at the end of their service contract."

"Opportunity knocks, in other words?" Kashi glanced at Conner with a slight smile on her face. "Shining Sun Shipping, and its partners, will work to provide a top-notch experience for Fleets personnel needs."

"Having enough food will likely be top notch enough for most of them, Ms. Tandon." Admiral Stephens smiled with a look at Barley before focusing on Conner again. "Now, Captain, to help with your real mission, I'm placing Captain Nokata of the *Soaring Eagle* in charge of the excess personnel. His personal experience of growing up inside Barley would give you someone who would make a great second-in-command. He'd also validate your orders to those in Fleet who might balk at taking orders from a civilian. Of course, whether Nigel's son is your First Officer or not is up to you, but that's my recommendation."

"You're expecting us to be attacked?" Zoeller spoke up, fear etching itself on the woman's face.

"To be frank? Yes." Admiral Stephens looked at everyone in turn. "Ms. Tandon, you and your father bought, or tried to buy, a military warship. Given how things have turned out, with Conrad Conner in the captain's seat, you have a real chance of surviving whatever is coming next. Captain?"

"Admiral," Conner said when the woman didn't immediately continue.

"Fleet is placing the lives of a great many people in your hands," Admiral Stephens said standing up. "While I don't expect you to let anyone down or needlessly die—"

"Not everyone in the Admiralty thinks the same as you." Conner finished for the woman. "While I might not want to be in this chair, I also won't be letting people just go around murdering my family."

"Admiral," Barley said, drawing everyone's gaze to him, "leaving Fleet service was not my idea nor something I wanted. Though I am upset about how I was pushed out and treated in that process,

I am not mad at Fleet in general. Fleet personnel sent to crew or merely travel aboard this ship will be treated as any Fleet crew would have been when I was in Fleet. Ground up and spit out as better spacers and defenders of the Sol-Humana Confederation. Just remember one thing. If I find out the people who did me wrong are involved in the attack on my captain's blood relations, there will be no place in this universe where they will be able to escape my wrath. Conner is my beloved friend and those youngsters now living within these corridors, whether he calls them his sons and daughters, or nephews and nieces, are all my family. My blood relations. Understand?"

"Loud and clear, Barley of the Hills," Admiral Stephens said, standing and giving a sharp nod. A slight hint of fear could be seen in the woman's eyes at Barley's statement.

"Veiled and open threats aside," Conner said tapping his desktop to get a diagram of the ship to appear. "The extra service members you mentioned. Just how bare bones of a skeleton crew can we expect?"

"Let's say you don't want to be too far from either Venus or Mars repair yards," Admiral Stephens said with an apologetic smile. "Some of those you're getting will have never set foot on anything as large as a frigate, let alone a star carrier. Others, will likely groan at having to set foot again on a star carrier, given their reputations."

"I will take exception to that statement, ma'am, on behalf of all of my siblings." Barley said with a hand to his chest and an indignant expression on his face.

"Said with love and affection, Barley," Admiral Stephens said smiling.

"Yes. Your family is lovably crazy, Barley." Conner said laughing.

"You say that now," Barley said crossing his arms.

"Yes, yes." Conner shook his head before returning his focus to the admiral. "One more item before we end this meeting."

"Yes?" Admiral Stephens furrowed her brow in curiosity.

"I want to make it clear that I, on Barley's behalf," Conner said with careful precision of his wording, "expect that any and all damage this ship, currently called *CSS Infinity*, ends up suffering during any conflict we are in, will be repaired with like or better by Fleet, per the judgement the Arbiters of the Accords made the night Barley and I left *Socrates*. Do you hear and understand,

Admiral Stephens?"

"Loud and clear, Captain Conner," Admiral Stephens said standing and giving a sharp nod. "On behalf of the Admiralty and all of Fleet, good hunting and safe travels. Fleet Operations out."

"*Infinity* out." Conner said as the admiral vanished.

"Conner?" Zoeller said meekly. "Do you think we'll really get into another battle?"

"What matters is that Fleet does," Conner said standing up to stretch his back. "Remember, our unknown enemy attacked Terra Prima, even if not their primary target. Whoever it is that fired those projectile weapons, they've declared war on not just the Conner family, but all of Sol-Humana. I wouldn't agree to do this if I thought it was just First Admiral Mori playing games."

"And if it turns out to be her playing games?" Kashi stood up as well, a stern look on her face. "What then?"

"Then she finally learns what it means to cross Conrad Conner once too often." Conner turned from the women and the desk to walk to the door out. "I'm going down to talk to Captain Nokata and see how the kids are doing."

"Your niece and nephew?" Barley walked beside him, bumping their shoulders together. "Or the Fleet crew members?"

"There's a difference?" Conner chuckled as he left the captain's office.

CHAPTER 15

"Well, Ezra, did you ever think you'd be standing on this bridge as one of Barley's commanding officers?" Conner looked at the black man in his Fleet uniform of blue with white shoulders for command staff. The pips on the collar, an eight-point gold star on each lapel, denoted his rank as captain.

"Given how hard it is to get a command berth on a star carrier, not in a million years, Captain," Ezra Nokata said with poorly suppressed joy in his voice and in his eyes. "Weird and exciting all at once is the only way I can describe the feeling."

"Well, at least you look better in that uniform than what I remember your father looking," Conner said smiling. "We can thank your mother for that."

"How much for me to not tell dad you said that?" Ezra smirked at Conner before jerking his head back forward. "Look sharp down there, you dogs. I don't want to hear needless yapping from you lot. We've got enemy ships hiding in our backyard who need to be found. Weapons, report."

Conner listened to Ezra hound everyone on the bridge to sound off their status. Zoeller let her displeasure be heard in her voice, but Doherty and Kashi both took to the disciplined method very quickly. Kandra occasionally giggled but otherwise slid right back into the military mindset. Sitting in the captain's chair, Conner watched the tan sphere of Venus with its blue and green veining slowly grow larger. This was the planet of his birth, where he grew up, and where he once had planned to marry and raise kids until old and decrepit. Lakes of lava, scars remaining from the hell unleashed on the planet a millennium ago during the Hive occupation of the Sol System, still dotted the planet. Centuries of terraforming, before and after the Hive occupation, showed how humanity still struggled to turn Venus into a twin of Earth.

"In final approach to Venus, Captain," Barley said with quick efficiency. "Lieutenant Betty is informing Fleet Operations on Eros Station of our approach in regard to the Shining Sun Shipping contract. Father and Arlene are busy working in your old tech division labs while Magnus and Ernie are out about telling busy random Fleeters raunchy jokes in an effort to crack their focus before team leads demand they leave. Ah, the memories it brings back. Right?"

"Magnus was really good at distracting people when he was that age, as I recall," Conner chuckled while shifting his focus to his chair's screen. A summary of the ship's status displayed as a miniature graphic of the ship with greens, yellows, and reds appearing and changing. "When Admiral Stephens said bare bones, she wasn't kidding."

Barley didn't respond. Conner looked up to find Barley staring off to his left with tears filling the artificial's holographic eyes. Before Conner could ask what was wrong, Kandra broke the brief silence.

"Commander Nokata, sensors are giving me odd readings in our orbital trajectory," Kandra said before the image of Venus had a tactical overlay. "Whatever they're registering is showing as debris, but this is supposed to be a swept orbital path."

"High Alert!" Ezra barked out before following it with further orders.

"Barley? What's wrong?" Conner looked back at the artificial, who now had tears trickling down his face.

"Oh Shin," Barley muttered, his image flickering when he wiped his face.

"Captain, we're being hailed by one *CSS Dragon's Hoard*," Betty said, glancing over her shoulder at Conner.

"Patch'em through, Lieutenant," Conner said turning away from Barley momentarily. He wanted to press Barley on what was wrong, considering the man was genuinely upset. The emotions artificials displayed usually mirrored the typical human range, which meant Barley had just gotten some very bad news.

A moment later, the open area at the front of the bridge lit up to show an older woman with a dark brown, almost black, skin and platinum-colored hair sitting in the middle of a simpler and much smaller bridge. "This is the *CSS Infinity*," Conner spoke warmly and with a broad smile, "and I'm Conrad Conner, Captain. What can I do for you?"

"You and that rusty bucket are blocking the shipping lanes, you stupid bolthead. Leave or you'll both vanish for good," the woman growled before the screen went dark.

"Well, she's a friendly bitch," Zoeller chuckled. "What company was she with?"

"What's a bolthead?" Doherty asked from the engineering station on the bridge's lower level.

"A bolthead refers to anyone that is or has ever served in any stellar government's military," Ezra explained. "It's derogatory slang that, I'm sure Kandra can tell us, any veteran from any star system will find offensive."

"Aye, commander." Kandra snarled the words.

"Betty?" Conner stared at the spot the woman had been. "What company operates that ship?"

"Black Hole Expeditors," Kashi said with disgust. "It's a Nicolas Danlen company."

"Captain," Betty spoke up. "We're being hailed again. This time by one *CSS Chesapeake Bay.*"

Conner turned to Barley. "You said Shin a moment ago, Barley. What's wrong?"

"Talk to this ship," Barley said softly while struggling to control his emotions. "I might be able to confirm it."

Conner watched Barley for a moment before he spoke again. "Put them in the main viewing area, Betty."

A moment later appeared an Indian man with no hair in a standard merchant uniform of dark grey with colored shoulders, which for this ship was a bright red. Conner noticed the man sat presumably on a bridge with nothing except a wall behind him. "You're going to get hurt, bolt boy. Leave and don't come back, or you'll regret it. Understand?"

Before Conner could even speak, the connection was severed by the other ship. Irritated, he turned toward Ezra on his right. "Tell me something about those ships. How much of a threat are they?"

A woman with the black hair and brown skin typical of the Indian subcontinent appeared beside Ezra. She wore a sari version of the Fleet uniform. What caught Conner's attention, though, were the tear-stained cheeks and fiery rage in her eyes.

"Sahalie. What are you doing here?" Ezra jumped, obviously not expecting his frigate's controlling artificial to appear. "What's wrong?"

"Have you told him, Barley?" Sahalie said with a mixture of rage and grief.

"I'm barely holding myself together." Barley sobbed.

"You said the name 'Shin', Barley," Conner said while recalling their conversation yesterday. "Is the ship, whose captain just threatened us, Abe?"

Barley nodded, the tears streaming down his face. Conner couldn't wait for Barley to get control of himself. "Talk to me, old man. What have those bastards done to our friends."

"I recognized slave subroutines present in both of them," Barley wailed as sobs wracked the man's suddenly ten-year-old body and gasps echoed from everyone. "And they've lobotomized Abe."

"Battle stations," Conner snarled as he stood up and stormed up to the railing overlooking the lower bridge. "Betty, broadcast me over all channels, but specifically to those two ships."

"Conner?" Ezra pulled Conner around to stare in shock at him. "What do you think you're doing? This is a star carrier. We have rules that have to be followed."

"This is the body of a person who is not technically in Fleet." Conner growled as a deep rage filled him. "Those two ships are the bodies of two people I fucking married more than a decade ago, Ezra. They are or were like uncles to you back before the Battle of Horus. I will not let them be abused like that anymore than I will let the bastards who killed my sister and her husband just do whatever they want."

"Do you need to be reminded we were sent here to investigate ghost images of ships in Venus space?" Ezra leaned in close with a mix of emotions playing across the face of a man Conner considered his nephew. "Not revenge."

"How much do you want to bet the debris which Kandra mentioned are mines." Conner hissed with barely contained fury. In his next breath, though, something clicked within his mind. "Voltaire."

"Voltaire?" Ezra and Barley said, confused.

"Yes. The Voltaire engagement which led up to Horus." Conner strode back to his chair and tapped hard on the screen attached to it. "I seem to recall Nigel ordering me to look at the way the Spartan ships' artificials were acting when communicating with you, Barley. You kept complaining about their timid attitudes toward others, which seemed contrary to other warships in both the Spartan and Sol-Humana fleets. We then ran into a field of mines."

"Full stop!" Ezra barked loudly, which silenced the growing

chatter. "Sensors! Systems! Give me a detailed sweep of our immediate space."

"Your analysis is what found the enslavement subroutines," Barley said, his crying and teary expression fading. "I'm using that same method to reason out what's happened to Shin and Abe. Especially since I have behavioral patterns in my memories to compare to the way they interacted with me and Sahalie just now on the subchannels we ship artificials use to talk to each other when in close proximity."

"Captain? Did you still want to do a general broadcast?" Betty pulled Conner's attention away from his search for info on the engagement in the Voltaire System, now a good fifteen years in the past. Both systems had been badly battered by the battles, with several moons of gas giants in both systems getting turned into small chunks of rock and ice.

"Yes." Conner said, powering off the screen for the moment. "Only me in the broadcast, please. Ezra and everyone else, stay back so you aren't in the image."

"This involves me as well, Conner," Barley said moving to stand on Conner's left. "These are my friends and family being harmed, and I have sworn to protect you and your family. So, let's make our stand together, and together warn the universe."

"Ready when you are, Captain," Betty said.

Conner nodded to Barley, standing up from the chair instead of staying seated. He understood the significance of him sitting and Barley standing. What they would say, Conner decided, would come from their hearts.

"We stand beside each other as equals, then, old man." Conner whispered before he looked at Betty and nodded. When she nodded back, he looked to the front of the bridge and spoke in a stern, steady voice. "Attention all ships in the Sol System and throughout the cosmos. I am Conrad Conner, president of The C5 Group, which has been contracted by this man beside me, Barley, the controlling artificial of the interstellar ship, *CSS Infinity*, to captain and hire a crew to help smoothly maintain and operate Barley's body. Thus, the reason for this open broadcast by the both of us."

"It has come to our attention," Barley said when Conner paused, "that individuals and or groups are placing enslavement and intelligence damaging limiters onto the controlling artificials of their ships, be they cargo carriers or other star-faring vessels, in violation of the Accords of Rights for Natural and Artificial Life of Twenty Ninety-Seven, commonly referred to as The AI Accords."

"Barley and I are hereby serving notice to each and every one of you, be you a civilian, a corporation, or even members of a stellar government or its military." Conner clenched his fists as he spoke, as much to keep from ranting as to keep himself standing still beside Barley. "We will not tolerate slavery and abuse of anyone, be they naturally born or artificially conceived. You will be brought forward before the Arbiters of those systems where you committed the crime, no matter where in the universe you run."

"Life is precious, no matter what form it takes," Barley said taking a half step forward. "I can be precise in my attacks, or as broad as necessary. We suggest you give yourself up before we have to take action."

"This is your only warning. Good day." Conner said, making a slight motion he hoped Betty understood he meant for her to stop recording.

"Message ended," Betty said. "Ready to broadcast on a loop via both System and open frequency."

"Do it," Conner said sitting back down.

The ship shook. Klaxons blared and the bridge crew erupted into controlled shouting. Weapons fire. Shields holding. Engines green and primed for action.

A clipboard appeared in Barley's hands, which he flipped through sheets of paper as Conner opened his mouth. Barley spoke first, though. "The *Dragon's Hoard* and *Chesapeake Bay* are both Rolchenkhov-class cargo carriers which have been modified to increase the number of weapons mounted on them, but not any visible outside of that allowed by interstellar law. In terms of size, they are no larger than us. To put it briefly, Captain, they are not a serious threat on the surface."

"However, Captain," Zoeller said from her station, "analysis of sensor sweeps of both ships indicate they are likely hiding armaments within their cargo holds. This is based on material and element analysis on the molecular and quantum levels. Barley, your sensors are amazing."

"Could we be dealing with dark world enforcement ships

intended to intimidate new shipping companies like Shining Sun Shipping?" Sahalie shifted to stand beside Barley. "And how do we stop this fight without hurting Abe and Shin?"

"How strong are their shields?" Conner said, trying to put everything in terms of a tech problem, which his mind could tackle. "I want to damage their engines, which I'm assuming are also powering their weapons."

"Weapons, I want a precision attack on the rear sections of those cargo ships," Ezra said as he moved to the railing. "Use the laser cannons, not torpedoes. We want to disable, not destroy. Those ships' controlling artificials are decorated Fleet veterans. Let's show them some respect. Sensors, get me readings on that debris field. What are we dealing with? I want to be able to maneuver Barley without worrying about blowing ourselves up."

"We could try and take control of the ships from Abe and Shin," Sahalie said with a hand smoothing her sari.

"We don't know the particulars of the enslavement protocols," Barley said softly. "What if they're more viral? A natural, such as Conner, needs to try to remove the enslavement first."

"And if those protocols can't be removed?" Conner looked at both as the lift doors opening sounded behind them.

"Then the ships will have to be destroyed." Sam said as he and Arlene walked onto the bridge.

Conner glanced over his shoulder at the pair before looking back at Barley and Sahalie. "Let's hope it doesn't come to that."

"Our shields are holding against the attacks, Captain," Ezra said, pulling Conner attention back to the attack itself. "Their weapons are powerful, but not enough to pierce Barley's military-grade shields."

"Targets acquired?" Conner's chair monitor displayed a small tactical of the two cargo ships, the *Infinity*, and then an arc of red dots on Barley's original orbital trajectory.

"Captain?" Betty called out louder than the cacophony of voices. "Admiral Stephens is hailing us. She's insisting to speak to you immediately."

Conner grumbled softly to himself about bosses. "On the main viewer."

"Finally! What in the hell are you doing broadcasting such an inflammatory statement?" Admiral Stephens glared at Conner.

Sam walked over to stand beside Barley on Conner's left. He spoke before Conner or Barley could. "Enslavement and lobotomizing of artificials who are veterans of Fleet. Specifically, Abraham, formerly of the *CSS Lincoln,* and Shin, formerly of the *CSS Shanghai*, Admiral. Both egregious violations of the AI Accords. I suggest you get Admiral Victoria, Earth's ConRad, and Venus's Aphrodite involved immediately. While they might have been allowed to retire from active Fleet duty earlier than their contracted time periods, they should never have been allowed out into the private sector without strict Fleet overwatch."

"And you are who?" Admiral Stephens glared at Sam.

"Samuel M. Youngs, Admiral Stephens," Sam said with a nod at the admiral, whose eyes widened slightly before returning to their glare. "And just because the company name might have changed, the contracts forged between Youngs Galactech and the Sol-Humana Stellar Fleet are still enforceable."

"Betty, help Barley and the destroyers send a packet of our sensor logs to Fleet Operations, Fleet Inner System Command, and Fleet Outer System Command," Conner said looking down at his screen as data on the debris field scrolled. Seeing the data brought understanding on why the bridge seemed so silent. Barley or Betty had erected a silence field around him and the captain's chair. "Be sure to include navigational sensor logs and your communication logs showing the translations you and Magnus have made, even if they're only partial translations."

"At once, Captain," Betty replied.

"In short, Admiral," Conner returned his gaze to the admiral. "During the brief communications we had with two different cargo ships, who both separately threatened us, Barley was able to determine the identities of those cargo ships' artificials. His determination of enslavement and intelligence tampering has been reviewed by Sahalie and by Mister Youngs here, correct you two?"

Sam nodded while Sahalie answered with, "Confirmed, Admiral."

"We have also identified a minefield," Conner continued as the admiral jerked as though slapped, "with the extent as yet unknown, in one of Venus's high orbital paths for large incoming ships. At this moment, those two cargo ships are continuing to attack us. Those cargo ships will be disabled, their controlling artificials isolated as safely as possible from afar, and their crews rendered harmless."

"And the minefield?" Admiral Stephens's expression settled into one of seeming calm.

"Still being laid, Admiral," Barley said, still standing beside the captain's chair. "Visually, they look like star mines, but don't have the magnetic signatures of star mines. My suspicion is they are housing more conventional explosives. I will get damaged if they go off but shouldn't be destroyed. Nonmilitary ships, though, won't have the heavy armor plating or enhanced shielding like myself or say the two frigates I'm transporting."

"Also, Admiral," Conner said leaning back in his chair. He tapped on his chair's screen. A heartbeat later, his tactical overlaid the admiral's image. "Please note we have not analyzed all of the mines you see in that tactical. Just a sampling. There could still be a few star mines lurking in the bunch. I don't think I need to say how much damage one star mine could do if it truly has stellar plasma contained within it, let alone there being even a dozen in the hundreds of mines currently being detected."

"I'll be in touch, *Infinity*," Admiral Stephens said suddenly, panic filling her eyes. "Operations out."

CHAPTER 16

The screen changed to the Fleet Operations logo over a star field. As he stared at it for a long moment, the sounds of the bridge returned. With his thoughts in turmoil, Conner wondered how he'd get anything done if Fleet tried to shackle him and Barley.

"Damn it!" he growled jumping up and storming to the railing, only to spin around toward Ezra. "Status report?"

"Through some Conner family brilliance," Ezra said with a growing smile, "your son and niece have used a long forgotten and presumed dead organ of Barley's body to sneak both Abe and Shin's matrix cores out of their respective ships. I've got a tech team heading down to start analyzing the artificials' true status now."

"My science project worked! It worked, Uncle Conner. It worked!" Arlene shouted as she rushed over from the station she'd been sitting at to slam into Conner with a bear hug.

"Not to be a killjoy, Arlene," Ezra chuckled at the teenager's enthusiasm, "but we won't know if it truly worked until the tech team reports back."

"Would someone mind telling me what is going on?" Conner glared at Ezra.

"My science fair project is about upgrading teleportation tech with modern security and field variance protocols," Arlene said in a rapid single breath.

"The coding looked valid to me," Sam said smiling a bit. "So, we'd come up here to ask if we could test it out on something. I was thinking snatching something out of their cargo hold."

"I gave the authorization for using it to grab Uncle Abe and Uncle Shin." Ezra grinned happily. "Now all we need is a miracle to happen so we hear the words we all want to hear about them."

Conner wondered if what they'd done was a good idea or not. He'd never heard of anyone solving the security issues teleportation systems had suffered from since their development for human use fifteen hundred years ago. "Well, first things first. Congratulations, Arlene. I look forward to looking over your work."

"Thanks, Uncle Conner." Arlene hugged Conner again before

grabbing Sam to drag him back to the station where they'd been working.

"Status of those cargo ships, Ezra?" Conner turned his focus back to their remaining threats. "Then we have to deal with the minefield."

"Which is still growing, Captain," Ezra said, his smile vanishing. "The cargo ships have lost their engines along with life support, which is active in only a select few locations. From our sensor sweeps, their bridges still have life support. Their power is purely by battery at the moment."

"The mines?" Conner looked back to the main viewer and the tactical still displayed.

"Neotitanium housings with magnetic attractors and drill-claw impalers," Kandra said from the sensor station.

"A typical mine mechanism that should explode upon impact with a hull." Barley waved a hand and the tactical was replaced by an extreme close up of a mine. "We've got a scattering of them attaching themselves to my belly. For some reason, they aren't detonating."

"Faulty actuators," Ezra said with a shrug. "Or maybe they're on timers."

"Remotely controlled is my guess," Sam said from one of the stations on the right of the upper bridge.

"Remotely controlled?" Conner latched onto that idea. "That makes the most sense for what we've got."

"What if we teleport the mines back onto the ship they came from?" Arlene looked at the adults. "Or off someplace where they won't hurt anything if they do explode."

"I've got a location," Zoeller said, drawing everyone's eyes to the woman.

"Okay, Zoeller. I'll bite," Barley said with raised eyebrows. "Where would you send a few hundred possible star mines."

"Here." Zoeller shifted the front viewer to display a graphic of the Sol System. A red dot sat as far above the sun's north pole as Jupiter was from the sun. "Betty mentioned there are transmissions going to the area marked by the red dot. Not knowing the distance limitation of these teleporters, couldn't we grab every single mine and just move them to this location and let the mines take care of whatever is up there?"

"Whatever we do," Barley said in a contemplative voice, "Fleet command should not be involved. If the mines are remotely controlled, those controlling them may detonate them early if they're able to listen in on our communications."

"What about the ship still laying the mines?" Conner looked at everyone. "We can't teleport an entire ship."

"With enough power, we probably could," Arlene said excitedly.

"Except we can't get an actual fix on the ship in question," Ezra countered. "We've just a general area."

"Warp tunnel," Doherty called out from the lower bridge. When everyone looked toward him, he continued. "Use one engine to create a small warp tunnel for the short distance between us and the target. Use the tunnel to suck up the mines and the ship setting them. Another engine can create a second warp tunnel to funnel the backflow of the explosion to another spot in the system and help hold us here on this end of the first tunnel."

"I've never heard of anyone doing something like that," Sam said, glancing at Barley. "Have you, Barley?"

"Not exactly." Barley shifted to his old man persona so he had a cane to wave about. "All these young'uns with their newfangled ideas. We old timers just ain't liking such changes. Yanking my guns off me belly afore, and now making me walk in two directions at once. Make up your damn minds."

"Crotchety old men aside," Doherty said snickering, "the engines currently powering this ship are Gommerson Mark Elevens. Manufactured about a century ago, they use Mercuriation protocols for modeling warp tunnels. Those protocols take advantage of Barley and his siblings greater tactical and multi-dimensional thinking. Or whatever type of thinking he actually has."

"I declare! Do you always go lifting a girl's dress to look at her engines?" Barley shifted into a young man just shy of twenty wearing a frilly dress and fanning himself with a huge folding fan. Conner hated the fact he could likely give the name of the ancient movie from which Barley pulled the outfit.

"Only the pretty ones," Doherty said with a cheesy grin. "Really, it was part of my doctoral dissertation. Well, one of my dissertations, at least. Anyway, I know the protocol set up, but not how well it'll actually work."

"Sensors have a second ghost ship closing in on our location," Kandra called out.

"Do it, Mr. Doherty," Conner said, making a snap decision. "Navigation, feed coordinates to engineering for the warp tunnels. The rest of you, we need a way to make sure both the ship setting them, and all of these mines, get swept up by the correct warp tunnel."

As Ezra barked out orders, Barley cleared his throat beside Conner. When Conner turned to the artificial, Barley motioned his head toward Arlene. "She could remove the mines attached to me with her new project. Give our Conner Junior genius something important to do?"

"Have we found any actual star mines yet?" Conner tried to recall from his own limited research into transportation tech whether stellar material could be moved by the devices.

"No," Barley said softly. "All semi-conventional explosives. The composition of the materials indicates a high yield explosive, though. Curiously, I think everything should be transportable by Arlene's new toy."

"And if things go wrong?" Conner furrowed his brow, worried about both his own and his sister's children.

"I can reconfigure some panels in the medical bay for her to use," Barley said, as though reading his mind.

"For her and Betty," Conner whispered, not sure he wanted to panic the girl. "Where are the boys?"

"Ernie is already in the med bay exchanging jokes with the doctor," Barley said in a low voice. "At least, when he's not sobbing about missing his dad and his horrible jokes."

Conner sighed softly. While the bridge wasn't on the exterior of the ship, it wasn't in what was considered the survival zone. He had to ensure the children, all of them, lived through this.

"Betty and Arlene," Conner said while looking at the tactical displayed on the main viewer, "would you both come here for a moment."

~ * ~

"You're free, Uncle Shin," Magnus said into the handheld comm unit the tech team had quickly set up in Shuttle Bay Three. It connected via thick cables to the half a dozen matrix cores Arlene had teleported out of the cargo ships. Each core sat in a ten-foot cube with a self-contained power unit, with everything suspended in a magnetic field to ensure stability and safety. "You and Uncle Abe are both onboard Barley. We yanked your cores out of those horrid prisons your bodies had become. My dad, Conrad Conner, is Barley's captain and as soon as he can, he'll come down here and fix you both back up. You'll be free of whatever's been done to you. I promise. Please, hang in there, uncles. We all need you back home with us."

"I'm getting response signals from this one, Mr. Conner," a tech officer shouted from one of the cores. "Give me a minute I'll get this comm unit reconfigured so this one can talk properly."

"This other core looks to have been shot with projectile weapons," another tech officer said with despair. "Who would do this?"

Magnus clenched his jaws and eyes shut to keep from wailing in grief. There would be time later to grieve if they couldn't save Abe. He had good memories and that's what mattered. His job right now was to keep Shin and Abe's spirits up and hopeful.

"Get me proper connections to talk to them both, people," Magnus shouted in his best imitation of Uncle Nigel from when the admiral had been captain of Barley. "Consider this field dressing of battle wounds. Let's stabilize these two and worry about full recovery later."

A flash drew Magnus's attention to his right. Barley stood there looking as old as his father. Tears formed in the ship's eyes as Barley watched the tech crew scurry about the cores, dragging and connecting wires to the huge cubes.

"Don't distract yourself from the battle, Pops." Magnus used his childhood affection for the ship's artificial. In many ways, Barley had become another parent to him during those eight years on board this ship. His real father didn't seem to mind.

"Shin can't hear us, can he?" Barley whispered the words, though the cavernous space echoed them back.

"Mic is off at the moment," Magnus said, making sure he spoke the truth. "Abe is badly damaged. I'm not sure even dad can work his tech magic on Uncle Abe."

"Conner wants you to report to the med bay at once," Barley said without looking away from the cores. Tears streamed down the man's face, carving wrinkles to age Barley to his old man persona. "I want you to let me make a copy of your matrix. Your father and I

…don't make me go through this with you as well, Maggie. Please."

"I'll be fine, pops," Magnus said with a chuckle. "My body has done at least one regular backup to your system.

Shifting his stance so he faced Barley, Magnus modulated his body's skin so he could touch Barley's holographic projection as though it was solid. A trick unique to this particular model. Wiping at Barley's tears, he smiled warmly for the artificial before leaning in to kiss his cheek.

"How?" Barley shifted back to a middle-aged man while furrowing his brow in confusion.

"The latest in artificial bodies," Magnus whispered. "You're the first I've tried it on, Pops. Now stop being such a worrywart and let me help the techies here by trying to distract my uncles."

Barley's eyes went wide just before the klaxons erupted. "Out! Everyone out! We've got incoming torpedoes."

Magnus rushed back to the comm unit. Thumbing it active, he hurriedly spoke into the unit as the ship shook. "We've got incoming, Uncle Shin. You aren't forgotten, but we have to evacuate for a moment. We'll be back as quick as we can."

"Now, Magnus!" Barley screamed with growing terror in his voice. "Get out of here."

"Aaagh!" A tech cried out from someplace. "My leg!"

Magnus leaped on top of the cores, jumping from one to another as he looked for the stuck tech. Finding the young woman pinned between the access door of one core and another core, he dropped down to her side. Grabbing the power cable wrapped around an ankle, Magnus saw the ankle's unnatural bend. Slamming the access door shut, Magnus pulled the power cable loose enough for the woman to pull her foot free. She collapsed, going unconscious from the pain.

"Fuck," Magnus swore. The entire ship shook, with the floor lifting before dropping back down. "Why am I like this?"

Pulling the woman into his arms, Magnus jumped with every ounce of his new body's strength. Overshooting the top of the core he stood beside, he could only watch in horror as the bay doors to space buckled. The shuttle he'd piloted to bring his cousins safely to Barley slid across the bay floor to slam into Abe's cores. A fireball filled the cavernous bay as he sailed through the air toward the open door to a corridor where the tech team leader stood waving at him.

"Shields at full," Magnus shouted, unable to hear anything but a rushing sound. "All power to suit in contact with mine."

He watched the door with the Fleet tech leader close even as he moved left of the door. Something slammed into his back, pain erupted up and down his body. An inside corner of the bay wall to a storage room approached. He extended his arms and legs, locking their joints, and bubbled his shields around the woman he held in his arms. Just before he struck the wall, Barley wailed into his ears. "Magnus!"

~ * ~

"Warp tunnels are working," Kandra shouted with excitement. "No sign of new mines and the existing ones are vanishing into tunnel one. Wait! We have four incoming bogies. Lower starboard upward bound."

"Evasive maneuvers!" Ezra ordered.

"No!" Doherty shouted. "We move and the warp tunnels collapse."

"More power to lower shields." Ezra shouted. "Weapons! Target bogies. Kill them first."

"Barley, order the evacuation of the lower three decks." Conner turned to his chair screen and tapped for crew assignments. "I told you to get Magnus to safe zone."

"Like father like son," Barley snapped back, though fear played across the artificial's face. "Fuck. Someone's stuck. Stop those torpedoes!"

The ship shook. Someone yelled cannon fire, which the shields could stop by dispersing the phased laser fire. Still, for cannon fire to shake the ship meant that ship packed one hell of a punch. More shaking. Flashes of light announced power overloads at various stations. Weapons missed one. Shields can't stop torpedoes very well, especially with cannon fire also pounding them.

"Brace for impact!" Ezra shouted as he dropped to a kneeling squat.

The ship jerked upwards, forcing everyone down into their seats. Power went out on the bridge momentarily but returned almost instantly. Conner's heart skipped a beat, as though something had just pierced his chest.

"Magnus!" Barley's panicked scream echoed throughout the

ship. The artificial staggered forward only to collapse to his hands and knees, sobbing and wailing for Magnus to respond.

"Damage reports!" Conner shouted as he pounded his chair's screen to come back on. "Where's my son? What the hell is going on?"

"Shuttle Bay Three has been vented to space." Zoeller said with a hollow sound to her voice. "I'm…I'm not…"

"One life sign, Captain," Kandra called out. "But it's a natural. No signal from your son's suit or body."

"Tell me you grabbed his matrix at the last moment, Barley," Conner gripped the arms of his chair with an iron grip. The creaking of the ship gave an ominous note to the welling grief within himself.

"He…his body didn't let me. He saved her life." Barley said between hiccupping sobs. "Those bastards took my baby boy. Took the only one who has ever called me Pops."

"Navigation isn't responding." Kashi said, glancing back at Conner and Barley. She too had tears staining her cheeks.

"Weapons are firing on their own, captains," the Fleet officer at the console to Conner's right on the upper bridge said with panic in his voice.

"Captain? Take a look at this," Zoeller said as tactical display on the main viewer vanished to show the smoky interior of the shuttle bay.

The camera shifted from the upturned shuttle partially laying on the six cores to a corner of the bay where a large section of what looked to be part of the bay doors leaned against two walls forming a corner. The center of the bay door section bulged out. Overlaid on the camera image was a sensor image showing the glow of suit shields and two bodies. A red flag tagged the body braced against two walls, as though holding back the door. The inner body had a yellow flag tag, with the letter "N" indicating that was a biological person.

"Get rescue crews down there now," Conner stood up. "Everyone, you're all relieved of duty. Get to the safe zone of the ship."

"With all due respect, Captain," Ezra said with tear-filled eyes and rage contorting the young man's face, "but we'll see this through to the end. Then we'll toast my brother as the hero he died being."

"Warp tunnels are…not collapsing?" Doherty called out in the momentary silence; his confused incredulity palpable. "The ends are moving with us. What the hell?"

Conner turned to Barley, who looked straight ahead on both feet, which were spread out to shoulder width. Rage contorted the face and darkened the skin to a bright red. "I will rain hellfire and brimstone down on your heads. Your children will be torn limb from limb. None of your bloodline will remain amongst the living for this crime!"

"All torpedo tubes have fired." The guy at weapons shouted. "Phase cannons are, dear stars, cannons are detaching from the ship. How in the blackness of space is he doing this?"

"My poor Barley," Conner stared at the tears pouring down Barley's face even as the artificial raged in the only manner left to him.

CHAPTER 17

"Come!" Conner barely spoke the word from his place on the bench in the captain's office. He looked down at Barley's short hair and the curve of the man's ear. Barley faced toward Conner's belly, the tears and sobbing having died down to the occasional sniffle.

The door opened to Ezra Nokata. "Sensors aren't finding any survivors amongst the wreckage of the enemy ships. So far, all of the dead we've found appear to be human. No artificials that we can detect. At least, not yet."

"What about at the far ends of the warp tunnels we created?" Conner stroked Barley's hair, remembering the few times he'd been able to do this for Magnus. The most memorable had been on the last day before he graduated from Fleet Academy. Magnus had hated the idea of leaving the academy and had thrown the biggest tantrum of the still young artificial's life. Only in one tech lab had Conner found holo-projectors that allowed artificials to become physical. Conner had hugged his son fiercely and promised to find more of these so they could hug like this more often. It had rarely happened. Yet another promise he'd made to his son and not kept.

"Ship and system-wide sensors are detecting debris fields at both ends," Ezra walked over to the corner of the desk closest to Conner. "Recon units have found the cores for a ship's artificial and hauled them into Shuttle Bay One, just so it's kept isolated from Abe and Shin's cores. I've got three tech teams already working on the data units to confirm some suspicions on who ordered them to attack. The tech team which evacuated Shuttle Bay Three are back at work on Abe and Shin's cores, which surprisingly survived that torpedo strike. Likely thanks to that shuttle getting blown over against them, which seems to have blocked the cores from the worst of the blast. Magnus's body is badly torn up, but the techs refuse to declare him dead yet. Something about how that particular model is designed to protect an artificial's core matrix. When I pressed them, they said chances of survival are slim, but Magnus saved one of their own, who it turns out is pregnant, so they won't give up on him until they've tried everything. Sam is down there helping them."

"How's the young woman Magnus protected?" Conner said softly, not sure what to think or believe anymore.

"Hysterical, thankful, and weeping all at once," Ezra said sagging as he rubbed his face with his hands. "Physically, she has a broken ankle and burns on her arms, legs, and head. She said she came to at some point to hear Magnus shouting something about all power to other suit. She sobbed when I told her Magnus is likely dead."

"The baby? Did she have a miscarriage?" Conner fought to keep his mind focused on good news. He couldn't let himself grieve yet.

"The doctor indicated the lieutenant needed to get to a station medical facility as soon as possible for the long-term viability of the fetus," Ezra said, his voice fading a bit. "He's keeping the woman strapped down in a biobed just for the safety of the baby. Getting her to Eros Station's medical facility should be our top priority. He was adamant about that."

"Any reports of more sensor ghosts?" Conner said, trying to think of what all he was supposed to do now.

"You need to tell Admiral Victoria and Terra Prima about Magnus, Uncle Conner," Ezra said with a growing tremble in the man's voice. "My dad should be told as well. God, the girls are going to weep. They always loved when he'd come visit as Maggie and play dress up with them."

Conner looked up to find Ezra verging on openly sobbing. Sniffling back the sobs and wiping his face, the black man stood up to turn away from Conner. In the silence that followed, the intercom beeped just before Betty's grief cracked voice filled the room.

"Admiral Stephens wishes to connect, daddy," Betty said, the grief palpable in her voice. "Permission for us to come up and get hugs?"

"Connect her and then you three can come up," Conner said with a wane smile. "We're in the captain's office."

"Thanks," Betty said, her voice cracking as she tried to not to openly sob before the connection ended.

When the Fleet logo of four stars and two ships circling them appeared on the wall, Conner considered moving to his desk. Deciding he didn't care, he sat there with Barley still laying on his lap. Ezra looked at the logo, shook his head, and tapped the top of the desk.

"Uncle Conner," Ezra said with a hardness in his voice Conner recognized from when Nigel got mad, "while I've no collaborating evidence as proof, the search teams have come across Fleet beacons used by Luna Command on high priority supplies. Also, among the dead being found are people in Fleet uniforms, but the insignia on the shoulders are not standard combat fleet issue like mine."

"What fleet insignia are they then?" Conner said as Barley sat up.

Ezra tapped on the desk until the image of a sword-shaped ship appeared overlaid with a stylized bird, their wings opened and claws gripping the sword's hand guard. Conner's gut dropped out of his body as his heart raced. He knew that old bat hated him, but for her to go to this extreme went beyond the pale.

"Ezra, who has seen these and knows what they mean?" Conner stood up and moved to sit at his desk.

"Only the recon units out looking for survivors," Ezra said with fists clenching and unclenching. "I've had the bodies pulled and placed into Barley's stasis pods since his power systems are more stable than either of the frigates at the moment. With your permission, I'd like to ask your doctor to do a memory grab out of the dead, if it's not too late."

"Barley, inquire privately with the doctor on that question," Conner ordered. "If he can, have him start immediately. Tell him we're looking for the names or visuals of their commanding officers. I believe that'll be enough for him to use as a guide without tipping our hand."

"Conferring with him now," Barley said in a calm voice. "The Admiral, Captain?"

"Remove the First Admiral's insignia and finish connecting Admiral Stephens," Conner said as he leaned back and tried to relax himself. The thought of going and blowing the moon to smithereens just so that old bitch of an admiral couldn't escape crossed his mind but didn't relax him.

"Captain?" Admiral Stephen's voice sounded as the woman appeared, the wall melding so their offices merged into one space. "Oh dear. What's happened out there?"

"I need you to connect Admirals Nokata and Victoria in on this stream," Conner said, deciding to find out where everyone's loyalty lay all at once. "You might also include both Earth and Venus's planetary artificials as well as Socrates and Treespinner. I think that's everyone who'll need to hear this. Oh, and make it as close to a Zeta level connection as possible. We don't want word to leak and cause a panic. Right?"

"I suppose," Admiral Stephens said with uncertainty from behind her desk. "Anything I can tell them as a warning to why we're doing such a large stream?"

"Tell them it's family meeting time," Conner said with a hard glare for the woman, "and that daddy is not a happy camper."

Admiral Stephens hesitated for a moment, her expression growing pensive. She finally nodded. "Give me a moment to verify they're all free."

When the fleet logo returned, Ezra leaned over to press the mute icon. "What are you planning, Uncle Conner? We can't accuse her of anything without proof, and dead people wearing a uniform can be faked."

"Magnus's body refused to let me copy his matrix," Barley said with venom as he sat up, "and must have lied to him about backing his matrix up when I asked him to let me back him up. Someone had to have changed those setting while my son was being placed in the body and given Treespinner's protectiveness of him, she wouldn't have done it nor allowed anyone to have done it."

"The only ones who can override a city-station artificial's security codes is a senior planetary artificial such as Earth," Conner said as he stared at the stars orbiting each other while the miniature ships flew about the stars leaving contrails, "or the Admiralty, with the First Admiral's security clearance being required."

"Blessed Stars of Andromeda," Ezra muttered, staggering back to drop into a chair. "That means—"

"Magnus was set up to die and make it appear as an accident or tech failure," Conner said with an icy tone.

"Murdered is the word you're wanting, Conner." Barley growled, hatred filling the artificial's face.

"Not her first murder nor her last if we can't stop her," Conner said drumming his fingers on the desk. "Either First Admiral Mori is faking aliens being after me, or she's been funding the dark world for her own purposes while seeding my name as someone whose been stealing from them all. I'm not going to spend my life running from her or her cronies. Nor am I going to put blinders on hoping it'll all go away like I did after Shima's murder. If either Socrates or

Treespinner still have backups of his primary matrix, then Sam and I might be able to reconstruct Magnus's primary matrix. If not, then Magnus is officially dead. At that point, she becomes responsible for killing Magnus, even if indirectly."

"There are also the contents of those cargo ships," Barley said as a new image took that of the Fleet logo. "During the rush of battle, I took the sensor logs and pushed them to the back of my mind, dismissing what was found as inconsequential to the priorities of the moment. However, in light of what you've revealed, I think it's become important."

The pair of cargo ships floated in the ether of the wall. One enlarged and discharged its cargo. "Dark matter storage containers, phase cannon blisters, empty star mine casings, empty torpedo casings, and a dozen other items, all of them in enough quantities on the two cargo ships to arm and outfit at least six ships like the ones we destroyed today. Also, there is a cargo hold on the *Dragon's Hoard* which is equipped with a life support system, but not to Earth standard. Sensors detected life-signs within that hold, but I don't recognize any of it as human or even Earth typical. What's unknown, however, is whether the lifeforms in that hold are guests or captives. Either way, the ships' manifest, which is freely accessible via commerce authorities, doesn't show any of the items my sensors are picking up."

"Fuck," Ezra whispered.

"Good people, besides Magnus, died because of these kinds of bastards," Conner clenched a hand into a fist before slamming it down on the desktop.

"Multiple connections incoming, Conner," Barley said with a hand resting on Conner's shoulder. "Our child will be avenged. One way or another."

The door to the office opened. Betty rushed straight to Conner. Arlene and Ernie followed close behind. As the Fleet logo returned, Conner stood and hugged the trio in one big bear hug. Slowly, holo-projections of those people Conner requested began appearing in the office, which grew outward into the wall.

"Love you three," Conner whispered to them before kissing each of their foreheads. "Go give Barley a hug as well. Magnus was like his son too."

As the trio hurried around the desk to hug Barley, Conner sat down and pressed the unmute icon on his desk. He noted the security icon wasn't a 'Z' as he'd hoped, but what he had would have to do. Clearing his throat, he waited until everyone looked at him before speaking.

"I wanted each of you to hear this directly from me," Conner said as he noted in his peripheral vision Betty and her cousins sat on the sofa to his left. Barley sat with them, which worried Conner immensely. "Today, we were attacked by two cargo ships controlled by former Fleet veteran artificials, Abraham Lincoln and Shin Shanghai. We were able to retrieve their matrix cores thanks to my niece's ingenuity and Barley's refusal to clean out his closets. Abe's core is badly damaged due to being fired upon by what is believed to have been projectile weapons and both Abe and Shin had been shackled with enslavement routines. Fleet technical teams are working now to try and restore both artificials, but the damage suffered by both while in those cargo ships and during the attack on the *Infinity* makes a full recovery doubtful."

"Where's Magnus," Admiral Vickie stepped up to Conner's desk, fear etching itself on her usual placid face.

"He suffered catastrophic damage to his body when an enemy torpedo struck Shuttle Bay Three," Conner said, his voice cracking. As he spoke, his own eyes teared up again. "Utilizing his body's greater strength and agility, he saved the life of a pregnant member of the tech team who was working on Abe and Shin's cores at the time of the attack. While the tech team he saved refuses to admit his demise, they have not gotten any response from his matrix."

"No," Admiral Vickie mouthed, no sound coming from her mouth. Tears streamed down her face even while shaking her head in denial.

"Due to unknown reasons, his body was not making backups of his matrix to a node in Barley's systems. So, unless there is a clean backup of his primary matrix on either *Socrates' Odyssey* or *Terra Prima*, my eldest child, Magnus Conner, is presumed deceased," Conner said, shaking from the struggle to not start wailing again himself. "Captain Nokata, I believe you have the total casualty numbers."

"Between *Infinity* and both frigates, seven dead and roughly three dozen injured," Ezra said as he stood to Conner's right. "The pregnant tech officer is the worst. She needs to get to a station-based medical facility to keep from losing her baby. The rest were minor injuries which our limited medical staff on the three ships are handling."

"I'm so sorry, Conner," Admiral Vickie said, unable to stop from crying. "He was so sweet and gentle."

"He'll be missed, but not forgotten," Barley said with a thick voice.

"Anyone else of note amongst the deceased?" Socrates said from where he stood beside Treespinner, who sobbed into the black man's shoulder.

"No," Conner said, knowing Socrates worried over his great grandson. "Sam is among those currently working to revive Magnus, otherwise I'd have invited him to join us. There is more I need you all to hear. None of it good."

"The ghost signals?" Admiral Stephens sat in a chair beside Admiral Nokata, both wearing dark, unreadable expressions.

"Ships cloaked using dark matter somehow bonded to or held against the exterior of the hulls," Ezra said, his tone hard and hateful. "Thanks to the hard work and ingenuity of both Fleet and civilian personnel, three ships and the mine field they were laying in orbit of Venus were destroyed and all hands onboard apparently dead. We have recon units combing the debris field of the one ship still in Venus space. We used short-range warp tunnels to relocate the mines and the ship setting the mines to locations where an additional ship or ships were suspected. Sensors indicated the explosions were of more than one ship or clump of mines."

"How did you find out about these additional ships, Conner?" Admiral Nokata leaned forward in his seat, his gaze growing intense.

"Communication signals between ships," Betty said with noticeable venom in her voice. "I want you to understand something, admirals and elder artificials, my brother's death lays squarely on the hands of First Admiral Mori. I expect her to be arrested and publicly executed for her crimes."

"Based on what evidence, child?" Aphrodite, Venus's planetary artificial, said from her spot beside ConRad. "And please note a gut feeling isn't evidence."

"That will be forthcoming," Conner said before Betty could speak. "This meeting is to—"

"I have recordings of her issuing orders to those on the cloaked ships which attacked us today," Betty said standing up and stepping right up to the admirals sitting on the front row of the group, "which attacked Barley during the Battle of Horus using alien technology to infiltrate Barley's systems in hopes of killing the commanding officers of each ship, and orders which sent hired assassins to kill my aunt and uncle along with, but failing to, kill my cousins sitting here either side of Barley. I have the original recordings, the encryption key which Magnus and I figured out, and decrypted messages to and from her personal combat wing."

"Sit down, Betty," Conner said softly, unwilling to make it an order.

"She's trying to kill us, daddy," Betty spun to face Conner, her hands slapping his desktop. "We have to stop her."

"You may just have," ConRad said with a low growl in his ancient voice. "Send everyone here a copy of your evidence, Betty. If it's as damning as you claim, and can be verified separately, then it can be used to unseat her and dismantle her power structure."

"None of which explains why she wants Uncle Conner dead," Ernie said from where he sat. "My dad was an engineer. He designed the skeletons of buildings. Sure, he told horrible and sometimes very crude jokes, but we had fun doing that. My mom was an artist. She never let Uncle Conner come visit, but never said a bad word about him either. When things got weird or she needed to vent, she'd contact Uncle Conner and he'd listen. We could call and talk to Maggie or Magnus whenever, but she urged us to keep it short so we didn't bother them, since they were so far away and in a different time zone. Still, Maggie would answer and be all playful no matter what time it was. Why did they have to die? Because they were related to Uncle Conner? Tell me, because I don't understand."

"Consider this meeting and what's been said as notice to you all," Conner said, watching Betty rush to Ernie's side to hug the now sobbing boy. "Each of you are better positioned to stop First Admiral Mori. If you can't or won't, Barley and I will be forced to deal with her in a very up front and violent manner. Should it come to that, anyone who tries to stop us will be seen as siding with the old hag. This is your only warning. Meeting ended."

Conner hit the disconnect icon before anyone could speak.

CHAPTER 18

Conner sat on one side of the long table in a large conference room on the same level as the bridge. To his right sat Ezra, while the Captain of the *Powell,* who was a lean white man with wavy brown hair and a prominent nose, sat to his left. Across from each man were the controlling artificials of the ships they commanded. Between the six of them sat two collections of nearly a dozen double-fist-sized memory crystals each, which were sealed in portable magnetic field containers. The containers had been coded to only allow access by a planetary artificial. Conner's fists hurt from how fiercely he clenched them.

"How stable is Abe?" Conner's voice trembled with barely contained rage.

"Father is still trying to determine that with the tech leads from all three ships," Barley said with an eerie calm. "However, father isn't hopeful. Abe is in a quantum state similar to a catatonic state in a human."

"None of us can get Shin to talk to us calmly," Sahalie said, her usually coifed and smooth appearance verging on disheveled. "He may never be able to control a ship again."

"You've been silent, Pollick," Ezra said in a low voice as the man stared at the memory crystals. "As I understand it, of all of us here, you're the one to have served with either Abe or Shin most recently. What are your thoughts on what we've seen?"

"That my brothers were beaten and tortured before their captors tried to or did murder Abraham in cold blood." Pollick's gaze shifted to his hands, which rested on the table. Appearing as a pure-blooded Native American, the man was thickly muscled with jet black hair and dark eyes. "She has dishonored not just the entirety of Fleet, be they natural or artificial service members in any body shape, but all of the peoples of the Sol-Humana Confederation. There is only one thing that can be done, but we aren't the group who can proclaim her fate."

"Father and the others are coming," Barley said, a catch in his voice spoke to the grief he struggled to contain.

Shortly, the doors behind the artificials opened to let Sam and three people in Fleet uniforms enter. Two of the Fleet officers were women, and they carried a container large enough to be another magnetic containment unit. Sam went to one side and pulled two chairs back for the women to set the unit on the table. Once the newcomers had moved to sit at that end of the table, Sam thumbed in a code on an unseen screen. The opaque exterior vanished to reveal another crystal from an artificial's core. However, this crystal had a large misshapen hole through it.

"We are here, captains and commanders," Sam said with a hoarse voice thick with emotion, "to report that Abraham Youngs, decorated Fleet veteran, and former controlling artificial of the Youngs-class destroyer *CSS Lincoln* and most recently the *CSS Chesapeake Bay*, arrived on board this vessel already deceased."

"No." Barley surged to his feet, his face contorted by grief and denial. "He couldn't speak, sure, but he wasn't—"

"Barley," Conner said softly before swallowing down his own desire to sob, "let Sam finish his report. This is difficult for all of us, but especially him since Abe and all of you are his children."

"Our findings," Sam continued when Barley sat down, "are contained in these memory crystals, with each of us having a complete copy of the findings and evidential recordings of our inspection and analysis."

Sam and the three officers who came with him pulled a much smaller crystal out of a pocket and set them on the table before themselves. Sam continued speaking. "In short, Abe had each of his processing crystals shot with both projectile and tightly focused high energy beam weaponry to burn a hole as you see in this crystal. Few other crystals were targeted, though the crystals destroyed besides processing units were those known to hold higher function matrix lobes. These crystals would be easily identifiable to a quantum technical team lead or engineer who has worked on Youngs-class vessels. A manual search of Abe's memory crystals yielded results on the persons who committed this crime."

"Wait a minute," Conner looked from Sam to the damaged crystal before him. "You're saying Abe was murdered? By who?"

"I'd rather not say any names, Captain," Sam said while looking straight ahead but not at anyone. "Suffice it to say, in my learned experience, a Class A assault has taken place against two artificials.

Unfortunately, this assault resulted in the murder of one of the victims. The other victim suffered enslavement and threats, both implied and stated, to keep them silent about the crimes. I formerly request a planetary guardian be contacted for guidance on how we proceed from here."

Conner took a deep breath, released it slowly, and took another breath before finally speaking. "Betty!"

"Captain?" Betty's reply seemed to come from all around him.

"Send a request to Earth for a secure stream connection with E. ConRad, the planetary artificial of Earth," Conner said without taking his eyes off the destroyed crystal. "Then, put me on a ship-wide broadcast. Tap me into both destroyers as well."

"At once, Captain," Betty said before she appeared, from the waist up, in the center of the table facing Conner. "Just to let you know, daddy, Socrates has requested a stream connection with you several times. He won't let me patch him through, saying it's a personal matter concerning Magnus. Thought I'd let you know while I had your attention."

"Understood." Conner let his head fall forward even as he closed his eyes for a moment. "Patch him through after I speak to everyone. Do the same with Earth's ConRad."

"Will do, Captain," Betty nodded before vanishing.

"This is bad," Ezra said from his place on Conner's right. "I don't think there's been a Class A violation of the accords in several centuries. Wasn't that what ended up toppling the Imperium's government and led to the formation of the Spartan Alliance?"

"How much of the evidence you four gathered has actually been watched by any of you?" Sahalie spoke softly while looking at the canister of memory crystals before her. "Do you have an idea of how widespread the ripple effect will be?"

"I don't think we should answer that, Commander Sahalie," the male tech officer said while glancing at Sam and the two women. "At least not until a planetary artificial is present."

Betty reappeared before anyone could say anything else. "The ships wide announcement is now possible, Captain. Do you want audio only, or also video?"

Conner looked at the captains to either side of him. When they both nodded, Conner looked at Betty and said, "Video as well, Betty. Just us three captains, though."

"You're live," Betty said. When she spoke next, her voice could be heard on the speakers throughout the ship calling for everyone's attention. "The captains will now be making a joint statement."

"This is Captain Conrad Conner of the *Infinity*," Conner said as he looked straight ahead. "Beside me is Captain Ezra Nokata of the *Soaring Eagle* and Captain Horatio Urlain of the *Powell*. We address you today to inform all of you, whether you're Fleet or civilian, that the team trying to restore Abraham, the badly damaged artificial rescued from one of the cargo ships which attacked us the other day, has been declared deceased. Abraham, or Abe to those of us lucky enough to have served with him, was truly a gentle soul whose desire was to protect those he loved. Who he loved was everyone and everyone was worthy of his protection."

"When his ship, the Youngs-class destroyer *Lincoln*," Captain Urlain said in a shaky voice, "was too badly damaged to be repaired, he requested to be allowed to retire so he could lead a more peaceful life. I had the honor of being the last Captain of the *Lincoln* and can attest to Captain Conner's description of Abe. He tried to stop battles before they happened with calm and peace. If forced into fighting, he did so with the goal of a quick win that minimized death on both sides."

When Urlain paused to wipe his face, Ezra spoke. "For those who don't know of me, I spent part of my childhood here onboard Barley when Abe and Shin were still in Fleet and assigned to Barley's carrier group. They quickly became my uncles who spoiled me with love and old action movies. Sadly, what should have been a relaxing retirement ended up being slavery and murder."

"We mention all of this because Abe was not just another warship," Conner said when emotions overwhelmed Ezra. "Like all of us, be we born to a biological or artificial body, Abe was a brother, a son, a friend, and to Shin, a husband and protector."

Everyone in the room said a soft, "Here. Here," to what Conner said. The doors into the room opened to reveal ConRad and Socrates walking in.

"So, to the list of those we have lost these last few days," Conner's voice thickened at the thought of having to bury yet another person in his life he considered family, "we add Abraham Lincoln Youngs. Give my little boy a hug, Abe, and regale my sister and her husband with embarrassing stories about me, even if they aren't completely true."

Ezra reached out to grip Conner's shoulder even as a sob escaped the man's lips. Captain Urlain spoke next. "Let's have a moment of silence and stillness in memory of Abe and all whom we have lost recently. They are gone from our lives, but never forgotten."

Barley lifted a whistle to his lips. As he blew into the thin short pipe, a sharp, high-pitched sound emerged. Most everyone in the room bowed their heads, letting their thoughts stay hidden from others. Conner couldn't help but think of Magnus back when he ran about on Barley doing whatever Barley let him get away with. Abe would drag him back from his ship to Conner's quarters, Magnus hanging upside down laughing and covered in grease or something. The pair would settle down to watch some weird two-dimensional movie that had to be a good three millennia old, the file half corrupted, and the story almost impossible to follow. Yet, it would hold Magnus's attention and get him fired up for the next day of living out in space.

Barley blew his whistle, creating two tones on it to signal the end of the silence. The man then spoke. "Abe and Shin's cores are down in my Shuttle Bay Three. Feel free to go pay your respects to Abe's remains if you wish. More importantly, let Shin know he's not alone and his husband will be missed by you. He needs to know he's loved by more than just the man who now only lives in his memories. Thank you all."

"Socrates and I offer our condolences to all of you," ConRad said with a somber voice and slight nod. "To have yet another death so soon after Magnus's demise is hard. Do we need to delay the meeting you requested, Captain Conner?"

"Please come in and have a seat, gentlemen," Conner said waving to the end of the table opposite Sam and the tech leads. "Abe's death is the reason we called on you. We need both of you on the highest security level connection you are capable of achieving with an undocked ship. Actually, if you'd both be willing to create local nodes for the duration of the security issues, we could achieve Zeta Clearance, I believe. Is that correct, Barley?"

Barley nodded. "I've guest nodes already prepared for both of you. Do you see them?"

Socrates and ConRad nodded. Their images flickered a moment

later. Once both had confirmed they were locally resident sub-matrixes and the security field in place, Conner took a breath and summarized what had already been said.

"Who or what organizations are implicated, Samuel?" ConRad said while staring at the bullet ridden crystal. "Much like Aphrodite told Betty the other day concerning her recordings, I and the other planetary guardians will need solid proof before we can render an enforceable verdict on these allegations."

"These small memory crystals before myself and the Fleet tech leads beside me each hold a copy of the pertinent memories from both Shin and Abe's memories we found, or rather, could stomach watching," Sam said holding up the crystal he'd pulled out a short time ago. "Those containers in the center of the table contain memories Shin gave us of each incident leading up to their enslavement. In Abe's memories, a group of people wearing Fleet uniforms, but with the personal insignia of the First Admiral, met with the crew of two cargo ships. Abe apparently had done or not done something which pissed off Admiral Mori, who was present in all of the memories we looked at. She used Abe to get her people to install the slave routines on Shin, with each time he refused, she shot another thinking or higher function crystal in each of Abe's cores. Once the slave routines were installed, she finished murdering Abe. She can be heard to say—"

"This is just a cargo tug, any idiot can run this piece of shit," one of the female tech leads said, dropping her head into her hands and sobbing.

"To watch your own spouse murdered," Socrates said with a thick voice. "That's a…pain I know well."

"I think most of us in this room have had some form of that pain happen to us," Ezra said with a hollowness. "The ship's wreckage we've been searching has yielded evidence of a corroborative nature. It might help you determine if Abe's murder truly is a Class A violation of the Accords, though I'm not clear on what that means?"

"That components of, or a majority of, a standing government or government body has committed widespread violations of the rights recognized and codified in the Accords to non-natural sentient beings, referred to as Artificials in the Accords," ConRad said, tapping on the table. Where each crystal or container holding a crystal sat, a circle lit up on the table. "A moment while I review the evidence gathered so far. Socrates, maybe you should discuss your reason for being here. This may take a bit of time."

"Very well, brother," Socrates said gripping both hands before him and tapping his thumbs together. "I am here to inform you, Conner, that the backups I and Treespinner had were infiltrated and corrupted beyond use. As such, Magnus Conner has been officially declared deceased. Upon that declaration, a filing which Magnus made just before his transit to *Terra Prima*, became active. While this is usually a private family matter, maybe the presence of everyone here can help soften the blow contained in what you are about to see, Conner."

Conner watched the artificial tear up and a catch become audible in the ancient city-station's voice. Swallowing hard, Conner forced himself to speak. "Is…this, um, a recording Magnus made for me?"

"Of a sort," Socrates said with a wave of both hands. Almost immediately, a two-feet-tall Magnus stood on the table between Conner and Barley. "Initiate the last will and testament of Magnus Conner Traxis, which is the name he took upon passing his adulthood tests."

"Hello, daddy," Magnus said with a weak smile for Conner before glancing around the room. "And others. Is…ah, there you are Pops, er, Barley. No cousins or sister, I see. Or Admiral Mom. Well, if they are with you, feel free to play this for them at another time, daddy. Most of what I wanted to say in this will and whatever is for you."

"You damn brat," Conner said as a sob bubbled out. Ezra gripped Conner's hand on the table, pulling his attention to the fellow captain. Tears streamed down the man's cheeks, reminding Conner how Magnus and Ezra had practically grown up together. It was one reason he and Nigel had gotten so close.

"I've not forgotten you, my brother of choice," Magnus said walking over to Ezra to rest a hand on the man's head. "Give your beautiful girls a tight hug from their Uncle Magnus for me, Ezra. I've a storage locker on *Socrates* that they, Betty, Arlene, and Ernie can sort through and pick things to keep as their own. You take a look and see if you want anything as well. I'm sorry I left before you. The only thing I have to give you, really, is the care and raising of my dad. Get him to actually activate the cleaning cycle on his smelly shirts. Don't let him fall into a deep depression like the one which the murder of his fiancé put him into after his marriage proposal was interrupted on Venus."

"I will, Magnus," Ezra said through his tearful sobbing with a nod of his head.

"Now, the real reason I made this recording," Magnus walked back to the middle of the table to sit on one of the magnetic holding canisters. "Father, a couple of years ago I met a wonderful man through a fan node for ancient movies. We bonded over them and grew really close. You may remember when I said a friend had come to visit and I'd be unavailable for a few days last year. After those few days, he returned to the cruise ship he served on as tech support. The ship was destroyed in the Gannadov nova a few weeks later. I've never heard from him since, so I've presumed he died. What neither of us knew, though, was that I, somehow, got pregnant with his child. I'm not sure how a natural and an artificial can have a child, but about three months ago, the artificial version of giving birth happened. This means that you and Barley are grandfathers to a baby boy, who I registered with the name Alexander Octavius Traxis."

Conner stared at the image of Magnus; not sure he'd heard correctly. Barley slowly stood up, drawing Magnus's attention. Tears trickled down Barley's face before the man grabbed up Magnus in a hug.

"I'll be the best granddaddy to your little boy," Barley said sobbing. "I'll make sure he grows up smart and strong, doing whatever he wants. He'll know what a hero you are and that he has the best daddy in the universe. Conner and I will make sure he knows he's loved, by you and by both of us."

Conner couldn't speak. His mind spun with questions. Who was this love of Magnus's life? Where did the baby's name come from? How, oh how, did Magnus get pregnant?

"Let the boy down, Barley," Sam said gently.

"While I don't expect you two to get married now or anything," Magnus said a bit red-faced as he looked from Barley to Conner, "especially since you two just reconnected, but neither of you can go off on some suicide run to avenge me or Aunt Emily or whoever else dear to you has died. There's a little baby boy sleeping in my node on *Socrates,* with a child matrix of Maggie watching over him. He needs his grandparents, aunts and uncles, and lots and lots of love. Little Alex is three months old and still a baby. I think his growth rate is close to that of human normal. You or someone who knows about this stuff can figure that out, maybe? Let him play like a baby and learn as close to human normal as you can, dad. Maybe get an actual apartment there on *Socrates* so everyone can have their own room. Oh, and Barley, get yourself a humanoid body. Stop letting a ship as a body limit your experiences."

"Why? Why the name?" Conner struggled to speak as a wave of grief, of having to someday explain to a little boy why his parents weren't there, overwhelmed him.

"Look at your birth certificate and watch the recording Aunt Emily sent to me around the time I first realized I was pregnant." Magnus stood up to face Conner as he spoke. "In short, Octavius is the father's first name. Alexander Traxis is the name of one of your fathers. Your true fathers, that is."

"Fathers? As in plural?" Conner stared at Magnus's image, unable to believe everything he was hearing.

"Alexander Traxis married Aunt Emily's older brother, Conner Underwood," Magnus said with a sad smile for Conner. A glance down the table at Socrates and ConRad, though, seemed to make the artificial say more. "Your fathers, well, were murdered when you were about four years old. I didn't want to go into details here since I know my sister and cousins will watch this, but you witnessed it, dad. Just, go watch the explanation recording made by your mother, which is what Aunt Emily sent me. Maybe with Socrates and ConRad, who can likely look up the answers to all the questions you'll have. None of this last bit will likely be repeated if others are watching. I don't have anything else, so I'm going to sign off."

"No," Barley whimpered, pulling Magnus back around. "Don't leave us, my little boy."

"Oh, Pops," Magnus said with a sad sigh. Walking across the table, Magnus leaned in to kiss Barley's forehead. "I'll always be with you, in your heart and your memories. Watch over my dad and my baby boy. You will forever be one of my fathers. Don't let anyone ever tell you otherwise."

"We love you, Magnus," Ezra said, his voice straining to sound normal and not like a sobbing mess. "Rest in peace knowing you are loved and will be remembered with love by all who knew you."

"I am and always was proud of you, my bratty little Maggie." Conner said through the tears and sobs which consumed him. "I love you, your sister loves you, and your cousins love and miss you. May you feel our love out there, wherever you have gone."

"All I am now is the love we had for each other, daddy," Magnus said, shifting from his traveling outfit to a blue sun dress with large yellow dots and her brown hair falling in waves around her head and shoulders. "Until we meet again. Just, don't hurry, daddy. The universe still needs you alive."

Maggie blew Conner a kiss, before doing the same to Ezra. For Barley, Maggie walked over and kissed him on the nose. "Live, Pops, and stop hiding from everyone."

Then, Maggie broke apart and vanished, as though a wind blew through the room.

Conner stared across the table at Barley. Both streamed tears down their faces. Sahalie and Pollick both struggled against their own emotions. Ezra sobbed beside him. One of the tech leads with Sam sniffled, drawing Conner's gaze to them. Sam wiped his eyes.

"Socrates?" Conner reached out to pull Ezra into a hug as he spoke. "Do you have repair yards capable of repairing the damage to *Infinity*?"

"The Jovian system's repair yards are more for the large cargo ships," Socrates said, also sounding choked up. "It may take a bit longer for the repairs to be made, though. I could bring the boy to you."

"I'd fear that him traveling by System transfer will cause the same fear in him as in Magnus," Conner said swallowing hard. "We need to see how stable his matrix is first."

"Arrange for a slot in your shipyards, brother," ConRad said standing up. "Push for the repairs to be expedited. Conner and Barley, you need to ensure Abraham and Shin's cores are thoroughly secured from tampering and damage before you start the trip across the system. Maybe erecting a physical barrier around them in addition to the force fields I understand are being used to pressurize the shuttle bay."

Barley merely nodded while wiping his face. Conner struggled to find something to say to distract both Barley and himself from this all-consuming grief. To his surprise, Sam spoke.

"I noticed you also accessed the memory crystals between the captains and the ships, uncle," Sam said reaching out to unhide the damaged crystal again. "How serious do you think it is? The same ships which attacked us, whose torpedo effectively killed Magnus, also attacked the shuttle sitting in the bay leaning against Abe's cores, fired on and destroyed a mooring on Terra Prima, also held those responsible for the murder of Conner's sister and husband. This isn't just about the control and enslavement of artificials, Uncle ConRad."

"Speaking of my sister," Conner said, gazing at Barley for lack of anyplace else to look, "I need to settle my sister and her husband's estate before I leave the inner system. There's also the contract between C5 and Kashi's company. What's that name? I can't remember suddenly. Magnus always took care of that stuff."

The tears and sobbing surged back into control. All he wanted to hear was Magnus's grumpy voice coming from his sleeve, teasing him about his stinky shirts and how abusive he was. None of that would ever happen again. For all of his adult life, starting from before he'd even entered high school, Magnus had been in his life. Everything he'd done in his life, from pushing Emily to follow her dreams of art, applying to Fleet's Academy, to standing his ground against Mori after the Battle of Horus, to leaving the big corporations and starting his own company, had been to show Magnus the ups and downs of life. That he could do what he wanted, and that even if you didn't succeed enough to become wealthy, you could still find happiness. Now, though, everything had no meaning. The struggles had yielded nothing but death.

"Betty is sending me a notice for attention, ConRad," Barley said in a soft voice, which still cut through Conner's grim thoughts. "Can I lower the security setting yet?"

"After I've had my say," ConRad said, now from behind Conner. The black man rested his hands on Conner's shoulders. "Nothing about how Abe was killed, or Shin's enslavement, can be discussed with anyone, even amongst yourselves. These crystals, both damaged and undamaged, are to be held in a secure space accessible only to the captain and ship's artificial. Barley and Conner, as the ship upon whom Abe and Shin's cores reside, I'm placing you two in control of them until you hard dock with *Socrates* and a physical transfer can happen. Do you both understand?"

Barley and Conner nodded, neither saying a word. ConRad leaned heavily on Conner's shoulders. "On a personal note, I grieve with you both over the loss of your son. However, take it from someone who has watched billions be executed in a day. Focus on the living, while securing the precious memories of the dead. You'll get through this horrible time. It'll be rough, you'll think death would be easier, but that's only going to make those who love you hurt even more. Betty, Arlene, and Ernie certainly need you both, but so does Ezra here and his daughters, along with everyone on three ships. Shin, especially, needs you both, even if it's as a silent presence. He's lost the man he loves and now is bodiless. Let him know he's needed, and you'll rediscover how much you both are needed. My words of useless wisdom."

Conner surged to his feet, pushing around the chair to hug ConRad. "You've done so much for me and my family. I can't thank you enough, ConRad."

"Just trying to pay down the very deep debt I owe you, Conner," ConRad whispered as the artificial hugged him back. "A debt I may never be able to fully repay."

CHAPTER 19

"Fleet Admiralty trying to connect with us, Captain," Betty said over the intercom as everyone stood up. "Shall I pipe them into there? They say it's urgent."

"They? Are we talking all five of the admirals?" Conner groaned inward.

"Yes, Captain," Betty said with a tone which told Conner his daughter was irritated to her last nerve.

"Let them hold while we finish up in here, Betty," Conner said, turning to Sam. "Conner out."

"We'll get these into secure storage with Barley watching over the process." Sam tapped the containment before him, the shielding reappearing. The tech leads each picked up their memory crystal.

"Oh, and ConRad's warning about this being of the highest security also extends to the other core in Shuttle Bay One," Conner said grimly. "Pass the warning on to those tech teams as well to not discuss any findings with anyone. Not even admirals or others outside of this room."

"I'm horrified anyone would kill so wantonly," a tech lead said. "My condolences, Captain Conner and Commander Barley, on the loss of your son. I'm sure I also speak for everyone on my team when I say Magnus saved all of us, not just Lieutenant Butler."

"Thank you, Lieutenant," Conner said nodding. "Dismissed."

"Mind if Socrates and I stay for your meeting with the Admiralty," ConRad said with a hand resting on Conner's shoulder.

"As you wish, ConRad," Conner said with a weak smile. "You can reign me in if I get too belligerent."

"Socrates, move to sit beside Captain Urlain while I'll sit down here beside Captain Nokata," ConRad said as the captains sat back down.

Once the five of them were seated again and the others had left, Conner called for Betty to connect the Admiralty. Admiral Stephens appeared first, followed by Nigel Nokata, Ezra's father. Two other women appeared, both older than Nigel. While easily close to their eighties, Conner noticed these women had the appearance and bearing of Earthborn humans. Admiral Mori appeared last, scowling at everyone and everything. The admirals all sat in chairs, with Mori sitting in the center opposite Conner. Nigel sat across from Ezra, with Admiral Stephens beside Nigel and the other two on the other side of Admiral Mori.

As Conner waited for the admirals to be seated, he could almost hear Magnus sighing from his sleeve. His genderfluid child would groan about how grating he could be and remind him to speak kindly and warmly or he'd lose business before ever getting it offered. The memory brought a smile to his face. As he spoke, just before Admiral Mori was fully situated, her dark scowl at not speaking first made him even happier.

"Good day, Admirals," Conner said keeping his smile, "I'm Conrad Conner, president of The C5 Group, which has been contracted by Barley to act as captain of the vessel he calls home and is now known as the *CSS Infinity*. I expect you all know Captains Urlain and Nokata on either side of me. We happen to have some guests who requested to remain. Beside Captain Nokata is the Earth planetary guardian, E. ConRad, while on the other side of Captain Urlain on my left is Socrates, who is the controlling artificial of the Jovian city-station *Socrates' Odyssey*. With the introductions on our side made, what business brings the Sol-Humana Confederation Fleet Admiralty to our doorstep?"

"Business? What in the hell do you think you're doing out there, you cretinous little waste of dust?" Admiral Mori glared at Conner.

"I'm sorry, Admiral, um, was it Morris?" Conner tilted his head slightly while putting on a confused look. "Mori! Mariko Mori, if I recall correctly. My apologies, Admiral, but it's been so long since I've seen you that I didn't recognize you. I see time hasn't really changed your personality. Admiral Nokata and Admiral Stephens, good to see you both again."

"You asshole!" Mori slapped her hands down, expecting them to hit the table. Instead, they passed through the table. Her look of shock pleased Conner to no end.

"Calm down, Admiral Mori," Admiral Vickie said, appearing behind the old woman's chair with a hard glare on her face. "Remember my warning and you'll be allowed to remain."

Conner quirked an eyebrow at the exchange but stayed silent.

He noted Admiral Mori's lips curling up into a snarl, but she stayed silent otherwise. The admiral on Mori's right, who sat across from Captain Urlain, cleared her throat before speaking.

"The Admiralty has been updated on recent events and all of us here wanted to convey our condolences on those lives lost," the admiral said with a stern, yet neutral tone.

"Conveyed and noted, Admirals," Conner said with a tight-lipped smile when the admiral didn't continue. "We don't have much time before our departure for home. Was there more the Admiralty wanted of us?"

Conner's statement drew both Vickie and Nigel's attention. It was Admiral Mori, though who spoke. "The Admiralty has need of a neutral party to help transport a diplomatic team to the Horus System in a month's time. Somehow, the Spartans learned of Barley's retirement and have requested he be the neutral party upon which negotiations of a final peace treaty be negotiated with the Sol-Humana Confederation."

Conner stared at the old woman, not sure whether to believe anything that came out of her mouth. "The *CSS Infinity* is contracted for long-term use by Shining Sun Shipping, Admirals. Any use as you've described will have to be negotiated with Kashi Tandon, president of Shining Sun Shipping. I will take this verbal request to Ms. Tandon and urge her to contact you directly."

"We can make this an order, you cretin," Admiral Mori hissed with venom.

"That, Admiral Mori, is a wrong assumption." Conner dropped his smile while keeping his expression on the stern side of neutral. "You may be the commanding officer to the Fleet captains sitting on either side of me, but I and this ship are both civilians."

"Just because that bucket of bolts was allowed to retire doesn't mean he can't be recalled to active duty, Conners." Admiral Mori leaned forward with open hatred on her face.

"Conner." ConRad said sharply. When Admiral Mori jerked her glare to the Earth artificial, ConRad continued. "His name is Conrad Conner. Not Conners. Get it right or one of the grief-stricken individuals here will shove the correct pronunciation down your increasingly senile old throat."

"Don't you threaten us," Mori snapped.

A flash behind Conner told him Barley had appeared behind

him. Yet, it wasn't Barley's voice which spoke. "Would you feel better if I threatened you, you hateful old hag?"

"Shin?" Conner spun his chair around to find the Asian-appearing artificial standing there, scarred and wearing a torn merchant fleet uniform.

"You remember what I said when you shot my husband?" Shin trembled, hatred filling the artificial's expression and clenching his fists.

Barley flashed in beside Shin, wrapping an arm around thin, almost withered shoulders. "My apologies. We connected him to my systems so he could use my holoprojectors. Come on, Shin. This isn't the time or place."

"You'll answer for your crimes, Mori." Shin said between sobs wracking his frame. "May Abe's dying screams haunt your afterlife!"

"This meeting is over," Admiral Mori said sharply, reaching out.

"No, it's not," Nigel said with cold fury while standing. "Shin, I want to offer you my deepest regrets and condolences on the loss of your beloved husband. I will personally investigate your accusations and bring all of the guilty parties to justice. Barley, take care of our friend. When you reach the Jupiter system, let me know what I can do, both personally and professionally."

"Thank you, Admiral," Barley said with a trembling smile and nod. "Come on, Shin. Let's go."

Shin trembled with tears pouring down his face. Conner stood up and positioned himself so the artificial had to look at him and not the admirals. "Go with Barley to the captain's quarters. Magnus's sister, Betty, and his cousins, who were orphaned recently, will join you. The projectors in those quarters will let you be solid. You can hug them, and they'll want to hug you. I'm sure they'd like someone they can just sob with, since they seem to struggle to not do so with me. Your father's also onboard. He'll come be with you as well, if you'd like that. What do you want to do?"

"He fought them, Captain," Shin whispered, his sobbing making his words hard to understand.

"I've got you, brother," Barley said weepy-eyed. "Let's go have a good cry. Lord knows I need one."

Conner started to reach out, but Shin flinched back into Barley. With an apologetic smile from Barley, the pair of artificial's vanished in a flash of light. As his own grief welled up, threatening to overtake his self-control, Conner gripped the back of his chair as he let his head drop forward while he clenched his eyes shut against the tears. Hands gripped his shoulders as both Ezra and Urlain whispered their own encouragement to him.

"The vote is unanimous," Vickie said from behind Conner. "Mariko Mori, you are removed as First Admiral and your commission as an Admiral within the Sol-Humana Confederation Stellar Fleet is rescinded. Upon final review and Arbiter declarations on the accused crimes of murder, your final discharge and retirement status will be decided. You are to vacate this office immediately and return to your quarters, where you will remain under house arrest. Guards, take her to her rooms."

Conner could see both Vickie and Admiral Mori's lips moving, but no sound could be heard. A second or two later, Mori's image vanished. Vickie stood there behind a now empty chair looking irritated.

"Apologies for that," Vickie said with a forced calm. "Fleet Operations, Inner System Command, will cooperate fully with any investigation that you will or have already started, ConRad. I feel terrible about what's happened to Shin and Abe. Losing Magnus suddenly is bad enough, after having him reenter my life so recently."

"While I don't want to disparage or doubt what I saw, everyone," the admiral to Conner's far left said slowly, "I think we all should be allowed to see the proof you find of Shin's accusations. I oversaw his and Abe's retirement a few years ago. We lost valued members of Fleet with their leaving, but I completely understood their reasons for wanting to leave. The battle which led to the *Lincoln* being retired from service killed nearly ninety percent of the crew and badly damaged Abe himself. While many thought Abe would recover fully and be back in a new Fleet ship, I'd seen such injuries in naturals who never recovered enough to return to active duty."

"The investigation is ongoing and cannot be commented on at this time, Admirals," ConRad said in a subdued tone. "Once all evidence is gathered and examined, the evidence and final declaration of the Arbiters will be released for everyone's review. Now, before I overstay my welcome, I will bid you all good-bye. Captain

Conner, please feel free to contact me again if you have need of me."

"Thanks, ConRad," Conner said with a nod to the artificial. As others started to say good-bye, Conner spoke quickly. "Vickie and Nigel, if you can stay a moment. I've something of a personal matter to discuss with you both."

"Do you think now, after what's just happened, is the time, Uncle Conner?" Ezra leaned in close to whisper his question.

"Is there ever a good time, Ezra?" Conner smiled sadly at younger man.

Once only the Nokatas, Vickie, and Socrates remained, Conner moved so they were all gathered around one end of the table. Feeling more like a personal gathering now, Conner glanced at Socrates before smiling at Vickie. "We were delayed connecting with the Admiralty due to Socrates coming to inform me of the official declaration of Magnus's death and having an unplanned reading of Magnus's will."

"He had a will?" Vickie leaned forward, surprised at what Conner had said.

"Of course that boy had a will," Nigel said chuckling. "He put himself through law school, after all. What I find surprising is that he had anything important enough to deal with via a will."

"Surprised us all," Ezra said smiling.

"The reason was guardianship over my and Barley's grandson," Conner said, slowly smiling as he watched shocked expressions spread across Vickie and Nigel's faces. "Yeah, that little boy of ours fell in love, got his heart broken when the guy, a natural I believe he said, died in that nova that happened last year, and then gave birth about three months ago."

"What? Where's the child? How did he even get pregnant?" Vickie said rapid-fire.

"Welcome to the old man club, Conner," Nigel said laughing. "Get back here as quick as you can. Sarah is going to go crazy with this news. Use some of that arbitration money to get yourself a better apartment. And baby supplies. Despite how we raised our boys, a warship is not a good place to raise kids."

"I still have to tell Betty and my sister's kids," Conner said sighing. "When we get back to *Socrates*, I'll give you a call so you can at least see the baby, Vickie."

"Also," Socrates said with a slight smile, "when you have time, you can watch the will. It may be rough, since it's Magnus interacting in a very limited manner. He may have a private message for you, Vickie."

"Thank you, Socrates," Vickie said, tears escaping her eyes as she smiled. "Can I tell Treespinner? She's taking his death really hard, Conner."

"Sure," Conner said smiling. "Maybe watch the will with her in case Magnus has something to say to her. I don't know when he recorded this, whether it was before or after he left for Terra Prima."

"Ah, Katie is calling. Can I give her the good news?" Nigel looked up from his desk to Conner before shifting to Ezra. "How are you holding up, son? Your mother and girls are worried sick."

"As well as can be expected after this one-two punch to the gut, dad," Ezra said with a shaky smile. "I expected Magnus to be the one giving my girls away at their weddings, not me doing the same for his son."

"The universe is a fickle mistress, as Barley read to me from some ancient tome," Nigel said with a sad sigh. "I need to go. Congrats again, Conner. Tell Barley his old man mojo will likely make his grandson giggle like a hyena. Let me know when you all get back here to *Socrates*. Nokata out."

"Bye, dad," Ezra said before Nigel's image vanished.

"I need to go as well, Conner," Vickie reached out to rest a hand on Conner's hand. "Magnus was a great kid. You raised him on your own but let me and Barley and so many others help along the way. He will always feel like my own son, and I can't thank you enough for those happy memories."

"Part of me still expects him to just chime in complaining about my stinky shirts at any moment," Conner said sadly. "Thank you for being the mother he needed when he needed you. I've got a daughter you can claim. I'm sure she could use a mother, or at least a motherly aunt."

"Sure thing, Conner," Vickie said smiling. "I'll wait for your call to show off the grandbaby."

With that, Vickie stood up and rushed over to hug Conner. As she vanished, Conner took a deep breath to calm his emotions, and let it out slowly. Ezra slapped his knees before standing up. Socrates patted Conner's back as he too stood up. Conner joined them in standing, suddenly realizing he had felt both Socrates and Vickie. He chuckled at how Barley had purposely made Mori not able to touch things.

"Thanks for staying connected for so long, Socrates," Conner said with a slight bow.

"You're important to members of my family, Conner," Socrates said with a very slight smile. "Let me know when the kids are ready to watch Magnus's will. I don't know if Shin will get anything out of seeing it or not. You and Barley decide that."

"Will do," Conner said. "We'll be in contact once we're underway."

CHAPTER 20

Conner stepped into the tech lab he used back when he served aboard Barley during his Fleet years. Now, it appeared, Sam used it for his own. A generic artificial body lay on one of the worktables in the long, skinny room. Barley and Shin stood close by watching Sam, Arlene, and two Fleet techs connect cables to various points along each side of the body.

"Is this one of the bodies Treespinner sent over?" Conner stepped up beside Barley. "Why the hard connections?"

"Treespinner said to use a hard connection to wipe the base command systems from the units before anyone's matrix, even if secondary in nature, used either unit." Barley said as Shin stood on Barley's other side looking pensive. "I'm still trying to convince Shin to at least try it."

"I'm not sure I should be allowed a physical presence anywhere on this ship outside of your quarters, Captain," Shin said softly. "My emotions, they're just so…"

Conner glanced over at the artificial now dressed in a ship's uniform, but without any rank pins. The man's hair was about shoulder length, with a few wisps of gray, and a face which looked about Conner's own forty-odd years. He couldn't see any form of joy in the artificial's expression, not that he really expected there to be any.

"I think a lot of us know what you mean, Shin," Conner said with a sad sigh. "I see Arlene, but not Ernie. I thought he was down here as well."

A hand waved from the far side of a worktable before Ernie's head popped up near the head of the artificial body. "Checking connections, Uncle Conner! Has Grandpa Socrates sent pics of the baby yet? I wanna see how much like Maggie he looks."

"Not yet," Conner called, smiling at both Arlene and Ernie's pouting expressions. "We're underway, though. So, we'll be able to see the little tyke in about six hours."

"Why so long?" Shin looked from Conner to Barley. "Is it because of me?"

"Not you, Shin," Conner said while watching the others work. "Rather, it's due to the young lieutenant Magnus saved. Her condition worsened at the last moment before being sent to Eros Station. The doctors there and here all agreed she and the baby wouldn't survive that trip. At the doctors' urging, we're not going to do any hard accelerations just in case. Socrates liked the extra time to hopefully get slots freed up so all three ships can be repaired at once."

"There are a few things we have to transfer from me over to Socrates's care first," Barley said with a meaningful look to Shin. "Remember what we talked about, brother."

Ernie hurried over to hug Conner. The boy faced Shin afterwards with a serious expression. "Uncle Shin, the blank is ready for you to take occupancy. Please do it. I don't want you to stay onboard here while we all go to see the baby. Magnus would want you to come and see your grandnephew."

"Yeah, Uncle Shin," Arlene came over to add her own pleading expression.

Conner smiled but stayed silent. Shin hesitated for a moment before sighing in defeat. "Fine. Because I know Abe will haunt me if I don't fawn over his precious Magnus's baby."

"Yeah!" Ernie shouted and ran back over to Sam.

"I'll help you get ready for the transfer, brother," Barley said with a hand to Shin's back.

Once the two artificials had vanished, leaving Conner and Arlene alone, the girl stepped close to wrap an arm around Conner's back while slipping under one of his arms. She rested her head against Conner's shoulder before speaking. "Love you, Uncle Conner."

"Love you too, Niece Arlene," Conner said pulling her tight against his side. "How are you and Ernie holding up?"

"Probably about like you and Barley." Sadness filled Arlene's voice. "Ernie comes and sleeps with me. We wake each other up sobbing."

"Betty can't sleep alone even though her projectors are off," Conner said softly. "If you guys want, come sleep in the other room of my quarters."

"Does Barley sleep with you? Or Sam?" Arlene whispered her questions, though her gaze remained on the activity centered on transferring Shin to the artificial body.

"Depends. Sam is father to every ship-based artificial here, and Magnus and Abe's deaths are affecting all of them," Conner whispered as he leaned down to kiss the top of Arlene's head. "I woke up last night to use the bathroom and had Sam along with all three ship's artificials looking like six-or seven-year-olds piled in the bed with us."

Arlene giggled. "Are you sure Ernie wasn't in there as well?"

"He was on the floor wrapped in a blanket hugging Betty's spine." Conner sighed, remembering the soft whimpering he heard coming from the pile of pillows and blankets on the floor. "He woke up when I was trying to crawl back into bed and said he heard Betty sobbing from across the corridor."

"We'd crawl into mom and dad's bed during storms because he'd get weird about thunder when little," Arlene said. "We all had to sleep together so he knew we were all safe."

"Well, you two take priority over Barley and his siblings," Conner whispered. "If you ask, Barley will gladly crawl into bed with you two as an adult or a kid. He'd do that for Magnus when I was assigned to Barley during my Fleet years. I didn't have access to projectors like in the captain's office and captain's quarters in those years, so I couldn't hold him when he got scared or upset. It was always Barley. Made me feel worthless as a father."

"Looks like Shin's in the body," Arlene said with a sniffle, pulling out of Conner's embrace. "Guess Sam and I can get back to trying to tweak Barley's sensors."

"Tweak his sensors?" Conner recognized a purposeful topic change when he heard one. "Fleet usually keeps them set at an optimal range."

"Sam said the sensors Barley got a year or so ago are multi-spectral and multi-dimensional." Arlene turned to face Conner. "I don't understand it all, but when he explained it to me for the third time, I said something that got him thinking the existing sensors can already see the ships, but the data interpretation coding was keeping things too confined. Or something. I couldn't follow the bit about the dark and normal matter interaction being at perpendicular angles to each other in the higher dimensions."

"Ugh," Conner said with a groan. "I hated working on the sensor array and Barley's central processing arrays. The multi-dimensional aspect of both makes my head hurt almost immediately. Like, physically hurt."

Arlene giggled. "He had to explain it three times before I could understand just what I said. I can at least help with the coding part."

At that moment, the body sat up on the worktable. As everyone watched, the silvery grey skin and blank face shifted and changed to become just as Shin had been portraying himself through the holo-projectors. The generic uniform shifted as the body itself altered slightly to appear a bit more Shin-like.

"How are you feeling, Shin?" Barley said from beside the table with a hand resting on Shin's shoulder.

"A bit claustrophobic," Shin said, his voice warbling just a bit. "Are you registering my auto-backup activating?"

"Yes." Barley smiled warmly nodding. "Running a triple check to be sure nothing is affecting the incoming data-stream before placing it in your personal node on my system."

"Magnus commented on the claustrophobic feeling as well," Sam said while gazing at a sliver of red crystal held out at Shin. "I'm not seeing any issues with the hard or wireless connections. Wiggle your fingers, bend your arms and legs, and turn your head and eyes for me."

Shin rolled his eyes before going through the motions. Conner smiled even as he thought how he missed experiencing this with Magnus. Yet another thing in which he failed his little boy. Magnus was never supposed to be in danger. Just go be present to take possession of his cousins until Conner could reach them. Just like during the Battle of Horus, he failed to keep his own son safe.

Turning away, Conner headed toward the door. Everything he saw here only brought to mind how he'd failed his children, his sister, and even his parents. At least he wasn't needed here. Whatever he tried would likely ruin yet another person's life.

Leaving the lab, Conner walked the corridors trying to think of something, anything, to keep from falling into a pit of grief. Yet, when he thought of the contracts which C5 needed to write and send to both Barley and Kashi, he thought of Magnus. Contracts were things his son took care of, allowing Conner to focus on his work. Letting his mind return to the years he worked on this ship under Nigel Nokata, he couldn't help but think of the times Ezra would run past him with Magnus chasing him, yelling about something the two were arguing over or teasing each other about. A time back before the war with Sparta erupted, forcing even the captain's child to stay back in the Sol System. His sister refused to take Magnus in, citing her university studies keeping her too busy.

"If not Magnus, then my sister Emily," Conner muttered around the lump of grief making his throat ache. "Too much death. So much damn death."

A door opened before Conner, making him jump in surprise. He found himself staring at ConRad who stood in a lift-pod with an eyebrow quirked at Conner. "Well, are you going to get on and cry into my shoulder or just stand there looking lost?"

"Who's died now?" Conner stepped onto the pod, leaning against a wall with his arms crossed over his chest.

"No one," ConRad said gazing at Conner while the door closed. Neither gave any direction, but the pod took off anyway. "I left a submatrix on board so I can observe the investigation of the cloaked ship's captured artificial cores. The techs took a food break, so I came to check on you. Thought you might want the company of someone who cares but doesn't require you to be strong or calm."

"Do I really look calm, ConRad?" Conner snorted with a forced chuckle even as tears escaped his eyes. "How calm can I be when my sister, her husband, and my son are all dead. Within days of each other. What do I do now? I was supposed to be the one to die. Not Emily or Frank, and certainly not my little Magnus."

Conner broke down, the tears and sobs escaping despite how much he tried to hold them inside. He wanted to say how he'd left the Inner System to keep his sister clear of the mess he'd made of his life. Talk about the times his brother-in-law would contact him to tell him about Emily's latest crazy idea or give him news on the kids. Wanted to explain his inability to get Magnus to talk to him about things, to confide in him, even as he sensed a growing darkness in Magnus. None of it could be spoken aloud. Each time he tried, he'd wail in despair. Finally, his knees gave out. Sliding down into a squat, Conner could only sob into his hands.

"Their children are taken care of financially thanks to healthy life insurance policies," ConRad said when Conner regained some control. "Your brother-in-law, Frank, left wills for both himself and your sister with a law firm. They named you as guardian of Arlene and Ernie. I've already arranged your sister and Frank's interment per their wills. Apparently, your sister was rather paranoid about dying and pushed her husband to have things prepared. Just in case, you know."

"Is that what their wills say?" Conner sniffed back the tears even as he spoke with some derision. "Emily always called me an imposter. She claimed I died on that cruise ship with our parents during the Valhalla Incident. Still, she never stopped the kids from contacting me, and apparently called Magnus on a semi-regular basis."

"Didn't your parents live in a low-tech town on Venus?" ConRad watched Conner stand up. "Might that have something to do with the claim?"

"I complained the entire time on the *Valhalla* because Venus is, or was, a haven for the anti-tech movement." Conner could remember the angry words he and his dad exchanged after Magnus had been exposed, all just an hour before the attack which killed at least half of the passengers and crew. "What happened during the explosions is fuzzy, but Emily always claimed she found me with a chest wound and no heartbeat. When she came back with help for me, panicking because she couldn't find our parents, I apparently had completely healed even though my clothes were soaked in blood. Reminds me of something Magnus once said about me dying during the Battle of Horus, but then being alive later. Crazy, hunh?"

"Given your fathers? Not really," ConRad said.

"My fathers? You mean Magnus was right?" Conner looked at the artificial, who looked down at the floor and not Conner. "Wait. Emily said something right before she was shot about us actually being cousins and not siblings. What the hell is going on, old man?"

"There are a lot of holes in the story still," ConRad said with a soft sigh. "I found a recording amongst your sister's personal data storage while searching for some reason to explain her and her husband's deaths. From what Magnus said in his will, this is likely the same video."

When ConRad didn't continue immediately, Conner whispered, "And?"

"The recording was made by your mother a few years after both of your real fathers were murdered." ConRad said, lifting his head to lock eyes with Conner. "She says her brother called after four-year-old you got hurt when something fell on you. Being a nurse, she rushed over to their place to help. She arrived about fifteen to twenty minutes after hanging up with her brother to find the house locked up, but a window left transparent enough she could see all three of you shot in the chest and not moving. A few minutes later, one of her brother's friends from Fleet showed up."

"That's got to be wrong," Conner said shaking his head in confusion. "I'm alive. We all know I'm alive."

"She claims this friend entered the house and brought you out to her," ConRad whispered with a slight tremble to the man's voice. "Brought a weak, unconscious, but now healed little boy out to her."

"Healed? That's not possible," Conner turned away from ConRad, uncertain what was real anymore. "You're talking about immortality, ConRad. Real, godlike immortality. The closest to immortality humanity has reached requires nanos to extend your life to around one hundred and fifty years. Even with those life-extending nanos, a gunshot to the chest or head will still kill you."

"Conner," ConRad said moving to force Conner to look at him, "your mother said this friend watched your chest wound heal on its own. When this friend urged her to take you and claim you were her child, she did just that. Left your fathers and left Earth with her new husband to live on Venus."

"Where they hid in a low-tech town out in the middle of no place Venus, afraid those same assassins would find them and kill me and them as well." Conner hung his head. Tears filled his eyes as he again remembered how scared his mother was that last night he saw her. "She must have expected an attack would come. Maybe even knew that cruise liner would be attacked and wanted me and Em as far away from our rooms as possible. It could be why dad was so harsh with me and Magnus. He wanted to give me and Emily a reason to leave the room for a time. To maybe survive."

"I've seen parents do some incredible things in hopes their children will live," ConRad whispered.

"You're a parent now, my little man," Conner spoke those last words his mother said to him, now three decades in the past. "You have to make the sacrifices to your own life so your child has what they need to grow up to be a strong, responsible, and loving member of society. Go and find Magnus, mom said to me after a fight between Magnus and my dad, and assure him his grandparents still love him, even if we're sometimes harsh with our words and our love. Five to ten minutes later, the first missile struck the ship. They knew. They knew and sent all three of us away deeper into the ship."

"There's more," ConRad said, the tone pulling Conner's gaze to the artificial's eyes. "Your mother names the friend who was there and saw you heal. That friend was her brother's childhood friend, Nigel Nokata."

Conner staggered back, hitting the pod wall with his back. His mind emptied of all thought for a moment, before his years on Barley with Nigel as captain flashed at high speed through his head. Every fatherly thing that man had done for him made so much sense now. How hurt Nigel had looked when Conner held Betty's rod before he and Sam left the hearing room. The seething anger when Nigel found out he'd been demoted and sent to FCOPS after getting Barley's entire carrier group and six enemy ships back from Horus. Even why he got the contract with Fleet for what would end up bringing Betty into his life.

"Your mother claimed he said both of your fathers worked for some hyper-secret Fleet division which wouldn't let them quit to raise you," ConRad said when Conner didn't respond. "She makes quite the case for your fathers' deaths to be an effort to keep them silent about something they had found out in space."

Conner ran his hands through his hair, and wondered if it was long enough Magnus would insist he get it cut. Rubbing his eyes, he pushed back down the grief that odd thought caused. "People I love keep dying, ConRad. My birth fathers, my mom and dad, my sister and brother-in-law, the woman I wanted to marry, and now my own son. How do I stop this? Stop her?"

"You're going to have to fight back, Conner," ConRad said with sadness in his eyes. "I know you hate confrontation. Hate to be in situations where you might have to hurt people. However, your family is the target, and always has been. Whatever it was that started all this is long gone, or long ago bound itself into you. My guess is that whatever is making you immortal is what Mori wants or wanted. Did you know she's almost two hundred years old? Has survived at least two assassination attempts in the last twenty years."

Conner laid his head back to stare up at the domed ceiling of the pod. What ConRad had told him swirled in his head. Arguments with his parents and Emily joined in the chaos that his mind became for a time. A dark-skinned woman in her late twenties coalesced out of his mental turmoil. Her dark brown, almost black, hair fell in ringlets to frame her tall face, which always seemed to have a smile on it. Looking up at her as he knelt on the stone paving, the sun set on the horizon beyond. The bullet, which passed through her head, struck the ring he held up to her, and got imbedded between two ribs of his back after ripping a massive hole in his chest.

"Do you remember Shima Oboro?" Conner spoke the woman's name, possibly for the first time in the ten years since her murder. "Do you know how she died?"

"No." ConRad said, a hand reaching out to wipe the tears falling down Conner's cheeks, though only a tingling occurred where he touched. "I only wanted to remember how hard you fell in love with her inner and outer beauty."

"Shot from behind with a high-powered bullet," Conner said with a trembling voice. "Just as I knelt to ask her to marry me. I may still have the ring and bullet imbedded in my back, for all I know. The sight of her head exploding, a bright flash in the sky from a speck of darkness, still occasionally haunts my dreams a decade later. She was why I was willing to return to that little backwater part of Venus. That and Magnus teased me about jumping between what few ancient computer systems exist out there. For the fun of it now, he said. You are so right when you describe her as beautiful inside as outside. When I decided I wanted to spend my life with her, every aspect of my life seemed to have happened just to prepare me for a life with her and the kids we'd have. She loved Magnus, thought he was a great young man who would make a wonderful big brother. I'm convinced Mori somehow was the one who pulled the trigger on that gun. She's somehow responsible for killing the woman I loved, but there's no way for me to prove it."

"There's also no way to prove you're immortal," ConRad whispered. "No medical records that I nor Venus can find make any claim to that effect. What wounds you suffered while in Fleet are all listed as minor, you're rarely ill, and the quiet life you've lived since leaving Fleet has allowed you to stay relatively healthy and uninjured. So, outside of the horrors the Hero of Horus, as some in the System call you, dealt with, the only time you seem to die and come back to life is when Mori tries to kill you."

"Don't ever leave me in a room alone with that woman,"

Conner said, snarling with sudden anger.

"Ripping her throat out, cutting her heart out, and chopping her head off her body should actually kill her," ConRad said with a smile. "That was what you were going to say you'd do, wasn't it?"

"As a start," Conner said, his anger collapsing at the sight of the Earth guardian's smile. "I'm that predictable?"

"We're ex-lovers, Conner," ConRad said with a wink. "You aren't predictable. Rather, there are certain aspects of you which are a known constant."

"Someone else recently called me constant as well." Conner shook his head smiling. "I still feel offended. And don't you dare call me an ex-lover, old man. We never got that far."

ConRad laughed. Loud and booming.

The sound of the man's belly laugh brought a bit of cheer to Conner's dour mood. Smiling, Conner still couldn't get the fact he might actually be immortal out of his head.

"There's some weird things which might lend credence to these aliens, and me being immortal, though," Conner said, again running his hands through his hair. "Magnus spoke of fighting what he called aliens infiltrating his lockdown during the Battle of Horus. And there was a hold on one of those cargo ships which Barley's sensors said had a non-Earth standard environment in it and non-terrestrial life signs. Add to that the non-human encryption Betty and Magnus cracked. Just what did my true fathers find out there in the universe?"

"And what did they bring home which Mori wanted for herself?" Conrad gave Conner a pointed look. "That may be the crux of why she hates you so much."

"Because I got the immortality, and she didn't?" Conner hesitated to believe everything he'd been through stemmed from one woman's jealousy or greed.

"You have a power which could be used to rule the universe, Conner." Sadness filled ConRad's voice. "Immortality without fear of death. Not even us artificials have that guarantee, my dear friend. Makes me wonder if you'll die with the universe. Or maybe you'll outlive even existence as we understand it."

"I could end everything now and find out, if you want?" Conner gazed down at the floor, the movement of the lift pod a gentle vibration against his back and hands, which pressed against the pod's wall. "After Shima's death, I took that job with Danlen Tech. Nothing felt real or worth staying around for. Mori seemed unreachable by me, so I did some research and figured out how to cause the universe to collapse in on itself. Simple really, ConRad. Nothing would be left of this or any other dimension. Possibly no other universes either. Nigel found out about Shima and how she died. He put the bug in my head to create Betty, though I didn't know she'd become my daughter at the time. Whatever else Nigel may be, he and Magnus are the reasons I never followed through on that desire. A desire which still comes up within me. I used to be able to just tap my sleeve and have Magnus call me abusive and stinky, which always reminded me of the reason why I don't want to end everything."

"Because you had him to raise," ConRad said with a knowing nod.

"No," Conner looked up at ConRad with a sad smile. "Because I'd be just like Mori if I did destroy everything, and I refuse to become like her. She's hatred and greed and jealousy personified. At least for me."

"So…" ConRad let the word drag on for a moment, a smile growing slowly across his worried face. "What you mean to tell me is that you plan on being the Guardian of All Creation, or GUAC for short?"

Conner stared at the artificial nonplussed for a moment, not sure what the heck he'd just heard. Then, a memory of himself being buried deep in one of ConRad's giant cores back in his FCOPS days came back to him. Having to listen to this ancient artificial drone on and on about the joys and wonders of some dish that just wasn't eatable anymore since the original fruit or vegetable, or what the heck ever the plant was, no longer existed.

"If you paint me green and call me your little dip, you festering pile of dog shit," Conner said trying to snarl but unable to keep a serious face.

"I'm the corn chip you know you want, my little Guacamole." ConRad burst out laughing.

"You're definitely corny, old man," Conner chuckled even as he stepped through ConRad to reach the lift's doors. "Let me off this damn thing."

ConRad moved to hug Conner from behind, though it translated into a soft tingling for Conner. In a low voice, the artificial spoke. "Life is worth letting it exist, Conner. Whether you grow old and die in a handful decades, or you outlive even the Sun and Earth both, there will always be someone who thinks they know what's best and what they want will be best for everyone. I just want you to stay the unassuming, loving, and protective father figure everyone wishes they had in their lives. Magnus and I didn't hit it off like he and Barley did, but I feel fairly confident your little boy will be happy if that's how you spend the rest of your life."

"Fathering everyone to death?" Conner smiled at the idea of his little boy's little boy hanging onto his arm, calling him cute, annoying names, and yet still trying to take care him like Magnus always seemed to do. "If that's what's left for me, then I can't exactly say that's an unfulfilling idea. Still, what's that phrase Barley's always using when he's an old cripple? Get off my lawn? Hmm, well, maybe I'll not age past what I am now. This is a good 'father forever' sort of age."

"Dear stars, I've created a monster," ConRad pulled his arms off Conner, giving Conner's head a playful shove. "The tech team has finished their meal break, so I better return my focus to them. Go back to your quarters and get some rest. We can talk again later."

The pod stopped, the level and quadrant displayed being closest to the captain's quarters. Conner turned to face the artificial, giving him a nod just as the lift pod doors opened.

CHAPTER 21

"I'm awake!" Conner sat up, not fully aware of where he was or who had called him. "I'm…awake?"

Yawning, Conner looked around his bedroom in the captain's quarters. The lights brightened slowly, allowing him to catch a glimpse of the stars beyond the narrow windows. No one was present in his room, yet he could hear wailing. Listening, he finally recognized the sound as a baby crying. Faint at first, the upset baby's sobbing grew louder, as though coming from the main room of his quarters.

Throwing the bedsheet off himself, Conner wondered when he had stripped off his uniform. Grabbing the shirt portion of his uniform, but remaining in his underwear, he walked to his bedroom's open doorway. What he saw made him stop dead in his tracks.

"It's okay, my little quantum byte," Maggie whispered while pacing in a circle. She wore a pale blue bathrobe over an extra-long t-shirt. Held in her arms was a blanket-wrapped baby crying its lungs out. "Mommy's here. You aren't all alone. Not yet at least. Magnus and grandpa and Aunt Betty will all return soon. You'll see. Grandpa's stinky shirts and his droning muttering as he works out whatever problem is vexing him will let us both get to sleep calm and worry free once again."

Conner watched the pair fade away, the baby's crying lingering for a long moment. A soft whimper to his left pulled his head around to find Betty standing in the open door to the corridor. Tears poured down her face as she too stared at the spot Maggie had last been.

"Betty." Conner rushed over to his daughter, pulling her into his arms.

"Why? Why did they have to die? Their baby is all alone now." Betty wailed into Conner's embrace.

"The baby will have us and our memories of Magnus and Maggie," Conner said with his own tears staining his cheeks. He wondered what exactly he'd seen. "Barley! How long before we reach Jupiter and the *Socrates*?"

"About forty minutes, Conner," Barley said as he flashed into view. "We just passed through the…what is that, um, smell?"

Conner quickly related what he and Betty had seen. As he spoke, both he and Betty regained some control of their emotions. Barley walked from one end of the room to the other before doing the same in both bedrooms. When he emerged from Conner's bedroom, Barley shook his head in confusion. He tossed the rest of Conner's uniform to him.

"I'm not sure what I'm sensing," Barley said scratching his head. "Sam, Arlene, and their tech team helpers have been updating my sensor array with their new parameters' algorithm. Maybe you saw a reflection of something in *Socrates'* systems? Magnus did say he'd left a child routine behind to care for the baby."

"Why Maggie and the baby specifically, and here in my quarters?" Conner pulled on the rest of his uniform.

"We're talking about quantum entanglement and randomness, Conner," Barley said with a shrug of his shoulders. "The range of the dimensional spectrums I am now able to look at and try to make sense of has increased by quite a lot. Maybe you had a dream which called out to Maggie and the baby specifically. Or the baby is looking for his grandfather and the rest of his mom. I don't know. We may never know."

"I was going to try and sleep for a bit," Betty said, standing partly behind Conner looking about nervously, "but not if Maggie is haunting us."

"The baby isn't dead, Betty," Barley said. "And if you want proof of that, contact Socrates and have him check on the baby."

"I will." Betty said walking over to the table on the far side of the room. Pressing a hand to surface, she said, "*Infinity* to *Socrates' Odyssey*. Socrates, this is Betty Conner. I need a baby status, please."

"Wailing throughout the city irritating every last one of the hundreds of millions of people who call me home." Socrates appeared across the table from Betty looking haggard. "I've no idea how it got ahold of my comm system, but that child is going to cause a rebellion if you and your father don't get here soon."

Conner walked over to stand beside Betty. "We just had a visit here by the baby and Maggie. We were worried it was a ghost come to haunt us."

"Oh god no," Socrates groaned. "He found the external comms as well? So sorry. Just hurry home. Please. Your bloodline is too freaking smart for everyone's well-being."

"Can you access a memory of me making notes during my development of Betty's systems?" Conner said, thinking of what Maggie had said. "Replay them in my room so it sounds like I'm there? Not sure if there's anything there with my smell on it, though."

"I'm getting desperate here, Conner," Socrates said looking away. "Hurry back while I try your idea. Complaints are pouring in from all over the city."

"Captain to the bridge. I repeat, Captain to the bridge," Zoeller said over the intercom, slight panic in her voice.

"Got to go, Socrates," Conner said glancing at Barley's angry grimace at Zoeller's incorrect word usage. "We'll be there in less than an hour, I'm told."

"Great news. See you soon," Socrates said before severing the connection.

Once Socrates vanished, Conner turned to Barley. "Status update. Connect me with the bridge so I can correct her word usage loudly if Ezra hasn't already."

"Multiple cloaked vessels are approaching from the direction of Ceres on an intercept course," Barley said as Conner sat to put on his boots, which sat by the sofa. "The exact number is hard to determine due to my sensors ongoing upgrade. Oh, and like uncle like nephew."

"How long until they're in weapons range?" Conner smirked at Barley's comment while sealing his boots and pants together by pressing the materials against each other.

"Fifteen minutes or less by our initial estimates, Captain," Ezra said before his image appeared standing nearby. "And we'll be about twenty from final approach to *Socrates* at that point. Do we accelerate and let the cities drive them away or do we slow and take them on before reaching Jovian space?"

"Socrates has a cranky baby who has figured out how to tap into the comm systems and is currently crying throughout the city wanting his mother and grandpa home," Barley said with a bemused smile. "Slowing down may result in a mass lynching of us when we finally limp to a mooring."

"Increase speed, but such that we don't risk the lieutenant's baby any more than necessary," Conner said, with thoughts racing through possible scenarios. "Sound battle stations and keep shields at full. Notify both Jovian Command and Inner System Command of our situation. Provide tactical from our sensors, but don't elaborate how we have that tactical. Then inform *Socrates* of our possible delay."

"And if the baby doesn't like the delay?" Ezra smiled with a twinkle in the man's eyes.

"Pray that an irritated, hungry, and sleep-deprived baby artificial who can take command of a station's internal and external comm systems doesn't figure out he has access to a city's defense systems." Conner stood up and gave the black man a hard look. "Socrates has already bemoaned my bloodline once. Let's not have the entire system glaring down on me."

"Like father like son," Ezra said laughing.

"Which bucket of crazy are you referring to, Captain?" Barley laughed as Ezra vanished from sight.

"No respect." Conner shook his head as he left his quarters. "Betty, round up your cousins and Sam before heading to the safe zone."

"Before you go, Betty," Barley said quickly while stopping them both. "The doctor wants you over in medical. Apparently, the lieutenant is hyper-stressed about Magnus's death which is causing the medical staff to worry about the stress's impact on her pregnancy. Could you and your cousins try to help calm her down? Or just distract her. Maybe it'll help both the mother and the baby."

"Will do," Betty said with a nod before leaving.

"Captain," Barley shifted his focus to Conner, "the doctor has extracted memories and says you need to see them immediately. My thought is that you also could talk to the lieutenant and assure her she is not responsible, without telling her who really is responsible. Once Betty, Arlene, and Ernie are there, you can slip away to watch the memories. Maybe she and Betty can bond. I think Betty could use a friend and the lieutenant needs reassurance you and your family don't hate or blame her. I really don't want her to lose that baby. Call me superstitious, but I want her and that baby to be strong enough she can sit up in a chair and leave this ship when we reach *Socrates*."

"Sure, Barley," Conner said, hugging Barley even as something told him the memories from the dead recovered from that cloaked ship back at Venus were going to make him angry. "Maybe her baby and our grandson can become friends."

~ * ~

Conner stepped out of the booth, his hands shaking from the memories he'd just experienced. Even without the emotions the dead had experienced at the time, Conner felt disgusted and furious all at once. Then there were the people present who were obviously not Fleet, but actual government officials. Everything he saw pointed to a major power grab coming, and who exactly was in charge was not clear. Mori definitely was up there, but possibly not at the top.

"You do recognize a number of the people in that memory, Captain?" Doctor Raui sat before a monitoring station looking pale despite his dark brown skin. "I can't even begin to believe what they did to that creature, whatever it was."

"Isolate the creature's speech and get it to my daughter for translation," Conner said while leaning on the counter beside the doctor. "We need to know where that facility is, doctor. Coordinates, star system, everything you can."

"Already done," Doctor Raui said, holding up a blue data crystal. "I'm from Humana Four, Captain. Our oceans are protected because nine hundred years ago, we got a rude awakening about what lived in them. An intelligent cephalopod race lives in those oceans and allows humans to live on their planet within very strict guidelines. They are non-spacefaring and fairly isolationist, but more advanced than us. Enough so that when factions tried to eradicate them, those groups and the cities they operated out of just vanished. Not a soul or building remained. Since then, the Humana Four planetary guardian has fiercely protected the oceans and the life it contains. Whatever race those creatures in these memories come from, they are more advanced than us and will not like what those idiots have done."

"They've stolen technology and possibly started a war we can't win," Conner said softly, lifting his head to stare at the doctor. "Bundle everything up for transfer to Socrates and the planetary guardians. Then make a list of what you need to get while the ship gets repaired. When the *Infinity* is ready, I plan on paying those bastards a visit."

"Be sure to knock on their door hard, Captain," Doctor Raui said with just as hard a tone as Conner. "What those bastards are doing to those beings offends me to my very core as a Humanan."

"I don't need to tell you that your extracting and recording must be kept completely secret," Conner straightened up and took the data crystal. He gazed at it, wondering if these people were also responsible for the deaths of his family, from his fathers down to Magnus.

"I hate extracting memories, Captain," Raui said standing up. "However, given the atrocities these people have committed, and likely are continuing to commit, I will do what is necessary to bring them to justice. Even if I have to pull the trigger of that justice."

"You focus on saving the lieutenant and her baby," Conner said walking over to the door out of the room. He stopped when it opened so Betty, Arlene, and Ernie could be seen laughing with the lieutenant in question. "Let me worry about how big the hammer will be that drops on their heads."

Conner left the doctor and the medical facility behind. He said nothing to Betty or the kids, wanting to be alone for a moment. He needed to get to the bridge and his office there as quickly as possible. As he approached the nearest lift pod, Barley flashed into existence beside him.

"So?" Barley said when they were alone in a pod. "What has the doctor found?"

Conner clenched his fist holding the data crystal. "War crimes." Snarling out the words, Conner relived that ride in a pod very much like this one which took him to the bridge and his one and only time as captain of a Fleet warship. "Loosen the locks on your cannon batteries, old man. I plan on cleaning out the scum in the Sol-Humana Confederation."

"What exactly did you see, Conner?" Barley stopped the pod, moving so they stood face-to-face. "Give me something more than vagueness."

"The dark matter cloaking of their ships is stolen alien technology." Conner growled out the words, the fury at what he'd seen rising from a simmer to low boil. "Stolen by extracting it with torture and murder of the aliens themselves. Not just Fleet members are involved, Barley. Government officials, some of whom are elected to office. What I saw in memories from multiple people all points to a coup to overthrow the elected Sol-Humana government and put one or a few people in control to rule as dictators or monarchs."

"Did you see anyone in Fleet whom we've dealt with in the last few days?" Barley paled as his eyes widened in shock. "Is—"

"One of the admirals in the Admiralty besides Mori," Conner spun away to face the pod doors. "Not Nokata nor Stephens. Get us to the bridge, Barley. Also, get Betty at a station down in medical. I want her monitoring communications. We need to hard dock with *Socrates* as soon as possible."

"We need to find a way to tell Nigel and Vickie," Barley said. The pod sped up, based on the soft chimes that denoted possible stops or levels. "Fleet encryption will be compromised."

"Betty!" Conner called out.

"Here, Captain," Betty said without appearing.

"Break out Magnus's lap encryption," Conner said as memories flickered to the surface of Magnus sending him information to decode on the fly. "I have information I need to send to Admiral Nokata, and he'll know the key phrases for that system."

"Aw, how sweet, daddy," Betty said affectionately.

"I want you to use those encryption methods for the time being." Conner said as the pod came to a stop. "Fleet encryption must be assumed to be compromised. Understand?"

"Perfectly." Betty said, all business. "Also, is Barley with you?"

"Yes. We're in a pod on our way to the bridge," Conner said with a glance at Barley.

"I'm decrypting the message Barley gave me which he said came in on a subchannel used by ships' artificials to talk to each other," Betty said as a scroll of text appeared on the door at Conner's eye level. "It's making me sick to my imaginary stomach, Captain."

Conner scanned the message, which he quickly saw was a list of ships and the artificials controlling them. Barley audibly growled as he also received the information. He recognized two ships which he knew had been scrapped, at least officially, years ago. Clenching his eyes shut, Conner took a deep breath and released it slowly. His heart still raced, but his mind cleared a little.

"Betty, encrypt this in Magnus's lap one zero code, then layer it in three Fleet high security encryptions," Conner said while his mind raced with one scenario after another involving an extended civil war and tens upon tens of millions of dead. "Then send it to Fleet Admiral Nokata on *Socrates*, his eyes only."

"Understood, Captain," Betty said. "I'll send it in a few moments. Betty out."

"Conner out." Conner looked at Barley as the scrolling text faded away.

"Can we just transport their cores out and leave the ships floating in space?" Barley shook with rage as his appearance changed to a bare-chested wild man with a giant axe. "Or can I go chop heads off and rip hearts out of their chests with my bare hands?"

"We aren't starting the fight, old man," Conner said softly, "but we damn sure will end it with them lying dead."

CHAPTER 22

"So, has everyone reviewed the proposal put before the Admiralty?" Nigel Nokata looked at each of the four other Fleet admirals sitting virtually in his office, who all nodded. The sound of a baby wailing could be heard through his office walls despite the security isolation field in place. "The proposal seems straight forward, the supporting documentation self-explanatory. Any comments or discussion by any of you before voting on whether to reverse the demotion of Conrad Conner and further promote both him and the ship artificial known as Barley?"

"I'm surprised it was you, Min, who put this proposal forward," Vickie said with a slight smile and pointed gaze.

"I've long felt there was an injustice done after that battle," Admiral Stephens said before taking a sip from the mug she held. "Let's put that battle in some context. The carrier group had been set upon in the Valiant system three days before. The Spartans harried all twelve ships until they got to the Horus System, where an all-out attack should have wiped them out to a ship. Even as both sides saw massive numbers of injured, and quite a few casualties, when Conrad Conner took command of Barley and his battle group, he used *Barley of the Hills* to its fullest design intent and more so. A then Lieutenant Commander Conner had spent most of the battle leading up to his rise as captain rewriting interface code on the fly for Barley as one system after another failed or was compromised. From the reports I've read, he even reconfigured Barley's primary cores, while taking enemy fire, to ensure Barley couldn't be forced into lockdown and killed by the Spartans. Let me repeat that. He reconfigured Barley's primary cores, while the Spartans were attacking his men, who were defending Barley's primary cores from Spartans who had boarded the carrier, all so the ship's controlling artificial, Barley, couldn't be destroyed or forced into lockdown. I've talked to a great many techs about just reworking a ship's primary core interface while the ship is docked for a refit and they would refuse, citing it taking too long and being too complicated for a human. Yet, Conrad Conner did it in the middle of a battle? Even getting shot at one point in an arm and having to finish his work one-handed. Genius doesn't even begin to describe the man's intellect. However, he returns with every ship in his carrier group, six of the Spartan's surviving ships in tow or under lockdown, and only a fraction of the casualties one would normally see after such a brutal battle, yet he's hit with a demotion from battle captain back down to lieutenant second-class for what? Having a non-Fleet and underage artificial on board? No. Rather, the supposed crime was merely an accusation by another officer who hadn't been on the ship for over a year and later was found to have lied about the whole thing. It smacks of a personal vendetta against Conrad Conner. That alone, is why I put this proposal before us."

"How does this further our mission of guiding Fleet, though?" A fourth admiral said, who tapped the desk she sat behind. "I'm not understanding why someone who didn't renew their service contract should be given special treatment?"

The door to Nigel's office slid open to reveal Nigel's aide standing there. Without waiting for permission to enter or to be asked for the reason he was breaking the security barrier, Colonel Horatio walked into the office to stand beside Nigel's desk. The sound of a wailing baby followed the colonel into the room, only to fade to a whisper after the door slid shut.

"My apologies for the intrusion, Admirals." Horatio tapped the top of Nigel's desk before snapping his fingers. "This just came in from the *CSS Infinity*. You'll all want to see this."

Rising up from the desktop was a graphical representation of the Jupiter system beside the colonel, a blue dot near the middle of the desk was labeled *Infinity*, and at the far end of the desk lay the Asteroid belt with Ceres noted. As they watched, a clump of red dots appeared from near Ceres headed toward the *Infinity*. The red dots were labeled as "3 to 5 cloaked ships."

"Ceres is a protected stellar body designated as a Cultural Heritage Body," Nigel said, leaning forward to examine the tactical closely. "Exploitation and use by anyone, be they Fleet, government, or private person or company, is expressly forbidden."

"I'm more worried about the possible five against one ratio," Vickie said staring at the graphic. "Was a time to intercept given, colonel?"

"Fifteen to twenty minutes, with *Infinity* increasing speed."

Horatio said motioning his hand to get the blue dot to expand into a visual of *Infinity*. "They cited their acceleration was a slow burn as they sought to not risk further harm to an injured lieutenant's unborn child."

"What is so special about this lieutenant and her baby that five of these ships are giving chase?" The fifth admiral looked from the graphic to the others. "Or is it Conner and his family they're after? What has this man done to draw such deadly attention?"

"Our focus needs to be where these ships came from and who is giving them orders," Min Stephens said, motioning *Infinity* away so the overall graphic returned.

"There is also the fact four city-stations here in Jovian space and the nearly billion souls who call them home are potentially at risk," Nigel said just as a baby's wailing suddenly erupted from the speakers overhead. "Sweet stars of Andromeda, he's broken our security barrier again. Horatio, can you try and reach Socrates again?"

"Whoever is allowing a child artificial to cause such havoc needs to be fired and imprisoned." The fourth admiral said, scowling at the sound.

"The infant artificial is hijacking Socrates's internal comm systems, Admirals," Horatio said sharply. "While you debate how many ships to send in aide to *Infinity* against these murderers, I'll go see if I can—"

A flash of light cut the colonel off as Socrates appeared standing beside the man. "No need. I just talked to the baby's grandparents after it apparently hijacked my external comms to broadcast himself and an image of Maggie into at least the captain's quarters aboard the *Infinity*. Given the security protocols I have in place, I feel the need to warn the Admiralty that this child is a true son of the Conner, or rather, Underwood bloodline. In other words, Alexander Octavius Traxis is obstinate, pigheaded, and way too smart for his own good. Get Captain Conner here safe and sound or you run the risk of an infant breaking through security encryptions no other natural nor artificial has been able to break since the first Human-Hive war broke out."

Nigel stared at Socrates, a sinking feeling making his pulse speed up. "What exactly are you saying, Socrates?"

"An upset baby is throwing a tantrum with a bullhorn at the moment," Socrates said looking at every one of the admirals. "He could turn that bullhorn into my defensive armaments at any moment, or any of Fleet's ships. My suggestion is you scramble every ship you have docked to this city's moorings and put them on a course to rendezvous with and give aide to the *Infinity* before that baby decrypts not just my security encryptions, but also Vickie's and every ship artificial's anti-intrusion encryptions. Now, if you'll excuse me, I'm going to see if I can calm the baby with some recordings of Conner muttering to himself while he works."

"I think my proposal has just been tabled," Min said chuckling, "and by a baby, no less."

"Hold on," the fourth admiral said gazing at the graphic of the cloaked ships chasing *Infinity*. "I move the proposal to rescind the demotion of Conrad Conner and to make permanent his field promotion to captain be accepted."

"Seconded," Vickie said quickly.

"All in favor?" Nigel looked at the rest of the admirals.

"Aye," the admirals all said in unison.

"The motion is approved," Nigel said with a thump of a finger to his desktop. "The next item up is, well, essentially grown men and women running away from a baby. My grandmother will haunt me for that, I'm sure."

"Don't feel bad, Nigel," Vickie said giggling. "Considering I first met that baby's mother inside the Academy library's high security restricted section muttering about finding nothing new or interesting, I think keeping that baby happy will keep humanity safe."

"That's a story I want to hear one of these days, Vickie," Min said smiling while tapping on her own desk so the graphic changed to include the inner system as well. "Nigel, scramble what you have in Jovian space. Inner System will investigate Ceres and the area right around it. We need to find out if there is a secret base we can destroy or capture."

"Keep any action you take between the Admiralty and the various ship captains," Nigel said with a nod to his aide. "We don't know if there are moles who will tip them off."

"Admirals," Vickie stood up from her chair. "The Sol-Humana planetary guardians are connecting with us."

"Which ones?" The fourth admiral jerked her head up.

"All fourteen of them," Vickie said as her expression paled.

CHAPTER 23

"Captain on the deck," Barley shouted as Conner exited the lift pod. Ezra Nokata stood up from the captain's chair. "Tactical on main viewer is current, Captain."

"Any aggressive moves by our shadows, Mr. Nokata?" Conner sat down to find his chair screen had a scenario in motion where five cloaked ships attacked at once. It didn't end well for *Infinity*. "How many confirmed ships do we have intercepting us?"

"Five ships with no aggression yet, Captain," Ezra said from his place to Conner's right. "They are moving into position where they'll be able to attack from all sides. Our enhanced sensors are giving us weapon capabilities and likely engine weak points."

"What about internal components of the ships?" Conner pulled up the sensor feeds on one of the ships. "How large a crew? Primary core locations of their controlling artificials? Things like that?"

"Each ship has a crew of between thirty and forty people," Ezra said without looking away from the various people manning every station on the upper and lower bridge levels. "From what we can determine, there is just one active core for the controlling artificial, though we can identify a second inactive core on each ship. The make-up of the ships are modified frigate-class Fleet ships. We just don't know if the ships have their original artificials or new ones."

"We also don't know if the artificials are there willingly or not," Conner said tapping the arm of his chair as he tried to figure out the best way to keep from having to engage in a fight.

"Sensors are detecting ships leaving Jovian space," Kandra shouted. "All have Fleet signatures, Captains."

"Numbers and headings, Kandra," Ezra said sharply.

"Barley, can you tell via our sensor scans how modified these ships are based on their original specs?" Conner tapped his monitor to pull up the specs of his niece's transporter security protocols. Scanning her code, he couldn't help but smile at how clean, concise, and thorough it appeared to be. Still, he quickly found several places which needed tightening up while other spots required changes to work in conjunction with a military ship's denser shields.

As he made the final adjustments, the actions took him back to the Battle of Horus. He couldn't remember how many of Barley's subsystems he'd had to recode on the fly like this. So many decisions on how to secure Barley from Spartan subversions had to be made with guesswork and personal grudges against Fleet in general at the time.

"There are additional secondary cores for controlling the dark matter cloaking," Barley said with some reluctance. "Also, the engines are new. So are the cannon blisters and torpedo launch systems."

"Life support, shield controls, and navigational systems are all the same, you think?" Conner looked up at Barley with a smile growing on his face, a plan quickly taking shape in his mind. "I mean, they do look like the two frigates we've got attached to our prow at the moment."

Barley jerked his head around to stare open-mouthed at Conner for a moment. "Surely they'll have overwritten the carrier group command codes."

"If the sensors are right and only one of the three primary cores are powered," Conner said tapping on the image of a ship shadowing them, then the controlling artificials have been either killed or lobotomized to the point of being legally dead. What you have could very well be a ploy to get us to grab all the cores, which would allow them to try and subvert you to their control."

"So, what? We try and do the same to them?" Ezra said stepping closer to Conner. "We try that and it could backfire on us."

"We wouldn't be taking control of their primary systems, Ezra," Barley said looking forward again. "It would be their secondary and tertiary systems, as had to be done with Abe during the Battle of Horus when he was nearly killed. Essentially, I took over their weapons and navigational systems while never touching Abe's primary command systems. It's an aspect of the ships in a carrier group working as a unit."

"And if they're expecting you to try that?" Ezra leaned in close to Conner hissing his question.

"The last battle I was in before retiring was a good four years ago, Captain Nokata," Barley said turning to smile at the black man. "During that battle, a traitor gave away Fleet command codes for ship control to the Spartans. When they tried it on me, security features written into my systems at some unknown time in my past activated. The enemy quickly surrendered so an ancient children's show theme song would stop playing at full volume throughout every ship the Spartans controlled."

"I love you," Conner sang softly as the annoyingly catchy tune returned to him. "You love me. We're a happy family."

"You tortured me and Magnus with that tune!" Ezra jumped away from Conner, his voice rising an octave in stark horror.

"If the creator of that show and music wasn't shot out of a torpedo tube into the sun," Conner said laughing, "I'm sure millions of people wanted to do just that to him three millennia ago."

"Remind me to not get you mad at me," Kashi said from her station chuckling.

"My luck is such that my grandson will probably love it," Conner said sighing and shaking his head. "My plan is to transport the weapon control cores off each of the ships around us. Then, while they're scrambling to block our transporter, Barley takes control of their navigational system and locks each ship into a collision course with Jupiter himself. I think the big guy can handle five starships plunging into him."

"And if I can't take control of the ships via the carrier command codes?" Barley gave Conner a hard look.

"If we grab their torpedoes and can turn off their shields," Ezra said crossing his arms while smiling, "your cannon blisters can take out their engines."

"I have a suggestion, Captain," Sam said walking from the open lift pod doors. "However, it needs to be between you and me in your office. Zeta level security, Barley."

"Is this really the time for secrets, father?" Barley glared at the man who created him.

"Considering the stories I've heard of what Conner did to you during the Battle of Horus," Sam said, raising his eyebrows and giving Barley a knowing smile.

"Into the office with you two," Barley said with shooing motions of his hands. "We don't want to risk lip readers out here, do we? Up and at 'em, you old coots."

A number of people, including Conner, laughed as he and Sam let themselves be herded into the captain's office. Once in the office, Conner sat on the edge of his desk and motioned Sam to a chair. When a purple 'Z' appeared on his desk, Conner smiled at Sam.

"The Z is now lit, Sam," Conner said while resting his hands on the edge of his desk. "Give me your super-secret suggestion."

"I kill the artificials on the other ships," Sam said without looking up at Conner.

"Excuse me?" Conner stood, shocked at what he'd heard.

"Betty told me about the message sent by one of the ships," Sam said with heavy sigh. "What none of the artificials I've created, which there are quite a few, know is that I buried a kill switch into their matrix. It's why I wanted to talk to you in private about this."

"Why would you do such a thing, Sam?" Conner moved to sit in the chair beside Sam. "I know you've lived a long life, but these are your children."

"Children created for the sole purpose of killing other people's children." Sam wrung his hands together in his lap, never lifting his eyes. "You have to understand, Conner, I lived through the most horrible years of the Hive-Human wars. When the Hive overran this system, killing every human they could find, I stayed and protected the stations, tricked the Hive ships into thinking ships full of humans were actually artificials, coming up with ways to kill artificials just so not all of the humans in the system would die. When they found me out, they forced me and Ares to watch them bombard Mars from orbit. In a few hours, they destroyed two millennia of terraforming that planet. That's why I put a kill code in any artificial I create whose purpose is to fight and kill other beings, be they naturals or artificials."

Conner reached out and gripped Sam's nearest knee. He had no words which could counter what he'd heard. After living through several battles himself, he could barely begin to grasp the horrors of what this man, this being, had lived through in his nearly two millennia of life. "I can't begin to claim to fully understand or comprehend what you've had to live through, Sam. To be honest, I think the crews of those ships following us have already killed or lobotomized their artificials."

"What? How do you know?" Sam jerked his head up, shock and horror filling the face.

Conner told Sam what had been found via the sensors, his theory on why only one of the normally three cores were powered, and his idea on how to hopefully stop a fight before one started. Sam sat there listening silently. When Conner finished, Sam didn't immediately respond. Conner considered standing so as to pace and voice out his own concerns on his plan, when the door to the bridge opened.

"Admiral Nokata wants to talk to you, Captain," Barley said from the doorway, which had a purplish haze filling the opening. "Press the 'Z' to lower the security field and accept his connection request. The security field will remain in place until then."

The door closed, leaving Conner unsure if Barley told the truth or not. Sam, though, leaned over to rest his head on Conner's shoulder. Sam spoke in a whisper. "I've only had to use the kill code twice in the roughly one thousand years since the first time I put it in place. The last time was at Dunns Four. By the time I got there, he was already in the planet's atmosphere. I still used it, hoping some of those on board could still save themselves. Everyone still died."

Conner wrapped his arm around Sam's shoulders. "We try and protect our babies with everything we have, but it's not always enough, Sam."

"Still hurts all these centuries later, Conner," Sam whispered. "I've not created an artificial since the last of the star carriers left my care. The desire is just not there anymore."

The desk beeped, reminding Conner of Nigel wanting to talk to him. Hating having to move, Conner turned his head to kiss the top of Sam's head. "Let's try something where you don't have to use your method of last resort. Okay?"

"Okay." Sam tilted his head back so they could kiss each other. When they just got into the kissing, the desk beeped again. Sam chuckled as he pulled his head off Conner's shoulder. "You better talk to the Admiral."

"He likely just wants to tell us about the Fleet ships headed our way." Conner stood up and moved to sit behind his desk. Tapping the 'Z', a soft beep preceded the appearance of the Fleet logo and the vanishing of the 'Z' from the desktop.

"Captain Conner," Nigel said with a smile from behind his desk while Vickie sat on the front edge of the same desk. "Ah, and I see Mr. Youngs is with you. Hope Vickie and I aren't interrupting anything important."

"Just bouncing ideas off each other's head, Admiral." Sam nodded, but his expression never showed even a hint of a smile. "If you'll excuse me, I'll—"

"Stay and be a witness to what we're going to say, Sam," Vickie said with a tight smile. It gave Conner flashbacks to the dressing downs he got when Vickie would catch Magnus breaking into the Academy library's restricted sections.

"I understand *Socrates' Odyssey* is experiencing some communication issues which makes it sound as though a baby is crying." Conner quirked an eyebrow at the very poorly hidden irritation by both admirals. Yet, he didn't want to openly comment on the ships all around them since this was not showing as a secure or encrypted connection. "Did Socrates get that resolved yet?"

"It comes and goes," Nigel said leaning forward with both hands gripping each other on the desk. "Much like the winds when you live on a habitable planet. I know you have a lot going on there, what with your son's death and the injured still recovering from the battle over Venus, so we'll try to be brief."

"So, let's get right to business," Vickie said while lightly scratching her neck, which drew Conner's eyes to the six admiral pins on her collar. "The Admiralty has started a review of select persons' service records in an effort to find and resolve issues created by the former First Admiral. Your service records were among the first we reviewed."

"In conjunction with discoveries concerning previous accusations made against you in the past," Nigel said with a half-smile on his face, "the demotion you received after returning from the Battle of Horus has been rescinded. Furthermore, your battle promotion to Captain has been reinstated and made permanent."

"Retroactively back to the date you had been demoted from lieutenant commander to lieutenant second class," Vickie said, throwing her hands out before her. "Surprise!"

"I…am honored, Admirals." Conner struggled not to spout derision at such an obviously political move at his expense. "A great wrong has truly been righted, if more than a decade late."

"With the change in rank being made retroactive," Nigel said while tapping his desktop, "comes a correction in the pay you would have received while still in Fleet and a change to your post service payout. While not a huge amount, still money that would have helped you in those first years after leaving Fleet."

Conner stared at the numbers which appeared on his desktop. Given all the lean years of begging for a free meal from Delilah or Nigel, having to say no to things Magnus had wanted, Conner found only anger inside himself. A hand gripped his shoulder as the faint sounds of a baby crying could be heard in the background.

"On behalf of my family, I thank the Fleet Admiralty for correcting the grave wrong committed to me and my son." Conner forced the words out in a mostly neutral tone.

"We aren't finished yet, Conner," Nigel said, drawing Conner's gaze back up to the admirals.

"Given the emergency contract made with The C5 Group," Vickie said, all humor gone from her face, "it has been decided that Barley and his body, now called *Infinity*, will be loaned additional ships effective immediately for the sole purpose of finding and eradicating all cloaked ships and any bases from which those ships may be operating. Your sensors should be able to pick up the ships by now. They were ordered to rendezvous with *Infinity* with all possible haste."

"As such, your rank for the duration of this contract shall be that of Commodore," Nigel said smiling. "The contract payment stipulations will be updated to reflect this new rank, and your authority over Fleet personnel will be the same as though you were still in Fleet service."

"Is that why you both look like you're eating nails?" Conner couldn't help but smile. Something about all of this was irritating the two admirals, and that fact pleased the petty part of himself.

"It's this next part that has us out of sorts, Conner," Vickie said pursing her lips.

"Just as the ships were ordered to head your way," Nigel said while resting his elbows on his desk and steepling his fingers before himself, "the planetary guardians paid the Admiralty a little visit."

"When you say guardians?" Conner's own smile vanished with the flip-flopping of his stomach.

"All fourteen guardians of the Sol-Humana Confederation appeared at once," Nigel paled slightly as he spoke the words. "While we can't say what all was discussed, the parts involving you can be mentioned. In short, the Admiralty is officially dissolved as it currently exists. There will never be another First Admiral. What will be called 'The Admiralty' will be composed of four Fleet-ranked admirals, with at least one being an artificial, and the fifth member being a civilian who has served in Fleet long enough to have reached at least the rank of captain and commanded a ship in at least one major battle, or for at least two years during times of peace."

"No," Conner said, seeing where this was going as fast as a comet streaking across a planet's sky.

"Yes," Vickie countered with a cruel smile. "You were proposed as the first civilian to serve on the reorganized Admiralty. Congratulations."

"Do I need to ask which planetary guardian I get to go punch in the gut for this stunt?" Conner snarled out as his anger boiled over.

"Huma Four's Descillian reportedly nominated you," Nigel said with a wry smile. "Aphrodite seconded the nomination while ConRad abstained, citing health concerns. When pressed, he said his health concerns involved you trying to beat him to a pulp over this idea. So, I think the planetary guardians are, what's the word I'm looking for?"

"Trolling ConRad is what I think they're doing," Sam said chuckling. "What do you think, Barley?"

"I think my job has just gone into the hazard pay area, Admirals," Barley said flashing into appearance. "Conner is going to be very pissy because of this. Can I get extra hazard pay because of you all making him hate the universe more now?"

"I think Socrates will have something to say about deserving hazard pay," Vickie said laughing. "Another in the Conner bloodline has shown an amazing talent for breaking supposedly unbreakable encryptions."

Conner's anger over what he was being pressured into doing broke apart at Vickie's words. Smiling, he nodded as he spoke. "Magnus apparently passed that annoyance on to his son. I'm going to have my hands full with little Alex."

"Well then," Sam said clapping Barley on the back as he headed toward the door, "you two had better get your buckets of crazy moving faster. We don't need that baby turning toward one of the planets to complain about his missing parents and grandparents."

Conner laughed hard and loud. The idea of a baby cracking

ConRad's control over the Earth's tech to broadcast himself wailing in anger to every home and business on the planet just sounded hilarious. Having a harried and exhausted ConRad appear before him, cursing and threatening his life, both amused and terrified him to no end.

"There will be a brief pause in the search, Admirals," Conner said as he forced some control over his laughing, "so I can calm down my grandson and assure him he won't be left alone again."

"Our cute grandson, you two," Vickie said smiling warmly. "I'm definitely going to be a doting grandma to that little boy."

Conner laughed. "Agreed, Vickie."

"One more thing, you three," Nigel said, which stopped Sam at the office door. "I received your message requesting guidance on Fleet personnel possibly being coerced into aiding those in control of the cloaked ships. The Admiralty and the planetary guardians all agreed the greater good requires a strong hand in dealing with those who are viewed as traitors to the Confederation and enemies of the state. Yes, there may be loyal citizens who die, but we cannot put the great majority of people in the Sol-Humana Confederation at risk to save a possible handful of lives. As a result, Commodore, you are authorized to take whatever actions, including the complete destruction of all enemy ships, you feel are necessary to end this threat as quickly as possible. Is that clear?"

"Perfectly clear, Admirals," Conner said with sharp nod. "Oh, and Nigel?"

"Yes, *Infinity*?" Nigel furrowed his brow at Conner.

"The Admiralty still has some dirty corners that need cleaning before I'll formerly accept the civilian membership appointment," Conner said, thinking about the memories he'd experienced. "I believe a lot of it is stashed away in Centauri Command's closet."

"We'll look into that and get it all cleaned up, Conner," Nigel said with a sharp nod. "Admiralty out."

"*Infinity* out." Conner said before ending the connection.

CHAPTER 24

"What do you mean she's gone?" Nigel slammed his hands down on his desk while glaring at the admiral in charge of operations at Fleet headquarters on Luna. Admiral Min Stephens had pulled him into this connection between her and Luna Central. "How long ago, Nevra?"

"Sometime in the last five or six hours, Nigel," Admiral Nevra said while glancing to her left. "Security cameras and sensor arrays don't show her leaving her room. We suspect transporter tech was used to get her out."

"Or she's had a way to bypass security for years, if not decades," Admiral Stephens said angrily. "Do a full-scale search of Luna Central, Nevra. Mori must be considered a traitor to the Confederation by this act."

"A…a traitor? That means we—" Nevra stared at Nigel and Min in shock.

"Use deadly force against her and anyone giving her aid," Nigel said snarling before slamming his hands down again. "Damn it! Find her! I've got to notify the planetary guardians."

"I've figured out what happened," Vickie said, appearing beside Nevra. "Her security detail ghosted her being taken to her quarters when she was actually taken elsewhere, likely to a shuttle ready to leave Luna. They had this planned just based on how good the ghosting images of her and her security team are."

"Vickie," Stephens said with a hardness in her voice, "I think it's time to clean house."

"Not just here in Sol," Nigel said while pressing the spot on his desktop which summoned Colonel Horatio. "I understand the Centauri System's pretty filthy."

"Chiron is already at work doing some spring cleaning." Vickie said. "I move that Nigel notifies the planetary guardians of this and requests all personal assets for certain people are frozen and or permanently seized. I'll send a preliminary list directly to ConRad shortly via secure connection."

"Seconded," Min said. "Inner System ships have been mobilized and all ship artificials put on notice to identify and isolate traitors. Most readily agreed. A few stated their personal objections but still agreed. A few had somehow heard about Abe but wouldn't say how they knew."

"Ships gossip with each other," Nigel said as Horatio walked into his office. "Barley would come into my office and tell me what he felt were the juiciest bits. Abe and Shin's romance was no secret to any of the ships, so the abuse of both and the murder of Abe was not going to stay a secret. My thought on cleaning house is that we need to be sure of our proof before we take extreme measures. The last thing we need is any of this coming back and slapping us in the face."

"Agreed," the other three said in unison.

"I'll begin the search for Mori," Min said.

"We've got our assignments," Vickie said. "Luna out."

"Outer System Command out." Nigel said.

"Inner System Command out." Min said before the connections ended.

"Trouble, Admiral?" Horatio asked, quirking one of his thin eyebrows.

"Yes, Horatio," Nigel said clenching a fist. "Get me a connection with one or all of the Sol System planetary guardians. Immediately."

"Crap," Horatio muttered before rushing back to his desk.

"Crap doesn't begin to describe this mess." Nigel muttered as he waited.

~ * ~

"Sam, are you able to get the transporter system to lock on anything in those ships?" Conner yelled as the ship rocked from yet another torpedo strike against the shields.

"Three ships have lost something," Sam shouted back, "but I've no idea what. The sensors aren't…wait. Something's changed."

"Sensors have weapons lock on one of the ships, Commodore," Ezra said from the railing between the navigation and weapons stations.

"Full barrage, destroy that ship!" Conner shouted as he looked at Barley, who'd been silent for a time. "Barley? No show tunes for this battle?"

"The shuttle in Bay Three has fallen over, Conner," Barley said turning toward Conner. "I can now hear Magnus whimpering in that bay. He's calling out 'Daddy? It hurts, Daddy.' Am I finally cracking up?"

"Let me hear it," Conner twisted in his chair to better see Barley.

For a moment, the only sound heard on the bridge was Magnus's pain-filled voice whimpering ever so softly just as Barley described. Conner didn't hear an adult Magnus, though. Something about the voice took him back to those first days when he finally got Magnus to come out of hiding and talk to him. His little boy had been just as scared and hurt sounding after running from system to system in that isolated little town on Venus where the tech was a good five hundred years old at the newest.

When another attack rocked the ship, Magnus cried out, "God damn! That hurts, you assholes. What are you doing? Someone help! Where are you, daddy?"

"Ezra, you have the bridge," Conner said standing up. "Barley, ready the Halo Star Weapons System. Pour every bit of your rage and pain at what's happened to Magnus into it."

"Where are you going, Conner?" Ezra rushed over to grab Conner's arm. "We're in the middle of a battle for our lives here. Magnus is dead. That can't be him."

"Ezra, I may be in command of everyone on board this ship, be they civilian or Fleet," Conner said, shaking with both rage and fear as he looked Ezra in the eyes, "but I know the sound of my little boy when I hear it. I don't know how he did it, but he's somehow alive. That boy was jumping systems from day one of his matrix's cohesion and awakening. I should have thought to look everywhere for him, including the shuttle."

"The shuttle's systems were shut off and depowered at the time of Magnus's death, Conner," Barley said, stepping up to both men. "There's no way he…"

Conner looked at Barley as the artificial's voice faded away. Nodding, Conner said, "The blast energy momentarily powered the shuttle's systems, giving Magnus a moment to jump out of his body and into the shuttle's more durable systems. He's been trapped inside a broken and damaged body for days, likely too weak to even try and speak until now. I'm going to go save what's left of my little boy. You two have this battle under control. We all know what our orders from the Admiralty are."

"They fired first, we fire last." Barley said with a sharp nod. "Three tech teams have already volunteered to help you, Commodore. Go rescue our boy."

"We'll smooth things out up here, Commodore." Ezra also nodded sharply, stepping back and turning around. "You heard Commodore Conner! Let's make those traitors regret ever messing with us. Weapons! Lock and load!"

Conner looked back to Barley. Tears filled the artificial's eyes, and the man smiled despite everything going on around them. Nodding to Barley, Conner slipped past him and headed to the lift.

"Zip tube one will get you to the same level as Bay Three faster, Conner," Barley called, drawing Conner's gaze for the moment. "Put on some extra oxygen just in case the fields keeping the bay pressurized fails. Oh, and take a power cable so Magnus has a hard connection to get out of that shuttle. Let's not take any chances this time."

"Sing to him, Pops," Conner said, purposely using Magnus's affection for Barley. "Let your little boy know help is on the way."

Conner went to the three zip tubes at the back of the bridge. He rather hated these things, but Barley was right. It would be the fastest way. As he stepped into the indicated tube, Barley started the countdown for deployment of what he most hated about his body, the separation of his cannon blisters as a separate but unified firing system. Using the shields of other ships in a carrier group, it created a huge web of high-powered laser fire around the carrier. Other ships in the group wouldn't be harmed, but any ships outside of the carrier's group would be badly damaged, if not outright destroyed. It reminded him of how Barley had sung show tunes, which he hated, as revenge for making him tear himself apart.

"Clang clang goes the trolley," a woman's voice sang over the ship's speakers as the tube pulled him down into the bowels of the ship.

As Conner flew through the ship wrapped in a force field bubble, the woman's voice brought back his mother's last words to him. He'd just had a huge fight with her and his dad over Magnus, who'd snuck along with them on the trip. His father had said some hateful things and Magnus had fled sobbing. Conner had been heading out to find Magnus when his mom had stopped him.

"You have to understand, Conrad," his mom had said in a low voice, "we are your parents and are only trying to keep you and your sister safe. Tech is dangerous. It's why we moved to Venus and that little town you hate so much. No matter how old you get or how far away you go from us, you will always be that little four-year-old boy sobbing because you fell and skinned your knee. As a parent, we are always trying to guide you to a healthy and safe life. Now, you go and find your little boy. He may seem like he's your age, but really, he's just a four-year-old who is hurt and scared of so many strange things and attitudes. Go be the daddy he needs right now. We'll always be here for you, one way or another."

Conner landed on the deck of the circular area he'd originally entered the ship on. Charlie stood waiting for him. In the memory of his mom, Conner found he remembered how his mom kept looking back to the windows of their rooms and back to him. For the first time, he truly understood why his parents had been so antagonistic. All of it had been to get him and Emily out of their quarters to someplace safer.

"They really knew," Conner whispered as tears trickled down his cheeks. "I truly was the target of that attack. Damn it."

"Put this on, Conner," Charlie said, moving Conner forward and around. Something got strapped to his back and wrapped around his wrists. Numbed by the memory, Conner did as he was told, only half listening to how there was both power, shielding, and a memory node all built into what he was wearing.

"We're here, Capt...um, Commodore," a woman said as the space suddenly filled with people. It took him a moment, but he recognized the leader of the tech team who'd been working on Abe and Shin's cores when Magnus had been killed. "I think we've come up with how Magnus might have jumped from his body to the shuttle. The explosion gave the shuttle's systems a burst of power, which your quick-thinking son took advantage of."

Conner looked around at the faces. A number of them, he saw, wielded energy rifles. "Why is security here?"

"The shuttle bay is open to space," a lieutenant said, as though that was explanation enough.

"Securing the perimeter and all of that?" Conner said, struggling to not start yelling at people here to help him and Magnus.

"Expect the worse and hope for the best, Commodore," someone else holding a rifle said with a sharp nod.

The ship shook. Sirens echoed in with the woman's voice, almost in time with the ancient musical's tune. It reminded Conner of the battle and how his life seemed to be filled with people dying in order to keep him alive.

"No more," Conner whispered to himself.

Focusing on the equipment he now wore, he recognized a tech teamwork-suit for vacuum situations, just newer than what he'd used back during his Fleet years. Looking at everyone, he gave them a sharp nod. "We'll want a power data cable long enough to stretch to the shuttle. Magnus typically has a fear of wireless transmission, and we don't know the extent of injuries his matrix has suffered. Based on how he sounded to me, I'm expecting memory loss or degradation due to the rough nature of his move from a body to the shuttle's likely already damaged core."

"Scared, confused, and in pain," the tech lieutenant said in summary. "We triage first and get him to safety. Then we work on restoring him once he's stable. You help keep him calm and distracted, Commodore, and let us focus on the extraction."

"If we get enemy infiltrators, my team will lay down suppression fire, Commodore," the rifle carrying lieutenant said with another sharp nod. "No one left behind. Right?"

"Right." Conner said as he turned to find Charlie already wearing his own suit of armor. "Where do you think you're going, Charlie?"

"With you, Commodore." Charlie said before lowering a helmet over his head. "Barley will wail like a little baby if you get hurt. I can't carry two buckets of crazy and the cabling you need, Conner. None of us are that young anymore."

Conner shook his head, actually smiling at the furry man's words. "Let's go, you old hound."

CHAPTER 25

"Let's get this done, folks," Conner said following the tech teams out into the bay. He huffed in frustration when he spotted the shuttle just beyond the barrier hastily built around Shin and Abe's cores. The shuttle had slid off the cores to lay upside down. "Security, do we see any threats headed our way?"

"Affirmative, Commodore," the lieutenant in charge said. "Multiples from both eleven and one o'clock, estimating arrival time now."

"Connection appears clear on this side," the tech lead announced. Two others, wearing backpacks similar to Conner's, rose off the deck.

"Barley? Are you still getting a signal from Magnus?" Conner looked up as he spoke.

"Yes, sir," Barley said slightly distracted. "Frigates are separating from the carrier. Incoming attempts to use Fleet override commands are invalid. Threat level raised to Protocol MC15. Enemy boarders verified. Initiating active defense systems."

Conner listened to something he'd never thought he'd hear again. In the middle of battle, as he rewrote secondary control systems, he altered the override protocols under the impression Fleet override codes had been compromised. He fully expected Fleet to change what he'd done back to Fleet standards.

"Have Sahalie and Pollick been compromised, Barley?" Conner glanced at the gaping hole to space where the bay doors would normally be. "We've spotted incoming enemy down here."

"Do you not remember how you wrote the override protocols, old man?" Barley chuckled into Conner's ears. "Whenever a ship connects to me, either physically or as part of my carrier group, their protocols alter to match mine automatically. The frigates are separating to help in the halo system."

"Commodore, we have a problem," the tech leader said walking up to him. "The exterior panel has been shot with a blaster. We're trying to get the rear hatch open, but the tumbling of the ship seems to have jammed it."

Conner glanced at the opening and the twelve security personnel lined up with easily fifteen feet between them. In the distance, a partial web of cannon fire crisscrossed around the ship. Silhouetted in the light were a dozen or two people fast approaching the opening. Turning back toward the lieutenant, the partially crumpled front end of the shuttle caught his gaze. "Has anyone tried the side door? It looks intact."

"The door is on the vacuum side of the force field." The lieutenant stated the obvious as though it was an answer in and of itself.

"So what?" Conner looked for the door, irritated at the woman's defeatist attitude. "My son is stuck in that ship and I'm getting him out. Barley! Will my suit let me pass through the force field? I need to get inside the shuttle from the other side."

"You? Why the hell do you need to do it?" Barley snapped. "Send the——"

"My son, my risk." Conner hissed as he strode toward Charlie and the tech team gathered at the back of the shuttle. "Besides, we've got a good two dozen enemy boarders headed toward us. The tech team will have to help repel them. Get more security down here stat."

Charlie slammed his booted heel down on the end of the data cable. The housing around the plug cracked. After his third strike, the housing shattered.

"Piece of crap Danlen cables," Charlie said with disgust as he ripped the remains of the housing away to expose a simple converter from an old-style connector attached to the cable and hidden by the housing. "Conner, get up there with this and do your battle magic. I bet a steak dinner that all their blaster shot did was make it easier to get the connection patch off."

"They changed connection types?" Conner grabbed the cable as Charlie yanked off the exposed connection converter. "Well look at this. Danlen hasn't changed at all, have they?"

"Please don't buy their crap, boss," Charlie said grinning.

"We'll get this connected, Commodore," the lieutenant said pulling the cable from his hands even as two other techs rose back to the damaged panel. "You take the portable node and talk your son into either it or through the cable to Barley."

Blaster fire erupted from the oncoming enemy. Conner moved to pull the techs down. As though reading his mind, Charlie stopped him with a hand to his shoulder.

"Let your people do their job, Commodore," Charlie said pulling him back to the door into the shuttle. "Our son needs saving."

Conner raised his brow at Charlie's phrasing but said nothing about it. Charlie had been on the star carrier when Conner was assigned to it. While Conner had aged, he couldn't tell if Charlie had at all.

"Is the door stuck or does it need power?" Conner followed Charlie over to the rear hatch. The access panel required Conner to use his suit's thrusters.

"My gut says it's been restricted to just you, Commodore." Charlie held out a briefcase-sized box with Fleet's Tech Division logo emblazoned on it. "Here's the node. Magnus should be able jump right into it if the projectors are still working inside. Good luck."

"You're not coming with me, fellow dad?" Conner smirked at Charlie, unable to resist teasing him after all.

"Everyone who fought at Horus claims some sort of parentage over Magnus," Charlie said with ears flattened with embarrassment. "I'll stay out here and defend your exit point."

Conner took the case and rose to the access panel. He noticed the panel said, "There is only Zuul." Shaking his head at the memories the movie quote elicited, Conner pressed his hand to the panel while using his stern father voice. "Zuul had better open this door or I'm crossing the streams on your behind."

"Just abusive," appeared on the control panel just before the door slid open. To Conner's surprise, the airlock's inner door already stood open. Despite the presence of air inside the shuttle, Conner flicked his eyes to pull up his suit's controls and activated its force fields as protection against blaster fire and depressurization.

"Magnus?" Conner said, hoping to get a response as he hovered inside the shuttle. "It's daddy. Can you hear me?"

"Yeah, daddy," Magnus said suddenly beside Conner, but upside down. The artificial appeared as a young teenage boy who obviously had been crying. "Being in this shuttle hurts. It's nothing more than scrap now. Core is behind you in the corner. You might need to press your hand against it since only about a quarter of the projectors work now."

Glancing around, Conner spotted the shuttle's core housing

with several blaster scorch marks on it. Still, he could see the blinking indicator lights confirming an artificial occupied the core. Flicking his eyes again, he activated the tech suit's built-in sensors to scan the core. The suit's dummy system automatically analyzed the issues and possible solutions. These suits usually irritated Conner, since he rarely agreed with the suggested courses of action. Even so, it pointed out the lack of power between the core and many of the ship's data transmitters. External communication transmitters worked only intermittently. The external receivers were nonfunctional.

"Your assessment looks to be right, Magnus," Conner said, pressing a palm flat on the core's scarred cover.

"Power is connected, Conner," Charlie yelled through the open door, now behind Conner. "Grab him and get out of there pronto."

Light levels rose inside the shuttle. At the front of the shuttle, the pilot's station started flashing. A massive explosion shook the shuttle, shoving it hard against Conner. Rending metal and hissing filled the inside of the shuttle. Lights flickered and Magnus vanished. Humming spoke of the engines coming online, as though someone prepped the ship for takeoff. Over his comm unit, Conner listened to those outside the shuttle struggling against what sounded like greater forces.

When the shuttle's interior lights stayed on, Conner spotted massive cracking on the front glass. Figures looked at him, locking eyes for a moment before three of them began firing at the shuttle. Twelve-year-old Magnus appeared for a moment; fear etched on the young face.

"Can you hear me, Mags?" Conner used his nickname for the artificial from back when he was in high school. "Jump into my suit's node and I'll get you someplace safer than here. Or take the cable to Barley, the artificial controlling the ship we're on. He's another dad, kiddo."

Magnus vanished. Charlie yelled as flashes of blaster fire from the open hatch competed with the blaster fire eating away at the front window. Suddenly, all power went out in the shuttle.

"Magnus!" Conner yelled, angling his boots so he moved to the open hatch.

"I'm in your suit, daddy," Magnus said. "Get out before my surprise goes off."

Conner didn't waste time in doing exactly what his son urged.

Once through the open doors, Conner reached out for the control panel. Before his hand touched the panel, both the inner and outer doors closed on their own. Another hand grabbed one of his arms. Before he could even turn his head, Conner sailed back away from the shuttle. He struck the barrier around the cores, the blow momentarily knocking the air from his lungs. Suddenly too weak to stand, he slid down onto his butt.

For a moment, he could only watch. Charlie lay on the deck nearby unconscious or dead, a man in a black uniform stood over him with a rifle pointed at him even as the battle raged in the rest the shuttle bay. Dozens of people on both sides fired blaster rifles at each other, their personal shields holding or failing. People lay on the ground with Conner not sure who was dead or just unconscious.

Then he spotted her striding across the bay. Mariko Mori crossed through the force shield keeping the bay pressurized, her wizen and wrinkled face announcing her presence.

"Shields at max!" Magnus screamed in his ears as the shuttle's engines sputtered to life. "Cover your face, dad!"

A roar filled the vast bay as engines, which the shuttle normally sat on, lit up with ion plasma. Curling into a ball with his head between his knees and his arms over his head, Conner could see nothing but a bright blue light and hear nothing but the roar of engines coming up to full throttle. Sharp screeching overpowered the engines' roar as metal ground against metal.

The glow and roar lessened. Conner risked a glance up. Only one engine remained on, causing the shuttle to spin across the bay. Like a giant hand sweeping across the bay, the shuttle prow slammed into enemy boarders, sending them back through the force field to bowl into more incoming boarders. A small burst of light announced the other engine coming to life. Skittering across the deck, the shuttle barely missed Mori. The first engine exploded, taking out a handful of people nearby. The second engine roared louder and brighter, sending the shuttle screaming into the jagged remains of the bay's outer doors. Getting twisted by competing forces, the shuttle pivoted on the door edge. Plasma at full force tore apart people indiscriminately.

The force field flickered for a second. Conner hunkered back down just as the shuttle exploded, the burst of light preceding the sharp jerk of the bay floor by a fraction. Klaxons sounded for a few seconds until the forced field collapsed, which let the air get sucked out. Pulled by the vacuum of space, Conner slid several yards before something struck him.

"Why won't you die?" Mori stood over Conner panting as the air returned.

Conner looked past the old woman to find most of the incoming enemy forces had simply vanished. A mix of people made it hard to determine which side now dominated. Looking up at the old woman, with her face contorted with hate and pain, Conner wondered if she'd actually shoot him point blank with the projectile gun she pointed at him.

"The universe must like me," Conner said, forcing a chuckle despite the pain wracking his body. "Why are you here?"

"With this star carrier under my command, I'll have your precious Barley execute you and everyone related to you. I'll then rip out of your body the secrets to your immortality and make them my own."

"Immortality?" Conner couldn't believe she actually thought he really was immortal. As memories of growing up and a neighbor, an older man of thirty years, who taught Conner all about ancient firearms, flittered through his head, Conner noted the gun's safety was still on. Feeling it somewhat safe to do so, he forced himself to stand. "Have you lost your mind? Humanity discovered immortality millennia ago and rejected it as obscene. Look at the emotional state of every artificial more than a few centuries old to see what happens. Besides, true human immortality is how your children, grandchildren, and their children remember you."

"You have no family left, you imbecile!" Mori screamed, pressing her gun's barrel to his chest. "I've executed your fathers and their parents, your aunt and uncle who raised you, set you up to die repeatedly while you were in Fleet, and even shot you through that insipid whore you were going to marry. Even now, those monstrous twins that whore and you had should be dead along with everyone in that ass-backwards town you grew up in. You should have died, or at least killed yourself, decades ago. Especially after those idiot creations of yours were destroyed."

Conner couldn't believe what he heard. "Idiot creations?" His voice snarled the words as rage turned his vision red. "Did you just call my son and daughter idiot creations?"

"No one denies me what I want, maggot," Mori hissed, lifting the gun to Conner's forehead. "Your fathers denied me their genius and the gift that stupid and gross insect race gave them for saving a few of their worthless lives. Everything and everyone belongs to me! I am your queen, and you will obey me!"

Conner grabbed the wrist holding the gun, twisting hard and fast even as he shoved it away from his head faster than she could react. Slamming his own head hard against her face, Conner grabbed her by the neck with his other hand.

"Idiots don't crack encryptions so strong no one in thousands of years have been able to crack them," Conner snarled as he slowly lifted the woman off the deck by her neck. "Idiots don't break into restricted sections of a library filled with the knowledge of an entire race and read it all in a few weeks and ask what else is there to learn. Idiots don't crack an alien language in a few days with only fragments of speech patterns. An idiot wouldn't quote ancient tomes of obscure arcana without expecting a response."

With Mori dangling from his outstretched arm, Conner roared with every ounce of his anger and hatred, "By the power of Grayskull!"

Crackling filled the air before bolts of electricity shot down from the bay ceiling to strike Mori and every other black suited invader still standing. Once the electrical barrage ended, Conner released Mori to let her fall to the deck. He staggered backwards a few steps panting.

Conner looked down at Mori, whose body twitched. When she slowly pushed herself up onto her arms, Conner wondered if he'd have to actually cut the old hag's head off, as though she were a vampire.

"A little electricity won't be enough to kill me, you waste of flesh," Mori lifted her head while cackling with mad laughter.

Conner noted the gun Mori had held lay on the deck partway between them. For a moment, he was again on the wide plateau on Venus known as the "Goddess's Bosom," due to the scenic beauty it overlooked. Stepping over to the gun, when a flash of light momentarily blinded him, he again knelt before and looked up at the most beautiful woman he'd ever met or who had graced his life up to that moment. The words, "Will you marry me," had already left his lips when Shima's face exploded downwards at him. Pain exploded in his chest. A cloud of red filled his vision, leaving an old woman's visage floating in the air over him.

"I knelt looking up at the most beautiful woman in my life," Conner said with tears filling his eyes and fury snarling the words with venomous hatred. "The words she'd wanted me to say for over a year left my lips as you blew her brains out. You aren't worthy of being a queen. Hell, you aren't worthy of being buried on a planet to feed new life."

Conner flicked his eyes to pull up his suit's interface. Opening the tech tools, Conner found the commands he wanted. With the gun in his right hand, Conner pressed his left hand to Mori's face, with two fingers sinking into her eyes. Using his own command authorization, he had the tech suit forcibly deactivate and power down her body and uniform's nano processes. Her screams echoed in the huge bay for a long moment.

"Commodore Conner," Barley said in a cold, officious voice from beside Conner, "the rebel ships have all been destroyed. The carrier group is even now combing the debris field for survivors. What are your orders concerning any survivors found?"

Conner wiped the wet remains of Mori's eyeballs off his fingers as he visually examined the pistol he held. An antique projectile weapon, that old Venusian's voice echoed out from the depths of his memories to tell him this was what had once been called a .44 mag auto-mag. A powerful weapon in its own right, but not always powerful enough to kill some of the wild animals that occasionally rampaged in that remote part of Venus. Ejecting the magazine, Conner wondered if a gun was where Magnus's name had come from. When the newly active matrix had first spoken to him, it had asked for a name.

"If they give up immediately, renounce any and all allegiance to Mariko Mori and anyone or any group other than that of the Sol-Humana Confederation, surrender their weapons, and deactivate their uniform once on a ship, they are to be held for trial as insurrectionists," Conner said slamming the magazine and its roughly seven bullets back into the gun.

Memories of his late fiancé replayed in his head. That long day they'd spent wandering Collette and the area around the small town flashed through his head at lightning speed. That day with his beautiful Shima had been the last time he'd held and used a projectile weapon, which had been at a practice range the town ran. This gun he pointed at Mori. "Those that refuse to surrender or refuse to renounce this rebellion are to be shot and killed on sight. That includes you, former Admiral Mariko Mori. What do you say?"

"You? A Commodore?" Mori snorted with disgusted laughter. Her face contorted with rage even as her eyes slowly started reforming. "I am the First Admiral. I approve promotions. Not any of those others on the Admiralty. Me! I am your queen. You will all bow to me!"

"I, Conrad Conner, as the duly appointed Commodore of this carrier group, which is currently between planets and undocked at any city-station or Fleet command facility," Conner said with as much gravitas and serious intonation as he could muster while flicking off the gun's safety switch, "find you, Mariko Mori, guilty of murder, slavery, and insurrection among many other crimes. Per interstellar law and under orders from the Sol-Humana Fleet Admiralty, I sentence you to death. Sentence to be carried out immediately."

Tightening his grip and stiffening the muscles in his arms, Conner fired the gun pointed at the bridge of Mori's nose. The bang was deafening and the recoil far stronger than he remembered. Mori's head jerked back, with blood and bone spraying out of the back of her head. Shima's soft gasp of surprise echoed out from the depths of his memories.

Not assuming Mori was dead, Conner shifted the gun slightly and fired a second time. This bullet tore through her throat. He and Shin and everyone else in the universe would never have to hear another hateful word in that awful, gravelly voice.

His third shot punched a hole into her chest right where her heart should be. Seeing the gaping wound and the blood spray brought up a horrible, nightmarish memory of this woman shooting two men in front of him, her angry voice demanding he give her something he didn't have. All he could do was scream for his papa and daddy.

As the echoing bang of the gunfire became the click of an empty gun, Barley laid a hand on Conner's arm. Gently pushing the arm down, Barley spoke in a soft, trembling voice. "That's enough, Conner."

Blood pooled quickly about Mori's unmoving body as Conner stood there staring down at the bullet-ridden body of the woman who'd tormented him his entire life. Behind Conner, the sound of people vomiting filled his ears even as the clang of weapons being dropped echoed loudly. The sounds rang with the death cries of his fathers, his mother, his sister, his brother-in-law, his fiancé, and thousands of others caught up in this mad woman's power-hungry schemes.

Conner absently flipped the safety back on and ejected the magazine. Letting the gun slip out of his hand, it and the magazine fell to the deck. Being able to remember how to do anything after learning it once had its charms at times. Other times, as he'd learned over the decades, it could be more of a curse.

"Conner? Look at me, Conner," Barley whispered into his ear urgently. "Focus on my voice. Did you get Magnus? Do you have your son?"

Conner tore his eyes away from Mori's unmoving body to look at Barley standing beside him. The fear and worry in the artificial's eyes pulled Conner out of the memories and sense of guilt over all the people who'd died because of him. No, he told himself, because of Mori's mad schemes.

"Magnus jumped into this suit's node," Conner said in a low voice, not liking how rough and hoarse he sounded. "You okay in there, Mags?"

"I want to go home," Magnus sobbed in that little boy's voice of earlier.

"So do I, kiddo," Conner said as he felt his strength ebbing. "Someone may have to carry us, though. I'm not feeling...crap."

"Conner?" Barley's eyes filled with panic. "Are you hurt? Did she—"

"Ion poisoning from the engine exhaust." Conner staggered away from Mori and the blood toward the barrier. "Everyone down here will need..."

Conner's vision blurred before going completely black. He heard Barley shouting at him and Magnus wailing so much like Alex had earlier in his quarters. Yet, he had no strength to move or speak. His body shook before the darkness took all awareness from him.

CHAPTER 26

Conner laid on the sofa in the captain's quarters facing the narrow windows. The sunlit side of Jupiter glowed through the windows, with the occasional ship, either leaving or approaching *Socrates*, passing in front of the planet. A baby lay on his chest asleep, with one of Conner's hands resting protectively on the infant. Conner, though, stared at Jupiter as he replayed the events of three days ago in the shuttle bay.

"Dad, you're supposed to be sleeping," Magnus said sitting backwards in a chair by the small table. Sam sat behind him working on the other body Treespinner had sent them before they'd left Earth space. "Not laying there brooding."

"I can't get something Mori said out of my head," Conner said softly.

"Her quip about an insect race?" Magnus lifted his chin off his crossed arms to look at Conner.

"That too," Conner said before looking down at the red-haired baby using him as a bed. "She said something about twins Shima and I had. Unless Shima got pregnant and never told me, she and I never had kids."

"Maybe the children Mori referred to belong to Shima's little sister," Magnus said. Turning his head slightly, he added, "How's it going back there, Sam? You've been worrisomely quiet."

"This body got banged about a bit during the battle," Sam said leaning back in his chair. "I like to verify all the little connections are still solid and undamaged. Back when I ran the company that is now Tandon Universal, people hated to see me visit the labs because I'd critique the small little details."

Conner chuckled. "I did the same thing back when I was head of Tech on Barley and in the FCOPS afterwards. Those poor ensigns later came back and thanked me for saving their lives. Sometimes quite literally."

"I found a few loose connections and fixed them easily, Magnus," Sam said before leaning forward again. "Let me close up and you can go rescue your son from the horror that is laying on

Conner's chest."

"You mean you want to replace Alex, you old lech," Magnus said snickering into his arms.

A flash and a chime happened simultaneously. Barley stood just inside the door to the corridor. Walking forward so Conner could see him, Barley sighed before speaking.

"Sorry for intruding in what the doctor said was needed rest and relaxation so your body could finish healing from the ion poisoning, Conner," Barley said with a chagrin look.

"Let me guess," Conner said with a growing smirk. "Someone leaked or spoke about what happened in the shuttle bay to the media and the Confederation is descending into anarchy. You're here on behalf of both the Admiralty and the planetary guardians to beg me to step up and tell everyone to shut up and stop being idiots. How close am I?"

Barley rolled his eyes and dropped into a chair within Conner's line of sight. "Fifty-fifty, you crazy bucket of something. Earth, Venus, and Mars, along with Nokata, Stephens and Vickie of the Admiralty, are all here wanting to speak to you as soon as possible. Also, word of Mori's rebellion and the Arbiters' decisions in my favor and concerning Betty have gotten out, which is causing far more government officials to resign than I, at least, would have expected to happen. Some or all of that may be why the big wigs want to talk to you."

"Not because I shot the former First Admiral with a projectile weapon?" Conner rubbed the baby's back as it began stirring. "It's okay, little Alex. Grandpa will speak softer. Go back to sleep."

"They won't say why they want to talk to you, Conner," Barley said followed by a heavy sigh. "I don't want to go back into Fleet. Being part of that little artificial's life, fighting for his right to exist in whatever manner he wants, is what I want now. Is this what it means to be a parent? Even if just a grandparent?"

"Yep," Sam said from behind Magnus before pushing his chair back. "All done and closed up, Magnus. Let me know if you notice any problems. Also, verify all backups with Barley for the short term."

"Definitely, Sam," Magnus said standing up and stretching. "So, Barley, are they all connecting for this meeting?"

"Well, Nigel wanted to come to us," Barley said with a tired look, "but the media is now hounding both his office and the public side of our mooring. Stars of Creation, all of the vid bots watching us transfer the cores to Socrates' secure holding was annoying and weird as all—"

"Language, Pops," Magnus said with a smile.

Conner sighed. "Let them all connect. Just make sure they understand I'm a mattress at the moment and anyone who upsets this little angel has to deal with the tantrum he broadcasts."

A bang out in the corridor made everyone jump slightly. Whimpering from Alex drew Magnus over, his appearance shifting to Maggie despite his clothes staying the same. Barley jumped to his feet and glared at the door.

"Ernie tried to pull a prank on his sister," Barley said shaking his head. "Arlene saw through it and made it blow up in her little brother's face. Almost literally."

"I'll go take care of the small fries, Conner," Sam said chuckling. "You get the big ones."

"What are fries, Conner?" Barley looked confused as Sam crossed the room. White smoke billowed into the room as Sam left, which worried Conner.

"Mommy's here, my mini byte of joy," Maggie said picking up the increasingly fussy baby.

A flash brought Admiral Vickie in first. She looked around, spotted Maggie and the baby, and rushed over to hug them both. Earth and Venus came next, with Admiral Stephens soon after them. Mars, a stern looking man with a long scar trailing down the left side of his face, onto his neck, and vanishing underneath the tunic and leather armor the olive-skinned man wore, appeared on the far side of the room with a wall to his back. Nigel Nokata connected last with a harried expression on his face.

As people connected, Conner sat up only to yawn. "Well, to what do I owe the honor of having so many luminaries in my humble captain's quarters?"

"Well, for starters, the news outlets are already reporting multiple scandals hitting Fleet," Nigel said while rubbing his face with both hands. "Add to those the judgement in Barley's favor, projectile weapon assassinations on Earth itself, the attack on Terra Prima with projectile weapons, and the battle between cargo ships over Venus, the markets are panicking. Tandon Universal, Danlen

Industries, and numerous shipping companies are all seeing their stocks plummeting."

Conner's thoughts returned to what Mori had claimed and done as he shifted his gaze from the admirals and planetary guardians to his eldest child and first grandson. "The rich losing a few million lunas, on paper at least, doesn't concern me. What I want to know is if my family, both immediate and extended, are safe from assassination by elements connected to Mori's power grab who might still be free. I still have to take my niece and nephew back to Earth to deal with the aftermath of their parents' murder."

"The reality, Conner," ConRad said standing beside the chair Aphrodite sat in, "is that your and your company's name have already been mentioned. By multiple people, in fact. Then there is the open threat you and Barley broadcast to the universe a few days ago. Your fame, or infamy, is guaranteed. The problems for your family are just getting started."

"I'm already seeing people trying to claim to be related to you." Aphrodite sipped at a glass of iced tea. "Human nature hasn't really changed much over the last few millennia."

"Mori claimed to have killed twins who were supposedly children of my dad and his late fiancé," Maggie said walking over to sit beside Conner on the sofa, having let Vickie take baby Alex. "A bigger problem is that anyone claiming a blood relationship is risking becoming the next target of the assassins."

"You need to look at the bigger picture, Mr. Conner," Ares, the planetary guardian for Mars, said. "We're seeing dozens of resignations as Mori's network collapses. Vids are being released anonymously implicating government officials on all levels in every star system in not just the Sol-Humana Confederation, but also the Sparta Alliance, the Rigellus Federation, and several other small independent systems. A rise in political anarchy will lead to armed conflict, which will lead to planetary damage and even destruction."

"I didn't want any of this," Conner said with a low growl leaning back. "Remember? I wanted to lead a nice, quiet life out here on *Socrates' Odyssey* so my sister and her family could have a nice quiet life back on Earth. Mori drew me into this. You all caused this to happen by not keeping tabs on her and her power-hungry machinations."

"Mariko Mori's actions and words have doomed all of

humanity to a period of turmoil and political chaos," ConRad said in a calm, even voice. "We are here to ask you to help us calm things down by using your sudden notoriety. The changes to the Admiralty were announced yesterday, which is part of what's led to this seeming chaos. Someone let the vid of Mori's boarding and execution by you be leaked. A rather quick following has already started calling on you to take charge and fix things just as quickly as you did Mori's bid for power. What are they calling themselves? The Grayskulls?"

"How?" Barley said before Conner could say, or yell, anything. "He is my captain and already has a contractual obligation to me."

"You were unanimously chosen as the planetary guardians' first civilian member of the reorganized Admiralty." ConRad kept his eyes fixed on Conner, as though trying to read his moves before he made any. "Your intellect is already well known, and you've made yourself a reputation as decisive and fiercely family oriented. Both naturals and artificials seem to be supportive of you. Having you serve for at least one ten-year term would give the people of the Sol-Humana Confederation some sense of reason and watchfulness over Fleet, especially as the wrongs committed to you and your family start coming to light."

"So, not about the insect race Mori mentioned or my dad's possible connection to them via some gift they gave my grandparents?" Maggie said from where she still sat on the sofa. "Because if your plan is to throw my dad in the supernova of mass hysteria over an alien threat so he takes the blame, my little boy's multi-city broadcast of his displeasure at his grandpa not being within easy reach will be nothing compared to the universe-ending holocaust I'll unleash on every occupied world in this part of the galaxy. Do I make myself clear?"

Silence reigned in the room at Maggie's pronouncement. Conner grabbed Maggie's leg just above the knee and squeezed tightly. Maggie cried out in pain, slapping Conner's arm to get him to release his grip. Conner glared at Maggie.

"Don't make those kinds of threats, Maggie," Conner said with a soft growl. "You've a child to raise and teach how to be a loving and kind person. The thing to worry about is whether or not Sparta truly wanted Barley and I to host a peace treaty signing. Given the horrors Mori committed, I find it doubtful a treaty is real. Am I wrong?"

Nigel cleared his throat softly. "First, the treaty is real. Sparta's new Chancellor is who demanded a peace treaty with you overseeing its signing. You might remember the man, considering he surrendered to you to end the Battle of Horus."

"Him?" Conner stared in shock at Nigel. "He's Chancellor of Sparta?"

"Yep," Nigel said with a sober nod. "Intel indicates he purged the Spartan fleet of anyone claiming to be able to kill you. Apparently, you scared the man to his core, Conner."

"That's my daddy," Maggie said grinning and bumping shoulders with him.

"Concerning the spacefaring alien race being a threat," Nigel said smiling, "that's being downplayed. I've reviewed several highly classified files concerning them. General consensus is in the short term, they are not a threat. Long term? No one can predict. What I've not been able to find is what Conner's connection to them actually is."

"Based on what Mori told me," Conner said standing up and walking to Vickie, "my fathers did something which saved some of this alien race, which resulted in my fathers getting a gift from them. A gift which Mori convinced herself properly belonged to her and not my fathers. My take on all of Mori's actions against me amounts to a deranged woman's personal vendetta against my fathers for refusing to play along with her delusions of grandeur and need for absolute power over all of humanity. When my fathers chose me over her, she decided everything was my fault."

"And when you found yourself with an ally who was personally invested in you and your family," Vickie said while passing a smiling Alex back to Conner, "you fought back against her and her forces. Protecting your children and your late sister's children with the fury of a parent in protection mode. Everyone, I think, understands and respects that mentality."

"Back to the question posed," Ares said sharply, obviously irritated. "Will you serve on the Admiralty or not?"

Conner looked back at Maggie, who nodded ever so slightly. Glancing at Barley, he only got a shrug and expression which Conner took as one of uncertainty. Turning back to the others, Conner took a breath. He didn't like what this would likely mean—

being in the spotlight and public eye. Yet, if it led back to stability and overall safety, he'd do it. After things were settled, he could slip once more into the background where he felt most comfortable. "Very well. Yes, I'll serve one ten-year term."

About the Author

Ted is an Oklahoma City-based architect, writer, gamer, and pithy observer of the human condition. As an architect, he's keenly aware of layout, design, and spatial relations, which also benefits him as a storyteller. With short stories published in various anthologies, Ted fills his copious free time filled with woodworking, friends, family, and endeavoring to create the perfect cheesecake.

Check out these Books from WolfSinger Publications

Borne in the Blood – edited by Carol Hightshoe

Delve into the mysterious and powerful world of blood

This collection of enthralling stories explores the multifaceted essence of blood—as a symbol of life, a medium of magic, and a bond of kinship. From the chilling tale of a minstrel haunted by a spectral king to the whimsical account of a vampire ice cream vendor, each story weaves a unique narrative around the theme of blood. Encounter a woman whose body bizarrely intertwines with metallic elements, and follow a girl's journey as she confronts her isolation due to her heritage. Feel chills as those who were wronged reach across the years to have their final revenge on the blood descendants of those who oppressed them.

Shifters, Vampires, Witches, and other ordinary and extraordinary folk—all bound together by that which they carry in their blood.

These tales will transport you through a spectrum of emotions, from the depths of fear to the heights of fantasy, as you unravel the mysteries and power that lie within the blood.

Proceeds from sales of Borne in the Blood will be donated to the Multiple Myeloma Research Foundation: themmrf.org/

Winter Emergence – Dana Bell

Kat has lived in the mountain her entire life. Going outside is allowed only to a select few, many of which never return, including her brother Ned. She doesn't want to believe he might be dead and tries every night to contact him via the coms. Silence is the only response.

Desperate to find an answer to his disappearance, Kat steals a snow cat and searches for her brother, putting the safety of everyone in jeopardy. She's joined by a cat who, for some reason, wants to come with her, and leaves once they reach the city, leaving her alone to face unknown challenges and threats for which she's not prepared.

In the city Word Warrior faces a new threat. A Striped One stalks the cats, wolves and snow ghosts killing any unfortunate enough to be caught as if they are rightful prey! He must find a way to stop the predator or all he has worked to accomplish might fail, forcing them to revert to the old laws of challenge and mate.

A new female appears bringing news of two legs, an enemy they all feared, who lived in a strange world where she had been forced to stay until she managed to escape. In fact, one was in the city and close by.

Faced with multiple threats, including worse snowstorms, Word Warrior faces the responsibility to protect their community from all dangers, knowing if he fails—they could all die.

Space Brides, LLC – edited by Dana Bell

Tired of those lonely dark nights? No one in your settlement suitable? We are here to help! We will help you find the bride or husband to keep you company, raise your children, and be your partner building a dream together. Contact us directly and give us your specifications. Success guaranteed.

In this collection of 15 testimonials read about the challenges and triumphs of some of our clients as they found love on the frontier of space.

From aliens to vampires, we brought these couples together and together they found acceptance and love—each in their own way.

A man with three kids finds an unexpected match in the brother of the woman he had contracted to marry when she runs away.

A woman running away from an abusive marriage finds acceptance and respect with a colony group that marries everyone to everyone in order to ensure they know they belong to a family.

A woman constantly rejected because of her skin color and origins finds acceptance and love with a wounded soldier.

Even though we encourage absolute honesty in your profile and correspondence with your potential spouse—many people don't. However, like some of the testimonials you'll read here; they still manage to expand their horizons—together.

Contact or walk into any of our offices 24/7. We are here to help you find that special someone and start a new future!

Other conditions apply.
Please ask for more information before contract is drawn up and signed.

The Dragon's Hoard – edited by Carol Hightshoe

Dragons are well known for their hoards—but not all hoards are created equal.

A young dragon starts his hoard with some very precious gifts.
One dragon shares her complaints about taxes with a friend as they wait for a lunch delivery.
Another dragon defends her most precious treasures against a group of greedy goblins.
And yet another may hold the solution to saving the Earth, after a devastating apocalypse, in his collection of bottled treasures.

In addition to the normal gold, silver and jewels here you will find dragons who collect many different treasures. 25 storytellers invite you to enter The Dragon's Hoard and share the treasures within.

The Dark See: Book Three of the MoleSkinCap
– M.R. Williamson

As Helen Durkin's journey to find out about herself continues, she finally realizes that she needs the help of someone with more knowledge than dwarves, elves, or even dragons. But, just how do you approach the old Wizard Andsell Phagan?

As she tries to solve that problem, yet another dangerous situation presents itself. This mysterious person is not a friend of the Phagan family. Helen quickly finds herself on a collision course with a halfling who most refer to as Scar—one who dabbles in the dark side of magic.

With this added pressure, the effort to approach and perhaps train under Andsell Phagan intensifies. As time progresses, an old friend comes to her aid. Now, the race is on, and the old Dragon Pragamore takes the lead in Helen's plight.

Will Helen finally find out why the Faes are calling her Bright

Helen?

What of Pragamore? Will his years keep him from helping?

And, who is Scar really after—Helen, the old wizard, or Pragamore?

The Steel Fist – Rob Jackson

The survivors of Recon 9 are needed in the Ozarks where some home-grown autocrats have taken over parts of Arkansas and parts of Missouri. They've looted National Guard armories and hoarded weapons, ammunition, and vital supplies, just waiting for the opportunity to take over the area. While most of their transport, armor, and aircraft are obsolete, they face people with no protection against such deadly equipment. And they're trying to get the local natural resources to gain control of weapons that even the military have no defense against.

Recon 9 has gained four new members and formed an alliance with locals, many of them veterans, against a common enemy. The locals have some grasp of tactics, an excellent knowledge of the hilly, forested countryside and a burning desire to be rid of the terrorists, who call themselves: THE STEEL FIST

Crisis in Big-G City – S.D. Matley

Olympus, Inc., is locked in battle with climate change!

Athena's Secret Ops program steps in when bad boy and technological genius Hermes can't come up with a carbon-curbing solution. Undercover agents Cleo Petra and Pan are deployed in the mortal world to vanquish the notorious East brothers, chthonic fossil fuel magnates who pass as human and eat humans, too...

Two-month-old Pablo, the one-quarter chthonic infant son of two fathers formerly known as P.B., employs his extraordinary abilities of adult speech and intellect in pursuit of climate justice!

Meanwhile, David Bernstein, whose hot romance with Cleo Petra meets a rocky end, recovers the memory of his century-old love affair with a beautiful Spanish nurse. He time travels to 1918 to find her and encounters love, loss, and the City of Mount Olympus —a dark and sinister place where every inhabitant lives in fear of a volatile and destructive Zeus!

David's birth father and Hera's former fling, Saul Crispin, is outed as a mortal made immortal. Will Hera's high crime of granting Saul eternal life land her before a jury of her peers for judgment?

And what of baby-crazy Queen of the Underworld, Persephone, pregnant at last but not by Hades?

Intrigue, espionage, crimes of passion, secret babies and looming existential threats—everywhere you look there's a Crisis in Big-G City!

Tree of Bones – Book Two: A Familiar's Tale
– Verna McKinnon

Two Curses

A curse of Darkness…Deep within the Thill forest, stands a tree made of human bones, crowned in black leaves and red thorns.

A curse of Light…Beneath the Wastelands of Skarros, a crystal imprisons a dark, immortal queen.

The Sorceress, Runa, is tormented by horrific images of this tree of bones in a distant, lifeless forest. Even as the visions debilitate her, Mellypip, her beloved familiar, also experiences these sinister dreams, bound by the same dream seer magic as his mistress. The tree of bones summons Runa, and she must risk madness and death as obsession drives her on. What she finds reveals a devastating truth.

Koll the Sorcerer awaits trial for his crimes. His familiar, Xabral, searches for allies to free him. Driven by his own dreams of dark prophecy, Koll seeks to free Obsydia, the Bloodstone Queen, from her prison. Determined to let nothing stop him, Koll will commit any evil to achieve his goal.

Runa and Mellypip's newest journey reveals truths behind ancient secrets, as Koll's obsessive hunt for a fallen queen threatens to doom the world forever. Runa and Koll, bound by opposing magical destinies of Light and Dark, will ultimately face frightening revelations and unimagined consequences.

Gate of Souls – Book One: A Familiar's Tale – Verna McKinnon

Familiars.
Magical animal companions of sorcerers.
Keepers of spells and secrets.
Most important, devoted friends for life.

When one such familiar, Mellypip, bonds with the young sorceress Runa, he shares in the wonders of magic. Together, Mellypip and Runa train under the tutelage of Runa's grandfather, Cathal, and his cantankerous mountain owl familiar, Belwyn. But secrets and spells do not make for good sorcery. Old friends begin to vanish even as enemies from Cathal's past return, threatening to reveal the truth of Runa's parents; a truth from which Cathal must protect his granddaughter at any cost. When Cathal is kidnapped, Runa and Mellypip rush against time to save their family and friends from dark sorcery that will not only destroy them, but shatter the Gate of Souls and release demonic creatures of The Otherworld into the mortal realms.

The Seven Exalted Orders – Deby Fredericks

Arkanost has Seven Exalted Orders. No more, no less. When a magus goes renegade in a far-off province, the Mage Lords demand something be done.

Ryamon is bitter and frustrated. He longs to be a Fire magus; as a Stone magus, he's miserable. If he can bring the rogue back, he has a chance—his last chance—to fulfill his dream.

It's a great plan—until he actually meets Valdira.

And more – check out our books at
www.wolfsingerpubs.com

www.ingramcontent.com/pod-product-compliance
Lightning Source LLC
Chambersburg PA
CBHW070927260626
47162CB00007B/2825